RoH

ALIEN LEGACY

© Don Hayward 2023

The sequel to Return

ISBN: 978-1-7752459-8-8 (Softcover)

Published 2023 by Don Hayward,
8 Huron Lane, Goderich, Ontario, Canada N7A 3Y2

Cover photo Stephan Keller Pixaby.com

Also by Don Hayward

Collapse
Book One of After the Last Day
ISBN 978-1-7752459-2-6 (Soft cover)

Under Shadows
Book Two of After the last Day
ISBN 978-1-7752459-4-0 (Softcover)

The End of shadows
Book Three of After the Last Day
ISBN 978-1-7752459-5-7 (Soft cover)

The Seventh Path
ISBN 978-1-62137-949-2 (Soft cover)

Journey's End
ISBN 978-1775-245933 (Soft cover)

Murder on the Goderich Local
ISBN 978-1-62137-993-5 (Soft cover)

Sherwood Green
ISBN 978-1-7752459-0-2 (Soft cover)

Return
ISBN 978-1-7752459-7-1 (Soft cover)

Echo of the Whip-poor-will
ISBN 978-1-7752459-1-9 (Soft cover)

High Falls
A pictorial history
ISBN 978-1-7752459-6-4 (Soft cover)

All of Don's books, except High Falls, are available in an electronic version from Smashwords.com and Amazon (and soft cover on Amazon). Most books are available through book sellers worldwide.

Contact Don,
haywardon@gmail.com

Acknowledgement

To Alex and Diane for their support and helpful corrections and advice.

Dedication

To everyone who dreams of the stars and struggles for a better Earth.

"The important thing is not to stop questioning. Curiosity has its own reason for existence. One cannot help but be in awe when they contemplate the mysteries of eternity, of life, of the marvellous structure of reality. It is enough if one tries merely to comprehend a little of this mystery each day."
—"Old Man's Advice to Youth: 'Never Lose a Holy Curiosity.'" *LIFE Magazine* (2 May 1955) p. 64"
— Albert Einstein

AND SO, IT BEGINS

Good morning, listeners, I am speaking from a farm near Goderich, Ontario.

RoH, the part alien, invited me here. I originally planned to take a few weeks to interview RoH's grandfather, Charlie Keys, and perhaps her mother, Ellie, if RoH allows it. So far, I have interviewed Charlie and then RoH, but to describe my conversations with the part alien girl as an interview would be deceitful. RoH interviewed me, but you have heard some of those recordings, and I have more to come.

That first night, I met RoH at the hotel. RoH's father and Kerri Grenier left for Charlie's house. The CIA had apparently murdered Kerrie, but the aliens returned her very much alive. RoH curled up in a big chair that night and sipped endless hot chocolates. She reassured me I was "Mom approved", and in an hour, RoH knew my life story. It seemed I had failed as a reporter, and I had not asked one question, yet I felt content. If you end up in RoH's presence and think that you will be in control, forget it. RoH, gently and stealthily, will direct the conversation. You likely never will meet her unless she invites you, but if you encounter RoH, it will be your privilege. Sorry, I sound like a fan.

RoH never tired that night, but I dozed off. When I awoke, I discovered RoH had covered me with a blanket, and she still sat in the same chair. I don't know if she slept at all, but she watched me with her piercing eyes, and her first words spooked me.

"Quantz, I'll see that your family comes to be with you in Canada."

How did she know about my desire to bring my family from Egypt? Then, I remembered I had dreamed of them over-night.

There are many aliens, and other part aliens on Earth, like RoH's mother Ellie, but RoH is the special one.

It would be wrong to say RoH leads the alien effort. The aliens who inhabit this part of the galaxy function as an autonomist collective. There is no leader, as humans might define one. The aliens have groupings only large enough to accomplish a particular task. Interstellar distances dictate that.

The original plan for Earth involved only three ships and a few dozen star travellers. Now, there are thousands of ships. Who knows the number of aliens in the solar system? The whole group discusses and decides together what to do, and then an individual, RoH, for instance, might be the one to put that plan into action. We saw how that works last September when Ellie returned to Earth with RoH. They immediately split up, each with her separate task.

Although there is a deep bond between Ellie and her mother Lisa in Seattle and father Charlie in Goderich, the aliens did not begin this effort for a family reunion. As Charlie Keys told me, the aliens want to learn empathy and how to be convivial, how to interact solely for the joy of being together, and not always for a purpose. The aliens think that is a necessary strength that they lost in learning how to travel the stars.

They hybridized that change with human genes. With their longevity, it will take thousands of Earth years to change their population. The star travellers had Charlie and Lisa conceive Ellie as part of this effort. RoH is the next generation; she denies she is their ultimate. Since they came to Earth, Ellie and RoH have focused on the goal of helping us avoid killing all life on Earth.

The events around New Year's Eve stunned me, and it astonished the entire planet. Before Ellie and RoH arrived, many aliens had been on the surface for years, some disguised as human in key roles associated with the return of the aliens. They have a few more "Ellie's" spread around the planet. Only now, the reports from Kenya, Australia and Europe are hinting at some of these others. I am convinced more of them exist, but no one has told me that.

Contrary to rumours, conspiracy theories and propaganda, I have seen no evidence that they have tried to infiltrate any government. They stopped the CIA's attempt to force them into service to the USA. They have no care for national governments except in hoping a popular, global demand for equity will force change.

The unexpected arrival and Mars impact of comet Clavette gave the aliens unplanned opportunities. They made Mars uninhabitable for several decades and enhance its atmosphere through natural terraforming. You have all seen the remarkable video record made by Jimmy Smith from an alien ship. When Clavette hit Mars, it added over four million cubic kilometres of water, and caused Olympus Mons to erupt. That forces humans to focus on our planet for a few decades and drop the Mars escape-hatch dream.

The aliens used the rescue of the one thousand Mars settlers as a spectacular self-introduction to the world as non-threatening friends.

Ironically, Clavette and Jimmy Smith upset their original plan. They wanted to take a year to prepare the masses for their arrival, but Jimmy Smith exposed Ellie's presence. The appearance of Clavette forced the aliens to take action with unexpected consequences. Perhaps the largest of the unforeseen problems came with their disarming all nations of nukes and heavy weapons. That has caused economic chaos. According to RoH, this act departs from their standard rules of contact, and they had not intended to intervene so deeply. The economic consequence surprised them too, and they see it as an additional difficulty for their plan.

Quantz Nedmar-CBC Radio for The Canadian Morning

CHAPTER I

Families and foreboding

The Martian X descended the long grade and sped deftly over the Maitland River at Donnybrook Bridge and up the steeper south side of the valley. Charlie dozed and dreamed as the autopilot took him through the night. He had been in Orangeville, training the factory people there, and looked forward to home and bed. He would go into the Goderich factory and check in with Kerri later tomorrow.

About one in the morning, the black car came to a gentle stop in his driveway. Soon he sat on his couch and sipped a drink, thinking of his bed. Idly, he flipped on the television cable news from the CBC.

"This just in," a voice overlaid a shaky image of a brilliant burst in the sky, "we have seen strange bright lights over parts of south-western Ontario."

His cell jingled, and a text popped up. Maybe Lisa had finally replied after her strange message early yesterday. Charlie frowned. A star symbol replaced the usual sender handle.

"Are you awake, Dad?"

The doorbell chimed.

Charlie stirred from a crazy dream that relived a distorted version of the night, four months ago, when his part-alien daughter, Ellie, had returned. He lay in his bed, but it seemed unfamiliar. Then he felt the warmth beside him and realized that for almost all of his life, he had slept alone.

The door once more demanded attention. The clock said after nine. They had enjoyed a lazy, satisfying week since the alien New Year's excitement. He had a father's pride in how his daughter, Ellie, mostly human, somewhat alien, had played a major role in the Goderich events.

Charlie slipped into his robe and hurried down the stairs.

"Hi, Father, we came for breakfast." Ellie walked in, followed by a hesitant Steve Jorgensen.

"Who is it, Charlie?" A voice sang from the upper hallway.

"It's Ellie, Kerri, and my friend Steve Jorgensen." Ellie lowered her voice. "Actually, Dad, Steve and I have become more than friends."

Charlie offered a lukewarm hand to Steve and frowned, but he suddenly brightened and gave his improbable son-in-law a hug. If Ellie had chosen Steve as her Earthly love, Charlie could only accept.

"Welcome to the family."

"I last saw you in the Dakotas, but we never met. You three ran for it," Steve smiled at Ellie, "and they sent me home."

Kerri descended and hugged Ellie.

"The family is growing," Ellie laughed. "I took Mom back to Seattle a few days ago. She says she is going to marry 'some weird guy' as she described Billy. I met him. He plays sax... a nice catch for an old drummer schoolmarm like Mom."

"I told them they had better hurry because we have a deadline. It might not be close, but it could happen, and we would have to withdraw."

It's a 55.5% probability, Mother.

RoH, where are you?

I'm at the farm with Quantz.

Having fun?

We had a lot of snow. I was going to blow it away, but Captain Fontaine insists she and her unit do all the maintenance. She says they need busy work.

Good, she will keep you from showing off.

Ghislaine reports to some General, and he doesn't want them just sitting around, so she sends him video of the work. Human soldiers sure do a lot of marching back and forth. Quantz and I discuss all this.

Mother...?

Yes...?

There are unintended consequences to what we did. It's serious.

I know, Sweetie. We are considering, but you keep to the plan so far... kisses...

Charlie noticed Ellie's frown.

"What's wrong, Ellie?"

"There is a fresh problem we did not predict. We don't know what it means, but we are analyzing it."

"Is it serious?"

"Yes..."

"What can we do?"

"Let's have breakfast," Ellie ignored her father's question.

"I'm cooking," Kerri headed to the kitchen. "Are omelettes okay?"

"Great, something for Dad to put ketchup on," Ellie smirked.

"At least Ellie didn't sneak up on me this time," Charlie said.

RoH watched out the farmhouse window as Captain Fontaine paraded her unit in morning muster. The fighters did not seem to mind the cold and snow. The Canadian Special Forces guarded a farm near Goderich, which the aliens chose as a main contact point on Earth. RoH noted the troops wore her Christmas gift of the red and white scarves as part of their uniform. They valued these as battle honours in the old British style, although they had not fought a battle.

The soldiers knotted the uniform additions identically, with one lead thrown over the left shoulder and the other hanging in front. By giving them the scarves, RoH had stolen their hearts and drawn them into her family. They wore the additions with pride as part of the uniform of what they now called the Alien Guard. To them, the alien meant RoH. The little half-alien girl, who commanded mechanical fireflies with the wave of her hand, but had asked them to teach her and be her friends. The unit did not know whom they might fight, but they had decided it was not an alien space invader.

RoH turned away in sadness. She knew the enemy and a growing certainty that humans would destroy the alien's hopes by committing ecocide on Earth. A dark player in that possibility would soon reveal themselves to RoH and the star travellers.

"Jaden," RoH brightened at a happier thought, "I'm so glad you have let me adopt you as my sister. I never thought I would have siblings, although my mother is working on that." RoH giggled. "My father on the ship doesn't see the need... yet."

"Honestly," Jaden smiled and sipped her herbal tea, "I don't think I have any choice. All I had before was my dorky brother and he's so smart and successful I could never measure up. Now, I feel I have something important to do, but I have no clue what that is."

Jaden's eyes questioned RoH.

"I could say it's making me happy," RoH said. "That would be true, but selfish. No, you have a minor job of helping the human species survive."

"My survival wasn't even on my mind before I met you." Jaden managed a weak smile.

"I know; I saw it in the photo your grandmother Emily showed me, but I also saw your strength. Despite what you believe, you are strong, Jaden. Most people who have survived struggle are stronger for it."

"How can a little girl like you be so smart?"

"I'm both a little girl, and not one, Jaden." RoH seemed sad. "Part of me is so old I can't fathom it. My brain is still developing, of course, along with my body. What I have already," RoH tapped her head, "runs efficiently and has absorbed learning beyond the undergraduate level of an Earth university. I know so little. I know I am mostly ignorant."

Jaden reached over and squeezed RoH's hand.

"For my whole life, I thought I was stupid." Jaden frowned. "Not anymore, but I don't know what to think; I'm ignorant for sure and can never measure up; a little girl who's lost at the foot of a steep hill."

"Let me be your walking stick and climb that hill together." RoH hugged Jaden. "We will find many paths to explore. At the top, the view will be breathtaking."

"First, let's have breakfast."

CHAPTER 2

We do not regret to inform you

President Harry Ascue splashed ketchup onto his home fries and sausage. Two sunny side eggs stared up from the plate. He took a gulp of black coffee and dug into the meal. The clock on his desk showed ten minutes before his telephone appointment.

For Harry, a down-home car dealer at heart, the next event, talking to foreign leaders, Russian President Lev Balakin and Chinese Premier, Wei Liu, seemed a waste of time.

These people think they are equal to these great United States.

If Ascue could be honest with himself, these confident foreign leaders made him feel stupid. His ego had made him believe that a small town car dealer could run the international corporation known as the United States of America. Reality differed from his simplistic dreaming. Mary had managed his career from a city councillor, governor of Iowa, to the White House. Otherwise, Harry would still hoodwink car buyers instead of world leaders. Mary remained as his irreplaceable political manager and security adviser.

He scanned the first page of a security brief.

Damned aliens, he thought.

"Harry," Mary arrived, "President Balakin and Premier Liu are on the video call in the Oval Office."

"Lev… Wei, how are you both?"

Harry blurted the greetings that Americans thought to be friendly, but most foreigners found obnoxious. It did not help that he mispronounced the names.

"Mr. President," Balakin started through a translator, "Premier Liu and I have been discussing our mutual problem for several days. We think it is in all our interests to cooperate to defeat these monsters from space."

"I agree," Premier Liu added without waiting for Harry to reply. "We must put our power together."

Harry waited for his translator.

"I don't think we can beat around the damned bush," Ascue began, "but what power can we all contribute?"

Both Balakin and Liu knew English, but Harry's slang confused them.

"If you mean being open about our forces, I agree," Balakin said. "We have many ballistic missiles ready."

Harry could see his face, and with the certainty of a salesman, knew the man lied. On the split screen, Liu appeared to agree with Harry; however, the Premier followed with equally impossible claims. Harry knew that none of them had anything operational, larger than a machine gun and a fixed amount of ammunition even then.

Harry considered following suit, or challenging the two, but he had political skill and pretended to believe them.

"That's great. I propose we set up a joint command team. I can send my Joint Chiefs of Staff to be in command."

Harry kept a neutral face, but the other two faces flashed brief anger. They spoke over one another, each suggesting that their military should be in charge. After a half hour of wrangling, they could only decide to hold another session in a few days.

"We have one mutual problem," Balakin said. "The aliens have kidnapped our citizens and hold them in Canada, but we want them back."

"Can you help?" Liu said.

"I suggest you call the Canadians," Ascue said. "They are not happy with America at the moment."

"I'll do that, Mr. President, and we'll show those aliens they can't push us around."

Liz Dafoe and Dawn Waasnodae stepped into the Canadian Prime Minister's office. The PM's Chief of Staff held the door but did not impress. Both MPs saw the woman as an ambitious bully. With a grand gesture, exaggerated to being cartoonish, the head of government waived the two onto one of the comfortable couches and sat opposite. The arrogant Chief of Staff hovered to one side, out of line of sight but ready.

"Have you had breakfast?" The PM asked and without waiting for an answer, gestured at the chief, who called through the still open door.

The women glanced around the room. They had not been here since their rookie-member orientations, years ago. Dawn thought the opulent space dripped of colonial history. Liz felt that the ostentation signified the distance between the government and her local voters.

The perfect metaphor of the problem, she thought.

An assistant arrived with a serving cart with various luxury pastries and silver pots of coffee and tea with delicate china cups; it magnified Liz's judgment.

"That is all," the Chief said to the server.

"No," Liz interjected, "he stays. Bring the other staff. The era of top-down decisions is over. Everyone must be involved from now on."

"Look, I'm..." the PM began, but Dawn showed him her hand.

"Not anymore," Dawn smiled with a look of confidence, not condescension or smugness, but she stated the new reality.

The head politician glowered. It seemed this woman had read his mind. It repulsed him he had to treat these insignificant backbenchers with such respect. The two had never conformed and had often been the object of scorn and rebuke, like children. The pair lacked the normal opportunism that kept a common member of Parliament in line, but that had always had been the Whip's problem.

Despite their closeness to Ellie Keys, neither woman considered themselves aliens or mind readers. They understood the predictability of the powerful, like the PM, as he strutted around Parliament. It made it seem that the women might be psychic or alien.

Six clerks and other assistants stood stiffly at a respectful distance.

"Everyone, take a seat," Dawn waved her hand, mimicking the grand gesture that the PM had used moments ago.

"Yes, please..." the PM tried to regain control of the hierarchy. It irked him that all eyes focused on his visitors. The others knew these women had a special relationship with the aliens. The PM could not accept Dawn's implication that he no longer qualified as the one in charge.

I loathe their ideology...

"We need cups for everyone," Liz smiled.

The Chief scurried out the door, more to get away from watching the humiliation of her boss than from a willingness to serve.

Is she powerful or just another token woman? Dawn thought. Everyone around Parliament assumed entitlement.

A frantic phone call brought more cups and another minion, who joined the group. Liz suggested that everyone have a pastry. No one accepted, still confused about who commanded.

"Okay, let's get going," Liz said. "You asked us to come," she nodded at the red-faced PM.

"The world is going to hell, and your alien friends caused it." His words dripped with sarcasm and his guests scowled. "Defence contractors are closing. Some of them declared bankruptcy with thousands of lay-offs. The markets collapsed because the aliens, with no right, disabled every military around the globe. There are no more markets."

"You left out," Dawn said, "that they disabled the factories that produce weapons and ammunition for all guns."

The PM waved a folder and flipped through the contents.

"The aliens destroyed over half of the economies of every industrial nation. NATO, Russia and China want a joint declaration of war on them. They will introduce a motion at the United Nations Security Council."

Liz and Dawn laughed. Staff watched the disrespect in stunned silence. The PM turned a deeper red. The Chief of Staff slumped against one of the louvered window shutters with a distracting clatter.

"Perhaps you should ask why over half of all industrial economies depend on war, but you did not call this meeting for that, Prime Minister. What do you want to talk about?"

"We want you to go to your alien friends and tell them to restore our militaries... or else."

"What are you going to do?" Liz asked. "Kick them out of the UN; refuse to buy their oil, or shoot down star ships with hunting rifles?"

"We won't give them what they want," the Prime Minister growled.

"It must frustrate you," Dawn said, "that they want nothing, at least nothing physical, but something we can't stop them from having. Humans have fallen in love or at least lust with aliens since 1947. We have been eagerly donating genetic material for decades. You still don't understand; you have no leverage."

"Prime Minister," Liz tried to remain polite, "I regret to inform you they do not want to talk with you. The star travelers have no desire or motive to negotiate, and Canada has no global power and influence. The world has always seen us as an echo the Americans. You could gain some importance now."

"Ellie has told us that when the time is right, they would meet with a great gathering of nations. Since the UN is already that, instead of war mongering and throwing a tantrum, the Security Council should move to request that meeting. I will tell you this; the visitors will not meet with the former great powers, but only the world. The General Assembly would be the place to start. If you want to be important, send that message to the American President."

Dawn Waasnodae and Liz Dafoe abruptly stood and walked out of the room. The Prime Minister sat in stunned silence. His Chief-of-Staff fumed. Minions eyed the pastries that remained untouched on the serving tray.

A phone rang beyond the doorway.

"Prime Minister," an aid hurried back from the outer office, "the Russian ambassador wants to talk with you."

Siglinde Hilfreich stared at the green handset of the high-security line to the White House. It gave the President direct access to the head of NAAP and had been ringing for a minute. Siglinde ignored it.

Siglinde and her team member, now lover Ted Kotwas, had flown in from Canada two days ago. Ted's revelation that he was an alien did not faze Siglinde. She knew the story of Ellie Keys' great-grandmother, who knowingly conceived with an alien. Siglinde found that story encouraging. She understood how a woman could love a being from the stars, especially one *as hot as Ted*, as Liz had exclaimed when she had learned of the relationship.

"Maybe I'll get me one of you alien hunks," Liz said when the three had group-hugged.

The bigoted preachers might think it disgusting, but Siglinde's feelings and understanding trumped it all. The miracle of Ellie and her daughter RoH confirmed Siglinde's desire.

"Elliana, I hate to ask, but would you answer him?"

"Siglinde Hilfreich's office..."

Elliana held the device well away from her ear. Siglinde heard her name as the only understandable part of the expletives that roared from the handset. She thought Ascue had meant her name in the same way. Elliana smiled and handed the phone to Siglinde.

"Yes, Mr. President?" Siglinde also held the device at a distance.

"Mr. President, I don't think the Canadian Prime Minister has such an active or perverse sex life, and I believe his parents were married. Perhaps you could calm down."

Siglinde sympathized with the man. The Commander-in-Chief had lost most of his power, and saw no hint he would retrieve it soon. The man felt diminished and helpless.

"I think you should take the Canadian's advice," Siglinde finally had a chance. "He's just repeating the message from the aliens."

...

"No, as far as we can tell, even if you had all your weapons, you could not deliberately destroy any of their ships. It is NAAP's assessment that they pose no physical threat. Politically and economically, they have had a tremendous impact, but not as bad for us as comet Clavette destroying the Mars settlements."

"Listen to the aliens, Mr. President. They control the situation, and we think they want to help humans survive."

...

"No, Mr. President, yours or any other government's political survival is unimportant to the star people."

...

"I say star people because, Mr. President, the word alien conjures an image that is not real. It's Hollywood's version of heartless invaders intent on eating us. Everyone needs to unlearn that bias. War of the Worlds was not a documentary. The worst damage the visitors will do is to abandon humans to our fate, and they calculate that means we destroy all advanced life on Earth."

...

"I know an election is coming soon, Mr. President. You need to advocate how to live in this new economic situation. We can't fight it."

...

"Yes, your opponent will want to 'kick alien ass', as you say. They might defeat you, but they won't be kicking any butt either. The visitors don't care who runs the USA."

...

"Yes, Mr. President, it will probably mean the country falls apart. To you, that seems like alien hostility. To the star visitors, it is a necessary step towards saving life here. All large countries will fragment."

...

"Yes, Mr. President, everyone must deal with political reality. You as well, but it's a new reality. Perhaps you could keep the country together by taking a rational approach."

The phone went dead.

Siglinde slumped into her seat. It appeared America, as a European wit had once said, would only try the correct solution after they had used up all the wrong ones. The Europeans were no better.

The President dropped the handset into the cradle and stared at the closed door separating his working office from the beehive in the next room.

"Mary, get your ass in here," he scowled into the intercom.

"Mary, I have a problem."

"Which one?" she fought a smile. She knew when not to poke the bear. Mary held the position of Chief-of-Staff for the President. Her role as his top political advisor went back to his successful election as governor of Iowa. He trusted her instincts and advice. Mary prided herself on knowing all the facts before she gave any advice. She had a large team of assistants with the resources of the executive branch and a nation-wide network of spies. The network included critics. Mary would not allow ass kissers to control her decisions.

"Who's the new girl?" The President's eyes lingered on the curvy young woman who handed Mary a file and undulated to the outer office.

"Oh, that's Daisy. She's the new one." Mary glanced towards the now-closed door. "One girl died in a car crash New Year's Eve... drunk driving, the cops said. Daisy worked for the CIA and they vetted her."

Mary sighed. The President's habit of philandering would have to be controlled. She would warn Daisy to stay clear.

Don't worry about that... the thought was fleeting, but it reassured Mary. *Why did that thought come?*

The mention of the CIA made the President frown.

"The CIA royally screwed things up," he growled, "that Greg guy."

"The Canadians still have him and his team." Mary said. "Don't be in a hurry to get them back. Having the Canadians hold them is better than reassigning them to data analysis."

"The Canadian PM called earlier," the President changed course. "He passed on an alien message that we should admit defeat and call for a forum at the UN to let the aliens speak to the world. Siglinde Hilfreich agrees. Her group says the aliens are not aggressive and only want the best for humanity. What's good for humanity is not good for me. The Canadian PM agrees that we have a political disaster."

"All governments worldwide think that," Mary said.

"Is there a way out?"

"My people have been going through the NAAP material. We have a countermove."

The President straightened from his slump. "Well...?"

Mary maintained her composure, but her thoughts were less than friendly at Harry's condescension.

What an ass. I'm no chump; if it wasn't for me, he would still run a car lot in Des Moines. He doesn't deserve me.

She took a moment to compose her thoughts.

"The aliens started a genetic experiment near Lubbock, Texas, in 1947. It seems they decided that this might be a good thing for them. We didn't understand why until Siglinde Hilfreich and NAAP pulled it all together."

"The aliens conducted many similar breeding experiments, but most failed, and some became horrors. We don't know if any succeeded, but news from Kenya, Australia and Europe suggests other healthy mutants."

"These are below the level of this Ellie woman who they bred, took, and now returned. The most interesting thing, and this came from Hilfreich, is that the little girl who is apparently Ellie's daughter is the next step of the experiment. Hilfreich says that they bred this RoH girl on a starship, making her a powerful hybrid between aliens and humans. The girl has more abilities than her mother."

"Why all this breeding nonsense...?" The President stood. "Sounds like a bunch of dairy farmers back home wanting the biggest udder."

"Hilfreich says the aliens want to learn empathy and conviviality from humans. Apparently, they lost it in learning to apply their science. They think our genetics are the key."

"Empathy... from humans...?" The President roared. The concept was foreign to the man and his vague idea of the definition.

"It is strange," Mary agreed. She also lacked the tools of caring that lay far outside their world of self-centred greed; however, Mary knew what empathy meant. She saw it as a weakness. Mary suffered from it once and had locked caring into a corner of her mind.

"Ellie and RoH have both, and mental powers we can't imagine."

"We considered one course of action, going after Ellie's mother and father and using them for leverage. Ellie's parents are Lisa Clarke in Seattle and Charlie Keys in Goderich, Canada. Ellie goes by the name of Keys. RoH uses no last name. Greg at the CIA took the parents and ended up in a Canadian jail. The aliens took over their base in Canada. For obvious reasons, we decided trying that again would be useless; however, we are keeping both parents under watch through NAAP, just in case."

"So, do you have a better idea?"

"If the aliens are trying to get something from us by inter-breeding, we can try that in reverse and gain some of their abilities for humans. According to Hilfreich, aliens live for thousands of years."

Mary knew the narcissistic President would find that attractive even if he would never benefit.

"Why would a cross-bred alien bastard work for us?"

"We think, if we could get a baby or babies like that, we could raise them to love us and hate aliens. Parents, teachers and preachers do that all the time, create haters, I mean."

"That will take years. It won't do me any good. I'll be dead by then."

Perhaps... Mary thought, *and maybe I'll be in charge.*

"That's where part two is important." Mary kept a straight face. "We have a strategy to delay the alien plans, maybe even make them retreat in disgust, as they threaten to do."

"How...?"

"Many churches are organizing against them. The economic collapse will unite billionaires with workers and those preachers. The billionaires and we will keep control, of course. We can create division and lots of killing, making the aliens leave. The more fighting on Earth amongst humans, the better. In the meantime, we figure out how to do our own breeding and get some goodies before they vanish. We must make sure the USA controls that power."

Mary's cold calculation unsettled Harry Ascue.

"It looks impossible. Who would do the breeding for us? What alien?"

"We believe we can convince or force that little girl, RoH, to be our breeder. If she won't cooperate, we will extract her genetic material. We have a team on the ground in Canada trying to locate the girl. Meanwhile, you need to organize a meeting between the rich and the angry masses."

CHAPTER 3

A long, cold winter

I regret to inform you...

Tens of thousands of industrial workers in many countries got a letter that "regretted to inform" them they no longer had a job. Those who handed out that message in the morning received their regrets in the afternoon. It would be the beginning of a cold winter of declining hope and growing destitution for millions.

As workers received terminations, the paper worth of billionaires and well-healed politicians evaporated. The equity casino markets eagerly converted almost every billionaire to a millionaire, or into poverty. Not even "the house" won. The oligarchs' anger matched that of the minions, and it created a brief alignment of interests.

Violent street demonstrations demanded quick action by the elite to reclaim control. This had reached Canada and the USA. Poorer and European countries with a rebellious culture,found their streets swarmed with protesters. They demanded either friendship or war with the alien visitors. Hunger, hopelessness, and propaganda had not made the majority hate the newcomers. No one on Earth had ever lived without the threat of nuclear annihilation before now, and many had a deep sense of relief and thankfulness.

The goodwill from the rescue of the Martian settlers persisted. Television repeated Jimmy Smith's video of Clavette hitting Mars and the aliens rescuing Martian settlers on New Year's Eve. Interviews with saved settlers praising the aliens held viewers' attention. At the beginning, all media eagerly supported the alien heroes. The billionaire owners of the media, and the self-serving religious leaders, would replace this with anti-alien attacks.

In Goderich, Ontario, on January 8th, Charlie Keys, Kerri Grenier, and Mike Hammersmith met at the Hammersmith factory.

"Bad times are coming." Mike sprawled on a stuffed chair in the corner of his office. Charlie and Kerrie shared a leather-covered couch. The low table between the seats held half-empty cups of coffee and a plate of sugar cookies. Kerri ignored the spot in front of Mike's desk where she had fallen when the CIA shot her. She had personal reasons for loving the aliens who had saved her life.

"Our order book is full," Charlie tried to be positive.

"I don't think for long." Mike sipped his lukewarm drink. "We'll see cancellations once the economic impact hits. Even if our customers want to go ahead, the banks will cancel credit. Maybe our credit will go too."

Mike gave his mug a disgusted look and set it on the table.

"We have inventory," Charlie said. "I doubt we can get a refund."

"So," Kerri touched Charlie's arm, "what's the situation overall?"

"The military supply chains collapsed, but everything else is still going strong; food delivery and that sort of thing."

"For how long…?" Kerri asked.

Charlie shrugged and looked at Mike. He received no support.

"I think it's going to get bad," Mike said. "We might have to lay-off everyone, and with no income and perhaps fewer deliveries, food and everything will be hard to get. I don't want to let anyone go."

"So what do we do?" Kerri spread her hands, palm up.

"Damn it, Kerri, stop asking hard questions. Here, have a cookie." Mike tried to smile and pushed the plate towards Kerri. They were her favourite.

"Do you know how the aliens work?" Charlie asked. "The aliens work together, as a collective. Maybe spending lots of time on ships leads to that, but Ellie said their entire society functions that way, even the populations on planets. No individual has a claim on any resources more than their need, and anyone appointed as a leader is only that until they finish what they had to do.”

“If you know super-computer technology, an individual alien mind operates at what we would think of as super-computer ability, maybe more. They can integrate individual minds to become a huge multi-node super-super-computer, if alien minds are nearby. Ellie never said if the light speed limits it, or if a size limit exists. Perhaps, with thousands of alien ships in the solar system,” Charlie glanced upwards, “a huge organic, sentient computer surrounds us.”

“That’s scary, like the Borg from science fiction.” Mike frowned.

“They don’t want to assimilate us, but just get samples of DNA and help us survive, but resistance is futile.” Charlie laughed.

“Ellie and RoH constantly discuss things between themselves and with whatever ships are involved. They make tactical decisions on Earth on the spot, but the overall plan is broadly based and to that common purpose.”

“What are you getting at?” Mike asked.

“I think,” Kerri jumped in, “we need to solve this predicament in the same way. If we want to keep Hammersmith Inc. and perhaps all of Goderich running, we all need to do it together; you, Charlie, me, and all the employees in the plants. Call a general meeting.”

The idea was not new to Mike, who had organized his business for teamwork. Charlie’s understanding of that had led to his promotion. He had struggled to get suspicious employees and reluctant front-line managers to work together. He had been returning from the Orangeville factory after team training on the fateful night last September, when Ellie and his imp granddaughter RoH had appeared. It seemed a long time ago in a more certain world.

“I walked through the factory last night.” Mike said. “We have two-inch lumber, plastic sheeting, and coils of plastic pipe. I’m worried about food supply. I think we can pre-fabricate hundreds of little greenhouses and give them to people to grow crops.”

“What about those piles of strand board?” Kerri felt excited. “We could make small animal enclosures, chicken coops and rabbit pens. We will need more than vegetables.”

“We’ll build a few samples and I’ll get the mayor and council in to look it over. Some Goderich by-laws will have to go. Meanwhile, we need to get the factory folks on side. I’d offer them first dibs on the things.”

"I'd like to offer a few to RoH and her bunch out on the farm," Charlie said. "Those soldiers have time on their hands."

"Farmland surrounds us," Kerri said. "People could convert from commercial to more locally useful crops, even mixed farming."

"Dream on, girl," Mike laughed.

The committee of three headed to the factory floor. Mike ordered a halt to working on orders until the customers confirmed them. Otherwise, they could apply the material to community use. After an afternoon-long mass employee meeting, the factory went dark. Everyone headed home, hoping that they might sustain themselves until some grander plan came from the higher governments.

The dark hulk of Marine One, the President's personal helicopter, loomed from the darkness. Despite the loud thrumming as the machine settled onto the White House lawn, Mary hoped that this late night trip would go unnoticed.

The noise drew a lone pool reporter into the Washington winter night.

Why do they have the helicopter here?

He watched the President, Mary, and staff climb into the machine. From habit, the President had turned and waved but there was no crowd to say goodbye. The reporter waved back, unseen. President Ascue boarded with stooped shoulders. The machine disappeared, and the echoes of the rotors and turbines faded to the north-west.

The helicopter landed a short walk from Air Force One, and the presidential party hurried across the windswept tarmac. Leaders from both parties in the House and Senate politely shivered at the gangway.

On the plane, the President turned left to his suite, hoping for some rest before they arrived in Des Moines. The politicians headed into the meeting room, and Mary escorted the support staff to the operations centre.

Mary stared at Daisy. Mary could not recall why she had included her on this trip. Daisy had superb skill in research, and Mary now relied on Daisy.

Once in the air, Mary briefed the politicians and easily convinced them. Out of sight of media, the politicians had a common interest in power and personal gain. Unlike the President, Mary had the advantage. In Washington, everyone, no matter the party, respected her, and if honest, they would admit they were afraid of her. Mary had ended the careers of several congressional representatives and one Senator whom she had judged wanting, or dangerous. She had released scandalous information to the media. Her information network spanned the city and beyond. No one important, even out of politics, could have a lover, a weakness, or usefulness hidden from Mary. People saw Mary as the President in all but name.

"Let him sleep," Mary said to the steward. "The Captain said we are facing a headwind and would be slow getting there. I'll brief him about..." she glanced at her watch, "five, Washington time. Bring everyone breakfast about half-past five."

Mary refused to acknowledge exhaustion. Her ambition overpowered personal convenience. Outside of politics, at 45 years old, Mary did not have a life, no family, no hobbies and no lovers, only a large regret.

"Gentlemen," Mary turned to the politicians. She frowned at the lack of women, but that was Washington. "We'll meet with the President at five-thirty for breakfast. Air Force One will touch down at 6:15. Five people will board and we will meet here about 7 AM local...8 AM Eastern time."

"The President will tell you we are in a bipartisan situation. We cannot solve the crisis with biased politics, even in this election year. Any attempt at political advantage will only aid the aliens and further destroy our power and economy. This is a confidential gathering, and there will be no mention of this meeting, let alone what we discuss. Am I clear?"

Mary stared everyone in the eye. The two members of the other party flared inwardly, but had enough political self-interest to agree. Everyone believed that to cross Mary would lead to political and perhaps actual death. Who knew how the aliens would react if they knew about this meeting?

"Daisy, could you type this up for the President, please?"

"Gentlemen," the President began. Mary sat to one side and behind at a separate small table. President Ascue could not see her, but everyone else at the big table could. Politicians had difficulty focusing on the President and not Mary. The religious and labour representatives vacantly smiled, and the three billionaires knew they owned them all.

"Gentlemen," the President repeated, "if we don't counter the alien threat, we will all be broke, and the United States of America finished."

"Why don't you get right to the point?" a rich man smirked.

"What do we do?" The labour representative shifted nervously.

"I have a plan," the President's eyes made a political sweep of the table, "each of you has a part to play."

Mary sat passively, allowing the man's theft of her plan.

"We need to reverse the media's cheering for the invaders. That's the first step in stirring up the mobs against them. Gentlemen," he looked at the billionaires, "you own the media. That's your job."

"It's already underway," said one.

The previous night, Mary had vetted all the plans with the representatives of the class that owned Washington.

"You two," the President turned to the preacher and the labour boss, "have gangs of followers. Organize against the aliens. Get your supporters into the streets."

"Here's the detailed plan," the President snapped his fingers at Mary. She stepped forward with nine folders of collated detail. It horrified the politicians that the man would treat the most dangerous person present as a servant. Mary was only the second most powerful person on the plane and the President third.

"What about us?" The Speaker of the House asked.

Everyone else present regarded the four politicians with annoyance and disgust. They saw the four as servants, bought, paid for and leashed.

"If you look in your folders," Mary treated the men with well-practiced false deference, "you will see an outline of legislation you can introduce. These will protect wealth with certain new banking and investment rules. Expand the definition of an enemy specifically to add non-humans and their hybrids. This will make it illegal to support the aliens without actually attacking freedom of speech."

The political leaders smiled. They would work in familiar territory.

Religious and labour leaders began a half hour of fruitless discussion. Politicians, who from habit had to fill a room with distracting chatter, joined in. The preacher returned to his private jet, and the labour man headed to the terminal for his flight to Seattle. The billionaires watched in the icy wind as Air force One rose and turned east. Then they headed into the warmth to plan for a presidential departure other than on an airplane.

CHAPTER 4

Diamonds are a girl's best friend

Unnoticed by human or alien, a man about sixty years old purchased a ticket at the Dallas airport. The passenger looked pleasant, but he projected an unsettling hawkishness. He would be in Toronto today and in Goderich, Ontario, in the morning. His credit card drew on an account of the Church of Heavenly Enlightenment in Dallas.

Robert Orville had founded the church and pastored a flock of a thousand adherents. Envious local pastors had commented on the unquestioning loyalty of Robert's flock. In comparison, their own congregations seemed like herds of cats. Every congregation had had at least one schism, while the Church of Heavenly Enlightenment had none. No one noticed that when Robert's congregation had reached exactly 1000, he stopped recruiting. His television revenues soared.

No one, including Orville's adherents, knew of his origins. People said he had been born in California. No one had a date. Robert Orville actually had been born in Nevada 20 years after RoH's great-grandfather had been born in Lubbock, Texas. His birth certificate said Rachel Nevada, the town closest to Homey Airport, and more popularly called Groom Lake. That same document listed his mother as Ruth Orville of Rachel, Nevada, and father as "unknown". No other documents referred to Robert, or his mother, until he appeared in Dallas. The only official record was a vagrancy arrest, thirty years ago, for a Robert Orville. After that, nothing until his name appeared on incorporating the Church of Heavenly Enlightenment.

Robert landed in Toronto just after lunch. He walked through customs and immigration without trouble, and rushed to catch a WestJet to London. There, he rented a car and hurried to Goderich. He had asked to meet Pastor George of the Holy Spirit Immersion of Huron. George had been preaching fire against the aliens and Robert found that encouraging. Orville also wanted to learn more about the alien operation centered in the town. He had to know more before he could realize his lifelong desire for revenge. He needed to find Ellie.

Captain Fontaine dozed in the comfortable chair, more relaxed than on any other field assignment. Ghislaine realized that she and her contingent guarding the powerful alien girl had the symbolic status of the British Palace Guard. She joked to the General that Ottawa supply greatcoats and busbies.

In her dazed condition, Ghislaine did not see RoH exit the front door. She snapped to wakefulness when a bright purple glow shone through the window. As Fontaine reached the porch, RoH rose gently skyward and silently disappeared in the low morning overcast.

Ghislaine shivered in the sub-zero cold when the purple column reappeared and RoH walked towards her.

"Nice show," Ghislaine managed. "The purple makes you seem regal."

RoH giggled.

"I'm just a little girl, Ghislaine. I'm sorry we disturbed you, but I could not help the timing." RoH fingered a sizeable diamond that hung on a chain around her neck.

"Diamonds are a girl's best friend," Fontaine laughed.

"It's not diamond. It's like what you call zirconium on Earth, but a bit more durable than either a diamond or its fake. We use quantum manipulation to arrange the atoms of natural material like this and the metal of our ships to be as hard as possible. That's why humans think they are some sort of strange elements, not in nature. This is an amplifier for quantum thoughts, so Mom and I can be in better touch. Mother received one just like it. My father gave it to me. Dad's a stuffed shirt, as you might say, but you would like him. He's special. My star cousins normally don't dote over their reproducts."

RoH examined the stone and tucked it beneath her shirt.

"Reproducts...?" Ghislaine asked.

"Children," RoH said. She found the descriptive words for her status uninteresting. She was simply, RoH.

"Have you had breakfast? I'm starved."

Captain Fontaine mounted the steps with a snow shovel in her hand. She and the squad had levelled a large area between the house and the old command building and hoped to make an ice rink. The last shipment of personal gear from Petawawa included their hockey equipment. They would use the opportunity to fight boredom. The Russian Martian was enthusiastic.

"What are you three up to?" Ghislaine found RoH, Elsie and Jake standing on the porch and looking towards the road.

"We are about to have company," Elsie said. "Muster your people."

"I don't think we will have a problem," RoH said, "but make them feel uneasy."

Ghislaine disappeared to assemble her squad into battle readiness.

RoH focused on the crystal around her neck. She could easily chat with her mother now, no matter the distance. The interstellar craft that RoH called the "Goderich Guardian" remained within easy reach above the atmosphere.

Mother, what did Liz Dafoe tell you?

RoH, she said the government is bringing Russian and Chinese diplomats to the farm. They want their three people back.

They don't want to go.

We know that, so convince the big shots.

A limousine service operated in Goderich, and they became the latest local beneficiary of the alien presence. The sleek, black car turned into the narrow lane. The four men who emerged wore expensive top coats. Two had bare heads; one had a fur cap in the best style of the czars, while a shorter man wore what seemed to be a civilian attempt at a Chinese military winter hat.

Captain Fontaine approached.

"I am Captain Fontaine of the 21st Special Regiment. Can I help you?"

"I'm Gilles Bertrand, liaison with the Ministry of Foreign Affairs," the diplomat said to Fontaine. "We might need your help if these people are stubborn."

"Let's see what happens before we decided what help you'll get." Fontaine stood stone-faced.

"Here," the diplomat extracted a paper from his briefcase and flourished it in a show of certainty, "we order you to help us."

Fontaine examined the paper, folded it neatly and slipped it into a back pocket of her camouflage battle dress.

"I will have use for that later." She patted her bum.

Bertrand scowled.

"I expect more respect from a soldier."

"Come this way. You look cold."

Ghislaine turned and headed to the house without looking back. The visitors followed.

No one took the men's outerwear or offered a chair, and they stood uncomfortably in the farm living room.

The Canadian in charge spotted RoH sitting on one side.

"Get that girl out of here. What are children doing here?"

"She stays," Fontaine said. "You don't know who she is."

"This is a man's job," he said and insulted both RoH and Ghislaine, but neither cared.

None of the delegation recognized RoH. In their circles, they worried more about social cocktails and diplomatic slights than the daily news. They had staff for details. RoH's big public appearance had been on Suncoast Boulevard throwing tractors around, and that had faded compared to other alien news. She remained relaxed in the chair.

"We demand to see the prisoners," the Russian diplomat stepped forward.

"They aren't prisoners." Captain Fontaine took the lead.

She signalled, and a soldier went to the kitchen. In a moment, the Martian refugees appeared. The Chinese couple held hands, drawing a frown from the short man in the army hat. The Russian nodded.

The Russian refugee and the diplomat exchanged words that ended in shouting.

"Nyet" was the last and only easily understood word from the Mars returnee. The diplomat's face turned red.

Fontaine always thought anyone speaking standard Chinese engaged in a shouting competition. She knew it was a tonal language and spoken differently from the romantic ones. After a few exchanges, Ghislaine believed there actually was a shouting match underway.

All three of the farm guests turned to Fontaine and said in English, "We wish to stay here."

"Well then, we'll just take you." The Russian diplomat said and yanked a pistol from his pocket.

"Hey, no weapons," the Canadian guide yelled. The weapon moved towards him. Captain Fontaine's hand went to her pistol, but she was no western quick draw gunslinger. One of her men, slightly out of sight, had his weapon out and pointed.

RoH stepped forward.

"You should put that away." She smiled at the gunman. The weapon now pointed directly at her face.

"Get out of my way." He snarled. We are taking our man.

For the second time since her arrival on Earth, RoH stared down a loaded gun. The weapon leapt from his hand and floated between it and RoH's head. She reached out and with a finger pushed the thing into a gentle spin. RoH smiled as the gun gradually spiralled towards the ceiling where it stopped beside the light fixture. Shock immobilized the Russian.

"These nice people are staying here for as long as they wish. They are not prisoners and may leave."

"Children don't talk," the Canadian said. RoH smiled.

"We recommend that the Russians and Chinese governments name these people as ambassadors. You think they were smart enough to send to Mars, but they are more intelligent than you think. They would be a good link with us."

"Who is us?" the Canadian asked.

"I and my star family are who you need to deal with."

Elsie appeared from the kitchen, in her true alien form. The four diplomats had never been close to a star traveller and cowered. Elsie reverted to her movie version of a farmer's wife.

"Would you boys like some breakfast?" Elsie smiled.

The four visitors ran to the door and the waiting limousine.

"Tell your governments," RoH called through the doorway.

"Jaden, let's go to town and chat with your grandmother," RoH pushed away from the breakfast table. "Ghislaine, please drive us?"

Captain Fontaine dropped RoH and Jaden in the town square and then headed to the mall to find treats for the troops.

Emily, Jaden's grandmother, sat on a bench, warmed by the sun in a January thaw. These warm winter days occurred frequently, and while people enjoyed these breaks from winter, they warned of climate change. RoH headed to the café for coffee and hot chocolate.

RoH stood on the steps of the café, holding a carrier of cups and a bag of treats, but she froze in startled awareness.

A whisper...?

Somewhere, the town hosted another individual with alien abilities. RoH knew where everyone should be, but not this person.

That should not happen... she frowned, slowly scanning the square. The disturbance was faint, not close. She only detected it because the crystal hanging from her neck had amplified.

Where is Ellie? The question came unmistakably. RoH tensed and drew a guard over her mind. Had the entity sensed her? The sensation of that question was sharper than the initial detection, as if the entity had shouted to itself and then amplified by her new diamond.

Father...

Yes, daughter...

Is a cousin on the ground here in Goderich looking for us? RoH thought of all the star-people as cousins.

No... Why...?

There is someone, or something here, a mentat.

No... That can't be.

Yes, father, RoH mentally stamped her foot. *I know it is real! Warn mother. They are looking for her.*

We have no record...no authorization.

Is it a reproduct like mother and I?

There was only silence from RoH's alien father.

RoH hurried to the bench with the goodies.

"I'll be back in a few minutes," she told the women.

The pair watched in horrified amazement as RoH deliberately walked into the middle of the street. Several vehicles, driving faster than they should, sped around her, but RoH stood in the centre lane without concern.

A purple light drew her into the sky. People leapt from vehicles or stood immobilized on the walkway.

"This alien thing is getting out of hand," one onlooker quipped. Goderich residents had not become used to strange happenings. Every demonstration of alien presence evoked both admiration and fear. The prettiest little town had taken on the title of the strangest, but it was good for business.

RoH appeared on the ship in her star-traveller form. Several of her star family had gathered, including her genetic father.

"What is this person I detected?" RoH's anger defeated the normal niceness filter of alien discussion. "I felt evil."

One of the grey shapes uneasily stirred at her emotion.

"We reviewed all our records, back to the beginning of your line. No breeding happened before that accident, but we have lost track of three of the known reproducts."

"How could we lose them?"

"We are sorry that we lost these experimental artefacts."

"These people aren't artefacts; they are beings, sentient beings, more like my great grandfather. They are I, and you. The one in Goderich is evil."

RoH's appearance flashed from star form to her human little girl. The figures surrounding her recoiled, not at the sight of a human, but they saw the depth of RoH's wrath. Anger did not live amongst star travelers, and they had no experience in it.

"You're right, I'm furious." RoH stamped a foot. "You had better get used to it. All human emotions come along for the ride with empathy and togetherness. It's how they sort out who they like to be with."

It's bad... the collective thought washed RoH.

"Damned right, it can be bad," RoH agreed, "but if it doesn't lead to humans killing each other, it strengthens a bond once resolved. I would like it if you stopped seeing me and Mom as lab samples."

She glanced around at the gathering of grey shapes. The conversation radiated outwards and caused a stir amongst the fleet.

"So let's decide what to do about your mistake, Father." she smiled.

RoH reappeared less dramatically to stand in the 10-centimetre snow on the courthouse lawn. She crossed the street and joined Emily and Jaden.

"I think your chocolate is cold," Emily handed over the cup. RoH held it in a mitten'd hand and the liquid reached acceptable warmth.

"Damn," Emily exclaimed, "you spook me whenever you do things like heating chocolate or standing in traffic!"

"I'm sorry about the exit. I was angry, but I'm okay now."

RoH felt through her jacket for the hard lump of crystal that hung on her chest. She searched with her mind, but she found no sign of the other hybrid. RoH snuggled against Emily. It felt nice to have friends.

Unknown to RoH, two pairs of eyes had watched her spectacular, exit to the ship. They had remained in their car when she made the less spectacular but equally alien return.

"Jaden and I need to return to the farm. Captain Fontaine will be here in a few minutes."

Ghislaine had just left Wal-Mart when she felt an urgency to collect RoH and head home. Minutes later, as they left the square, another vehicle, a nondescript rental, followed them to Victoria Street and out of town. RoH twisted to look out the rear window. The car followed onto the County Road.

Mother...

It is the Americans, Love. They are looking for you. They want to kidnap you and breed you.

Father says I won't morph to the breeding age until next year.

They will take your genetic signature if they can't breed you. That's their plan.

I have a job to do. There is a rogue evil hybrid. It's looking for you.

Your father told me. I think you will have to endure some of the American ordeal before you can track down the outlier. Great-grandfather just told me they have located two of the three. One is dead, why is unknown, the other disappeared into the Australian outback. It seems to have been a breeding attempt at Alice Springs, which is in the middle of nowhere, worse than Lubbock, where we came from. We think the third one came from Nevada, USA. It must be the evil one.

I want to go to Australia.

You will, dear, but first you have to give the Americans another setback. Make sure everyone on the farm is safe.

Love you, Mother.

Love you, RoH.

"That car didn't follow us down here," Fontaine said as they turned into the farm lane.

"You saw it?" Captain Fontaine surprised RoH.

"It's my training," Ghislaine said. "Knowing what's behind you might keep you alive."

"It's Americans," RoH said. "They know how the CIA set this place up, so they didn't need to get closer. Now they know where I am."

"You...?" Ghislaine asked.

"They are going to kidnap me." RoH climbed from the SUV.

"We'll stop them," Captain Fontaine became professional.

"You probably can, at least for a bit," RoH said. "I don't want anyone hurt, including them, but especially you and our friends."

Jaden had overheard and sobbed.

"Don't worry, sister, you all will be safe. I must go with them. None of you should get angry or hate. That makes us weaker. Believe me; we are stronger than they are."

RoH hugged Jaden.

CHAPTER 5

Who's zoomin' Who?

The first request for a meeting with the alien representatives at the United Nations General Assembly came through NAAP. Siglinde Hilfreich received a coldly polite call from Mary, the President's Chief-of-Staff. Siglinde had met the woman at her last visit to the President. Apparently, Mary resented that the head of NAAP had not stayed in Washington. It caused one of the few times in her career when Mary did not have control.

The American invitation attempted to pre-empt the Secretary General of the UN, and that caused a problem. The Secretary rebelled and refused the meeting until he had consulted all member states. Even though it was a foregone conclusion in the rapidly deteriorating global economy, the United Nations chief would not let the Americans usurp his limited authority. After a week of wrangling, UN headquarters in New York issued a formal invitation. The United Nations ignored Washington and channelled the request through the Canadian Prime Minister. He resented being a messenger boy that once more had to ask Liz Dafoe and Dawn Waasnodae for help. The aliens refused all other contact. In due course, they agreed and scheduled the gathering for February 2.

Robert Orville finally contacted Pastor George. George had seen Orville preach on television, and he harboured both envy and dislike. The two had differing views on the scriptures, but Robert preached more power than George did. It had only been since the undisputed aliens that the Holy

Spirit Immersion of Huron, as led by Pastor George, had become a popular and powerful voice. Pastor George earned this new prominence on New Year's Eve in the Goderich square. His well-publicized condemnation of the aliens to hell along with treasonous scientists and the Martian settlement survivors had spread.

"You have come a long way to meet me," Pastor George eyed Robert Orville and stroked his scruffy beard. "I'm honoured."

Looks like a cartoon of a guru, Orville thought. Robert had the appearance, copied from an actor in an old television series, of a mature father with wisdom. He chose an investment adviser look designed to make people trust and send money.

"I saw you preaching about the alien devils." Robert smiled. "You impressed me, and I share your sentiments, but we have had no local interactions in Texas. I thought I would visit the centre of the alien universe, so to speak."

"It's a scary place," Pastor George frowned. "More people doubt the faith, and I can't preach from Genesis anymore. Even firm believers are wondering about Adam and Eve."

"My flock are smarter than that," Robert bragged, but George thought he detected cynicism.

Could Orville be a phoney?

Pastor George held complete faith in the word's truth. His carless appearance reflected a genuine disdain for worldly things. The wild hair gave added emphasis when he preached the Book of Revelation. He seemed then to be a present-day version of Saint John the Divine, but he did not have the wit or dishonesty to do it deliberately.

Robert Orville frowned at George's hesitation.

Phoney or not, I'll be in charge.

"I would like to meet these aliens," Robert said, "and sort them out about where the actual power in the universe lies."

"I've met them," George shuddered. "They don't fear us. The little girl actually froze us in our tracks and pushed our vehicles out of the way so the cowards who fled Mars could escape our enforcing God's wrath. Then she just put everything back to the way it was, as if we had no importance, the arrogant little snipe. If you assume you have power, you will make a mistake."

"I have a power that you do not have." Robert said. "They don't know of me. They aren't ready for me."

One human vice Robert possessed, or perhaps possessed Robert, was hatred for those who had abandoned him in Rachel, Nevada.

Pastor George laughed. "I think you assume too much."

"I assume nothing," Robert flared. "I want Ellie, my real enemy."

"How..."

The church office door opened with a knock and the secretary entered.

"I'm leaving now, Pastor."

"That's okay, Gail, I'll lock up."

"Can you please deliver the parcel to Elder Vanderdam?" Gail said as she went out the door.

"So, we are alone?" Robert noticed that night had fallen. He looked at George. "Don't you have security?"

"Nothing bad ever happens here."

A wind whipped small swirls of snow about his feet as Pastor George backed his SUV to the side door of the church and struggled to load a large parcel into the back. Satisfied that he had secured the church doors, he drove into the bitter January night, abandoning the snowy parking lot to a lone rental car.

The following Sunday, Pastor George preached the most fiery sermon the congregation had ever heard.

On January 28th, Ellie called Bobby Briscoe at the television studio.

"Can you and Jimmy Smith join Quantz and RoH on the farm on February 1st? Come prepared to stay overnight. I promise you some interesting footage, but again, you'll have to sit on it for a bit."

"Damn, you are always teasing me," Bobby laughed.

"Yes, but the results have always been worth it."

Bobby could not argue. Both he and Jimmy Smith had received accolades, and media groups nominated them for several journalism awards. The follow-up program from London, the day after the aliens had staged the spectacular rescue of the Martian settlers and the comet Clavette hitting Mars, had been the most widely viewed news presentation globally ever. The broadcast had far exceeded the record previously held by a sports event. More significantly, both now had huge salaries paid from a global network pool. No other reporters had the inside edge with the aliens.

"Business in Canada...?" The Canadian border agent seemed to be bored.

"We're going to the casino," the young man driving said. There were three others in the car, about the same age. The agent peered into the SUV.

"How about the Red Wings last night?" The agent said.

"Red Wings... oh the Red Wings, I don't follow hockey. How did they do?"

"Beat the Leafs six to nothing. Enjoy the casino." He handed the man's papers back. *Who doesn't watch hockey?*

On January 31st, in ones, twos and fours, young people from the USA crossed into Canada at Fort Erie, Windsor and Sarnia and claimed they were visiting the casinos. All twelve ended up in motels in Goderich.

Silhouetted in the setting sun that same day, a large American Coast guard icebreaker eased into Goderich harbour. Small bits of harbour ice swirled away to the stern. Deep blasts from the ship's horn raised a similar greeting from the Canadian vessel moored at the coastguard base. The mild winter had given little work to the breaker and a good excuse for a courtesy call. It moored up the harbour from the Canadian base in a place that normally hosted a wintering freighter. It was late in the day. They scheduled the greeting party for the next night, and the visiting vessel would leave on February 3rd.

About 3 AM, long after quiet had descended on Goderich, a black SUV made a U-turn on the wharf that separated the harbour from the river and pulled up alongside the American boat. The duty watch knocked on the captain's door, and soon crewmembers lowered several large duffle bags from the ship. No one spoke as the two people in the SUV stowed the bags, and in twenty minutes, the vehicle sped up North Harbour Road towards the Comfort Inn.

"What a dead hick town this is," the man in the passenger seat said.

"It works for us," replied the woman behind the wheel.

"We need sleep," the man said. "Tomorrow, we plan the raid. There are some Canadian soldiers there who we'll have to take out."

Bobby Briscoe turned into the farm lane.

"It's rustic, eh." Jimmy looked out at the snowy scene that could have been a Christmas card.

"We'll shoot filler stuff of this. Producers love that sort of thing."

RoH and Ghislaine greeted the reporters. They did not need to hurry. Nothing would happen until daybreak the next day.

RoH waited until late in the afternoon, after everyone had become acquainted. She then gathered them into the renovated space where the CIA had ripped out a wall and joined the dining room and the old farmhouse parlour. It felt crowded, as the eleven soldiers seemed to take up a lot of space. Jaden and RoH sat together with the reporters mixed with the troops and the aliens, disguised as an old farm couple, hovered near the kitchen door.

"The Americans are going to kidnap me tomorrow morning." RoH ignored pleasantries, and her matter-of-fact voice kept everyone calm.

"We'll deal with them," Captain Fontaine muttered.

"No," RoH smiled at the Ghislaine, "we don't want anyone, not even the kidnappers, to get hurt. We didn't come up with this, but we will use it. The first part must happen to their plan. They will be ready to shoot, but we have to make sure they don't hurt any of you."

"Who's behind it?" Bobby interviewed while Jimmy videoed.

"The American government, specifically the White House and the CIA…"

This would be dynamite when broadcast. Bobby saw more accolades but wondered if that might seem meaningless soon.

"How do you know?" Bobby hoped the answer would prevent a libel suit.

"We have been working to save Earth for a long time," RoH looked at the reporter. "We follow most key places, including the American White House, where they hatched this plot."

She looked into Jimmy's camera.

"You will notice we don't start a fight. We let them plot and see if we can use it to help life on Earth. My kidnapping will serve for part of that."

"So here's the strategy for tomorrow."

"Can I keep filming?" Jimmy asked.

"The more the world knows, the better it is. We don't want to suppress anything. I know it sounds arrogant, but humans cannot repel us directly. If we give up and leave, it will be on our decision, made in sadness, but it will mean we have decided that the human cause is hopeless."

Everyone fell silent.

"At four in the morning, gather in the operations building." She nodded toward the steel structure set away from the house. "The kidnappers will ignore it at first. All you have to do is to be ready, but do nothing except to defend yourselves. Hopefully, I will be a distraction to keep you safe."

The room remained quiet. This little girl amazed them with her calm assessment and instructions. Some, like Quantz, understood more of RoH's ability. The others had gained that insight. Jimmy's video, when eventually shown to the world, would raise reactions of admiration and trust, but it would also deepen the fear of aliens. Many would think it a horror that some non-human could appear as a little human girl, innocent and seemingly harmless, and yet could hold armed people at bay.

RoH followed her friends' thoughts.

"I'm still a little Earth girl," she said, "but I am probably the end point of the experiment to create a human-star variant. When I am an adult, if that concept works, they will imitate my existence throughout the galaxy."

"What happens if it isn't a success?" Jaden shivered.

"Oh, sweetie," RoH giggled, "They'll give me some minor planet to live, where I might be happy and not cause mischief. It might be Earth."

The sparkle in RoH's eye said she teased. Her abilities and wealth of empathy already awed her star family and her human relatives. It seemed she followed the oft repeated but mostly ignored saying, love your enemies as yourself. No one that day, in that farm parlour, thought this little girl, this powerful entity, could ever be a threat.

RoH wandered their minds.

"It helps," she said, "to know the galaxy does not harbour real enemies."

Inwardly, RoH thought of the evil she had detected in Goderich. That enemy she might not love. It perhaps had the power to be a threat. The evil represented the first sentient individual who RoH believed she might kill.

Still, she thought, *few humans are neither purely evil nor purely good, but this enemy is not all human.*

The attack came long before the eastern sky lightened. The American agents, dressed in winter white, quietly eased down the concession road. A stealth foot approach in the pre-dawn darkness would allow them to be in control of the yard before the defenders detected them. They saw only infrared signatures from the chimney.

Captain Fontaine's troop waited at the ready, clutching assault rifles inside the large command building. Their night-vision revealed ten infiltrators. They followed RoH's instructions and held fire. Ghislaine sympathized with her sniper. She held her weapon ready, and she saw the targets. In fact, all members of the troop had easily qualified as sharpshooters at the distance of the road.

"Obviously," Ghislaine whispered, "they don't expect us to be awake."

The approaching force came down the lane, fast and spaced well apart. *Professional...,* Ghislaine thought.

The team spread out in the yard and two of the kidnappers prepared to assault the front door. The door opened and RoH stepped out. A swarm of shining insects rose from the oak tree and flooded the yard in light.

"I think you are looking for me."

The team leader, startled by the sudden brightness, rushed up and roughly bound RoH's hands behind her back with a zip tie.

"Check all the buildings," he ordered.

Several attackers levelled their weapons and advanced to the command building. Jimmy followed them in his camera frame. Ghislaine's force slipped safeties off.

"You don't need to check the buildings. You have me. I'm alone." RoH stared at the leader.

"Forget the buildings. We have her. She's alone." The man called out.

A black SUV hurried down the lane. Ghislaine and the others watched the kidnappers push RoH into the back and speed off. The rest of the force hurried to their vehicles hidden just over the brow of the hill. Jimmy had everything on video from the time the attackers walked into the yard light until the last of the kidnappers vanished down the lane.

CHAPTER 6

War drums and a hollow drum

The runway lights activated as a Gulfstream 550 marked Agency Air with an American registration number touched down at the Goderich Airport. The craft turned at the end of the runway beside Highway 21 and an SUV sped down the general aviation strip. Three figures boarded the plane, and both vehicles departed. The Gulfstream climbed rapidly into the Detroit ATC air space. The SUV turned towards town and headed to the border at Sarnia.

The Gulfstream arrived at Joint Base Andrews in Washington, DC as a Canadian government Challenger left London, Ontario. It carried Ellie Keys and Steve Jorgensen to New York City and the United Nations. Although they had travelled in a more conventional way, a protective ship followed above the atmosphere.

RoH paused at the bottom of the Gulfstream steps and surveyed the air base. Several rows of military aircraft, mostly jet fighters, filled the ramp area at the far edge of the field. All were dead. Not even the ground support carts could provide power. An agent gripped RoH's arm and led her to a waiting limousine. The car had no flags or insignia and blended into Washington traffic in a city jaded by self-important comings and goings.

"You don't need this." RoH paused at the car, handed the agent her zip tie, and climbed into the rear seat between him and another agent. The kidnapper kept a nervous hand on his pistol all the way to the White House. Everywhere he looked along the way, he saw buildings razed by bombing and fire. It was a war zone. The acrid smell of smoke penetrated the armoured limousine's anti-gas-attack system.

"Washington's burning," he cried. "Why weren't we warned?"

"What the hell are you talking about?" the agent on the other side of RoH eyed his apparently unstable partner.

"Someone destroyed all the buildings. Look out the window."

"Everything looks fine to me," the other said and signalled the woman who rode shotgun to be ready.

"What...?" the first agent exclaimed. Out his window, a destroyed building he had been watching appeared whole and normal. A few people moved on the sidewalk with no concern. Sweat beaded on his forehead. RoH smiled.

It's too late to tell you to behave; was that necessary?

Mother, he is actually a nice man. He has a wife and three cute kids. He would really like to be a carpenter.

Don't worry, dear. He won't have this job much longer.

What do you mean?

We have calculated that based on the culture of the U.S.A. there will be a violent change in government.

How...?

That is unpredictable right now. We don't know who the other forces are yet. The hatred that they are manufacturing against us must first reach its peak. Siglinde, Ted and their friend Liz are leaving until it all settles down. Steven and I will soon arrive in New York City on our way to the United Nations. You have your fun; we'll do our work.

Love...

Love you too...

In contrast to RoH's clandestine journey to the White House, Ellie and Steve received VIP treatment. Officials handled them as dangerous rather than allies. They rode from Laguardia to the United Nations in a stretch limousine that flew the blue and white flag of the UN above the front fender. The American version of pomp came in the usual form of a dozen escorting police cars with flashing lights and sirens. Spiteful religious demonstrators appeared at a few spots, but their hateful chanting did not penetrate the limousine.

The convoy sped down 1ˢᵗ Avenue, and the black car swung through the gate onto the circle drive. Every available space hosted reporters and camera crews who hoped to see an alien up close. The aliens would give them a bonus.

The driver intended to swing left and under the portico where the Secretary General waited, but the engine died. Ellie and Steve climbed out, followed by their mystified handlers. The Secretary General stepped into the drive beneath the portico to see what had happened.

Cheers and boos rose from the crowd gathered on First Ave. A preacher bellowed through a bullhorn to condemn the aliens to death and made misogynistic and racist comments about Ellie. A cop grabbed the bullhorn and two others slammed the man on the pavement. The issue was not what he was saying, but the Council made using a bullhorn in New York City illegal after the anti-Wall Street insurrection.

Ellie and Steve walked a few steps to the middle of the circular drive. A shaft of purple light shot down, and an alien walked from the light and touched Ellie and Steve. The trio approached the stunned Secretary General.

They stopped under the portico with the alien clasping its hands waist high. The visitor said something that grated on all ears.

"Thank you for inviting us," Steve translated.

The Secretary General gaped and could not respond.

"It's okay, Mr. Secretary," Ellie said, "Great-grandfather is not a threat."

The diplomat suddenly came to life and extended his hand in reflex. Grandfather shook it, followed by Steve and Ellie. The Secretary General would later say that the alien's grip was firm, warm and comforting. To the chagrin of the mob of reporters, the party disappeared into the General Assembly building. The United Nations carefully controlled all video feed.

"The Security Council has directed me to make a statement and ask a list of questions." The Secretary General stood with the newcomers in an anteroom by the entrance to the dais of the General Assembly.

"We will only speak in front of the assembly," Steve translated.

"But..." the Secretary General began. Ellie waved her hand.

"We are not here to negotiate," Ellie said. "We will state the situation plainly, so that the world knows, unfiltered by any government or their servants like the United Nations. I don't mean to belittle you, Secretary General, but we would like to proceed to the assembly."

The Secretary General smiled. He knew that their control of the television coverage would only allow what the Security Council wanted the world to hear.

The alien made a sound to Ellie. She smiled.

"Sorry, Mr. Secretary," Ellie said, "but we have by-passed your television control room. All the raw feed is going to the world. We have been broadcasting this conversation. Unfortunately, we could not share your recent thought about censorship."

The annoyed diplomat escorted them to the assembly hall. The place had a grand appearance, common with those spaces that humans designated as important. Delegate seats swept up and away from the front. A large recessed dome dominated the space. Graphics created by a celebrated artist, devoid of meaning but overpowering in scale, decorated the sidewalls.

There was no need to call the assembly to order in this informal session, but the hall had seldom overflowed as now. The Secretary General introduced the visitors and stumbled over how to address the alien.

"You can call me Grandfather," Steve translated. He glanced up at the windows where the professional translators observed the scene.

At least they only need to translate from my English. Steve smiled upwards.

Your English is good, dear, Ellie giggled.

Stop reading my mind you wench...

If an alien face could show a frown, Grandfather directed one towards his great-granddaughter and Steve.

As Grandfather reached the podium, a police strike force moved up the hallway and stopped just outside the door. Police presence violated diplomatic protocol, but the Security Council wanted to neutralize the delegation. The major powers liked coercion, and the police waited.

Steve went to work as Grandfather began.

"My Earth friends," Steve translated, "Our species has had a scientific curiosity about Earth for over one of your centuries. Our interest is still strong."

"Fortunately, in 1947, our plan of quiet observation and sampling met a minor disaster and a success. Grandfather and Steve looked at Ellie. A craft that I travelled on crashed in the American state of New Mexico, near a little place called Roswell. One of the crew had died of natural causes and that led to the mishap. The American government impounded the craft along with several of my crewmembers. For our research, we allowed the USA to keep those for some decades."

"The crash injured me, and I made my way to Lubbock, Texas. There, completely unintended, I fell in what you humans call love with a human woman, and she loved me, even after she knew my real identity. We parented a child whose lineage has resulted in my great-granddaughter, Ellie, who is standing beside me."

Grandfather reached out to touch Ellie's arm.

"Our research to that point had been cold and meddling. It caused harm to some humans. My experience introduced another element into our thinking, human emotions, and part of that is love, empathy and the desire to socialize. Those things a woman's love in Texas gave to me. After that, we began a programme of purposely creating hybrids. In our ignorance, we created several disasters."

He let Steve catch up. The force beyond the door grew restless, but no one had issued the order.

"Ellie has been more than an experiment," Grandfather glanced towards her. "As she matured with us amongst the stars, we learned more of what we missed, of what perhaps you humans could give us."

A general gasp rose from an audience that still considered science fiction as having documentary meaning. They waited for the demand for ransom.

"You are thinking we want some physical resources from Earth? I must repeat what we have said several times since New Year's Eve. We want nothing physical and no tribute. We want to incorporate into our civilization empathy and the desire for socialization from humans, nothing more. You are a unique species. Ellie brought a taste of that to our community. She has been an example while travelling many light-years from Earth. Now, she has returned to the source, and with her daughter, whom you know as RoH. While Ellie may be the example, RoH is perhaps the ultimate in what a star traveller should be; what we hope will be. RoH has great power, but also a huge amount of empathy and caring. We see RoH as the next step in the evolution of galactic life."

"We had not decided how to, or even if we would reveal ourselves until the looming disaster of comet Clavette hitting Mars forced us to rescue the settlers. Not to do so would be, as Ellie taught us, inhuman." Grandfather allowed an ironic smile. "So here we are, more by accident than planned."

"Because we had to do that, we realized we had to neutralize all of your militaries."

This raised a hostile murmur.

"Ellie, and now RoH, and several others on Earth unite humans and we star travellers into an extended family. We would like to see you succeed and do what is necessary to survive and perhaps reach the stars. If you could do that, you would be a valuable species in the void. Unfortunately, you are on the way to committing suicide. Either you will destroy your climate, or go to war and irradiate the planet. None of the known species who travel the stars is hostile or aggressive, and all have a feeling of group responsibility. They all threw away extreme individualism and greed. Those species who did not overcome those characteristics failed to reach the stars. We give you the time to pause and think. We hope you decide wisely."

Both Ellie and Grandfather scanned the audience members' minds. Every delegate had thoughts about how to defeat the growing mass movements in their countries and the aliens who had instigated them.

"You are all thinking of how to kill us and our human supporters," Ellie replaced Grandfather at the podium and spoke in English. "We do not want to kill any of you. We do not need to do that. If you do not listen to your people and take care of their needs, and all life on this planet, you will die by your own doing, after we are gone, and we surely will go. If you cannot stop yourselves, we won't do it for you. Sorry, but that must be the way to the stars."

She waved to the ceiling in an expansive gesture. The audience gasped as the vast decorative ceiling displayed a bleak planetary landscape with an eerie red sun hanging in a dusty sky.

"That is a planet not too far from here, but that would be your future, or more correctly, the future of the rocky ball we love and call Earth, if you don't choose wisely. A technical culture once lived on that planet," she again waved, "and more advanced than Earth is now. They took the wrong path."

"I have searched most of your minds, you exalted leaders of the nations, and I find you wanting." Grandfather spoke and Steve rushed to keep up. Rippling anger and perhaps fear ran through the hall as self-defined elite leaders felt violated and helpless.

"Most of you are shallow opportunists, enjoying the fruits of inequality. You are here because you want to appear at the centre of significant events. Most of you," Grandfather stared at representatives of the three strongest countries, "want to have your militaries restored to attack us. My Ellie's heart is breaking over that. Earth is her home. This exploitation of the many by you few to feed your grotesque power and comfort at the expense of all living things on Earth attacks her soul. It also assaults your souls. You have sold your humanity for comfort and vanity, and if you do not change, most life on Earth will die, and you will die with it. The curse you exploiters have brought on yourselves is that you will die last. You will have more time to suffer the horror of it than most humans and other living things."

"We travellers will neither speed that up nor will we stop it. It is up to you."

Grandfather waved his hand over the room and fell silent. Ellie took the podium.

"I'm mostly human. I want you to succeed. It will break my heart otherwise. Please..."

Her face pleaded as Ellie sighed and stepped back.

The cavernous place hung in total silence. The ceiling returned to its empty decorative glory. Several representatives applauded and clapping rose from small delegations. The rest remained stone-faced and silent.

Ellie sighed again. Steve became nervous at the restless crowd. The Secretary General pressed a button on the dais. The doors behind burst open and a dozen armed agents rushed onto the platform.

Steve ran to protect Ellie. One agent raised a rifle towards Steve. Ellie pointed her hand, and the weapon wrenched from the man's hands and flew up to spear into the ceiling.

Ellie, Grandfather, and Steve grouped together. Shouting and screams came from the auditorium. Some people ran for the exits. A few rushed towards the platform, crying, "No... No..."

The attackers encircled the three on the platform.

The witnesses could not agree on the details of events that only involved a few seconds. The round dome above the chamber flew skywards. Instantly, a purple light surrounded the trio and the attacking force. The trio, the Secretary General and the police flew out of the hole created by the missing dome, so quickly most thought they had simply vanished.

Watchers further away at the back of the room, and the television cameras saw them soar into the sky. The room became deathly silent except for falling debris. Fragments from the roof pelted the area around the building. Many people suffered minor injuries, but the main section of the dome roof flew into the river. The media outside first reported a terror attack and a bomb explosion, but the intact dome, bobbing upside down in the East River, told otherwise. Ellie, Steve, Grandfather and about a dozen cops and the Secretary had disappeared.

They sat RoH in the Cabinet Room near the President's office. The cavernous place and the table that had room for 40 people could intimidate. While waiting, RoH made an origami swan from the linen napkin at her place. A man in a white coat brought in breakfast. RoH chose the omelette. The wonderful cook in Captain Fontaine's troop, along with Elsie, had given RoH a love of eggs and toast.

As she ate, RoH searched the building with her mind. She sensed darkness. Several minds radiated hostility. It was not Mary or the President. These were further away and conspiratorial.

Perhaps the hostiles are the violent ones from Mother's warning.

CHAPTER 7

Hello and Goodbye
To the moon... Siglinde, to the honeymoon...

"It's time for us to have a honeymoon," Ted drew Siglinde closer beneath the covers. He pondered how wonderful, how alien it felt to sleep beside a human, especially this human woman. Ellie's great-grandfather had explained it all, but he had not conveyed the pleasure and feelings that accompanied it. Ellie and RoH called it love.

"I thought we were having one," Siglinde snuggled against Ted.

"I mean a trip," Ted smiled and kissed Siglinde on the forehead. "To where there's a waterfall and good food."

"I've been to Niagara Falls," Siglinde smirked. "Found it overrated when you leave the hotel room, and I had a room to myself."

"I'm thinking of a great place. It actually is a moon, but much further away, about 19 light-years to be exact. We give it the romantic designation of catalogue number Z263-A."

"You don't make our honeymoon moon sound attractive."

"Our community only designates planets and stars with symbols that translate to numbers and letters. The native species' word for Z263-A is softer and translates to Jewel in English."

"Well, a diamond is a girl's best friend, and a diamond is a jewel. I haven't seen a diamond from you yet." Siglinde's sense of humour had shallow roots.

"They have experts in quantum processes." Ted suggested.

"Even better... I'm in. You're a gem."

"Good, because NAAP no longer has anything useful to do except baby-sit the politicians. I thought you might like something more interesting and going back to MIT is out. Z263-A has waterfalls and forests, too."

"So we will close NAAP."

"Not so fast, Professor; we are sending in replacements."

"The President will never approve, and he wants to exercise the little authority the aliens left him."

"The President will never know, nor anyone else. Three star-travellers are coming down, and while they are not doppelgangers, they will look like us."

"Three? I only count two in this bed," Siglinde snickered, but Ted had puzzled her.

"We are taking Liz with us to Jewel."

"Oh, great, every girl's dream, a female third on the honeymoon."

"I hadn't thought of that," Ted laughed. "Remember, we aliens have explored all human cultural material... all of it, and some of that internet stuff is..."

"Don't even think it, lover-boy."

"Just kidding," Ted felt satisfied with his human humour, "but Liz will get to explore a new culture. That'll keep the anthropologist in her busy. You and I will sneak off to the delights of Jewel, or at least to the quiet places where the native intellectuals sit at waterfalls and think about the universe."

"Does Liz know?"

"She jumped at the chance when I described Z263-A. She's interested in their self-naming the planet Jewel while we use Earth, the ground at our feet."

"That reminds me," Siglinde jumped out of bed and dressed, "what do you call your planet?"

"I don't have one," Ted seemed sad. "They bred me on a ship, and by the time I became self-aware, we were flitting around star systems far away from where they had fertilized my zygote."

"That sounds cold and unsettling."

"I now find it sad from a human perspective, but I have been on Earth for over twenty revolutions. Earth is the closest to a home planet I have ever had."

Siglinde counted backwards.

"So you turned up here about the age Ted Kotwas would finish high school?"

"Yup, up-state New York, South Jefferson High... Go Spartans Go. They never went far, though." Ted laughed. "They were good times. I had to become a teenager, and even nerds went to the games."

"No girlfriend?"

"The chicks didn't find a guy who got perfect in math to be sexy."

"I do," Siglinde kissed Ted.

"But there is Laura Grey," Ted sounded wistful. Siglinde gave him a harder than normal shoulder punch.

"Laura's a nerd too, an astronaut prepping for the Jupiter mission. They will cancel it. We were just friends. Nerd girls were social misfits too, so we stumbled around, but that was it."

"Hey, I'm a nerd girl, and I don't stumble."

"I noticed," Ted had dressed and headed to the door, "let's grab breakfast on the way to the office. Our ship leaves tomorrow."

Historians, looking back at the beginnings of alien contact, would call February 2nd as a key day at the beginning of the story. Only the spectacle that introduced the aliens to humans on the previous New Year's Eve surpassed it. On this day; the aliens challenged all the Earth governments; arranged it so the American government became ineffective, and the first humans left for Jewel.

Siglinde and Liz almost panicked when they met their replacement selves on the morning of departure. Ted showed no emotion, but he and Elliana reassured the women.

"They don't have your souls, or whatever," Elliana laughed. "They have their own life force, and are real, just like Ted and I. We harmed no Siglinde or Liz in the making of this charade."

The three new comers flashed into alien form, produced the star equivalent of smiles and reverted to perfect copies of the Earth scientists.

"I found," Siglinde 2 looked at Siglinde, "the conversation you had with RoH a few months ago to be amusing. I will cherish that memory forever.

That girl needs a little sharpening of her physics, but that's not my job or her purpose."

Siglinde looked confused.

"I have absorbed all of your memories, Siglinde," her pseudo-twin smiled. "You have a wonderful mind, and I'm happy to share it. No wonder Teddy boy loves you. Maybe I'll love this doppelgänger Ted." She soft-punched Ted's duplicate, who responded with a wink.

"See," Elliana smirked, "they have been on Earth only a few minutes and have already picked up bad, or perhaps good, habits."

"I am concerned, if I ever meet any of your colleagues in physics, that I might talk from my knowledge and not at the current human level of understanding. If I did, they will think Siglinde Hilfreich had gone nuts."

"They already do, because I like you star folks." Siglinde resisted the desire to hug her stand in version. If she had a therapist, she would have had to explain why she liked herself so much.

"I'll be the team coordinator here," Elliana said, "to keep us from making mistakes or getting into bad human habits." She giggled. "See, I'm already corrupted. It would be worse if you three appeared to know too much other than not enough. I don't think we will slip up, but if we do, I guess we would have to alter a few memories."

"Give the President a lobotomy," Siglinde laughed.

"We won't have to," Elliana frowned. "He does not have long to live, but won't directly die from anything we do."

CHAPTER 8

Unplanned parenthood

The President strode into the room, comfortable in his domain. Mary trailed, and several others, including Daisy, followed her at a safe distance. He looked at the little girl with disdain and took a seat at the opposite end of the vast table. RoH glanced at him and played with her linen swan. The man reddened and held out a hand for a file from Mary. He flipped through it for show, but the President seldom read briefing notes. He took pride in his memory and felt verbal briefings were enough. His forgetfulness had made him the butt of jokes.

"For a kid, you cause a lot of trouble," the President snapped.

"Can you make these?" RoH offered her hand-folded swan towards the far end of the table. Her eyes pierced the President. "They are a lot of trouble, but fun."

RoH held the swan in her hand and made a flying motion. She glanced at Daisy and smiled.

"Stop playing games, little girl," sarcasm dominated the President's conversation even on his best days. This had turned into a poorer day.

"We are in charge here. I am meeting you out of curiosity. My people will deal with you."

Mary frowned. She believed RoH did not know what faced her, and Mary preferred to keep her ignorant.

"You are going to help us defeat those aliens, whether you like it." The President bulled through. "Children like you don't have any power or influence, nothing to compare to a president, but you will help."

"I don't think so," RoH said. "Do you have any hot chocolate?"

The President signalled Mary. She beckoned Daisy, who followed her into the corridor.

"Get the hot chocolate," Mary said and turned towards the washroom.

"Okay," Daisy followed Mary into the washroom and rinsed her hands. Mary disappeared into the stall and Daisy left, reassured that there were no other humans in the space, and headed to the kitchen.

When Mary came out of the stall, she found a man lounging against the vanity. She gasped.

"Mr. President, do you mind? Get out..."

"Now, Mary," the President said, "you know you want me. No one can resist. I want some fun, just like you."

Mary closed her eyes in anger and fear. She knew the President was a philanderer but did not think he was a rapist. The image of the one man she had ever loved flashed from her memory. It was Nathan, the only man Mary had genuinely loved, but that was years ago and he had died. She had hidden her grief deep. Nathan would lean against his car, the car he later died in, with that smug, loveable smirk. Nathan's death had devastated Mary and built her a hard shell.

She opened her eyes. The President had disappeared, and Nathan lounged at the sink as if it were his car.

"You are... Get out!" Her shout echoed from the mahogany-panelled walls. "You aren't the real Nathan. You're a..."

"Alien," Nathan said.

Mary reached for her phone.

"Mary, I am real as long as you remember me, as long as you remember our love, don't, Mary; you want me. You have always wanted me. I always wanted you, only you. It is our turn now."

The words were the same ones Nathan had said the time he seduced Mary. He had said the truth, then.

Mary had carefully guarded her love and grief all of her adult life, for all of her career as a cynic. It all burst out. She felt her long dead love. Nathan's arms engulfed her. Love washed away all logic. She had always dreamt of this more than she longed for anything else, even power.

... but it's not real; Nathan's not real. The aliens... but even that doubt evaporated in her need.

"That took long enough," the President snarled at Mary as Daisy set the delicate cup of chocolate in front of RoH. Daisy looked down and winked.

Mother, isn't getting a human pregnant without the love a violation of our policy?

Sweetie, humans who speak English have a saying, "In for a dime; in for a dollar."

What does that mean?

We have already destroyed their military, industrial economies. Getting one woman pregnant seems like a little thing, a dime for the dollar we already spent. Remember, you are sitting there because they want to do worse to you. Mary created most of that plan, but it is a step to convert an enemy to a friend. She felt that as an act of love. It has restored her a bit.

Fine, Mother, will I see you for dinner?

We'll be there soon, but, dear, you are going to Australia.

"Okay, girl," the President resumed, "tell me about your mother."

RoH sipped; savouring the best hot chocolate that she had ever tasted.

Money and power buy many things, she thought.

"Nothing to tell. Like me, she is human, but slightly improved."

"You look pretty ordinary," he muttered.

"So do you, Henry," RoH said, "but you don't feel or question. You think you know."

The President scowled. No one but his long dead mother had called him Henry. He had adopted Harry when he went into politics. It sounded more homey and referred to one of Henry's heroes, a long ago president and the only one to drop a nuclear weapon. Henry admired that.

The small cup did not match the mugs and fast-food cups that RoH normally used. She finished the chocolate.

"Henry, there is a group inside the White House plotting to fight you." RoH paused.

Father...

It is a 70% probability, Daughter...

"They will kill you, Henry," from RoH, it seemed a friendly warning.

"How can you know that?" The President shouted. This little girl knew about the plot. He had been trying to track down that rumour since New Year's Eve. He had never believed it threatened his life, only his career.

RoH waved her hand and the linen swan lifted from the polished table and sailed gracefully down to land at the President's hand.

"I know lots of things, Henry." RoH smiled and stared down the length of the table into the President's eyes. The President looked down at the linen swan and his face turned white. His hands trembled. He saw his inert body slumped over the ceremonial desk in the Oval Office.

The President jumped up from the table and backed away as if the linen creation were a bomb. Everyone in the room eased back from the table.

"Get her out of here, get that bitch out of here," he shouted at Mary. "Do what you want with her. Breed her."

"I don't think so," RoH said. "There's been enough breeding today."
She smiled at Mary.

"I'm going to leave now. I have to deal with more dangerous people than you are. You have your own problems."

RoH headed out of the room. Everyone, including the agents who had kidnapped her, remained unable to move. Only the trembling President, Mary and Daisy, remained free, but did nothing to stop her.

RoH walked out to the rose garden and rode a purple light into the sky. She left a dozen confused New York City cops and the dazed Secretary General of the United Nations in her place.

CHAPTER 9

Altyerre, dreaming becomes real

"Werte, Johnny Bray," RoH looked at the man. "Ankeleatye..."

"unte-arlke..." the man stood, sounding the phrase into a question. "unte itelareme..."

"Ayenge mpwareme..."

"Unte nthenharenye…?"

"Can we speak English?" RoH had not had time to become fluent with Mparntwe.

"I do it for the tourists all the time," the old man smiled. "How did you know my name? How can we be cousins?"

"You might say a galactic computer tracked you down. We owe you much, cousin, and I carry a small payment for your suffering. I am here to introduce you to yourself."

"I come from the sky, but lately from Canada. We are cousins, but you are more like my great-grandfather."

"Crikey, that's a relief, I reckon. I was having trouble with being cousins to a little girl. Being your cousin, maybe a lot removed, has not been good for me until now. I have felt so alone even though many love me and I love them. My dream time seemed only mine, but finally, time to share."

He pointed to a framed photo on the wall beside the service counter. It depicted a large family of three generations, with everyone smiling and surrounding Johnny Bray. The engaged minds of every star traveller in the solar system had finally found Johnny thriving in the dusty outback. In the background stood the jagged red ridge of the MacDonnell Range at Heavitree Gap. The green treetops seemed to flow through the gap like water, as the gums followed the usually dusty course of the Todd River.

"My wife, children and grandchildren, my mother was long gone by then. That was last year."

"Mother was of the Mparntwe. She told me my father was an alien. I just thought it was a drunken story; she was always drunk. She had drifted, and drank herself to death after he abandoned her, and me fatherless."

"You hate," RoH said.

"Why wouldn't I? Someone, I guess an alien, used my mother and left her pregnant and alone. Yes, I hate."

"Yet you don't," RoH added. "You long to know, to understand, to find answers that might make your life, your mother's death, worthwhile."

"I think nothing can repair that in my heart."

"It is hard," RoH sighed. "I'm part human, so I feel and love and wish to understand and heal your anguish. I can't share it, but empathy drives me to embrace your heart. They made arrogant mistakes back then."

"You are like my great-grandfather. He and his mother had no guidance, and he suffered much like you, but the star people followed his life and his offspring, and then, eventually, they made me. You did not get that comfort. I know the one who started my line, my great-grandfather's father. I don't know who your father is."

"My mother tried to run from it all," Johnny resumed. "She went into the land and finally washed up a drunk on the banks of the Todd River. Cheap wine and casual sex did the rest."

"Here's her picture." Johnny drew an album from beneath the counter. A smiling young woman looked at RoH. Her beauty shone through a well-worn face. "Her name was Anna Mackenzie."

RoH sobbed. She saw the same anguish and hopelessness that she had seen in Emily's photo of Jaden. RoH briefly reached out in her mind to confirm Jaden's safety. Johnny reached out and used one rough finger gently to wipe away RoH's tear.

"We are cousins," he whispered. "Our faces feel the salted wetness. We are one."

"One…" said RoH.

"I was lucky. An aunt took me in, saved my life from the riverbed. I went to school, but for a reason I did not understand, something drew me to art. What you see here is my work."

Johnny waved his hand around the room, highlighting his paintings. RoH stared. Every image had a light in the sky, and a background shadow that RoH could not resolve into detail, as if the darkness were an infinite void.

"I see longing in your work," RoH said. "You have a memory from your dream time. Even in your mother's womb, you knew of the sky, and her dark void."

"It is my soul," Johnny replied. "I must include the bright, or the dark."

"You have embraced the light," RoH observed. "You resisted the darkness. There is one like you, in the USA, who embraced the shadows."

"I think I would go mad in the darkness," Johnny said.

"He has," said RoH. "I came to make sure you had not. I hope I comfort you."

She looked at the images once more.

"Johnny, would you like to go to the light someday?"

Johnny gripped the counter, feeling a sudden weakness.

"Yes, but I fear the shadow."

"Don't worry, cousin, you won't find the shadow there. I will return one day soon and we will travel together. We will not feel the salted wet, but the warmth of many suns. There will be a strangeness and wonder, but it will never replace the longing."

"Where do you wish to die, ankeleatye?"

Johnny felt no threat. It seemed he had known this star cousin all his life.

"There…" he pointed once more to the family portrait, and felt the joy of the green canopy of the timeless river, to die surrounded by the loves of his life. "There…"

"It will be so, cousin, but no time soon. We need your light to counter the dark sometime soon."

A whistle sounded loudly. The tourist train would depart for Darwin in an hour and called its passengers. Several travellers in the shop lined up to pay for cheap trinkets, although a woman had selected one of Johnny's fine acrylic works. It depicted a ghost-gum in the moonlight whose branches reached for the sky. Still, the shadow of the bush intruded.

"Your train wants you." Johnny said. He assumed RoH had arrived on this shiny tourist version of the old Ghan.

"I didn't come by train."

Johnny followed RoH into the street. The Wet would soon end. The monsoons had not visited Alice Springs this season, and the hot wind had coated the asphalt with dust.

"Goodbye for now, Cousin. Think about the light."

A purple haze, almost indiscernible in the glaring outback sun, engulfed RoH. She rose, at first slowly, with their eyes locked, and then she shot high and disappeared.

Johnny stood in the baking sun, staring at where the light seemed to linger in the clear blue sky.

I'm an alien, he thought. The idea settled Johnny. He had felt like an alien in his own land, in the dark skin of his people for his whole life. For the first time in that life, Johnny Bray felt peace. He closed the shop and went into the studio in the rear. On a new canvas, the image grew rapidly. A purple shaft descended from a prominent bright light hanging in a desert-blue sky. The purple made a halo around a small white girl, but Johnny had dressed her as traditional Mparntwe. She peered from the canvas into the viewer's eyes. In a lower corner, a rock cast a shadow, not as deep as normal, and its darkness flowed away.

CHAPTER 10

Alien Atonement—Dancing for the Stars

"Steve, dear, I'm so sorry we put you through that wild ride at the UN. We expected trouble, but had not thought they would be so foolish."

Ellie watched as her love cleared the breakfast table and loaded the dishwasher. She switched between following the ongoing discussion on the ships, her scolding RoH for being a drama queen, and sharing with Steve.

"It's okay, dear." Steve hit the start button. "I didn't have to buy a ticket. The discussion with some of those tough cops, even for the few minutes before Washington, intrigued me. We scared them."

"A ship ride once scared me like that," Ellie said, "and the one cried so much. I discovered his wife is dying of cancer. He believed he would be dead before her without even a goodbye. I soothed him and offered to have an expert on a ship cure her cancer. To his credit, he said his wife would have to decide. I gave him your card. They might call, I'm not sure."

"Is that a metaphor for the entire human problem?"

"I guess we could think so. It is a personal equivalent to us neutering the nukes, I think. If we do things like curing that woman, it won't be reversible, like us leaving and letting humans have their suicide toys."

"From the television, the chaos in the Rose Garden after we picked up RoH looked scary."

"They had more to fear from other humans than we star travellers. It could have been murderous. The first response of the Secret Service could not oppose a dozen well-armed New York SWAT fighters. A fight would have hurt many."

"Killed," said Steve, "but someone in the White House could think."

"Did you notice how the news cut away when those cops praised aliens?"

"Anti-alien stuff is all over the media now. The owners want nothing positive said about you. Demonstrations by religions and jobless workers are growing. Cops join them. I think it won't include the twelve we met."

"The President organized the hostility, but we can't say how it will go. We know powerful Americans hope to cause so much violence and killing that we leave and let them have their power back. It's their primary plan."

The television displayed a cable news programme. A large late winter storm had paralyzed much of north-eastern USA. A reporter interviewed a man in Boston leaning on a snow shovel.

"I tell you," the man drawled, "it's them aliens done this. Last night there were flashing lights in the sky, just like how aliens attack."

"There you have it, folks. It seems these aliens are up to no good again." The feed switched to scenes of cars sliding on ice and snow-drifted streets.

"The war propaganda has begun." Ellie frowned. "I had to study all of recent Earth history. In the last half-dozen wars fought with mass media, they spouted lies, distortions and half-truths. Later, good historical analysis showed how badly the media behaved, but it's worse now. This storm coverage is a good example. The reporter deliberately ignored the silliness of that person. He never asked if he had ever seen an alien ship, or said that lightning is common in a big blizzard. It didn't matter that star people have never attacked. Even our disarming of everything on New Year's Eve was unspectacular. I think this will cause a lot of sadness."

While she pondered the potential tragedy, Ellie wandered to the window overlooking the street. Steve's apartment occupied the ground floor in a two-apartment conversion of a century old mansion near the university. A nondescript compact car sat opposite. A different one had been there overnight.

"They watch us," Ellie said, and stood well away from the window.

"I think it's the Mounties," Steve said. "Are we bugged?"

Ellie did a mental sweep. "Not yet..."

She slipped on a coat.

“Where are you going?”

“I’m going to say hello to our friends in the car.”

“I don’t think that’s safe.”

“Steve...” Ellie looked at her partner.

“Oh, yah...” Steve laughed. Ellie had jogged his memory of the events in the Dakotas.

“Good morning, gentlemen,” Ellie smiled at the driver. “Would you like some coffee?”

“Oh, hello,” he lowered the window. “We’re just checking the street for the city.”

The man had volunteered a defence before Ellie accused them of anything. The police manual said that meant guilt.

“Well, we know better, don’t we?” Ellie put a mitten enclosed hand on the window frame as she imitated a good cop. “Doctor Jorgensen and I are about to leave for the university. Why don’t you give me your cell number? We can call you and let you know where we are.”

The cop in the far seat chuckled.

“We are here to protect you,” the driver went to story B.

“You are wasting your time. We don’t need protection, and if we got away, you would never know we had left.”

“You underestimate us,” the man said.

Ellie looked into his eyes.

“Your wife, Doreen, and the kids miss you. I hope you get sent home soon, and you,” she glanced at the passenger, “your girlfriend will not cheat on you.”

Ellie ignored the stunned looks and glanced at the idling gasoline-powered car.

“At least, if you insist on following us, get an electric vehicle. This thing is making climate change worse. Anyway, if you ever need a coffee or donut, just knock.”

Ellie frowned at Steve as she stowed her coat. The minds of the two Mounties had revealed detail.

“Those Mounties don’t want to be here. They sent them from Toronto to reinforce the London cops. The anti-alien demonstrations downtown are occupying a lot of police time, and the governments are desperate to control things.”

"There's lots of weird stuff going on. The bigoted talk shows are over the top, but there are pro-visitor rallies and opinions too. Both sides are evolving into irrationality, like cults."

"It isn't only governments who are trying to exploit our visit."

The Mounties dutifully followed Steve and Ellie to Steve's office. Rachel sat at the front desk.

"About time you two love birds got here. Is your shirt ripped, Steve?" Rachel laughed.

"You upstart... the ink isn't even dry on your Fud."

"Hey, I have a job offer. Can you come up with 100-K plus benefits, so I can stay here? I'm never going to find anything as fun as here."

"You're out of my league, kid. Where is it?"

"A little school, called Stanford. It's an assistant-professorship plus fast-track to tenure."

"We need a west coast office," Ellie said. "I suppose they want you because of us."

"Yes, they want to start a research project called 'Extra-planetary linguistics'. I think they are jealous of Western."

"When...?" Steve Jorgensen had become fond of Rachel in the years he had advised her on her doctoral research.

"June, so we can have it all set up for the August classes."

"Congratulations." both Ellie and Steve hugged Rachel.

"You know," Rachel said, "there are anti-alien organisations all around the world now. I feel safer here." She looked at Ellie.

Ellie hugged her again.

"We will assign a watch-dog to you. Years ago, they protected Mom from government punks so I could be born. You'll be safe and be our friend out there."

"Okay, here's some of the fun stuff I will miss. Bobby Briscoe from the television network called. He says there's something wild you need to see. He said someone he called 'Crazy Jim' tipped him off. Who's Crazy Jim?"

"Jim is not really insane, but his ex-wife's crazy cockatoo keeps calling him that." Ellie said. "They abducted Jim years ago when they bumbled and scared people. He has PTSD from it, as do most taken survivors. I should be angry at him because he tipped Bobby off about me and forced our hand last fall."

"What's it about?"

Rachel laughed, "Bobby said that it seems to be a cross between country gospel and a barn dance. He and Jimmy Smith will be here soon."

They could not meet Crazy Jim until late afternoon. He squeezed into the back seat of Bobby's car beside Ellie. Jim wore blue denim coveralls beneath a warm parka.

"When we get there," Jim said, "let me do the talking. I've been there a lot. They see me as an alien abduction hero. Don't tell them you are reporters, and for God's sake," Jim looked at Ellie, "don't tell them you are even part-alien. They would turn you into a goddess."

They approached a farm that occupied a side road hilltop along Highway 8 between Clinton and Goderich. A bank of squall clouds obscured the setting sun. In the deepening gloom, a shaft of light shone skyward from a field just past the barnyard. Ice crystals in the frigid February air shone as a silver pillar beckoning those on the ground and in the sky.

"That's the landing pad," Jim smiled. Jimmy Smith videoed the spectacle. A car pulled up on the road's shoulder. The Mounties waited.

"Make sure no one sees that camera," Jim repeated.

The barnyard served as a makeshift parking lot and held several vehicles. A line of portable toilets ran along the eastern side. The parking area ended at a vast structure that had once been a chicken barn. Double doors embellished with fanciful graphics of aliens and flying saucers marked the main entrance. A large LED roof-beacon flashed random pulses, and Ellie read the Morse code for SOS. An older man wearing a more refined version of Jim's coveralls approached from the barn.

"Hello, friends, hello Jim," his smile welcomed, and he nodded at Crazy Jim. "We welcome everyone who seeks the truth, especially friends of Jim, whom the aliens chose."

He noticed Ellie looking at the beacon.

"That is our help call to the stars," he said, confirming Ellie's coding ability. "My son rigged that. He programmes computerized machinery. Nice, huh?"

Everyone nodded.

"Those star travelling aliens need to come and save our bacon." He frowned and then sent a questioning glance to Jim.

"These are my friends from London," Jim said. "We share a relationship with aliens."

"Come for the tour," the host turned towards the corner of the barn. "The ceremony won't start for an hour. People gotta eat. Let me show you the landing zone."

They had cleared the snow from a large area beyond the barn. Flood lamps normally for back-yard hockey rinks illuminated two sides. An elaborate system of coloured lights filled the barn wall.

"It's beautiful," the owner did not ask for confirmation. "Them lights are for sending greetings when they're landing, just like that old movie. We put a big arrow made from round bales in the field, pointing to the landing pad. If our friends don't come first, next summer my lad's going to replace it with a light arrow, just like at an airport. It's cold; let's get a coffee before things get going."

They sipped burnt hot coffee at the back of the barn interior where a saucer-shaped table held a variety of pastries. Someone had polished the concrete floor. In a throwback to long ago high school gymnasiums on a Friday night, they had spread dance wax over the surface. High above, a disco ball spun below the rafters and shone a whirling cosmos onto the walls. Chairs lined the edges of the still empty floor. A stage spanned the width at the front, supporting music stands and a pole microphone, with a large sound system and speakers mounted above a piano. Two elaborate chairs sat to the left, the larger rose slightly above the other.

People streamed in. Everyone dressed like Jim and the owner, although there was much variation. A man with a guitar, another with a fiddle mounted the stage, and a woman took her seat at the piano. In a grand entrance, two individuals dressed as green aliens entered to a loud ovation. One went to the centre of the floor. The other stood at the mic on the platform.

"They know now they should be grey," Crazy Jim whispered, "but these costumes were from last year. They'll fix it soon."

"Okay, let's get going," the alien impersonator gripped the mic pole. "Take your places. Those with this week's green tickets circle Gar."

The floor filled with circles of four couples. One of these gathered around the second green alien. The musicians blared out a crescendo. Winston strummed the guitar; Walter fiddled; Florence tickled the ivories. The crowd chanted, "alien" several times to a beat of rising chords.

"Here we go," the alien caller cried.

"Grab your partners," and then he began a musical chant.

The dancers wheeled about in well-practiced coordination with the caller's instructions. Everyone looked at the alien in the middle on cue and kept their eyes fixed on them during the dosey doe.

Ellie's eyes teared.

"It makes you want to weep," Steve squeezed her hand.

"Oh, Steve, it's sad, yet hilarious. They want us as rescuers, but they don't understand us, and that they are their own saviours."

"They want good old-fashioned salvation," Crazy Jim said. "I nearly got sucked into those rabbit holes of TV preachers. I thought my feelings were my fault and maybe if I got right with God, they would go away. That didn't work, but you coming back sure helped." Jim smiled at Ellie. "I actually know where we stand."

"I'm in with this bunch for the fun and a woman I like. It beats the isolation. Usually, I ride with other abductees from London. None of us taken ones believes this nonsense, but it's fun and has other perks."

"These people want to get right with you star travellers. Some even believe you're God's angels. They think you're mad at them and that's why you haven't rescued all Earthlings from whatever they consider their suffering. They think that hooting, hollering, landing zones and beacons will bring you back to forgive them and bring them paradise. It's like a church service, complete with altar and aliens as gods."

"We'll have to discuss this in the ships." Ellie said. "I can't say if it's a good or bad thing."

"Bad," Jimmy Smith muttered. "It's the same at Roswell North by Ottawa at the barn we escaped. A cult formed there. They say, 'All hail the mighty barn-blowers.' These people scare the hell out of me."

"How did they organize this so fast after New Year's Eve?" Steve asked.

"This has been going on for years," Crazy Jim said. "Many of us abductees hated the aliens for what they did, but a significant bunch think of them as holy and powerful. The farmer here is one of those. What you did on New Year's just filled the parking lot with people who have never been near a star ship but were at the Goderich square. Most believe you aliens chose the residents of Huron County as favourites."

"The chosen one thing never turns out well." Steve said.

A woman, perhaps 60 years old, hugged Crazy Jim.

"Who are your friends?" She smiled at Jim.

Jim made the introductions.

"Everyone should dance and have fun," she said. "Wait here."

She returned, dragging two others along, and turned out to be an efficient organizer. Before long, she had paired the others with Jimmy and Bobby as she latched onto Crazy Jim. The eight formed another square, and the so-called fun began. The newbies had never square danced, and the results were predictable. Still, the woman had not lied, and they enjoyed it. Ellie felt the seduction of body movement and again understood why humans relished both dancing and music. Ellie could not help but love music because of her musician mother, Lisa. She saw how it could be a unifying part of any sort of worship or cult activity.

After the first attempt, the alien imposter hurried over to stand in the middle of their formation. Seeing the opportunity to draw the visitors in deeper, the caller repeated the original call,

> *Bow to the alien*
> *That ain't got hair*
> *Dosey doe.*

The dancers stared at the fake alien. They ignored Ellie. The alien who had hair swayed with the others and enjoyed the accidental joke. Then the alien stand-in, Gar, hurried into another square.

After several more squares, done with traditional lyrics, the old-time musicians disappeared. The dancing changed into gyrations to a loud thumping beat from the massive sound system. Few in the room had been born before rock and roll music. One of these was the farmer who owned the property. The majority tolerated the old time music in deference to their host's tastes, but enticed the younger crowd with something more modern. The farmer took his place as patriarch in the elaborate chair, to the right and secondary to a more ornate seat resembling a throne. This higher seat awaited the omnipotent, an alien saviour.

The five onlookers slipped from the barn, and Crazy Jim remained to flirt with his friend. The floodlit landing pad cast the building's shadow over the yard full of cars and pickups.

"There are many UFO nuts and believers," Steve eased into Bobby's car beside Ellie, "here and in the USA."

"You know," Steve Jorgensen watched the farm gate slip past, "there are those who live on the moon and those who dance naked before it. Aliens are the moon. These people dance in love and hope to their alien moon."

"A brilliant linguist, a legend in my undergraduate days, postulated what she called the contact zone. Created, she said, when cultures interact, usually a powerful and a weaker one, the invader and the oppressed. It seems to me, all-powerful star-travellers fit that perfectly. It has reversed that contact zone relationship between the powerful and the weak on Earth. Dominant nations are suddenly the weak ones. The powerful resent it, and the formerly oppressed on Earth, as we see in that chicken barn, find hope in it. That cult may be a stand in for all the oppressed around the world. They have their own language and culture. We judge it, belittle it, but rarely understand it."

"There is more," Ellie said. "Contact has affected my star family. It showed them what they had lost while becoming scientific star people. Earth is an outlier. Most planetary civilizations are long extinct or not yet developed. Earth is in that spot of almost being there. I could find no record of a similar contact over the millennia."

"We are a quantum-based race," Ellie pondered, "and ours is a classic example from quantum physics of how observation affects the results. It reflects how our language influences our understanding, how new understanding influences our language. For instance, before the events that led to me, aliens had no words for empathy and love. Our biased uncertainty has collapsed into reality. This contact zone is an exciting place if we can open our minds."

The dutiful Mounties followed them back to London.

CHAPTER II

Rachel was a harsh mistress

Rachel, Nevada, sat on Nevada Highway 375, also known as The Extraterrestrial Highway. Rachel shared the fate of thousands of small towns across the USA. It had gradually faded away as water vaporized on the baked plain between two mountain ranges. The flatland once supported a decent cattle industry. The growing drought from climate change had reduced its liveability. A few irrigated operations made up the last gasp of agriculture but sucked down an aquifer and would soon lead to disaster.

Rachel had a secondary commercial base... aliens. More precisely, its nearness to the secret operations of Groom Lake attracted visitors. UFO conspirators had convinced the public that the American government hid an alien spacecraft and bodies at the test facility.

Most space tourists came at the shoulders of the year... spring and fall, between the unfriendly winter winds and the furnace of summer. In the moderate months, they found it more comfortable in their futile attempts to sneak around Groom Lake security.

Jas watched a young girl walk along the highway and approach his gas bar. He could not have understood the irony that an alien walked The Extraterrestrial Highway.

That gal has no hat, he thought... *full sun too, but winter, so it's cool out. Few here this time of year.*

The girl stopped opposite the store and gazed at the window. Jas stepped back; embarrassed that she had caught him, but he hoped that she could not see through the sun's glare on the window.

The door opened.

"Hello," she did not sound local, "have you lived in Rachel long?"

"Bred and born here," Jas replied, "fourth generation."

"So you know all about the aliens then," she smiled.

"Never took no truck in that nonsense," Jas frowned. "Tourists and whackos come a lot. It's good for business, but I'm scared one could be a dangerous nutcase, and I don't mean the aliens."

"I'm not dangerous, or a nutcase," RoH laughed.

"Try the Taken Inn down the road," he nodded further up the highway. "They got lots of alien stuff there."

"So your grandparents were here in the 1950s?" RoH stared at Jas.

The question spooked Jas. The 1950s were taboo here in the dusty valley. There had been too many comings and goings, too many lights, too many crazy stories back then. He actually thought his grandparents had gone senile, repeating those tales.

"What did your grandparents see?"

Jas' thought of his grandparents had been fleeting. Jas shook.

"Nothing... nothing..."

"Please tell me," the girl soothed. Jas weakened. He feared people would call his whole family crazy. Still, aliens made for good business.

"Would you like a soda, girl... just 50 cents?"

RoH laid an American dollar onto the counter. "Orange, please, and have one with me."

Jas broke out a cold orange and a root beer. He walked to the corner where worn chairs and small tables made a place for tourists and locals to sit out of the summer heat and watch the dry lands across the highway. For a change, the boys who normally haunted this corner were out on the range, annoying what few cattle remained.

"Plenty of strange things happened back then, ever since the late 40s. The military had lots of traffic over to the Lake, Groom Lake. I know you're here because of them, Area 51 and all that."

"What did your grandparents see?"

"They said, one night, a big air ship floated over the town, towing something big and black. It was night, so who knows, but they said it disappeared over the mountains to Homey Airport. That was in 1957. I know balloons are only for sports now, television game coverage, but in the 1950s they had a use, no heavy lift airplanes or helicopters back then."

"Was that all?" RoH stared. Jas had more.

"There was lots of coming and going after 1955 and not just military, but suits in government cars and aircraft all the time. The runway approach takes them just west of Rachel. We see 'em a lot, some are ginormous. It's quietened down since them aliens; down east, screwed us… we haven't seen jet fighters since then, just a few transports. Our pastor says we should kill aliens. They ain't from Genesis, they's from the devil, though that might not be good for business in Rachel."

Jas language was a wonderful foil to the stilted Washington-speak she had recently endured. His hatred and confused motives weakened her optimism about humanity.

"Did they ever see any aliens?"

Jas paused, considering what to say.

"They… didn't." The way he had said, 'they' implied more to the story.

"Who saw an alien?"

"Would you like another, on the house?" Jas gulped the last of his root beer and wished it had been whisky. RoH had stirred up memories he had hoped to forget.

"Yes, thanks…" RoH followed Jas' example and gulped the orange. She wanted him at ease.

"Well, lots of folks claim they saw little green men." Jas sat new bottles on the table.

"Did they all say 'green'?"

"Everyone…"

"They are grey, Jas."

"Huh? You know my name?"

"It's on your shirt," RoH laughed. Jas blushed.

"How do you know they are grey?"

"Just a guess, maybe from the movies." RoH had decided not to enlighten Jas, considering his hate.

"Who's everyone?"

"My Aunt Ruth, Gran and Gramps said so. I met my great-aunt Ruth later, but they said she claimed she actually met one, about 1967. Ruth and I didn't talk when she came home. She never told me nothing. There were others. A rancher out there." Jas pointed across the highway. Where Groom Lake lay hidden behind the mountains. "He claimed he saw a flying saucer and a green guy get taken up into it."

"When was that?" RoH sipped. Jas seemed to have forgotten a little girl interrogated him.

"In 67, the inn down there has the story in a display. I was born twenty years later. We all thought the old guy was a cuckoo. He died when I was about your age. Maybe these aliens on the TV came here for real."

"I think they did," RoH sipped, "but I don't think they chose Rachel on purpose."

"No, I don't think so either," Jas worked on the root beer, but slowly this time. "I think grandma and gramps really saw the balloon. The government brought them here. The rancher, I'm not so sure. He was a kook."

"Seems likely," RoH agreed. "Tell me about your aunt, Ruthie."

"Not much to tell. I never met her until later, about your age. Gran said she got pregnant and left town when the kid was born. Gran blamed the doctor. They were all young. Gramps said Ruth claimed an alien knocked her up, uh... sorry; that made her pregnant. Grandma blamed the doctor that delivered the kid and then left right after Ruth did. It's a sin to commit adultery, you know."

RoH considered how a sin in rural Nevada appeared as breeding in Washington and among the far-flung stars, or as recreation just down the highway in Vegas.

"But she came back?"

"As an older woman, she stayed and died here. She never talked to me about it, but my nosy sister said Ruth told her the kid had run away as soon as he was 18 and left her cold, not even a 'good bye Mom'. Ruth never seemed happy. She was always angry. She would walk around in the dark, cursing the sky. It's a wonder she didn't die of snakebite. Ruth just withered away and died a couple of years later, too young even then."

"All her stuff is down to the Inn at their museum. As far as I know, they keep it locked up and never show it. I ain't never seen it. Sis says it's all Ruth's papers."

"Thank you, Jas. You're interesting. How would I get to Homey airport?"

"Get arrested," Jas laughed. "You ain't getting anywhere near there. They won't let you. You can't even see it unless you know the back way."

"Who knows the back way?"

"Me," Jas smiled.

"Thanks, Jas. Can we talk again, maybe?"

"Sure, anytime... the drinks are on me."

Jas did not know why he liked this strange little girl.

RoH headed up the highway on the short walk to The Taken Inn. The town, never thriving in the good years, displayed general decay.

"Can I get a room, please?"

"We don't rent to kids," the pleasant woman was friendly but firm.

"Mom will be here soon. She went to take some photographs. Here's mommy's credit card. She works for the government."

The woman became attentive. The card drew her in deeper. It was Siglinde's credit card from NAAP.

"The National Agency for Aerial Phenomena," the woman repeated. "That's them flying saucer people been in the news since last fall. I have all the newscasts recorded. It would honour us to have a real scientist at the Inn. There's a lot of anti-alien hatred going on now."

The woman examined the card again. "I saw your mommy on television."

"Yes," RoH tried to sound proud. "Mommy's a real scientist."

"She'll have to sign when she arrives." The credit card slipped through the machine. "You're in room six."

RoH accepted the old-fashioned metal key with a plastic tag bearing a distorted head of a green alien.

"Is the museum open?"

"Right this way," the woman said.

"Peg," she called out, "watch the counter."

"This time of year, we don't see many customers."

"Does mommy have anything to do with the Lake?" The woman nodded towards the mountains. "I'm Corrine."

"Not directly, I don't think." RoH smiled. "We are supposed to be on vacation. I'm RoH."

"Sounds like a busman's holiday to me." the woman laughed. RoH searched for a reference to understand the humour. She would ask her grandfather.

"That's a strange name."

"It's short for Roberta Heather, but I like RoH. It sounds special."

"It sure is different," Corrine said. "It'd be a good name in an alien story. Here's the museum." She opened the door and flipped a light switch. "It's dusty… didn't expect anyone until Easter."

Corrine escorted RoH through the displays and explained them all. Some were just tourist catching representations, but some were authentic if only marginally to do with aliens. Most were accidental artefacts, like a licence plate from a 1949 army vehicle. Corrine claimed a General had driven it.

"What's in there?" RoH pointed to a door.

"That's the archives." Corrine tensed. "It's private stuff. Sometimes a real investigator looks at it, but it's not for the tourists. That room has the real McCoy. Some things we don't share with the UFO guys. Even the best of them seem dodgy. Peg and I are writing a book about it."

"That sounds like mommy's work," RoH smiled. "Maybe you could show her."

Corrine stopped and examined RoH. She decided a little girl could not be devious.

"That would be an honour," Corrine said, "but we couldn't let her have it. She has to promise not to reveal the contents. Your mother will be the first real scientist to see the stuff."

"She'll promise," RoH promised. "Maybe she already knows that material."

"Yes, could be. The government has been covering up since Roswell. We think this has something to do with that; seems it all started 'bout 1947."

"That's what Jas at the gas station said."

"You talked to Jas?"

"I had a soda with him… nice guy."

"He's a bit of a Bible thumper, but pleasant. You know his family is at the nub of this alien stuff. His great aunt claimed she had an alien kid."

"Jas suggested that, but thought the doctor did it."

"Ruthie's stuff is in there," Corrine smiled. "And so is the doctor's. I read it all. I know it wasn't the doc."

"What was Ruth's last name?"

"Orville… same family as Jas' grandmother. Ruthie was her sister."

RoH yawned. "Can I please go to the room? Thank you for the tour. Mommy will love talking with you."

At suppertime, a woman walked into the Taken Inn office.

"I'm Siglinde Hilfreich. Where do I sign?"

After a half hour of questions from both Corrine and Peg, most of which Siglinde answered with the word "classified", Siglinde reached the privacy of the room. RoH lay down for a nap. She needed to wait until after midnight to check the archives.

Siglinde, by that time, had made it halfway to Z263-A. Siglinde 2 dozed in Siglinde Hilfreich's apartment in Virginia with Ted 2 and Elliana.

At one in the morning, RoH quietly left room six and passed through the museum door. The inn struggled financially, and primitive mechanical trips on the outside doors and windows composed the security. RoH slipped into the archive and scanned the shelves. She did not need lights. She saw a file box labelled "photos" that held some clear pictures of a ship. It was genuine, of the type used on small-scale surveys that had crashed at Roswell, New Mexico in 1947. The mountains in the image suggested it had passed near Rachel. The date on the back said 1967. It could have been from the crazy rancher that Jas had mentioned. The back of the photograph did not have any other information.

It looks like Ruth's lover actually went home, but why can't we find him?

Other pictures were obvious fakes. She found a birth certificate for Robert Orville, born in Rachel in 1967 and delivered by Doctor Newhouse in a folder of documents labelled "Ruth Orville". It held Ruth's driver licence, expired in 1996, with an address in Las Vegas. Various school records for Robert made the bulk of the find, with several photos of a frowning boy and another of a teenager with a forced smile. RoH knew he had not been happy. She thought of Jaden, but this look was darker... angry, worse than the shadows in a Johnny Bray painting.

Sadly, Ruth's precious memories were mostly of her son. She had loved Robert. He seemed to be the focus of her life, and she had loved and longed for her lover. In those days, in this dusty Nevada backwater, even a slick-talking dude from Vegas mesmerized the girls. A lover from beyond the sky made a far larger impression.

A photo showed a middle-aged woman, probably Ruth, with a group in a restaurant. The caption said, "Congratulations Ruth, on your retirement-1996." She seemed too young to retire.

A memoir in a readable script told Ruth's story. RoH sped through the pages. Robert had graduated from high school and then disappeared. Ruth bitterly wrote, "I sacrificed everything for him and he hated me. I hate his son-of-a-bitch alien father." A note in the margin said, "No, I love him."

At the bottom of the pile, she found a postcard depicting a long-horned beef cow. It read, "Mom, I'm sorry. I'm okay. I'm in Texas now." It did not mention love.

RoH sat, absorbed in the harm that this alien carelessness had caused. She already knew of it from discussions, but the sad story of Ruth and Robert made the disaster real. Robert was the missing reproduct. RoH stared at the picture of the teen boy. He was the danger, the enemy. She hoped he had no extra abilities beyond what her great-grandfather had possessed. RoH could handle those.

RoH lived with empathy. She pondered if she could save Robert. The entity that she had felt in Goderich had radiated evil. RoH felt certain that the reproduct was Robert Orville.

Can I help evil become good?

RoH should have detected an intruder, but her concentration on Robert had distracted her.

"What the hell are you doing?" Corrine's shout accompanied the lights coming on. RoH sighed. She had not decided if she would let any local know the truth. It seemed her inattention had decided.

"Can we talk, Corrine?"

"Damned right we will," Corrine took an angry step towards RoH. "I'll call the sheriff."

"Sit down, Corrine." RoH pointed to a chair and smiled. Corrine sat, but not sure why.

"I never thought a little girl would be a thief. I guess that's city folks. Vegas is too close."

"I'm from much further than Las Vegas, Corrine." RoH took a vacant chair. "Would you like to hear the story?"

"Damned right, get talking." Corrine's anger had softened. She felt something had pushed her into the chair.

"I'm part alien, Corrine."

"Sure, lots of our guests claim to be alien. Never a little girl, though."

Suddenly, Siglinde sat in front of Corrine, and then RoH reappeared.

"Would you like to see my alien form?"

Corrine could not speak. She had never been so scared in her life. The growing anti-alien propaganda had affected her, although not as bad as religious believers. Years of alien monster movies did not help.

RoH briefly appeared in her alien shimmering grey, and then RoH stared into Corrine's eyes. She instantly knew the complete story of RoH.

"I won't hurt you, Corrine. I am part alien. What you see now is my genuine human form. I prefer it especially here on Earth. The biggest fear you should have of us is that we will leave you humans to your own devices. That won't turn out well."

"I only pretended about aliens. It was a business opportunity and why we called the place as a joke, Taken Inn, the gullible... until Ruth gave us her stuff. Then I knew, but Peg and I wanted to get rich from our book."

"Publish your book, Corrine. I don't know if you will get rich, actually I hope human's lust for wealth will go away, but you may help humanity survive."

"Have you read anything by Richard Locke? He was my great-great uncle. He did not die rich, but he helped prepare humans for us. All of his later works are true."

"His books are in the shop. The later ones contradict his earlier beliefs. They sell well."

"I needed to see your archives, Corrine. I needed to find out about Ruth, and especially Robert, her son. He's alive and seems to have become evil. I don't know why for sure, but I think alien bumbling, abandoning him and his mother. I think it made him hate, but I must look further to find out. Did Ruth say anything about him, where he might have gone?"

"Texas, I know he went to Texas."

"Yes, I saw the postcard. Did Ruth say more?"

"Just before she died, she seemed happier. She told Jas' sister that Robert had joined a church in Dallas where he had become the pastor. It made her happy. She said, 'If he found God, I can die happy'. She only lived a few more weeks, as if knowing about her son gave her permission to go."

Corrine sobbed. RoH hugged. Somehow, the sad tale of Ruth Orville had become a magnificent testament to love.

Perhaps a mother's love can yet save Robert Orville, RoH wondered. RoH did not know that another yet unknown human mother's love would pass through a generation and heal.

"Corrine," RoH touched her arm, "you are a good woman. Ruth was a good woman, a victim of bumbling. I hope I can reverse some of the harm. My mother and I want humanity and all life here to survive."

"Your mother...?"

"My mother isn't Siglinde whom you saw. Siglinde is a real scientist, and is the head of NAAP, and a key to your hope. If you read Uncle Richard's second last book, my mother is the little girl who the aliens took in Texas. It makes the Taken Inn name legitimate. You know it all now, and you probably saw her on TV. She was my age then. If you write your book, maybe I'll write a chapter for you."

"The credit card is good," RoH said. "Siglinde is on an all-inclusive holiday, but gave me the card before she left. I want to stay for another two nights, anyway."

"What are you going to do for two days?"

"We can't find the alien who mated with Ruth. Jas told me a rancher saw him leave on a ship in 1967, but we have identified no one in the community as Robert's father. I suspect he never left here. I do not know who or what got onto that ship in the picture."

"Maybe your alien's too scared or embarrassed to fess up."

"Feeling guilty or embarrassed would not be a factor. There are no black marks for errors with the star people. There are only data points to consider, even if an action was a mistake. Judgement and punishment are another thing humans have to abandon. The father is probably dead, but I need to know."

"What about humans murdering each other?"

"It won't be easy to get to a place where no one commits murder or other violent crimes. It all starts with equity. Sharing resources and fair decision making must come before you have a hope of stopping violence."

"Impossible..."

"I hope not," RoH frowned. "Anyway, the father's body might still be at Groom Lake. I need to check. All aliens, including alien-human hybrids like me, function as powerful computers. We can join our minds to create a huge, sentient computational matrix."

"What the hell is that?" Corrine had not been a scholar.

"It's an organic super-computer with the power of learning, like the human mind. We can be like a powerful artificial intelligence, except a natural one and much more realistic. The father should be part of that, but he isn't. We can withdraw and shield our minds, but seldom do it. Usually we pull away to ponder some idea or minor decision before involving a larger group. That is normal. I have shielded my mind once while on Earth to protect myself from a dangerous mind. To hide from Robert Orville, I think. It's safer to stay in the loop. Right now, I have an open interface with every star-mind in range. They know we are talking, but not the details unless I deliberately share them. It would make it too noisy otherwise. If I felt danger, they would know immediately. The nearest ship, which is right above us now, would intervene."

Corrine frowned at the ceiling.

"If Robert's father is on Earth, he's deliberately or being forced to shield his mind. I expect if I find anything, it will be a body."

"Who on Earth could threaten you?" Corrine felt two emotions. That she talked to an alien as if it were an everyday thing stunned her. She had genuine concern for the safety of this little girl alien. She pulled her sweater tighter. RoH noticed.

"This room is chilly and you should control the temperature and humidity. You have some valuable stuff here." RoH looked around and only saw a small space heater and a silent window air conditioner that seemed about to fall into the dusty yard.

"That old electric heater is a fire hazard, and the AC is useless in this drafty building. You need better."

"We can't afford it."

"I'll have someone install a power-unit with a heat-exchanger that will run for years on its own. We will give you a small one, only a terawatt-hour of energy."

"What does that mean? How much will it cost me?"

RoH looked around and calculated.

"It's a gift, Corrine. This building will probably use a kilowatt of power. That unit should," she paused for an instant, "run for 100 million years...plus. I think that might do. It could run Rachel for 110,000 years, if you shared the power."

"I'll be dead by then."

"Maybe...," said RoH. "It'll arrive soon and someone will install it."

"What if this thing incinerates the valley if something goes wrong? Is there a warranty?"

"It's a quantum energy device and no danger. If it stops, no one will notice because the universe will have stopped."

"Robert Orville is the danger." RoH frowned more deeply. "I have to get to Groom Lake."

When RoH walked into the little store at the gas station the following afternoon, she found Jas stocking shelves with the lights dimmed.

"Jas," she startled him. "Show me the back-way to Groom Lake."

Jas turned white beneath his two-day-old stubble. He set an orange and a root beer onto the little table by the window and sat so that RoH faced the bright opening. He had sampled some whisky last night.

"Why do you want to go there?" The cold soda soothed his head.

"Your aunt Ruthie," RoH sipped, "to explain what happened after her lover left."

"That's sinning stuff. She's long dead. Best leave it all dead."

"You have always wondered, Jas. This thing has eaten at you."

Jas leaned towards RoH and stared.

"How'd you know that? Yah, Ruthie was good to me, better than Ma was. She weren't crazy, just hurt bad. I lied the other day. She loved the alien, and she said he loved her."

Jas took a long drag of soda and closed his eyes.

"She said he looked like that Guy Williams actor on Bonanza. Ruthie loved that show, set here in Nevada. She'd been watching re-runs the night he showed up... dressed in a Stetson and cowboy vest. She said he was the sexiest thing she had seen in the valley, but why not? If Dakota Fanning dropped in here, I'd be in love for sure, even if she's named for the wrong state. Ruthie said she figured out it weren't Williams, and that's when she found out he was an alien. He'd taken the Williams character out of her head because she'd been watching those Bonanza reruns. She was smitten, so it didn't make no difference. She walked around at night cursing the sky because she thought the aliens had made him go home."

"We don't think we took him." RoH said.

"Who's 'we'," Jas frowned.

"Oh, the bunch my mother works for... government stuff."

"Why don't she just go there then? Who are you, little girl, Nancy Drew?"

"I'm just RoH. Take me to Groom Lake. I'll pay your guiding fee."

RoH took a wad of bills from her pocket and placed it on the table. Jas saw pictures of Andrew Jackson. He gripped the soda bottle to keep from snatching the pile. It looked like more than the station made in a week.

"Tonight, nine o'clock," Jas said, "no moon will help. They have sensors everywhere, but I know a clean path, at least to the mountains. It's easy through there to the lake, but they likely have traps on it. I only went there to hunt. Damned game knows they're safer inside that perimeter. Show up here at midnight, in good boots and a warm jacket, if you have 'em."

RoH shoved half the pile to Jas. He counted $300.

"The rest will be at the inn when we get back."

They drove across the plain into a little gully. Jas parked his pickup in a draw that hid it from anyone on the ground, checked his compass and headed southwest. Jas pointed a dim light at the ground to keep from stumbling, and once he stopped to let a sidewinder clear the trail.

The snake coiled with a menacing rattle. Jas fumbled for his sidearm. RoH touched Jas' gun hand and stepped towards the reptile.

RoH stared at the creature, and it suddenly raised its head 20 centimetres and focused on RoH. The two locked eyes for several seconds, and the snake suddenly flipped backwards, rolled to its belly, and slithered away.

"Okay, let's go," RoH said.

"Fool thing doesn't know it's winter," Jas muttered. "I didn't expect any snakes, but today was warmer."

"It was hungry", RoH replied.

The hills became more difficult and then a hard climb up a dry stream took them to a ridge.

"It's downhill from here. There's a path, but I ain't never gone past here. The government gets snarly, this side of the ridge. I'll stop here."

"Jas, I'd like you to come with me."

"No reason," Jas said, "we would just be learning new ground past here. You're as good as me when we both knows nothing. You should stop here too. I don't like no little girl down there in the dark."

RoH peered into the black canyon. Her mind reached out to the base. *There's a spark... faint... gone...*

"Jas, you must come. You need to see what's there. I'll protect you."

Jas laughed. "That's ripe, a little girl protecting me."

"Jas, look at me."

RoH took Jas' hand and directed his lamp at her face.

Jas then knew. He took it better than most humans who experienced RoH's identity. Only a subdued gasp betrayed him. Perhaps a generation of alien stories had prepared him for the real thing.

"Ruthie once told me you would all come in ways that we would never know unless you wanted us to. She also said that you ain't bad. I been hoping my whole life to meet you. I always knew the preacher was wrong. Between Ruthie and those good things on TV about you rescuing the Martians and such, you didn't seem like no space invaders."

"Jas," RoH softly said, "I think we will find the answer to Ruth's sadness down there on the base. My human part is angry that humans would treat any sentient, any other life, in such a cruel way as I think we will soon see. My alien part sees an opportunity to save a life, and it is holding my anger down. Let's go."

"RoH," Jas said, "what happened back there with the sidewinder?"

"We had a little chat," RoH laughed. "I told it where to find a mouse."

As Jas predicted, they did not get far before base security ambushed them in a narrow gully. Jas and RoH surrendered peacefully and submitted to the inevitable wrist-ties. Jas struggle against the discomfort, but RoH remained quiet. Perhaps because RoH was a little girl, and the security people actually knew Jas, they treated the captives gently.

"Jas, why the hell did you want to come here? You knew what to expect. Now you have heaps of trouble." The soldier had frequented the gas-bar.

"The angel made me do it," Jas managed a joke. RoH said she would protect him. He hoped she could keep him from a military court and firing squad. He had read every exaggerated story and anti-government diatribe from most of the UFO nuts. In reality, they might just send Jas home and tell him, if he ever tried to come back, they would shoot him. RoH would face much harsher treatment once they could not identify her.

We'll be okay, Jas...

The security room contained uncomfortable chairs, a table, and harsh lighting. A large man in a captain's uniform strode in, slammed the door, and sat down abruptly. They had roused him from his bed. An armed guard stood ramrod at the door.

"Who the hell are you two?" The officer leafed through the patrol's report.

"Where do you have the alien?" RoH's face remained passive.

"Oh, so you're more UFO nuts... that's boring. We don't have any aliens here. I was hoping for Ruskies."

"Not Ruskies," RoH smiled, "but we have little time. You have an alien. Where is he?"

RoH saw an image of a nearby building flash through the interrogator's mind. He did not know what the building housed, but RoH guessed.

"I'm asking the questions here, young lady. Where I come from, children shut up and do as they are told."

"You have guarded an alien for a long time, and you don't know." RoH stood and handed her zip tie to the captain. The guard dropped his rifle. Jas felt his zip tie fall to the floor. The captain sat catatonic.

"Take us to your alien."

The captain discovered he could stand. He cried for help, but the guard saluted and began singing the Star-Spangled Banner.

The aliens did not have entertainment, but in the past five months the expanded swarm in range of Earth looked forward to replaying the record of RoH's antics. Ellie called it the RoH Show. All aliens claimed watching RoH was necessary research to evaluate hybrid behaviour.

Just don't crash into a planet while you're watching the RoH Show. Ellie would tease RoH's father.

She had him singing the anthem. Ellie's heart contained a mixture of pride and embarrassment. *RoH needs a playmate.*

The captain and the guard exchanged salutes as if all were normal.

"This way..."

No one guarded the outer door of a bunker with thick concrete walls and roof. RoH stared at the electronic security panel. It required retinal identification and a thumbprint after the insertion of an electronic key. The door swung open untouched and slammed shut behind them.

In the middle of the night, no one worked inside. In fact, no one had been here for several months. The single room, 20 meters square, housed a central three-meter cube tank made from thick acrylic sheet. Soft light emanated from the transparent tank and illuminated the surrounding space. Liquid, more viscous than water, filled the tank and glowed slightly blue from electronic lights embedded in the opaque top. An alien corpse floated gently in the liquid.

Jas stood in amazement. He had seen dead people before, but not an alien.

The captain backed against the wall. He had never known of the prize he guarded. The Pentagon said that the building housed a secret super-computer; a story closer to the truth than people connected with the project understood. For decades, they had shielded this node from that super-network. A grounded lattice of copper cable embedded in the concrete outer walls made the structure into a large Faraday Cage. A powerful mind like RoHs, amplified by the crystal hanging from her neck, easily penetrated the shield. The suffering alien floating in limbo could not.

The project had languished with little funding. NAAP had not been aware that it existed. Everyone officially involved believed the alien's brain had died, but the body functioned in some mysterious way. Years before, someone suggested the alien corpse might hold clues to longevity, but no one had investigated the proposal. The military refused to release the cadaver for civilian scientists to study.

Loud banging resonated against the door. The first wave of guards had arrived. When RoH penetrated the security, the sensors had alerted the garrison.

RoH ignored the mayhem outside and approached the tank. She examined the alien. Its eyes were open, but aliens seldom closed their eyes, even in death. RoH understood that the bluish liquid nourished the body, but at first, she thought it preserved a corpse. Then it moved.

He senses me...

The alien twisted his neck and made eye contact. RoH saw fear, frustration, and pleading.

He knows what I am.

She projected reassurance towards the star-mind. The body writhed slightly, as if flexing long disused muscles.

"What is that?" Jas stammered.

"Jas," RoH said, "I believe this is Ruthie's lover. He's alive."

Banging vibrated the door. Jas wanted to run; now certain he would die, but the room only had the one exit. It would take a few minutes for someone to arrive with the security clearance for the door.

RoH examined the rest of the room. Shelves along one wall held glass containers of what looked like dismembered alien body parts. Her human half wanted to vomit.

Grandfather...

Yes RoH...

What happened to everyone on your ship in 1947?

One died, and that caused the crash. The impact threw me out of my restraint and I crawled away into the desert. Even then I nearly died. Another had died in his control seat. We retrieved the corpse a year before we rescued your mother. The remaining two stopped interacting with the network and we assumed they had died.

They thought I was dead, because the injury interfered with my abilities, but when I healed enough in Lubbock, they detected my signal. When I was ready, they picked me up.

So we can't verify two of the crew.

They must be dead.

Yet there is a non-zero possibility they are not, or perhaps one is not and another died years later.

That possibility has always been in our calculations, but we had no data.

RoH looked at the vat, and then at the horrifying wall.

I have data. One is dead, and they dismembered the body. Another is here and still alive, barely. I'm not sure I can rescue him. I want to find out if he fathered Robert Orville.

Alive or dead, we must bring him here and the remains of the other.

Okay, here is where I am. There are three of us. You had better take his tank, and me and a human whom I can't leave. Take the shelves from the wall to my left.

A military officer is in the room. Leave him unharmed. There is a concrete roof and walls and armed guards at the door.

Almost immediately, the sounds of shattering concrete and ripping of steel reinforcing rods filled the space. Dust fell. The door banging stopped. A low hiss began. RoH realized that the security included a way to fill the chamber with gas. Perhaps it killed; perhaps it only knocked intruders out.

"Jas, cover your mouth, don't breath, and stay by me."

RoH moved beside the tank where the alien body floated in the nutrient bath. The roof was gone and she could see the black sky and stars. A purple shaft took RoH, Jas, the containers of a dismembered alien, and the tank into the sky. The army captain lay flat on the floor, horrified and unmoving.

A five-ton truck rolled to a top in front of the Taken Inn. The logo on the door said, "Star Energy".

"Are you Corrine?" A pleasant-looking young woman leaned on the registration counter.

"That's me."

"Siglinde Hilfreich sent us to hook up a power unit. Can you show me your primary power source?"

Corrine overcame her puzzlement. "Oh, you mean the breaker panel... come this way."

After her midnight encounter with RoH, Corrine guessed that this young woman was an alien. An old comedy movie crossed her mind about a beautiful alien becoming someone's stepmother.

These aliens understand us humans, Corrine thought.

This female visitor knew electricity. A handsome young man with a tool belt slung from his hip joined them where the line from NV Energy linked the building to the grid. The male looked identical to the actor in the feel-good advertising by NV Energy.

"Wires," the man said, "... primitive."

He looked towards the pole near the road and the fused disconnect popped open. The inn went dark.

"It'll just take a few minutes," the woman reassured. Corrine panicked at any power failure. A summer without air conditioning in Rachel would be deadly. Late winter held less of a threat. "I'll back the truck around. Bill, we need to have a transfer switch under the meter. Corrine, what's behind that wall?" She pointed to a spot beside the power meter.

"Nothing..."

"Bill, make the hole for the unit right there."

The pair removed a large metal box from the vehicle and slipped it into the neat hole that Bill had made. The thing seemed much lighter than one would expect, and the two handled it with ease. When Corrine tried, it seemed to be impossibly heavy. Three leads came from the box. Bill ran them through a switch that separated the building from the meter.

"Okay, let's give it a go."

The woman knelt beside the enclosure and stared for a few seconds. The inn's lights suddenly came on. She smiled and patted the box.

"Let's go inside," Bill said. The box protruded into the inn's main lobby.

"Feel this," the woman guided Corrine's hand onto the white surface. It felt cool.

"What temperatures do you like in here?"

"Oh, about 72," Corrine said.

"That's a local scale." Bill smiled and knelt beside the box. Corrine felt the surface warm.

"It will sense the room temperature and adjust to cool the place in summer. Just touch it and think of whatever room temperature you want. It will give you all the electricity you need. Replace those electric heaters." The woman looked around, "and the AC units too."

"We don't have enough money," Corrine sighed.

"Sell your book," the young woman said.

Corrine slumped into a chair, overwhelmed by the inn changing overnight from a tourist trap to an alien beehive.

"You can sell electricity to your neighbours," Jim said, "but that needs heavy wires. Call this number if you want to do that. We will come back."

He handed Corrine a business card with Elliana's name on it and NAAP's toll-free number.

"What do I tell NV Energy when I'm not using power?"

"Tell them you have gone off-grid using star energy." The woman smiled. "Get them to take their wires away. You won't need them."

"Why are you doing all this?" Corrine felt a little fear that it might be some horrible alien plot.

"RoH," said the woman, "you are her latest dandelion."

As a courtesy to Corrine and Peg, RoH arranged for her and Jas to return into the front yard of the inn during what passed for a rush hour in Rachel. That meant about half the population observed a bright light in the sky. A purple shaft descended to the dusty barren patch between the office and the highway, causing several near collisions. RoH and Jas emerged, and the light disappeared. Jas' status in Rachel instantly shot to almost god-like or a devil, depending on which side of the judgement line a person stood. His humility, reinforced by RoH, kept him as a teacher and friend to all.

"Corrine, Jas will tell the story and be your main tourist attraction. Here's the chapter I promised about my life." RoH handed a few dozen typed pages to a shocked Corrine. "I might have more about Robert later."

"They had the alien who loved Ruth in a tank at the base. He had escaped from Groom Lake, found Ruth in Rachel and surrendered voluntarily to save the other one that we found dissected in jars. He's home now." RoH pointed skyward.

"They murdered that other one, but we don't seek revenge. She would not have suffered. If they tortured, she would have just used her mind to kill herself, but they threatened her to lure Ruth's lover back to the base."

"Robert's father did not commit suicide, even though that vat tormented him for decades. It seems his love for Ruth made him want to survive, hoping to see her again. Believe me, the one in the tank and my great-grandfather was unique back then. This idea of love has required an extra word in star language.”

“Ruth’s lover is Robert Orville’s father. He should be the one fixing the problem, but he’s too weak. It is up to me to get Robert Orville.”

CHAPTER 12

Dallas and the army of evil

RoH sat on a bench opposite a building that dominated the far side of the street. A gilded spire crowned with a cross topped the sprawling establishment that included a few acres of parkland and several outbuildings. The old church failed to adapt to the growing lust for the certainty and simplicity of fundamentalism. The Episcopalians had sold the old cathedral to the Church of Heavenly Enlightenment. That church satisfied the modern population's hunger for easy slogans and judgemental ranting. Cynics called the message from these sects, "The Gospel according to Saint Twitter." The Enlightenment owned no other edifice, although they rented a television studio down town. The sanctuary held 1200 souls, but every service called exactly 1000 adherents to the Enlightenment.

Several large vans filled the rear of the driveway, and people off-loaded crates into an out-building at the back. RoH did not have to guess at the contents. Every container was military deep green. The Heavenly Enlightenment had converted the property into an armoury. There seemed to be every type of light weapon and ammunition available in America.

On New Year's Eve, the aliens had stopped the production of light arms and ammunition. Texans and Americans everywhere had stripped gun shops bare of stock. The militaries around the world saw outstanding orders for weapons cancelled by suppliers. Everyone only had what was on hand, and with no possibility of receiving fresh supplies, handmade cartridges would never fill the gap.

The USA military suffered a woeful lack of resupply. The church had responded to the rumour that the government intended to seize private weapons and ammunition. In Texas, with its culture of six-shooter swagger, this threat became a call for civil war. Heavenly Enlightenment armed itself with earthly firepower to prepare for war. Donating weapons and ammunition became part of the expected tithing and a basis of status within the congregation.

RoH had hoped to see Robert Orville here, but realized that would not happen. She had spent the few days since her time in Rachel, Nevada, reviewing all public information about Orville and the church. She had replayed the Sunday broadcasts. In recent weeks, an assistant pastor had delivered the message in the strident manner of a true cult believer.

Something puzzled RoH about what she saw. Only now, sitting and observing these believers at work, she found the solution. All of their faces, including that of the fill-in preacher, lacked unique emotions. In the services, people responded with proper reactions. They stood, waved and chanted the worship songs with smiles, but then, and now, workers showed no spontaneous expressions. They moved normally but did not exchange banter, as would any random workers. It seemed they were emotionally absent, soldiers in an evil army.

The situation worried RoH. Robert Orville had manipulated the minds of his 1000. This suggested he had enough power to influence some people. RoH decided 1000 reflected a limit to Robert's control. After all, they had bred Robert in the same way as her great-grandfather. The records showed that her ancestor had limited abilities and great-grandfather had some empathy. Perhaps Robert's alien father had less compassion. Until he recovered from the Groom Lake ordeal, she would not know.

Would that have removed limitations to Robert's ability? Could it have doomed him to evil even at birth?

On a ship, a newborn matured in a teaching and caring, if not loving, community, but unlike RoH's ancestor, Orville had not had even that. *Is his power limited?*

RoH needed to examine the church records and find where Orville had gone. Goderich seemed the most probable. She passed unnoticed through the workers. RoH felt tempted to tamper with the side arms slung on each worker's belt, but humans had to decide on their own to stop killing each other. The door to the warehouse gaped beyond, but she needed the church office. The assistant pastor carried his own 9 mm automatic and supervised the work from an open rear door to the main building. RoH eased around the man and into the gloom. She found a door with a brass plate that read, "Robert Orville". An assistant worked over a large desk with a computer to one side and a layout of a brochure spread over the surface. The words "Call to Arms" in impressive font shouted from the front page. RoH surveyed the various filing cabinets. She guessed what she needed lay beyond an inner door. That door opened and then closed on its own.

RoH did not hurry. Unlike Corrine in Rachel, Nevada, no one would surprise her here. She had examined the minds of the people she had passed. What she found gave more worry; ordinary humans, not artefacts that Orville had manufactured. Orville had implanted unquestioning loyalty into their minds, subtly, but RoH knew. She had used the same ability often on Earth, but never made it permanent. In fact, no alien could make it permanent. The quantum decay process acted as entropy of the human mind, another road to forgetfulness that had to have regular repairs. If Robert Orville did not reinforce his changes, they would weaken and eventually disappear into deep memory. This necessity probably limited him to the 1000 loyal followers.

RoH felt empathy for the reproduct. Orville must have found restoring minds every day to be a tedious chore. It also meant that in his absence, the allegiance of his congregation weakened. RoH rejected the idea of doing an experiment in the rate of quantum decay in the human brain.

What would be worse, a well-armed gang of rogue believers or a closely controlled weapon of an angry hybrid alien?

RoH resisted the temptation to restore these human minds. If done now, Robert Orville would know that an alien had been here as soon as he found the alterations. Worse, he would know that the aliens knew about him. RoH did not want to drive him into hiding after the effort she had made to track him down. RoH still could not imagine Robert Orville's motives, although his mother's note in Rachel, Nevada, hinted at hatred.

It had been lucky that he had chosen a public persona as his source of power and his cover. As difficult as tracking him had been, it might have been impossible if he had remained anonymous. RoH had a startling thought. A better strategy for him would have been to lead this church from a pew, manipulating the leadership and congregation with no one knowing. She decided Robert Orville had an ego problem. Her assumption would lead to problems.

RoH returned to the mind of the woman in the outer office. She sought clues about Orville's character. The woman radiated a deep love for the pastor, but it was an innocent believer's love, not sexual. RoH searched for memories, gossip, details. She had no recollection of any impropriety, sexual or otherwise, from Orville. The woman knew everything about the church. Since she lacked RoH's abilities, she did not know she had all the names, addresses, and biographies of each member of the church in her memory. RoH filed these away. The one memory she did not have frustrated RoH. The woman did not know Robert Orville's current whereabouts. His location remained RoH's biggest unclaimed prize.

Mary sat patiently in Pastor George's office. Pastor worked on his next sermon while that new member, Brother Orr, leafed through sheets of paper on his desk and ignored the church secretary. Mary had noticed that in the past few weeks, while Pastor George preached with new, inspiring fire, he had become distracted otherwise. She had often flirted with the man, hoping for more. In her zealotry, being the Pastor's wife would have been Heaven on Earth. Now he seemed distant and unresponsive.

Two sides to the coin, she thought. Brother Orr's instant acceptance into the pastor's confidence annoyed long-time members and the elders.

The papers on George's desk held the biographical information for each member of his church. At least, as much information as Brother Orr could gather. It seemed to be a contrasting bunch. It ranged from workers and farmers to business people with a good smattering of professionals, mostly small-town lawyers. He did not see these people as representing an intellectual pinnacle, and that pleased him. These country lawyers would not think too deeply and ask hard questions. Pastor George preached the obvious, and he delivered it with emotion designed to incite unthinking reaction. Manipulation of true believers came easily.

"Pastor," Mary interrupted, "we have several calls from that church in Texas. Would you like to call back?"

From long practice, George's face did not reflect his annoyance. Mary filled the role of faithful servant, and he liked her. The Texas situation seemed to be a minor distraction. The church in Dallas might not even be necessary anymore. He needed to make plans to exploit the alien presence for his goals. He had too little information.

Where is their weakness, he wondered, *who is their Judas?*

The answer eluded him, but he was sure it would come.

"Yes, Mary, call and tell me when the pastor is on the line."

RoH searched through the bits of paper on the pastor's desk. So far, she saw no hint of Robert Orville. She felt a growing frustration.

Records for the previous Sunday lay beside the bank deposit slip. The record from the service showed the faithful had donated $100,000 in cash. The deposit slip showed $25,000 went to the bank account.

Where is the rest?

RoH looked around the room. A finely crafted wooden armoire took up a corner. It hid a massive safe with an electronic lock. The impressive vault seemed too small for the loot if all normal Sunday donations matched the previous service.

Someone takes a regular load of cash somewhere else.

That seems obvious. Why hoard so much money? Who is getting it? The store of weapons came to mind.

Where does Robert live? It's strange that woman doesn't know.

The phone rang in the outer office. Footsteps retreated and then returned. Heavier shoes approached. The assistant pastor locked the door, sat at his desk and took the handset.

"Pastor George, finally..."

Pastor George? RoH perked up from her perch on a side cupboard. *Why is this man talking to the Goderich troublemaker?*

"Everything is coming together here. The other churches are ready, but they are amateurs. We will lead when the time comes."

He listened.

"There's no sign of aliens. Someone saw a bright light last night, but it was a spotlight from Love Field."

He paused once more.

"Of course I'm sure. It was not an alien ship. There is one minor problem, though. The roof blowing off at the UN created a conspiracy theory claiming the aliens will destroy the UN. Anyone supporting the UN is an agent of a one-world government. We are solid, but some churches lost anti-UN believers to the pro-alien camp. One preacher changed his tune to supporting the aliens, but more because of his lost revenue than believing the conspiracy."

RoH smiled at the irony. They would have temporary allies with some of the more backward elements of humanity. She knew this would only last until the next conspiracy sent their allegiance in another direction.

"Okay, I'll only call if there is a crisis. Sorry, Robert,"

RoH almost fell from her perch.

Robert...? Pastor George...?

She knew now where the enemy hid. She had to get home immediately.

Father!!!!

Coming...

RoH headed for the door as the assistant pastor endured a loud verbal lashing from the other end of the call. He had made a mistake in using Orville's name. Neither he nor Orville knew the seriousness of the slip. In his chagrin, the local did not notice the locked door spring open and remain that way. The woman in the outer room felt a gust of air that blew her artwork onto the floor.

A shaft of purple light snatched RoH from the front yard of the church, but the adherents stowing the weapons did not understand what they had seen.

CHAPTER 13

Bang… Bang, he shot me down

That same cool, clear morning, in El Paso, Texas, as RoH rushed home from Dallas, Noah Lee, as he often did, sat hunched over his computer. Noah preferred to draw the heavy drapes and bring gloom to his spacious bedroom. When his mother had complained, he said he needed it dark for the computer screen.

Today, he would take action.

Noah was not a nerd, at least in the Hollywood cliché sense. He starred in athletics at Franklin High before graduating last summer. As with other natural athletes, he had excelled at several sports, from track to basketball. His popularity only exaggerated Noah's sense of entitlement. It also hid his profound emotional isolation and lack of empathy. Noah scored high academically, especially in anything related to computing, and could pick from most universities in the state. Instead of enrolling last fall, he secluded himself. Noah spent his time alone except for Sunday church, occasional visits with friends or to gun shops and computer stores.

The Lees lived in an up-scale part of El Paso, Falcon Hills. It was not the most elite neighbourhood. It reflected his father's status as a real-estate lawyer, and his mother's role as a senior teacher in a private girl's school. Noah's peers considered him privileged, but reality overpowered image. Throughout his childhood, Noah had experienced the care of strangers more than from his parents. His father travelled and worked long hours. His mother placed her job and its social rewards above mothering.

Noah entered day care as a baby, with various nannies before and after school. Noah felt rejected and had longed for his parents. Once, about grade six, when his father had been angry with him, he had said that Noah was an only child because they would not have any more inconvenient babies. Since then, Noah remembered always being angry with his parents.

His self-isolation became his life after he had graduated and lost the daily routine of school. He had worked hard in sports and class in his desperate need of his parents' recognition and approval, but they had seldom attended a game. His father had been away and his mother arrived late for his graduation. The adoration of his peers could not fill the hole.

One place he still received approval was at church. Pastor Mike shouted a steady stream of racism, leaning heavily on choice quotes from the Old Testament for justification. This being El Paso, much of the hatred focused upon the constant stream of desperate Hispanics crossing the Mexican border. For many years, Noah had heard this message about what Pastor called "illegal alien rapists and murdering drug dealers". When the message had recently switched to hatred of the space aliens neutering of the greatest military on Earth, the target had blurred in Noah's mind. He knew the difference between immigrants and star-travelers, but the word "alien" put them into the same bucket of hate. Noah became an example of how hatred could pervert intelligence.

Noah's life of isolation, religion, and internet addiction led him to Robert Orville. He never met Orville, but the services of the Church of Heavenly Enlightenment streamed on the internet. The strident message had a more sophisticated feel than that of the local preacher. To Noah Lee, Pastor Orville built a logical, Bible based reason to hate and fear aliens.

The Church of Heavenly Enlightenment told people to attack aliens and their supporters. They were agents of Satan. This led to the final fatal influence of the internet.

In his obsession, Noah roamed the dark web where conspiracy, bigotry, and lies became truth. A new site named AlienStrike had appeared after the New Year's Eve alien rescue of the Martian settlers. AlienStrike encouraged violence towards any "godless aliens, bastard crossbreeds, and human sympathizers". It suggested, with accidental truth, that many aliens disguised themselves as humans. The discussion forum on AlienStrike spread plans for attacking aliens. A plot to invade Canada and destroy Goderich had popularity, full of fanciful ideas and much hatred. Apparently, an alliance of "libtards, Commies, gays, perverts, and Arab terrorists" ran Canada.

The horde of American participants had a sketchy idea of where Canada might be. Goderich wandered from British Columbia to Newfoundland but popularly seemed to be near Buffalo, New York.

Aside from impractical nonsense and a smattering of dangerous conspiracy, the key for Noah Lee was the El Paso node for AlienStrike. No one knew who owned the website, but a user listed El Paso as home. Noah chatted with this person several times; however, they would not meet.

"It's best we don't know each other," they said. "The feds are watching."

This element of danger and rebellion against the government excited Noah. He believed everything the El Paso contact said. Even in his internet sophistication, it did not occur to Noah that the other could easily be in a bistro in St. Petersburg, Russia or a coffee shop in Washington, D.C. The person claimed they had inside information from the El Paso police.

Noah believed the Undocumented Alien Support Services on East Sixth Avenue was a front for inter-stellar aliens. That these volunteers belonged to other Christian churches did not reduce Noah's hate. AlienStrike claimed space-aliens disguised as murderers and rapists had crossed the Mexican border. His pastor accused those churches of being prostitutes of the federal government, since they accepted federal grants. Worse, they did not follow the sacred word of King James.

The three-pronged assault on his judgement by his pastor, AlienStrike, and Robert Orville led to Noah's dark plan. He would be a hero, a martyr, admired by all, and would finally show his parents what "inconvenient" might be. If Noah had not been intelligent, the outcome might have been less horrific. Unfortunately, an automatic assault rifle is a great magnifier of perverted intelligence and ignorance.

On a golf course in Florida, a shooting took place that would push Noah to a greater level of horror.

"Watch where you are hitting... " the old golfer snarled at the younger man who had driven a ball into their preceding foursome. It had been accidental, but the young man was inconsiderate.

"Ah, you old fart, I didn't hit anyone."

"You young jerks just don't care about anyone but yourself." The older man, full of righteousness, stepped aggressively towards the transgressor. He waved his putter at the upstart.

The intruder stepped back to his cart and, in a flash, levelled a semi-automatic handgun at the threat.

"You don't scare me," the putter waved in the air. The gun spoke, and the putter hit the ground before its dead owner. The rest of the dead man's foursome rushed towards the shooter. He did not just own a gun, but knew how to use it. He had been in war. The four bodies did not bother him. He chipped onto the green and teed off.

The police caught up to the man two holes later. He and a cop joined the list of the dead.

Of the four other mass shootings that had happened in the USA that morning, the Florida golf course grabbed most of the headlines. Noah lamented the attention on Florida. People might not notice his heroic act.

I'll have to make it spectacular, so they will remember Noah Lee in the fight against aliens.

Today was the day for Noah to answer the call. Noah had made several scouting trips downtown. The busiest time was on a weekday afternoon, and that made for the best target.

The one thing Noah's parents did for him, out of guilt, he thought; they showered him with money. He had the best computers and clothes. They gave him a self-driving electric car as a graduation present. They had held a graduation party, invited all their friends and none of Noah's. The party was about their bragging rights. His parents made a big deal of the gift, and then ignored Noah as they worked the room full of important or useful people. Noah eventually drove off in his new car to sulk in a pizza joint.

The clock edged towards noon. Noah set his in-room camera to record and pulled a long steel container from under his bed. He lifted the rifle from the lock-box and cradled it. His parents did not know that their guilt money bought the best weapons available in El Paso. Noah retrieved a 9 mm pistol from the case, doffed a cop's shoulder holster and hid it beneath a loose combat jacket. He tested his quick draw and smiled into the camera. At every step, Noah narrated his actions. His track bag came from the closet and Noah inspected the high-capacity clips. He locked one into the rifle and slipped two into his jacket pockets.

Noah had been an army cadet in high school, and while he did not enjoy it, he learned to shoot and quick-change clips. He resented a system where he was not the centre of attention and self-important officers and lead cadets bullied everyone else. He liked the shooting-range trainer, a veteran instructor from Fort Bliss who had become an El Paso police officer and volunteered with the cadet corps. The man kept Noah from quitting until the end of his first year. By then, he could shoot a handgun at 450 and make clusters with a rifle at 200 yards.

Noah wrapped the rifle in a blanket and gathered it and a bag full of spare clips. He typed one last message to AlienStrike and posted a copy on all of his internet platforms.

Today is the first strike in the fight against Satan's aliens. Today will be a glorious victory in El Paso. Watch the news, Praise God; praise Pastor Mike; praise Pastor Orville.

The video of his preparations joined the upload.

He placed the weapon and the bag into the back seat and had a pleasant lunch at his favourite pizza shop.

"Have a great day," the cute clerk smiled as he left.

"Oh, it will be a wonderful day," Noah replied.

He stopped, looked at the girl, and considered staying for another soda. Perhaps, if Noah had actually fallen in love, it might have changed history. A pretty face almost succeeded.

He climbed into his car and punched in the auto-drive to the address on East Sixth Avenue.

In front of Undocumented Alien Support Services, a dozen recent arrivals enjoyed the warming winter sun. Mandy Rice passed out sandwiches and water to the throng. Each day saw many nationalities asking for help, but today seemed to be Guatemala Day. Many more were inside talking to counsellors. Mandy found joy and purpose in helping others, and these people had fled suffering she could only imagine from their stories. She watched a small red car pull up to the curb. It was a no-parking zone, and Mandy debated whether to make an issue of it. A good-looking young man jumped out and opened the rear door on the street side. Mandy thought he was nervous.

Noah did not give Mandy or anyone time to consider the situation. His first clip sprayed the crowd. Six were dead and many more gravely wounded. Mandy lay, eyes open amongst her spilled treats.

Noah charged into the building, squeezing off shots as he went. His first victims were behind the reception counter. The packed crowd presented an easy target. Many of these people had experienced high levels of violence in their home countries and hit the floor when they heard shots. This may have saved a few. Noah slipped another clip into the rifle. His distraction would prove fatal. Noah had wounded the security guard in the first barrage. While Noah felt for a clip, the man raised his handgun and fired. In his pain, he could not aim to kill, but his bullet passed through Noah's leg and severed the femoral artery. The gravely wounded guard slipped into unconsciousness. Noah screamed in pain and dropped to one knee, his purpose forgotten. While the death toll already had reached 18, with another 13 gravely wounded, the security guard's last conscious act saved many lives.

Noah dragged his leg and left a river of blood to his car. He slumped into the driver's seat and punched in auto-drive. The car auto-selected the programmes to take Noah home and sped down the street, obeying all the traffic laws. The car dutifully pulled to the curb to allow several police vehicles and ambulances to pass as they screamed towards the carnage. All the while, Noah's heart pumped away his life. In a half hour, the car came to a stop in Noah's driveway. Unconscious and unable to move, Noah died in the driver's seat ten minutes later. A neighbour, watering her flowers, found the body.

CHAPTER 14

Bait bucket

RoH, I should be the one in this fight.

No, Mother, we don't know exactly how much power Robert has. He's of the same sequence as great-grandfather and that first reproduct's abilities were undeveloped. His hatred magnifies Robert's capability. I'm not sure you have the tools, but I don't think he can handle me. Father is ready to back me, and we have the crystal. I must surprise him when he is vulnerable. I'm not sure of the situation, so it may be a few days or weeks, unless Robert starts a problem.

Can we save Robert?

I don't know, Mother. I'll try to pop him into a bucket and take him home.

RoH returned her attention to Jaden, Captain Fontaine, Jake and Elsie at the kitchen table, trying to enjoy breakfast. The ugly news on the television had destroyed the joy of RoH's return. Yesterday had been the worst day for mass killings in the USA in over two years. Altogether, there were six tragedies totalling 49 dead, 50 if one counted Noah Lee, and many more wounded. Noah Lee's massacre in El Paso had been the worst and grabbed most of the international headlines. According to the police, Noah had committed the only specifically anti-alien atrocity.

"The police are saying little," the voiceover of the carnage in El Paso said, "but they have confirmed that Lee acted alone. Many fear this might inspire other anti-alien violence that will kill humans instead of the dangerous alien invaders. Police seized his computer and phone and the data stored in his electric car. Lee had connections to internet conspiracy sites advocating violence, and to two churches, one in El Paso and the other in Dallas."

"A few months ago, this network did a 'tell all' on the hateful racism of the El Paso pastor. Sources tell us that the pastor's message has become a diatribe against star travelling aliens who have recently attacked us."

"The aliens operate with impunity. We must oppose their attack on our property and power, but not kill Americans. Mr. President, where are you? The police have not said what Dallas church Lee contacted."

"I think I know," RoH said. "This news implies it might be okay to kill aliens, just not humans. I must stop Robert Orville before he causes more killing. He won't kill us, but many humans might die because of him. We aren't invaders."

"My squad is ready," Captain Fontaine said.

"Ghislaine," RoH said, "if it ever comes to that, I will have failed. We star people owe it to Robert to save him. I owe it to him and especially to his long-dead mother. He is the way he is because of alien bumbling, or circumstance. So far, the star-cousin I rescued cannot give a full account. He floated in life support tank for over 60 years and that has damaged him. If we can't salvage Robert, I'm afraid I will have to kill him."

"How can you even think that?" Jaden trembled. Her heart hated violence. "Can't you just make gunpowder stop working?"

"Star travellers can't change the laws of physics, Jaden. It would be dangerous and suicidal if we could and likely have killed ourselves years ago. We didn't stop nuclear reactions when we neutralized the weapons. We simply tweaked both the electrical and other mechanisms. If humans avoid suicide, they will have to dismantle all of those bombs. Most of the world's warships and airplanes are scrap. We calculate that there are not enough cheap resources on Earth to replace everything."

"Robert Orville is impersonating Pastor George. The real pastor George might be dead. If Robert killed him, it raises a genuine issue with us. We do not have a protocol for dealing with criminals in our community. There has never been a recorded crime since before we left our home world.

Humans use brutal systems you call justice, but they magnify the problem. The possibility that Robert is a killer has caused a discussion far beyond the solar system and ranges over the part of the galaxy we call home."

"I have to wait until Sunday to confront Robert when he is preaching. I hope to pop him into a bucket and send him to a ship."

"In the meantime," RoH looked at her alien companions, Jake and Elsie, "we need to keep a mental shield here. Robert might search for our minds. If he finds out where I am, or any alien, that will endanger humans."

"I still want to back you up?" Captain Fontaine expected to lead her combat group into action.

"No, thank you." RoH appreciated Ghislaine's eagerness. "There will be too many innocent people there. I don't want to hurt them. We must wait."

Pastor George's church sat on a rural side road just a few kilometres from the cult of the alien worshiper's chicken barn and flying saucer landing pad. It reflected the popular trend to build drive-in churches on cheaper rural land. Everyone drove to the site. Pastor George attracted a huge congregation from much of Huron County. Cynics quipped, without data, that these churches in North America generated a million tonnes of carbon pollution every week. In fact, many members owned high-end electric vehicles and others car-pooled. Unlike the cargo cult, Pastor George wanted to be isolated. It played into the siege mentality he shared with most fundamental believers.

"Mrs. Grenier, please drop by the office after service?"

Pastor George's request puzzled Jody Grenier. She did not think she had made any transgression. Still, Jody worried as she entered the office. The service had been especially inspiring with the faithful raised to a new frenzy that made the idea of killing aliens a logical step.

Brother Orr had been evaluating the congregation and the name Grenier stuck out. He had heard it before. After searching through past news stories, he discovered Jody shared the same last name as the woman, Kerri Grenier, whom the CIA had supposedly shot. A more recent report suggested Kerri was Charlie Keys' lover. Keys had fathered the alien half-breed, Ellie Keys.

"Sit down, Jody. Don't worry, I would like to ask a few questions and make a proposal." Pastor nodded to Mary. Bob Orr sat nearby.

"We want to propose that you work with Mary as an assistant. Her workload exceeds what one person can handle."

"I would like that. Mary has been so helpful to me."

"I see your last name is the same as the woman who works with the father of that alien woman

My husband, Gary, is Kerri's brother, and she now lives with Charlie Keys. I have never mentioned it because she's a horrible person cozying up to that alien lover. When the cops reported her murder, we cried, but then we found out that she's an alien-lover. Frankly, we don't know what happened in that supposed shooting and her miraculous reappearance after New Year's. Either the cops faked it, or the aliens kept her alive and made her into a monster. I hate her. Gary cut her out of his life."

"Where is she now?" Bob Orr asked.

"She's shacked up with Keys."

"Where does Keys live?"

"I don't know. We never thought about him until they got together. They work at the Hammersmith place on Industrial Road in Goderich."

Pastor George nodded at Mary.

"Come with me, Jody," Mary said. "Let's talk about the job."

The women left. Bob Orr quietly followed while the Pastor stayed to work on his next sermon.

Brother Orr walk into the reception area of Hammersmith Inc. Mike had added a receptionist as gatekeeper to control the reporters and the curious.

"Can I please see Kerri Grenier?" Orr asked. "I have a message from her brother."

Kerri had felt bad about the recent split with her family, and soon Brother Orr stood at her workstation.

"Hello, Kerri," Brother Orr smiled and pulled out a pistol, "take me to Charlie Keys."

Kerri trembled. Her fear caused flashbacks to the day the CIA shot her. Her body tingled. They found Charlie puzzling over paperwork. The gun gave him the same fearful reaction, including the warm wave surging through his body.

"You two, come with me. If your alien friends cooperate, you'll live."

Charlie eased his hand towards his cell, hoping to press the 911 button.

"Leave that alone," Brother Orr levelled the gun, "no tricks."

Charlie hung his hands to his side as Orr herded them out.

Perhaps I can warn Sangha at the desk.

Strangely, Sangha had left her post.

Damn...

The cold air wrapped around them, and a chill replaced the warm flush. Gloom had settled in the late winter afternoon. A squall threatened along the lakeshore and the wind swirled light snow from the ploughed-up embankments. Orr ordered them to Pastor George's SUV in the snowy parking lot.

The burst of brilliance above the factory came with no warning. A vivid purple glow, accompanied by a loud roar, shot to the surface and surrounded Kerri and Charlie. The sonic burst flung Brother Orr into a nearby pile of snow. Kerri and Charlie shot up and disappeared into the low clouds.

I guess you can't die twice, Kerri thought as they rushed skywards.

The parking lot returned to winter gloom.

Brother Orr did not suffer any physical damage beyond ringing ears. He slid from the bank, stared skywards, and shook a raised fist. Bob Orr drove away in defeat. He did not know how the aliens knew what he had been doing.

Charlie and Kerri's nervous systems had sent a help signal as soon as they felt fear. The star vessel that RoH called "The Goderich Guardian" always lurked between the farm and the town. This had led to an early rescue. The ship could have saved the pair earlier, but having them out in the open simplified the effort, and they did not have to damage a building. RoH thought neutralizing Robert Orville was tricky enough. She did not want the complication of hostages, especially Grandpa and Kerri. Destroying buildings would leave a poor impression.

Mother, where are Grandpa and Kerri?

Your father is briefing them. We will return them to the factory. The system works and they will always be safe. We could have rescued them in Dad's office, but we did not want to wreck Mike's factory.

I'm doing it Sunday, Mother.

Your father will be watching.

CHAPTER 15

Doctor, you are kidding

One month after the fiasco of trying to subvert RoH to aid the human breeding attempt, Washington had become a depressed centre of helplessness. Political turmoil threatened the Union, and the President spent his days trying to suppress opposition inside and outside of his party. He spent long hours brooding in his office. His staff, and especially his most trusted advisor, Mary, reassured him they would soon have a new solution. The kidnapping of RoH had gone so badly that even Mary had lost some influence with the despondent politician.

"We aren't making progress. I can't calm the old man down." Mary dropped a file and looked at Dawn.

"What progress are you looking for?"

"I don't know. The fiasco with that little alien bitch was my best. I see no way to counter the aliens. They sit and wait for us to choose... something."

"My grandfather used to say that most times, the right way is the hardest." Daisy invented the saying based on her experience with American movies. Walter, someone had been in that one, playing the wise grandfather. "Maybe the aliens have shown us that way."

"I'm not taking advice from some damned interlopers," Mary snapped. "The politicians are abandoning the President. They think he's useless, worse, a loser, and that makes me powerless. I used to have leverage. I have info on them all. Everyone but six is immoral, and I have the evidence, but now they don't care. They think shouting against the invaders will elect them. I have power if they fear me, and that is gone."

Daisy thought Mary shared the President's depression.

An early March storm blew snow against the glass. The view echoed Mary's mood.

"The March Lion," the down-home wisdom from Iowa comforted Mary. "We don't always get them now."

"I read somewhere that there will be bad hurricanes in Texas this year." Actually, Daisy had access to the massive alien organic computing power. They had analyzed Earth's climate in a detail no human system could duplicate. Long-term disaster lurked, but they knew a massive storm would devastate south Texas in September.

"I don't think I'll be here long," Mary continued her gloomy assessment. "If the old man lasts for the next election, he might not even get nominated. His strongest allies in congress have been pressuring me to get him to resign. The V-P hates me, so if Harry goes, I go."

Mary sobbed. That had become more common over the last month. Since the star travellers knew the President would be dead soon, likely by assassination, Daisy considered what might need to be done to have Mary remain influential with the new woman president. The plan they had started with Mary did not include her losing influence in Washington. Daisy could ensure that the V-P would not be a problem as president.

"What can you do?" Daisy handed Mary a tissue.

"Nothing..."

Mary leapt from her chair.

"I have to pee." She ran from the room with her stomach heaving.

Mary left the washroom and gripped the doorframe for support. The last few mornings had become nightmares of fatigue and nausea. Today had started the same way. She had to urinate a lot and often felt sick, although she seldom vomited. This time had been an exception.

"Are you okay, Mary?" Daisy appeared. "You look pale."

"What the hell is it to you?" Mary snapped, but then regretted it. "I'm sorry, Daisy. I have been feeling a little under the weather lately."

"Mary," Daisy replaced the doorway to steady Mary, "let's get a coffee."

"Water," Mary said. "I've been feeling sick lately; food puts me off."

Daisy held Mary's hand and drew her into the little kitchen near the President's office. She made sure no one lingered and locked the door. Daisy eased Mary into a chair.

"Mary," Daisy took her hand, "you are pregnant."

"No," Mary screamed, "No..."

The worry had gripped her ever since her tryst with whatever had impersonated Nathan. She had thought of the diagnosis, but Daisy confirmed it. *But I'm too old for that...*

"How do you know? You're not a doctor." Mary trembled.

"I'll get to that in a minute, but you have shown all the early signs, so many, in fact, that your situation should be in medical texts." Daisy annoyed Mary with her laugh. "Just so you know, I'm pregnant too, but a few months further on than you."

"No way." The news temporarily took Mary's mind from her discomfort. For reasons she had not understood, she had felt a connection with Daisy the day she interviewed her for the job. Motherhood became a deeper bond.

"You don't look, or act pregnant. You're a ball of fire, and I'm always tired. Do I know the father?"

"He's a nice doctor in Canada," Daisy smiled. She and Mary's inseminations had occurred deceitfully. For Daisy, it had combined human lust that seemed to be a part of her masquerading as a human, with their ongoing breeding objectives. The star people on the surface of Earth had some situational independence, but they all had to conform to the plan. Daisy would not have had her fun with Dr. Kai if the group had not allowed it, or if Kai had not been eager and willing.

I have to make it up to Kai sometime soon, Daisy thought.

She felt privileged to conceive a baby. Few star travellers ever had the chance, and as Ellie had with RoH, Daisy insisted she carry the baby to term instead of into the gestation vat. Daisy had learned much from Ellie as she had aged from a little girl into womanhood and a mother. The birth of RoH was a powerful incentive. *They will not hatch my child in an incubator.*

They had impregnated Mary partly as an experiment in hybridization. Mary was a strong woman and the star travellers wanted to see if that might produce another RoH without an Ellie as an intermediate step. A more important aim was to draw a powerful figure in Washington into supporting the alien objectives. They hoped it might reduce the potential bloodshed.

"Canada... but we checked you out. You haven't left the country, ever."

"Mary, look at me. Why I don't look pregnant, and why I know you are."

Mary screamed louder than she had at the pregnancy news. The slightly shimmering grey entity opposite at the table smiled and took Mary's hand. Immediately, the tyrant of Washington politics calmed. Daisy reappeared.

"Oh, God," Mary exclaimed. "I'm carrying an alien." She could not prevent the image, from old movies, of a monster erupting from her belly.

"I must have an abortion."

"We won't let you, Mary." Daisy shared the cruel calculation that had seemed practical and progressive among the stars. "We want your baby to be alive. Either you carry it to term or we can remove it and incubate it on a ship. I hope you carry him. It's something you and I can share as he grows. I will birth before you, on a ship. You can be there to support me. I can help you, and our biology people can give us the medical help we need. Please, Mary..."

Daisy earnestly hoped the woman would agree. She wanted to share the bond. Somehow, because of her imitating a human, some humanity had crept into her being. Daisy would discuss it with Ellie and RoH, the resident star-travelling experts on the human species.

Mary closed her eyes. Her heart felt the grief and confusion, remembering the day they had buried Nathan.

Nathan, it's part of Nathan... him, she said, him...

Confusion grasped Mary. She knew she could not, for her career, but... she lifted the water bottle, replaced it, raised it once more, sipped... The room threatened to go dark. Daisy waited.

"Yes..." only Daisy could hear the whisper. She squeezed Mary's hand.

"We will do it together," Daisy hugged her new friend. Mary tried to remember if she had ever had a friend before.

"You said 'him'."

"It's a male," Daisy said, "but now we have a debate going on up there. Some think that a first-generation child conceived between a star traveller and a human must be anatomically male. Mine is too. So far, it's about three to one in that way. There is a female in Africa."

"There's a push to conduct more experiments. Ellie, RoH and I fight that. Sentient species on planets should not be lab rats."

"I feel like a lab specimen now," Mary reverted to gloom.

"Well, you are, a little, but you won't lose your humanity, and you will get to nurture him to adulthood. Ellie set that precedent with RoH. You can deliver on Earth, or in space. Mary, he will look like Nathan."

Daisy let Mary sit quietly, absorbing the shocks. Ellie said any human first exposed to aliens needed time, and they needed a mentor, a caring mentor. Ellie received that from her great grandfather. Daisy would comfort Mary. They did not want another Robert Orville.

The walls and doors muffled a distinct gunshot that ended the reverie.

"It came from the Oval Office." Mary raced to the door, not considering there might be danger beyond.

A door slammed, somewhere, as they ran down the corridor, and Mary flung open the door to the Oval Office.

The President sat in his chair, slumped onto the desk. A revolver lay on the floor beside him. Mary pushed the emergency button and felt for a pulse. Harry had died, probably instantly. Blood seeped from beneath his chest. The Secret Service agent burst in. Daisy closed the patio door that allowed snow in from the raging storm.

"He's dead," Mary told the first agent. "Get the Vice-president. I'll call the Chief Justice."

There would be a female president before lunch. Mary stared at the body and thought about clearing out her office. She had no love for Harry, but her ticket to power had expired.

At least I won't need to explain about my little boy, she thought.

CHAPTER 16

G'day, Mate

Johnny Bray had never been on an airplane, let alone out of the country. He felt compelled to track down the alien hybrid girl who had visited him. She had said she had come from Canada, and research on line led to Goderich Ontario. The Qantas flight would get him near there.

Johnny had his itinerary safely tucked into his shirt pocket. The friendly folks at Worldwide Tours had worked out every detail. They had realized he had never travelled before. The agent gave detailed instructions about the Air Canada flight in Vancouver, and the local from Toronto to London. He would have to decide how to get to Goderich from there. Johnny had no driver's licence, but he had the name of that reporter in the videos, Bobby Briscoe. It might help if he told Briscoe he was a hybrid alien.

Johnny learned two things from the trip. The first lesson showed that in the wider world, skin colour did not raise an immediate look of disdain. The second occurred because one of the flight attendants collected Australian art. She knew of Johnny Bray and had one of his acrylics in her apartment. Fewer people travelled these days and there were empty first-class seats. Johnny enjoyed some derivative luxury courtesy of his art-collecting friend. He promised her free pick of his shop when he returned.

"No thanks," Johnny said when offered wine. The many sad stories at home, especially that of his mother at the plonk shop, and the help of a strict aunt, had ensured that Johnny would never drink alcohol.

"Mr. Briscoe," Johnny cradled the telephone handset in the concourse of London Airport, "you don't know me. I'm Johnny Bray, a friend of an alien girl named RoH."

"Mr. Bray?" Bobby assumed the black man dozing on the bench was his recent caller. He had seen some Australian Aboriginal characters in movies, and this older man with a weathered black face and a wild white beard looked the part.

"You didn't tell me much on the phone," Bobby smiled, "but dropping RoH's name is always a clincher."

Johnny was no bush tracker, but when someone suffers racism, they learn to look at people. He examined Bobby. The young man's earnest face reassured. Johnny had watched most of the reports from Canada, and Johnny knew Bobby liked aliens.

"G'day, mate, I'm here because I think I am needed in Goderich. I do not know why, but I'm sure of it."

Johnny sat straight and found his water bottle. "RoH came to visit me in Alice about a month ago because I am a human-alien half-breed. I never knew until she showed up. Her visit made my life make sense."

Bobby processed this shock.

"Can I interview you on television?"

"I'm not sure I want the world to know, especially everyone back home. My going walkabout already has them thinking I'm crazy."

"I tell you what," Bobby said. "I'll take you to RoH's mother. She's here in town. Let her decide what you should do. I would be happy to drive you to Goderich and RoH."

RoH, your friend, our cousin, Johnny Bray, from Australia is here.

Johnny... that's a surprise.

He wants to meet you.; something told him to come. It must be important, but he doesn't know why.

Johnny?... Mother, I think I know why. I think Johnny and I can save Robert Orville. I'll be right there.

Father...

Coming...

"Would you like a coffee?" Steve Jorgensen played the host. The last Australian Aboriginal he had met was a post-doctoral fellow at a linguistics conference in Canberra.

"Tea, if you have it, mate."

Steve had not had time to boil water before there was a burst of purple light from the street. RoH let herself in.

"Hi, Mom, hi step-Dad," she giggled. Ellie hugged her tight.

"Stop scaring the natives, RoH. London will be complaining."

"Mother, so far I haven't blown up a barn on TV." RoH peeked around her mother's hug and smiled at Johnny.

"That was Jimmy and Bobbie's fault." Ellie tried to glare at the reporter recording the scene.

"Does Bobby know about Robert?"

"Until today, he didn't know any lost reproducts existed. Johnny ended that."

"Bobby," RoH said, "you can record and listen, but don't share yet. It would wreck my plan."

"Don't worry, RoH, the American President's suicide is taking all the news time. They won't want anything from me until the audience drops off, or until someone blows up a barn." He winked at Ellie.

"Mother, Johnny is the key to any hope of saving Robert. Johnny survived the same abandonment as Robert, but he worked out a solution."

"Johnny, I told you about our cousin. He's younger than you are. He has become a danger. If I can get him alone, would you talk to him? Unlike you, who can choose to stay or go, we eventually must either get Robert off Earth or kill him."

Ellie gasped at RoH's bluntness.

"I don't want to kill him."

In reflex, RoH touched the diamond-like jewel hanging around her neck and hidden beneath her shirt.

I don't want to kill.

"Is it that serious, sweetie?" Ellie felt RoH's distress.

"I have touched his mind, Mother; yes it is."

Bobby and Steve did not know about the failed hybrids and did not know what Ellie and RoH talked about.

"A life of hatred," Johnny mused from the couch, "a life of hatred... the darkness took him..."

Johnny knew how close he had come to having hate consume his life. He had put that black void onto canvas where he could control it.

"Johnny," RoH said, "I want you to stay here with Mom and Steve until I need you. It will be safer. If Robert found out about you before we are ready, it might be bad."

Steve retrieved the steeped tea for Johnny and delivered the habitual hot chocolate to his adopted stepdaughter.

"I am going to get Robert next Sunday. When I do, we'll need you in Goderich, Johnny. Father will let you know."

"Will you be okay?" Ellie knew about RoH's abilities, but Robert Orville still had unknown capabilities.

"I just hope I don't need to kill him on the spot. I want to get him calm enough to talk. He'll be preaching on Sunday, and, I hope, distracted for the instant I need. Pastor George's congregation is going to be confused. They don't know that Robert eliminated their real pastor and replaced him with an impersonation. Then the aliens will have snatched even that away from them."

"That will end up creating more hatred for star travellers." Ellie said.

"You know," Steve said, "that in the movies Orville would become a good guy but still die to pay for killing the real Pastor George."

"That's a moral calculation we do not make," Ellie said. "If we accepted tit for tat, the whole star-travelling species would have to die. We made Robert Orville."

"This Orville thing is distracting us from our primary goal," Ellie said. "It is such a waste."

"I don't think it's a waste," Johnny Bray said. "I suffered my whole life until you showed up, RoH. For me, that's wonderful."

"We created your suffering too, Johnny. Even with our abilities, we can't give that life back to you."

"In the outback, in the night, the moonlit ghost gums shine and dance for the joy of the spirits," Johnny said. His eyes closed as if he watched something in his mind. "The spirits made the gums for their pleasure, and the gums suffer long days in the baking sun to fulfil their destiny. I suffered, like a ghost, my whole life to fulfil this destiny. If I help our cousin, our suffering and our spirits will merge into the ghostly dance of the gums. We both will be happy with our purpose."

In Steve's living room, Johnny's dark wrinkled face and white grizzled beard conveyed learning from thousands of years. He had faced all the sunsets, felt the dusty winds of all his ancestors, and kept the learning and patience from each. Johnny had visited a million stars and touched a million minds.

Bobby recorded this wisdom from the red dust of Australia. He decided that whatever he might show about these new hybrids, he would begin and end the piece with Johnny's poetic acceptance of his life.

"Can I get art supplies?" Johnny tried to enjoy Steve's tea. He had looked at the bleak Canadian winter scape and hoped to capture it with his newfound joy.

"That's why your most wonderful paintings are of the white gums." RoH smiled and shared Johnny's pleasure. "They dominate the darkness."

CHAPTER 17

There's a hole in the bucket

RoH eased the Martin X into the far corner of the parking lot of the Holy Spirit Immersion of Huron. Neat rows of vehicles from rusty pickup trucks to luxury sedans filled the lot. A high-end SUV occupied Pastor George's reserved parking. RoH walked past the vehicle and through the front doors.

She had visited the place during the week, to learn the approaches and to be familiar with who might be with Pastor George on other days. It seemed to be the pastor, Mary and Jody, the secretaries, and Brother Orr. The latter's clumsy attempt to harm Charlie and Kerri had made him known throughout the fleet. It seemed Robert had recruited Orr as his chief helper. RoH had decided that Orr was under Orville's total control.

While it might have been easier to handle Robert during the week and snatch him into a ship, RoH wanted to make an impression on this full house of the faithful. A good scare might do them good, but she wanted to expose them to the reality of whom they had idolized. She had a theory that congregations worshiped their pastor more than they worshiped the God he espoused. She based this on the evidence that in the splits of churches, adherents either left to follow one pastor or stayed because of the other. It surprised her that catechisms left so much wiggle room for interpretation. Charisma usually triumphed.

The star travellers knew much, but the universe held an unexplained mystery. They saw that as an opportunity to explore and learn and not to explain the unknown through non-scientific stories. They would allow that mystical explanation may actually be correct, but in the millennia of their existence, they had verified none. On Earth, mystic beliefs dominated the human psyche and differed little from those of sentient species on many other planets. This had formed part of the attractiveness of humans. They coloured human culture and provided interesting and often enjoyable distraction. It gave a clue to the development of the humanoid brain.

The service had begun, and the congregation sang in wild intensity, standing, waving arms in the air and most eyes closed in ecstasy. Everyone had crowded the front seats. RoH slipped, unnoticed, into an empty chair at the aisle about a third of the way up. She did not want to stand out and the closed eyes frenzy helped. She looked about. Pastor stood on the stage singing into a microphone. A casual band of a drummer, guitar, harp, and a saxophone provided the musical accompaniment. RoH thought they were quite good. She noted that Brother Orr occupied the sound booth at the rear corner, near to the door.

RoH focused on Pastor George. She had no firm plan but waited for the moment of maximum effect. The worship music lasted for twenty minutes, allowing her to wander a few minds. Orville had not altered these, as he had done to the adherents in Dallas. That encouraged her.

Business came first. Four children passed collection baskets down the aisles. RoH had a few coins. As the youngsters waited for the offering-basket to travel down the row, RoH noticed a woman on the opposite side of the aisle frowning at her.

She's wondering who I am.

The woman searched for RoH's non-existent parents. RoH resisted sending a calming message to the woman. Listening to minds was one thing, sending a signal might alert Robert. Pastor George approached the dais.

"Praise the Lord,"

"Praise the Lord" echoed the congregation.

"Children," Pastor George began, "in the face of the abhorrent alien attack, God leads me to revisit the story of David and Goliath. Please turn to First Samuel 17 in the holy book of King James."

Pastor George insisted on reading the complete chapter. The congregants constantly interrupted him with cries of Amen and Hallelujah. He finally reached verse 40,

"And he took his staff in his hand, and chose him five smooth stones out of the brook, and put them in a shepherd's bag which he had, even in a scrip; and his sling was in his hand: and he drew near to the Philistine."

RoH rose from her seat, stepped into the aisle, and walked towards Pastor George. She had no stones from the brook. He loomed on the raised platform, formidable in a black robe, starched collar with a large spear-like candle flickering to his side on a meter long brass holder. The massive emblem fixed to the support of the dais resembled a shield. He broke stride with the text.

"How dare you interrupt me, little girl, you little snip with a child's face and unkempt hair?"

Pastor George suddenly grimaced as he recognized RoH. She had thrown farm tractors to the side with a wave of her hand.

"I'm not a dog you can muzzle," he screamed and pointed at her.

The adherents shouted, "Sit down", "go away". A few joined the pastor in their horrific recognition.

"This is not your pastor," RoH shouted. "He's an imposter."

She raised her hand, but paused in surprise. Pastor George had suddenly changed into an enormous dog that towered towards the apex of the sanctuary, snapping and growling. Foam poured from its mouth. The congregation screamed in fear. RoH had not done that. She ran forward. RoH still saw the human Pastor George, although she knew what they all saw. Orville had manipulated the minds of the congregants and had not actually changed. RoH left the people's minds to Robert Orville and concentrated on his apparition as Pastor George. The beast with its gaping toothy mouth leapt from the stage, arching towards her. RoH raised a hand and the thing, Pastor George, hung twisting and growling high above the aisle. RoH suspended the pastor in mid-flight.

To do it all, RoH had unshielded herself and a sense of evil washed through.

I hate you.

No, Robert, you hate yourself.

Evil witch...

Let me help you.

Die, bitch, die...

She fought off the attempt to control her mind. These few seconds of mental sparing proved that Orville was no match for RoH. His withdraw felt physical, and it jolted her.

Behind me...

RoH spun as Brother Orr disappeared through the slamming front door of the church. She turned and waved. As Robert withdrew, the rabid dog suddenly became Pastor George to everyone and eased, lifeless, onto the floor. RoH ran for the doors. The congregation, at least the part that had not frozen in shock and fear, rushed to help the pastor.

Pastor George's SUV skidded out of the driveway and sped towards the highway. RoH watched in dismay.

Too far...

Father...

We can't follow him.

Follow me...

RoH rushed to the Martian X. It had pursuit mode. At the highway, she guessed Robert had headed east.

The radar unit in the OPP patrol car screamed at the bored cop. The number said 140 as Pastor George's SUV flew by. Just as the police car hit full speed on the highway, a Martin X shot past, apparently under the reckless control of a little girl who waved as she charged ahead. The radar screamed at 240. He sped after the disappearing car and called for backup. On a Sunday, the nearest patrol was 50 kilometres away. RoH could see the police car with its blazing lights, but the hybrids that the OPP used could not match the power of a Martin X in full pursuit mode. She sped out of sight.

RoH zoomed through Clinton and turned towards London. Robert would try to disappear into the city.

The cop met an ambulance rushing in the opposite direction. The congregation had called EMS. Pastor George lay on the carpet, alive but catatonic. At the crossroads in Clinton, the OPP car stopped. The officer could not decide which way the offending vehicles had gone. The radio diverted him back to the Holy Spirit Immersion of Huron church on County Road 31. He would soon investigate the crazy story of a mysterious little girl who turned people into devil-dogs. Perhaps she had kidnapped that fine Brother Orr. Except for the unconscious pastor, he found little evidence of any crime.

Sunday morning had light traffic and RoH could see the SUV far ahead on this dead-straight road. She could feel evil and desperation. Robert now knew her power, and he feared RoH. Snow shot up like a rooster tail behind the speeding Martin X. The AI self-driving ignored it all. They were closing in on the fleeing Robert Orville. She needed to be about a kilometre away to deal with his mind.

Just south of Kippen, the Martin X suddenly died. The battery said 10% and they had programmed the software to shut down at ten. It supposedly left enough charge to reach a plug-in. No one had recharged the car in the madness of the attempted kidnapping of Charlie and Kerri. The SUV had long disappeared. She slapped the steering yoke in frustration. Then RoH smiled.

This is just like an old television show I watched on the ship. Too bad Daisy isn't in the car too.

RoH checked the rear-view camera for a pursuing sheriff.

Father, take the car and me back to Grandpa's house...

Later that afternoon in London, Robert boarded a direct flight to Dallas-Fort Worth. RoH had made a mistake in assuming Robert had killed and impersonated Pastor George instead of turning him into a puppet. She had learned a sobering lesson not to make assumptions.

Robert Orville had escaped through a hole in RoH's carefully crafted bucket.

CHAPTER 18

The President is dead, long live the President

"Everything is going to hell in a handcart. I'm not sure I can paddle this canoe up a creek full of poop." Newly sworn President Cortez delivered the clichés without embarrassment and eyed the two women opposite. They sat in her study, not a formal office, and everyone had relaxed. Strangely, both of the other women had refused alcohol. They had just returned from the state funeral dominated by tiring pomp and platitudes about a dead President few of the hypocrites liked.

"I'm surprised you have kept me on as chief," Mary said. "I thought you didn't like me."

"I don't," Cortez said, "but I need you. You are the best. Everyone believed you were the real president, and I do too. Harry stole all of your ideas and called them his own."

The President eyed Mary.

"Don't think I won't do the same, but keep those ideas coming. How do we get out of this mess these aliens put us into?"

"We surrender," Mary said. "We decide to work for the good of all and not the usual bunch."

"We won't have any money and the people will turf me out on my ear. I won't even get the nomination."

Cortez had been the third female vice-president and the second non-white female. She was the only one to become President. Fortunately, the investigation had immediately cleared her of suspicion. The police had ruled Harry had killed himself, even though the formal Senate inquiry had not begun. Like most of Washington, the Justice Committee had fallen into a partisan quagmire.

"President Cortez," Mary said, "every politician wants to attack the aliens. Everyone blamed Harry, and they will blame you. I don't think your chances of re-election are good, anyway. If you take the high road, you can at least go out with integrity. You might win as a non-partisan third candidate. The alien question has split the people."

Mary had never admitted possible defeat. Her trauma with being pregnant, Daisy being an alien, and then Harry's death had forced some re-thinking. She had savoured winning and political power. She now thought these things as meaningless in her new view of the sweep of history and the place of this small blue planet in the galactic immensity.

"When is the last time anyone in Washington took the high road?" Cortez laughed.

"You can either hold your head high, or someone is going to serve it on a platter. They already got Harry's head."

"What do you mean?"

"Emalia," Mary used the President's given name, "I knew Harry. I've been with him since he ran for city council back home. Harry would never kill himself. He told me he might resign, and he agreed with the assessment I just gave you. Like you, he believed it to be political suicide. I have no proof. I don't know how they did it, but Harry did not kill himself."

"There's a conspiracy to take power centred here in the White House." Daisy chipped in.

"Who are you, again? Mary, why is this woman here?"

"Emalia, Daisy is my irreplaceable right hand. She ferrets out information that I can't even think of."

Mary and Daisy had discussed how to get the conspiracy information to Cortez without having to reveal that Daisy was an alien.

"There is this," Daisy slipped a slightly crumpled sheet of paper from a file. "When we had that alien girl here, I did the cleanup after the fiasco. I found this."

Daisy handed the paper to Emalia.

"The alien girl wrote, 'There is evil here, in the basement. It will kill the president.' If they murdered Harry, you, Emalia, are now the one in their way."

No one had any idea what RoH's handwriting might look like. None, including President Cortez, could challenge the message's legitimacy.

"Emalia, the CIA office is in the basement, as well as the facilities for the household support staff. I think you need to clean the house immediately, all of them." Mary placed her hands on her hips as if she were a schoolteacher lecturing a class of naughty third-graders. "You need to bring in your own staff and ban the CIA from the building."

"I'll get the Secret Service on it right away."

Mary glanced at Daisy and then back to Cortez.

"We aren't sure you can trust even them." Mary continued her lecturing pose. "Daisy and I were in the kitchen when we heard the shot. As we hurried to the Oval Office, a door slammed somewhere past the staff offices. The police established that none of the staff had done anything but rush to the scene. Someone else slammed that door. It may mean something, even though the cops pooh-poohed it."

"Someone left the patio door open. I closed it as Mary examined the President. The cops think Harry had opened it. We aren't so sure. Maybe the killer came in that way. The storm hid any tracks, but the cops didn't even look."

"One problem," Mary said, "is how anyone, including the president, could get a gun inside. Even the President walks through a metal detector. It would have been easier for Harry to shoot himself somewhere else."

"So, what can we do?" Emalia Cortez slumped in her chair.

"The Secret Service has all the weapons, and that makes one of them the likely suspect. Let Mary and I interview each Secret Service agent here. We have some questions that will help us decide if they are okay. When we cull the rotten apples, you can swap them out for others. We will interview the replacements as well."

"Once you have trustworthy agents, then call the CIA Director and tell him to order his people out of the building." Mary sat. "I have a draft of a procedure to maintain CIA contact once they are gone. Remember, the Director may be in on it." Mary handed over another document.

"Here is a list of support staff. We will vet each one and let you know whom I will be replacing."

They left President Cortez on the phone engaged in political firefighting.

Mary and Daisy had a list of routine questions for the Secret Service agents except one who had transferred the day after Harry died. They disguised the interviews as part of the political handover to the new president. In reality, while Mary asked meaningless questions, Daisy examined each mind. Daisy would be the one to decide.

Scheduling problems stretched the Secret Service replacements over two days. They replaced three agents, none of whom was the killer. The support staff went much quicker and Daisy only found two connected to the plot. Mary sent these to work at the capitol building. Daisy planted a small seed of self-doubt in each of the offenders' minds. None would be useful to the leaders of the plot and new recruiting would delay any threat.

The CIA left amidst shouted recriminations and threats from the Director. President Cortez shrugged it off. She felt safer, but remained nervous. The conspirators now knew that the President was aware of them and would hide even deeper.

In her efficient way, Mary had a detailed list of every potential accomplice. Daisy said no one knew if the CIA Director was involved. Mary passed her list on to her clandestine network. Anyone involved who she could not send to the equivalent of Alaska might become accident-prone. Daisy's mental tinkering with the plotters saved their lives.

President Cortez moved on to her next problem of selecting a vice-president. "Mary, I must make the appointment today or tomorrow. It has been two weeks. The party suggested an old white man. I want to appoint you."

Mary blushed, a rare occurrence, and shook her head.

"No Emalia, I am flattered, considering you don't like me, but I'm happier where I am. Frankly, I have more influence than a V-P."

"I like you more since you dealt with the conspiracy. Whom can I appoint? I don't want party hacks. I would prefer someone with no political ambitions."

"You should appoint Siglinde Hilfreich, the head of NAAP. She has no political goals, and she would give you a back channel to the aliens. I think that is extremely important."

"What good is she to me? Congress will never approve. She's famous, or notorious, if you hate aliens. I think she will be an anchor, politically."

"Leave that to me," Mary smiled. "People vote for names they know more than for their policies. You can pick a politician for your running mate in the next election."

It was time for Mary to call in about 500 markers at the Capitol. Not even Mary knew the real identity of Siglinde2, who would become vice-president. Mary accepted Daisy's arguments when she suggested Siglinde.

The star travellers had no desire to wield power on the planet. They wanted leaders like Cortez to steer their populations to save Earth's biosphere and themselves. Siglinde2 would provide extra security for Emalia Cortez but not manipulate her.

The star project to absorb human empathy by producing alien-human hybrids remained the important activity. Daisy had a full-time assignment of keeping Mary and her baby safe.

A small ship, the type used to approach a planet without alarming sentient native species, lurked in synchronous orbit above Washington. They constantly monitored all activity in the Washington area. If a black-swan menace developed, the craft was seconds away from saving any threatened aliens or designated humans. Several such operations circled the globe. Almost as much planning had gone into this operation as for the rescue of the Martian settlers. If a problem developed, the farm near Goderich might host new arrivals.

"You know," President Cortez had a good grasp of political subtleties. "If I appoint a known friend of aliens, I will send a signal that I have taken sides, and that goes against my political instincts. It's best to sail down the middle of the river, safer from the pot-shots from both banks."

"You sound like Harry and his Iowa down-home sayings." Mary laughed. "Another one he liked said the opposite. He would joke that if you stand in the middle of the road, you'll soon be road-kill."

"Dead on the bumper or dead in the ditch." Cortez stared out the window. Spring had invaded the White House grounds. The happy sunshine mocked the President's gloom.

CHAPTER 19

In the beholder's eye

Johnny Bray found himself at loose ends. Robert Orville's escape gave Johnny time to wander around London and sketch. He experienced new things. He had never been in a place where the ground held a snow cover, and the daytime here often felt much worse than the coldest night of a central Australian winter. Even stranger, the citizens of this town worked and played in this cold with casual comfort. He contrasted this with the heat of summer's day in Alice Springs. In that furnace, few moved about and found air-conditioned comfort as soon as possible. Bundled in the new winter clothes, Johnny shivered. He decided that when he returned to Alice, he would capture that contrast in a two-part image. One would be his old dog, Shep, in his usual mid-day heat pose of lying belly up in the shade. The other a dog he had sketched trying to catch large snowflakes in what the locals called a "little squall" and Johnny thought to be a blizzard.

Johnny decided it was impractical to do a large canvas. He accumulated sketches and notes to use in his studio. There would be one exception. He began a large painting of RoH, standing in the doorway of his shop as he had first seen her. He laboured to capture that mix of humour, knowledge and out-of-place wisdom in one so young. Johnny had to put love and empathy onto her face. Behind RoH, he had defined the Alice streetscape shimmering through a purple glow.

"This is the flip side of having a cold one under a gum tree in Alice." Johnny said. He and Ellie sat at an outdoor table of a coffee shop, placed so the late-winter sun warmed them with the aid of overhead infrared heaters. "We could never imagine doing it in sub-zero."

"It is a nice day," Ellie replied. "Don't get the idea that it is always this pleasant. January and February are usually brutal, although climate change has made a difference in that. March isn't over yet. We could get buried under 30 centimetres."

Johnny stirred his tea slowly, allowing time to frame his thoughts. If he had been a smoker, he might have filled a pipe for the same reason.

"She's special, isn't she?" Johnny looked past Ellie. A bicyclist raced down the street, oblivious to ice and snow. "RoH, I mean."

Ellie's face filled with love and pride.

"Yes, she is, Johnny. She may be the best hope for humanity and for the star travellers."

"Why?" Johnny sipped.

"My star family," Johnny noted a slight flash of that same love, "stagnated millennia ago. Oh, they kept exploring and found Earth, but they have turned inward. They struggle with large scientific questions and no emotional existence. The technical and engineering aspects of living carried on and even improved, but the whole felt emptiness. They asked questions about their purpose in the universe, and that departure from the scientific upsets them."

"Another species we know about, much older than us and we aren't sure if they are more advanced, about 1000 Earth years ago stopped all exploring and contact. I have heard native legends. That species actually visited Earth. They occupy a small region in an arm of the galaxy, but we know little more. They behaved friendly enough before. We think we match them in ability and knowledge."

Ellie sipped her coffee.

"When our species discovered sentient life on Earth, excitement returned. Most habitable planets either had no surviving advanced life or are in a primitive stage. We do not interfere in those. Most planets that developed technical civilizations like Earth destroyed themselves. Only a few died in asteroid impacts or nearby exploding stars. Earth and its cultures held promise, so we stayed and meddled. Maybe stumbled about would be a better description. Then, accidentally in 1947, a star traveller and a human woman conceived my grandfather.”

“I say, accidental, because there had been no plan. He impersonated a human. We think that transfers some human emotion to an alien. My grandmother stirred something in him, a feeling star-travellers had long forgotten, and she taught him about love and empathy. Suddenly, everyone decided the species lacked that vital thing. So they went from simply probing specimens, humans that is, to proactively tinkering. They bumbled around. You suffered from that, but the big problem is Orville. Anyway, they learned and debated and eventually they made me, on purpose.”

“When I agreed to become pregnant, years later, I gave birth to RoH. I’m almost all human; RoH is more alien than human. We are all in awe, and perhaps the star family is a little frightened. RoH, at eleven years old, can control her quantum abilities and influence star travellers, humans, whatever species it may be, with her empathy and love. In fact, she draws emotions from star-travellers that had lain dormant since before memory. Her love is the difference between the RoH we adore and one who could be exponentially more powerful and evil than Robert Orville.”

“I know one thing. RoH does not belong to me anymore.”

Ellie exuded love and sadness. Johnny knew where RoH found her love.

“The thing that worries me,” Ellie asked the server for a refill, “is that RoH takes the weight of the galaxy onto herself. She thinks she is a fulcrum balancing the future of the galaxy, or at least our species. When I raise that, she says ‘Oh, Mother...’ and changes the subject, but I know it is on her mind. I know when something worries my daughter.”

“I sometimes see her examining some living thing, dandelions she calls all life, but then suddenly she looks up to the sky, and to me, it seems her mind has gone to infinity. RoH embraces it all. I can’t pretend to understand. She is special.”

Ellie shed a tear and hid it behind the rim of her mug.

Johnny reached out with his mind to comfort her.

With my mind... I did that; she didn’t... I did...

Johnny stiffened in surprise. That had never happened in his long life. He had never knowingly used the ability before. It had always hid from him.

Ellie smiled. Her mind had felt Johnny’s comfort.

"Behold," Ellie said, "the real Johnny Bray, part alien, part human. I
think that ability you just used is why RoH thinks she needs you to help
defeat Robert Orville."

CHAPTER 20

Heavenly Hash

The Church of Heavenly Enlightenment in Dallas, Texas sat on the far side of the street from a huge and popular park. Food vendors of various types frequently appeared at the park entrances. In the heat of early spring, the timely arrival of an ice cream truck opposite the church raised no special notice. The jovial older man who ran it would become a favourite to both park visitors and many of the congregation from the Heavenly Enlightenment. The vendor would joke with the church members that he had made his Heavenly Hash flavour just for them. These folks would smile in a welcome change from their normally dour faces.

The ice cream truck also became an interesting curiosity to city officials who had followed up on the temporary vendor licence.

"Y'all don't make noise or have a tail pipe on this thing. It's great for a park." The city man said between licks of the most delicious strawberry swirl cone he had ever eaten.

"It's battery powered," the vendor gently smiled. "I adapted the old truck with one of those newfangled cesium-osmium things they make for that long range truck."

In fact, the power unit had much lower weight than any battery, and the quantum process lay far beyond the understanding of human physics.

"We should make that a city standard." The inspector wiped his lips and took a long sip of water to remove the lingering taste from the treat. Ice cream could remain in a mouth and not be enjoyable in Texas heat.

"It's expensive," the ice cream man said. "I only did it as a hobby."

He did not want to open an alien battery factory. His cooling unit and the larger one serving the Taken Inn and Rachel, Nevada, were the only two on Earth. They had nothing to do with cesium-osmium mumbo-jumbo.

If humans beat the long odds and survived, a quantum energy device would be the first application of the effect, long before it powered faster than light travel. Star travellers refused to intervene to allow humans to skip steps. Normal human scientific progress would put that breakthrough about 100 years into the future. Propulsion systems would take even more Earth time. Even if they dismantled the two units now on the surface, humans could not reverse-engineer them without the scientific understanding. They would puzzle over the cultured organic unit resembling a rat's brain that moderates the quantum interaction inside a sealed box. The only human close to having that knowledge was Siglinde Hilfreich. She honeymooned on Z263-A.

Between sales, the ice-cream man watched the comings and goings across the road. Robert Orville had returned, but little had happened. Anti-alien rallies and those supporting Texas leaving the Union became more frequent, but the church seemed to stay out of it. For now, it pleased them to know where Orville was. A new plan had to be developed, and the collective decision left that in RoH's hands.

"Jaden," RoH had found her friend in the kitchen, chatting with Elsie the alien. "I would like to discuss something with you. It's personal and would be a big decision."

"What?" Jaden completely trusted RoH, but her friend sounded more serious than she had when contemplating her own kidnapping.

"My mother was about your age when she became pregnant with me," RoH eyed Jaden. She would not violate Jaden's mind for this.

"What?" Jaden emphatically raised her voice. She knew exactly what RoH had asked.

"I don't want to pressure you, or even advocate. Everyone agrees with me. You are a special human, and would be a wonderful mother for a new branch of the galactic population."

Jaden trembled. "Four months ago, I thought about suicide. Now, my best friend ever suggests I have a special place in the stars."

"I have to think about it," Jaden frowned. "You make it sound as if I would be responsible for thousands of future lives."

"You would be, but likely, as a fondly remembered matriarch. There are several old star travellers, many still alive, whom star people think of as what we call progenitors. We don't have hierarchy amongst the stars, but keep honour and memory, no fancy robes and rituals, of course, but a thing as close to deference as we can allow. There is a similar thing on Earth amongst tribal people who respect their elders. The thousands of star travellers now in the solar system have only two progenitors. One of them is still alive and involved here."

RoH looked at Elsie. Elsie smiled and slid a bread pan into the oven.

"Elsie...?"

"Yes..."

Elsie came and sat beside RoH.

"RoH represents the latest in my line." Elsie smiled fondly. "I am honoured, that is so. There is no other entity like RoH in the galaxy."

"How old are you?" Jaden's astonishment grew.

Elsie closed her eyes and thought.

"Translated into Earth terms, I would say about 10,000 of Earth's revolutions around the sun. Galactic time scales are hard to resolve. We visit, work, or live on so many systems. Relative time, like Earth's Coordinated Universal Time, is only necessary to organize local activity on Earth. For instance, we have laid the foundation for a relationship between Earth and a planet, a moon actually, we refer to as Z263-A, or Jewel as the locals call the place. It does not matter what time it is there for us or here for them."

"There is an old, famous set of fictional stories about a galactic empire," RoH added, "that used a time coordinate based on the imperial planet. Since there are and can never be galactic empires, that idea is meaningless and we use nothing like that."

"And you want little Earthling nobody Jaden to be part of that? It blows my mind."

"You can take all the time you want," RoH touched Jaden's hand. "There is no pressure and you can decide not to do it, and I will still love you. You are not a nobody, Jaden. You are exquisite, as is every life in the universe.

Life is precious amongst the stars, a struggle against entropy, and we need to value it all, even microbes. That is a reality that humans must embrace."

"It doesn't sound romantic," Jaden said. "I expected candy and flowers and fooling around in the back seat of a car."

"We can arrange that," RoH laughed. "It could be clinical as well, but I prefer how my great-great-grandparents did it. It was sweet, and it was love. That's what I want when I decide to reproduce."

"You...?" Jaden startled, "You're too young."

"Yes, not for a few Earth years anyway, but my body is already changing." RoH's flowering towards adulthood seemed to give her joy. "My physical body seems to differ from a normal human. I thought only my mind had advanced, but I think I'll be through puberty by the end of the year, or sooner. Still, I have too much to do for me to be pregnant. That must wait until later. Besides, for all of us, there is no rush. We control star populations. Most newborns are to replace a death, but sometimes we have a need for expansion, usually only a few individuals even then. Your line would take a long time to have a third generation."

"We do; however," Elsie added, "want RoH's line to propagate faster, as long as her offspring have her characteristics. Time will tell on that one."

"Mother and I will have to raise them that way," RoH said.

"One more question," Jaden said. "What is entropy?"

"Let me try," Elsie laughed. "Did you ever study science?"

"No, I hated science in school."

"You asked a profound scientific question," Elsie began, "and this is a less than a scientific hint of how it works. Do you see RoH's mug of hot chocolate? It used to be hotter when she first made it. She boiled water, and scientifically, she added heat energy from an electric resistor to the water. We won't get into how that is also an entropic process, but let's say it concentrated energy as heat in the water. She poured it into the mug and made that concoction she loves."

"We could say," RoH added, "that the energy did the work of dissolving the chocolate powder and converted it and the water into an enjoyable drink."

Elsie made a less than appreciative face. RoH stuck out her tongue at Elsie.

"That mug absorbed some of the heat from the water. Boiling the water concentrated energy and made it useful before it dispersed. The heat keeps flowing out of the mug and becomes disorganized and useless. That is how entropy works. Concentrated energy becomes disordered and useless to do anything."

"Life," RoH added, "is like me boiling the water. It concentrates energy in an organism. Eventually, the living thing dies and, like my cooling mug, that energy disperses... entropy."

"That's depressing," Jaden scowled.

"And makes life so special," RoH sipped chocolate and pondered how to value Robert Orville's life.

Mother, does the existence of Robert reveal a potential danger in our breeding effort?

It might, sweetie, but I think Robert was the victim and the product of a unique situation.

When you rescued, Ellie used an unpronounceable alien name for the star traveller whom RoH had extracted from the vat at Groom Lake. *We discovered he had intended to go back to Ruth.*

Ruth was not as strong as my great-grandmother, and since they had parted without even a goodbye, she had bitterness. We think all this addled Robert's head, and that's why he is psychopathic.

Can we save and reform him?

I think we owe it to him to try.

That's what I think, Mother. We owe it to Ruth Orville too. I need to save Robert.

Robert Orville sat at his desk watching a television news feed of a Texas separatist rally at the governor's mansion. Orville approved of the anti-alien undercurrent. According to the latest poll, 80% of Texans supported leaving the Union while a slightly lower majority hated aliens. He tried to think through the opportunity Texas provided; that it supported his desire to attack the star travellers who had made his horrible life.

The problem of when to act came in second, behind his worry about RoH. Somehow, the little girl had discovered him and his threat. Robert made the same mistake most adult humans made, thinking of RoH as a youngster without understanding her abilities. Orville constantly examined the minds of his adherents and anyone within range to see if she had impersonated somebody. He had gained a brief glimpse of her mind as he fled Pastor George's church and thought he knew her mental signature.

None of the churchgoers or anyone passing on the street was RoH; the carefully shielded alien mind at the ice-cream truck eluded detection.

Robert examined the airplane ticket that had arrived by courier. A billionaire had invited him and several other pastors to a meeting to plot an anti-alien campaign. Soon, Robert would be in Aspen, Colorado.

Robert discounted the linking of his name to the anti-alien massacre in El Paso. He felt anyone could randomly pick his name from the streamed services of the Church of Heavenly Enlightenment. His arrogance made this a serious mistake.

In El Paso, the FBI tried to overcome city and state hostility while it investigated a federal hate crime. The locals considered the case closed since the perpetrator had died. They filed all the details, and like most city politicians, they wanted to forget. The hated FBI had other ideas.

Noah Lee's posts and notes hinted at a larger conspiracy, or at the least, a massive problem that involved the hate preached in many places. The FBI classified the local pastor as the largest culprit in distorting Lee's thinking. They also believed that the internet conspiracy group had given him the ideas and details of how to attack.

The FBI seized Lee's computer and phone on a federal warrant, and so they had access to all of his contacts and his VPN. Local police had done a superficial examination of Lee's electronics but only bothered with the obvious details. The media constantly re-ran Lee's live stream of his preparations and arrival at the mission. The horror after that lay beyond what the media could stomach. As a regrettable consequence, the bigoted local pastor saw his congregation swell because of the free publicity.

Lee had been lazy and had saved all of his log-ins.

"Jen," an agent looked up from his laptop, "I'm into this AlienStrike site. What a god-awful zoo that is. If these guys ever met an alien, they wouldn't stand a chance."

"No one would stand a chance. Look what happened at HQ on New Year's Eve."

"Yah, but they didn't even hurt anyone. Maybe the aliens are soft."

"The one guy had a broken finger when he tried to shoot and the purple light yanked his gun out of his hand. He got a sore ass too when he landed in the street. I never want to meet an alien that's angry."

Both agents ignored the reality that the aliens had disabled military weaponry and manufacturing capability. The only weapons left were lighter, powder driven ballistics they could not replace. The agency had recently issued a directive to conserve ammunition. They had suspended all target practice. Another thing that the agents and most humans did not understand, anger and revenge were outside of the alien psychological make-up. If they were not, Groom Lake would have been a molten pool of slag seconds after RoH had left the place. Every action the visitors took had resulted from cold calculation. The only other option for them was to do nothing or leave.

"Is there any history of Lee's contacts?"

"He had a regular on AlienStrike, Paso Posse but there's no real name. I'm downloading all of their interactions. Maybe Virginia can tease out the meta-data."

"So we have a racist pastor in El Paso and a violence preaching conspiracy website. Is there anything else?"

"Lee contacted the Church of Heavenly Enlightenment in Dallas. He exchanged e-mail with a secretary. There is nothing too bad, but the church bragged about the big fight against aliens. They invited Lee to create the El Paso brigade of what they called the holy army to fight the devil's angels. Fortunately, Lee was a dysfunctional loner."

"Too bad he hadn't been stupid too. He might have shot himself before he killed anyone else."

"It sounds like Dallas is another threat, but what? Call the office."

The next day, a Tex-Mex food wagon, "Taco and Soda: $5", appeared beside the ice-cream truck opposite the Church of Heavenly Enlightenment.

"It's nice to have a taco once in a while," the ice cream vendor leaned against the dropdown counter of the Tex-Mex outlet. "Bringing food from home is a drag. Y'all make nice ones, too."

The grizzled taco maker smiled. Field agents normally did not conform to the television Barbie and Ken version of police heroes.

"Thank y'all, been doin' it for years."

"One complaint," the ice cream man said, "that generator of yours is noisy and smelly. How much electricity do y'all need?"

The agent frowned. The extra electronics demanded a good amount of electricity. His cooker used bottled gas, so one would expect electricity for lights and the bank machine.

"Oh, about 30 amps at 240," he hoped the ice cream seller would not think that strange.

"I have lots extra juice from my battery, a lot over 30. Can I hook y'all up and turn off that damned generator?"

"What will it cost me?"

"At the skyrocketing price of gas, it saves me a bundle, and it will for you too, but a free taco and soda a day will cover it."

A day later, a tech from the FBI Houston office arrived to make the connection. She held the cable that the ice cream vendor had provided and turned it over in puzzlement. The wire had a connector from the ice-cream battery inverter, and a similar one on the opposite end. They had provided a receptacle for the Tex-Mex truck. The wiring was obvious, but she had never seen the polarity profile of the insulated moulding. This one had the shape of a starburst, leaving only one way to join the two. All the markings on the thing were alien to her. She guessed it came from Asia.

In an hour, the truck drew its power from the battery, and the gasoline generator died. In reverse, the ice cream vendor had access to all the digital material in the Tex-Mex electronics. The FBI had a vast array of sensors monitoring everything except thought-waves from the church.

"I'd love to see that battery and inverter y'all have there," the tech said as she licked a free triple-butterscotch.

"It's all in a closed unit," the vendor flipped up a panel at the back of the truck, revealing an unblemished metal box about the size of a truck bench-seat. The cover had bolt heads formed into a shape the tech had never seen. They required a special tool. Only three electrical leads exited and connected to the truck's panel.

"That battery runs cooler than any I've ever seen, especially that powerful." She held her hand against the casing. "It must have good ventilation. I don't see a heat sink, and it feels cold."

The box enclosed its volume of the universal continuum. It harvested energy from a closed loop in the entropic interaction of Base and type 1 energy. The small artificial organic brain modulated this interface using quantum effects. Energy wise, it superficially seemed the unit qualified as a perpetual motion generator, but it violated no physics. It could either cool or heat the surface of the box. The alloy was beyond human ability to make on Earth, but it had heat flow characteristics that chilled the ice cream. They could reverse the heat flow and make the box into a heater as had happened in the Rachel, Nevada winter. Every star ship, every galactic installation had similar units.

"I have never seen inside." The vendor noticed the woman's puzzlement. "If it goes bad, I would have to get a service tech from LA. They guarantee it for ten years." His tone expressed the normal cynicism of people towards company assurances.

"Promises, promises," the tech reinforced the sceptic attitude.

A small possibility existed that the organic unit would fail, probably by dying. In that case, the process would simply stop. A smaller but real possibility would be an unpredictable failure in the manufactured brain, equivalent to a psychotic episode in a human. That would turn the generator into a propulsion unit. The ice cream truck would likely shoot skyward towards the speed of light. It would become a reverse meteoroid and violently burn up in the atmosphere a few dozen kilometres above the surface. They had tested these possibilities millennia earlier in a stellar system full of asteroid debris many light-years from Earth. In a psychotic failure, the test unit shot from the surface of one asteroid. It collided, at a fraction of the speed of light, with a rock at a million kilometres' distance, obliterating itself and that asteroid in a massive fireball. A super-heated ice cream truck, accelerating to the stars, would suffer thermal catastrophe in the lower atmosphere and break a lot of glass in Dallas.

CHAPTER 21

When he opened the seventh seal...

A key slipped into the lock of the side entrance door to the church. A figure concealed by a black balaclava followed a hand lit path into the basement. They poured a can of diesel fuel over the floor of the banquet room. Some gasoline followed, and from the safety of the doorway, a burning brand of church bulletins ignited everything. They fled up the stairs ahead of the acrid smoke. One more task would complete the job.

The beautiful stained glass window of the Holy Spirit Immersion of Huron church building burst inwards. Shards showered the spacious lobby. A gasoline filled beer bottle landed amongst the carnage and burst into a bright fireball. Two more projectiles of gasoline and lamp oil followed. A car sped away into a dark morning, illuminated by lightning flashes.

The spring storm seemed a fitting beginning to the conflict between those worshiping star travellers and those wishing to kill aliens. As the loudest local voice against aliens, Pastor George had notoriety. Most congregations remained quiet as they tried to navigate the mere existence of aliens. Alien life questioned dearly held origin stories. Every religion and many tribal mythologies suffered the same crisis.

No one noticed the fire until it had burst through the roof. A driver passing on Highway 8 called 911 half an hour after the attack. Volunteer fire units arrived in time to see the roof collapse with a ground-shaking roar as the building writhed in its death throes. Exploding ammunition in the burning rubble sent the volunteers for cover. The Fire marshal discovered they had stored a large amount of ammunition and some long guns in the basement. The elders argued with the authorities and the insurance company that they did not know who had hidden the weapons. Rebuilding appeared to be in the distant future.

They had transported Pastor George to a London hospital where he lay catatonic. The doctors could not penetrate his withdrawn mind. Tales from the congregation of a monster dog and a little girl with magical powers attacking the pastor seemed like a fantasy. The adherents felt it was good that the Pastor had not seen the destruction of his beloved building.

Although Pastor George's congregation knew RoH was the little girl, they recognized that the aliens and RoH had not burnt the church. They had watched her throw tractors around on Suncoast Boulevard, and they guessed the monster did not need a Molotov cocktail to destroy a building. Rumours spread about the real culprits: "That group of wackos in the chicken barn."

They planned "fire and brimstone" revenge, but as March turned into April, the home front remained quiet. In a speedy decision, the insurance company had allowed rebuilding. They ignored the careless weapons storage charge that the church faced in the Goderich court. The congregation had builders who could do the work. The only outside expense would be material.

"Mr. Hammersmith," the head of the elder's committee sat opposite Mike in his office, "we need a lot of material for rebuilding. Can you give us a good price? We were hoping you might donate some."

Mike looked at Charlie. This bunch of zealots preached long and hard that his friend's family should die.

"No, I don't think so," Mike said. "I love someone you want to kill."

Mike thought of the first time he had met RoH and she had him kneeling on Charlie's lawn talking to dandelions. "You should love her too."

"Do you have the spec and the drawings?" Charlie sat on one side with Kerri. Not only was this a big job, it was the only new one available in the rapidly fragmenting economy. Other than the ongoing manufacture of small greenhouses, business was dismal. These small units had already begun producing early salad greens on farms and more filling crops matured in the earliest ones. So far, the chain stores had supplied enough food, but prices soared. April planting would begin soon.

Charlie did not see supplying building material to the church as aiding the enemy. He knew RoH and Ellie could deal with this crowd if necessary. He did not want Mike to lose the business in these hard times.

"We are rebuilding exactly what we had," the elder handed Charlie a roll of drawings and a copy of the original specifications. Either he had forgotten, or ignored, the well-known fact that Charlie Keys was the grandfather of the hated alien half-breed.

Charlie handed the paperwork to Kerri. Hammersmith Inc. had supplied the material for the original building and had copies of that quote on file.

"Mike," Charlie said, "this involves an enormous amount. We have to see if suppliers can deliver. At the new prices, I think we have to wait for those quotes before we can bid."

"We will need 25% up front to cover extra material cost," Mike said.

The elders blanched and looked at each other. They guessed the church account might cover that, but leave them penniless. Still, the insurance cheque was as good as in the mail.

"Agreed," said the senior elder. "We need to get this done quickly. The church is everything to us."

Kerri resisted asking if they worshiped a building or their saviour, but that would have been bad for business. The alienation from her brother angered her. She had no empathy over the firebombing.

With any luck, the damned place will burn down again. Kerri thought of her brother and his zealot wife.

"I can get the take-offs from the first time," Charlie said, "and we can see what we need to order in."

"Two weeks," Mike said.

"Good," the elder smiled, "the foundation should be ready by then."

Kerri and Charlie relaxed in the living room. It had been a long afternoon. She had just put her feet up when her cell buzzed. She read her brother's name, Gary, on the display. Kerri had not heard from Gary since he had called to tell her they would never talk to them again. They blamed her apparent murder by the CIA on the aliens. He had not even said that he was glad she was alive. She had tried to tell him they had shot her because of the aliens, and she had lived for the same reason, especially because of an alien named RoH.

"You called..." Kerri tried not to sound resentful.

"I need to talk, Sis."

"Why are you whispering?"

"Oh, sorry, habit, I'm afraid Jodi would hear, but I'm out in the Tims parking lot. I was wrong and acted like a jerk. Jody totally believes Pastor George's bigotry, but I don't, and I love you."

"That's good news, Gary. I love you too," Kerri's aching heart burst. She smiled. Charlie watched and wondered at the call and her happier mood.

"My brother..." she mouthed and confused Charlie more.

"What woke you up?"

"Everyone thinks those crazy alien cultists in the chicken barn burned the church. They want revenge, and some are planning it. People are going to get hurt. It's bad, more so because those crazies didn't do it."

"How do you know, Gary?"

"I know, but don't ask why."

Kerri knew her brother's tone when he was sure of something. His cocksure attitude had aggravated her in high school. Gary used that same snootiness, but there seemed to be a catch. The "don't ask" implied that he knew who had burnt the church.

"Gary, I have to tell Ellie Keys. The aliens don't want anyone hurt. They would never burn your church or want anyone else to do it."

"That's why I called," Gary said, "and it isn't my church any more. I'm leaving and splitting with Jody."

"What are they planning?"

"I don't know details. I've stayed out of it."

"Don't quit or dump Jody yet," Kerri had a thought. "Find out the details. I'll talk to Ellie."

"Jody is on the inside. She works with the church secretary. I'll call from work as soon as I know."

"Love you, sis."

"Love you, Gary. I'm sorry I alienated you." Kerri giggled.

Kerri hugged Charlie and burst into tears. Reconciling with her brother held more importance than the rest of the nonsense. She used the old-fashioned telephone system to reach Ellie in London.

"Gary's going to call when he knows. He thinks it's soon."

Ellie and Steve drove up from London. Her star family decided that she should try to prevent bloodshed.

"The incident with Pastor George and the hybrid Orville weakened many of those people's faith," Ellie said. "Perhaps we can convince them, despite their belief about where the universe came from. We need to know what the extremists are going to do. The mobs in London are scary and the news from elsewhere is worse. Maybe we can prevent more violence. Ask Gary if I can meet him."

Ellie's desire to prevent conflict faced human opposition. She saw the contradiction between the star traveller's objectives and the chaos that their actions had already created.

RoH, this has me questioning what we think we are doing.

Mother, I understand. Father and the others are in a great debate about it. There's an opinion we should just leave humans to their fate. I think of it differently, and I hope this minor story is true of humans. I watched a caterpillar that spun a cocoon. It is ready to burst out, but not as the old worm crawling about the debris of the forest, but as a beautiful creature that can fly. It will reach a level of existence that the caterpillar could never imagine. However, it had seemingly to die before it achieved its wonderful purpose.

Humanity is the caterpillar, and the Earth is its cocoon. The process of rebirth is a dying of the old ways, a struggle, and then success. I like to think humans will do that, and the pain we have caused is part of the chrysalis bursting. Most times, the pupa evolves into a butterfly. The alternative is the destruction of the nest. With humans, it is likely to be from within.

While the chaos we see now is painful, it must happen for humans to burst into the universe. We should try to ease the pain, but it is necessary. At least we have kept them from blowing up the planet.

RoH, your insight overwhelms.

It is of you, Mother; your heart guides me always.

In El Paso, Texas, Sam Rice had cried at his sister's funeral. Her death tore his heart into pieces. Mandy had been his hero, friend, and teacher. She loved people and dedicated her life to help everyone. Her love had ended with a bullet from Noah Lee. Sam felt confused that a loving church had led her to practice that love, and a place of hate, founded on the same scriptures, had spit out her killer.

Sam shared Mandy's love for people, but his love for her had been deeper. No amount of platitudes, such as "she died doing what she loved", or "she died defending others" from their gentle, loving pastor or helpless friends, eased his pain.

Noah Lee had been the trigger for a hateful monster beyond the imagination of the best horror writers. He was a human monster, bred not from the fires of hell, or alien invaders, but from the corrupted hearts of humans. Sam would do all he could to kill this evil creature and cut out its heart.

On the Sunday, a month after Mandy's funeral, Sam Rice attended church. This was not the comfort of his home congregation, The Loving Gospel Assembly. Sam passed through what he thought as the portal of hell into the church of The Southern True Christian Gathering. This hateful bunch had bent Noah Lee into a killer.

Sam endured what he considered the most detestable, even blasphemous, lecture from a pulpit that he had ever heard. He saw a preacher make hate by misquoting the scriptures and twisting biblical platitudes and parables into un-Christian lies. The monster in the pulpit spent twenty minutes torturing Sam Rice. He justified Mandy's murder as deserving since she had prostituted herself to aliens. Sam realized that while the congregants in this place were superficially respectable, they confused nice with good. They suffered from the delusion that they only had to love each other and not "the other". Mandy had loved the other, and that included inter-galactic aliens who, she had once said, "must be God's creatures". These "fine folks" had caused her death. Thankfully, this first ordeal ended and Sam joined the flow into the lobby.

"Y'all are new here, young man; why don't y'all come over to our place for brunch?" The effusive middle-aged woman seemed sincere. "I'm Lila; what's your name?"

"I'm Sam. Where do y'all live?" Sam asked.

"That's a nice name, like Samson from the Bible. Y'all got cute, long hair. Can y'all do great things?" Her smile warmed Sam.

"I like to think so," Sam said. "It's still from the Bible, but Samuel."

"That's good," Lila tousled Sam's long hair.

He's a good-looking man.

His home congregation had no problem with anyone's appearance. Sam had feared that this narrow church might be too judgemental, but Lila seemed to like his locks.

"I live just over there," Lila pointed from the front steps of the church to a lavish house about 100 meters away. "It's a handy walk, and I help with the church. All the houses belong to my friends here in the congregation. We wanted to be close to the Lord."

Large dwellings surrounded the church. "Closer to the Lord" involved the church building all the adjacent houses and then selling them to willing parishioners. A flow of mortgage money augmented the church coffers. A circle of meadow and parking lot separated the church from the houses. The cloister gave Sam a new plan. He worked as a gas fitter and suddenly knew what to do.

"That would be generous of y'all, thank you." Sam thought he might get more useful information from this couple as Lila escorted him to a house facing the street. He looked around for Mr. Lila as they entered.

"Oh, Bo-Bob's away on a business trip." Lila escorted Sam to the living room. The delicious smell of barbeque came from the kitchen.

"Would y'all like a drink?" Lila showed a bar towards the dining room.

"A Coke would be great." Sam had never liked liquor, and he reserved beer for times with his buddies cheering on the Cowboys. Besides, he had to drive home.

"So, do y'all have a gal?"

"No," Sam sipped. He had recently graduated from his HVAC course and worked for a contractor. There had been no time for a serious relationship, and none of the women at church interested him or seemed interested in him.

"That's too bad, a nice boy like you." Lila had made a large Mojito for herself. She sat beside Sam on the couch and sipped in silence for a moment.

"I'm guessing you're a muscular guy," Lila felt his biceps. "Yes, I thought so. How did y'all get so strong?"

"I'd like to say it's my good looks," Sam joked, "but I work out twice a week. It's a habit from high school. I played football."

"I have a gym in the basement. That's how I keep my girlish figure." Lila ran her hands down her sides and over her hips. She had a trim body for a woman in her forties. Normal Texas parlance referred to middle-aged women like Lila as handsome. In reality, she was an attractive woman who spent much time not to look her age. Sam noticed.

"I wonder if y'all could put that muscle to use for me," Lila smiled. "I want this couch," she slapped the seat and somehow her hand came to rest on Sam's leg, "turned around. It's heavy and I'm just a weak girl."

"Sure, no problem," he said. "I can do it right now."

"Y'all wait until after lunch," Lila smiled, "you'll need your strength. The ribs are ready."

Lila knew how to cook.

"You should open a restaurant," Sam said. He had cleaned his plate of ribs, baked potato, and broiled asparagus.

"I only serve the best to special people," Lila brushed against him as she cleared the plates.

"Okay, I'll take care of that couch," Sam said.

The couch gave Sam more trouble than he had expected. It was heavy and had no convenient handholds. When he was done, making several minor adjustments for Lila, he slumped into the seat with sweat dripping despite the air conditioning. The couch now faced the window. Sam could see the church across the lawn.

"Let me get y'all another cold Coke." Lila stood behind Sam, reaching around over the back of the couch to hand him the drink, pressing against his head. She used a hand to wipe sweat from his forehead and then massaged his shoulders.

"Oh my, I have tired y'all out."

"I'm good to go," Sam said.

"Good," Lila said, "come with me. There is one more little thing I need taken care of."

When Sam woke from a light nap, the afternoon sun streamed through the bedroom window. Lila noticed and snuggled against him.

Sam considered his sinning. Apparently, the seventh and tenth commandments held little sway in Lila's faith. Sam's own church taught that they should approach the commandments in forgiveness and grace. He had noticed that even in his congregation, many flirted with, if not shattered, those two commands. He looked around the room.

"This is one of those old-fashioned plantation style beds." Sam appreciated the polished walnut headboard and stout corner posts supporting a canopy.

"It's good for tying people up," Lila laughed. "For y'all, they would have to be more than little strings."

"Sure would." Sam flexed his arm. After this initiation into manhood, he felt macho.

The sun neared the horizon when Sam finally left.

"I'll be back, soon." Sam's smile carried a subtlety that Lila missed.

Lila had introduced an element that Sam had not expected. Considering a love affair with an older woman, certainly one as eager as Lila, Sam felt confused. Should he go through with his plan? Lila was a member of the hated congregation and they had not had a serious conversation about her beliefs. Theology was not a popular topic during the act of adultery.

Does she hold those horrible beliefs? Is she one of those responsible for Mandy's death?

Sam decided that avenging Mandy had more importance than his simple pleasure.

Even if Lila seduced me, it doesn't mean she loves me. I must destroy this evil, even if I die trying.

Sam sincerely believed in the Gospel message, and he struggled with how attacking Satan might not conform to the message. After all, Jesus restored the ear that Peter cut off. Sam; however, saw his plan as being like his saviour overturning the tables of the evil moneychangers in the temple. They, too, exploited their faith and its laws and the Lord's sanctuary for base purposes. Sam understood the gospel replaced those laws with love and grace. Sam felt that to be a good thing, considering he just broke at least one commandment and was not sure that his hiding his identity did not qualify as "false witness". He had dug deep into the grace reserves. Sam resolved to try not to hurt anyone. The man who indeed loved his sister and others did not see that as an alien concept.

The following Sunday, Sam once more attended the soul-destroying service. He slipped out during the message and asked about the washroom. An usher directed him to the basement stairs. Sam wandered the lower level, checking the furnace room with a professional eye. Natural gas provided the heating and shrubs surrounded the meter just outside a small window. Sam placed an altered cell phone out of sight on top of the furnace. A wire extended from the case and Sam wrapped it around the power cable and bent the stiff wire to make a small gap between it and the grounded gas pipe. Sam test-dialled the number for the device and smiled as a spark jumped from the wire to the pipe. He only needed that brief flash. Sam checked the window. It did not have an alarm because a solid grid of bars protected the outside. A person could not get through, but he did not need that. The window hinged inwards. Sam released the lock. Before exiting, Sam disabled the gas-leak detector and left the furnace-room door ajar. It would make for a perfect air-gas mix. He returned to the sanctuary as the congregation clapped and waved their arms through the last songs.

"Lunch" progressed the same way it had done the previous week. At sunset, Sam left Lila for home, clutching the church bulletin that listed the bible study in the early evening. The place would be empty after that. Sam now had Lila's phone numbers. Last week, he had thought he had only broken the seventh commandment. After today, he felt like he had placed the tenth in peril. Sam tried not to covet his neighbour's wife, but Lila was a seductive woman. Now he had an extra problem of making sure he did not hurt Lila. Her house would suffer if the plan worked.

Arriving at the church around 11 PM created some risk. People still moved about and might see him, but later in the night, Sam would look like a prowler even if a white man had some leeway. He drove along the street, past the church driveway, and stopped at the second house. He placed a black backpack into a few shrubs and then parked two blocks down near a variety store, but on the street and out of sight of any cameras.

Sam strolled back, retrieved the pack, and slipped quickly into the shadows beside the church. Every door had a floodlight and a camera, but the side with the furnace window lay in darkness. Streetlights allowed him to see without using his hand light. Sam checked Lila's house. Her bedroom light was on and in the direct line of the impending blast.

Sam extracted a medium pipe wrench from the bag and quickly closed the main gas valve. The same wrench loosened a cap on a small pipe usually used to bleed the building side of the meter. He allowed the hissing to stop and gently removed the cap. A spark here might be fatal. A length of flexible hose came from the bag. It had a female connector in pipe thread. The gas company used this as a bleeder hose during repairs. Sam chose it because it was all plastic to avoid metal on metal sparks. He hoped it would completely melt. Sam pushed the window inwards and shoved the hose into the basement. Sam opened the main valve and disappeared towards the street as gas hissed into the basement. It would take some time for the gas to flow out the open furnace room door and create the right air mixture through the basement. Lila's light still shone.

Sam drove the opposite way from home to a fast-food joint on the far side of the army base. Eating a burger combo and Coke and fiddling on the internet took an hour. His drive home took him far away from the impending disaster.

Sam sat in the car in his driveway. He set his cell to private number and made two calls.

"This is a friend," Sam spoke in falsetto, and hoped Lila would not recognize him. "Something bad is going to happen in five minutes. Get out and run away from the church. Get out now."

Sam knew he had taken an enormous risk with the warning, but he did not want to kill anyone, and certainly not Lila. Five agonizing minutes later, Sam dialled the number of the cell attached to the furnace pipe. He hoped Lila had not called the fire department. People would die if she had. He did not hear the blast, but Sam saw a glow in the right direction.

Confined to a fiery hell, he thought. *I'm done here. I'll go to Dallas and confront that evil preacher the way Christ struggled with the Devil on the tall tower. However, this time, we need to throw the Devil down with no saviour.*

Sam sat in his car and asked for forgiveness as the church disintegrated.

Most of the roof remained recognizable but landed in the street. The shock wave demolished the two nearest houses, including Lila's. Flying concrete foundation and fragmented lumber severely damaged many more. Wreckage blazed vigorously in the debris-filled crater that had replaced the basement. Flames from the ruptured gas line flared high and hot for the hour it took the El Paso Natural Gas Company to cut supply.

They found a severely hurt family in the second destroyed home, and flying glass lacerated a few others in a wide circle. Unfortunately, Sam's attempt at making it look like an accident failed. They found the gas meter with a bit of the hose still attached on a roof half a block away. After puzzling over the meter for a few days, the investigators decided it had been deliberate sabotage. The hunt began, but the police had no suspects.

Lila, being good looking, articulate and having had her house destroyed became a favourite for television interviews. Lila appeared remarkably compose despite her loss. She put it into Biblical terms. Lila told a reporter that the ground shook and the sky shouted loudly. It was the Book of Revelation finally revealed.

"That quaking and the alien devils coming... someone opened the seventh seal. It's the end times for sure. I hoped to be raptured by now."

The journalist nodded in agreement. It fit what he heard in church. He did not notice Lila's sly smile.

"Do y'all think the aliens did this?" The reporter asked.

"For sure, just like I saw on television and read on the net. Y'all know them aliens blow up barns and buildings and kill folks."

Lila smiled at the irony. The aliens rising to their ships that she had seen on television mimicked the popular imagining of the rapture.

"How did you escape?"

"I went for my usual after midnight walk. I was lucky."

Sam watched Lila's interviews with a combination of relief and lust. When she mentioned her lucky habit of the late night walk, Sam believed she looked into the camera and winked. Was that for him? Did she know he did it? Did she know his last name? She had never asked. Blaming aliens might distract the police.

The unquestioned belief that aliens had demolished a sacred holy site swept the religious networks and the internet. Re-energized anti-alien riots erupted across the United States, Canada, and Australia. They joined the growing demonstrations of jobless workers. Separatist rallies swept Texas. Lila refused every attempt by her vindictive pastor, to draw her into this violence.

Sam called Lila, but the turmoil made a meeting impossible for the near future.

Sam Rice planned a trip to Dallas.

CHAPTER 22

All the President's women

"Mary," President Cortez set a thick folder on her desk, "Texas is getting out of hand, especially in Austin and Dallas. They want to separate from the Union and kill aliens at the same time. I guess one good aim out of two ain't bad."

Emalia Cortez had a habit of reverting to slang when upset.

Mary winced. Her view of aliens had reversed course.

"On the bright side, since I kicked the CIA out and have an FBI direct contact, I find out more than we used to see." She touched the file on her desk. "Unfortunately, what I get seems to be all bad news."

"Emalia," Cortez insisted that they be on a first name basis in private, "the same things are happening elsewhere. The obvious political choice is to side with the alien haters, but the correct course is to push the opportunities the visitors provide."

"What opportunities...?" Cortez snarled.

"What is the first question any of our billionaire backers would ask?"

"How do we make money from this?" Cortez smiled. "So how would they and us make money or get votes from this?"

"Why don't you ask those rich guys to come up with a Plan B. Tell them it would be more beneficial than a losing fight."

"One thing, make sure they understand the aliens will not engage in any commercial activity or favour any group." Daisy said. "The plan has to deal with human activity on this planet." Daisy had sat quietly on one side. Emalia Cortez gave her a sideways glance.

Since when do secretaries give advice? Cortez thought.

"Mary promoted me to assistant advisor," Daisy smiled at the President.

Cortez wondered if Daisy could read minds, but discounted the thought.

"The confirmation of Siglinde as VP is near. She handled that senator from Alabama nicely... damned misogynist bigot." Mary said. "It would be good to get her involved. She understands aliens better than we do."

Mary did not understand how much the entity she called Siglinde knew about aliens.

"We need someone to figure out all the crazy people running around this damned country." The President's discouragement shone through.

"Sadly, that might be the aliens," Daisy said. "The fiasco at the UN will make it hard to convince them to give specific help, but Ellie Keys might be willing. She's mostly human."

Daisy knew that if her people did anything in this, it would be a collective decision, including her ongoing, real-time input. They had already begun the discussion, and they would have decided long before the human politicians asked. Like Ellie and RoH, Daisy advocated tactical intervention where needed.

President Cortez leaned back in her chair and closed her eyes. Mary and Daisy waited. Unlike Harry Ascue had, Emalia mulled over things beyond the immediate political opportunity or problem. She played a mean game of chess, and her political work reflected that world of thrust, counter, and planning several moves ahead.

"The aliens won't deal with us directly. That Ellie woman said so." Cortez sat upright. "I'm meeting the Secretary General today. I'll ask him to approach them once more."

"He'll have to grovel a bit, or at least apologize." Daisy said. "Suggest that he go through the Canadians. The star travellers aren't taking direct calls, especially from us."

"You look like crap, Emalia." Mary's duties involved how the President presented herself to the world. "I bet you aren't sleeping much."

"Not much," Emalia admitted. "Would you rest easy with all this?"

"Let's bring in your hairdresser and the rest of the Emalia dress-up crew," Mary said. "The Secretary General will be here in two hours."

"President Cortez," the Secretary General began, "I am on a world tour to every major capital. I want a unified approach to the alien problem."

"Coming here first might not have been your best move." Cortez said. "Since the aliens sabotaged all the militaries, the other nations are getting restless and building on old resentments. We have lost influence."

Cortez eyed the man opposite. They sat on stuffed chairs in the Oval Office. The Security Council had chosen this Secretary General with the usual acrimony between the members. He represented a painful compromise. While a career diplomat, he had shown initiative and independence from the Council, as if he did not care if they elected him for a second term. Emalia Cortez knew that her former boss had forced the Secretary General to approve the ill-conceived attack on Ellie and the others at the Assembly.

She eyed him once more.

Perhaps he and I are in the same boat, she thought. *Neither of us is likely to be re-elected.*

"Madam President," he replied, "I see it as more than restless. There is widespread sentiment that the aliens cut the super-powers down to size. A growing movement supports the alien cause, or their suggestions for humans, at least. Admittedly, many dictators think they can use it to gain more power and resent losing the big powers' patronage. My casual discussions tell me that a majority want to form a second United Nations free of the Security Council. My tour is to prevent that, but I would like the current UN reformed. I need your commitment to change the Charter."

Emalia knew that Mary, watching on the recording circuit, would think that the Secretary's message gave hope.

"We need to get rid of the Security Council's power. You founding victors of World War 2 created it so that you always held control. That has to end if the world is to change. I sense that most humanity is demanding change. If we don't do it legally, then I fear an alliance of small nations will decide to do it by force."

"You know," Cortez said, "that the aliens have little hope humans will do the right thing."

"Since they revealed their presence on New Year's Eve, we have been doing a great job of proving them right." The Secretary General sipped his tea. "That stupid attack at the Assembly did nothing to help."

"That was Harry's foolishness. I am leaning to taking the high road on this," Cortez sipped an orange juice. "My new Vice-President knows more about the aliens than anyone else. Siglinde Hilfreich led our alien-hunting agency. She told me she has had contact with that Ellie Keys entity, and they get along fine."

"I'm just dealing with the political reality at the UN, but can we trust the aliens?" The Secretary frowned. "In the movies, the ones that seem good turn out to want to eat us or something."

"That alien food cliché began with the first novel by Wells in the 1800s. Almost everyone has used it since. I have never met an alien," Cortez said without insincerity, "but I think they are who they say they are. If they leave, and that is the worst thing they could do to us now, I want to have a deep hole in Idaho with 25 years of supplies. There's a good chance we would irradiate ourselves."

The pair sat in silence for a few minutes.

"Will you commit to reforming the United Nations?"

"I support it," Cortez smiled, "but I need to do a lot of politicking to get real backing. You have seen the riots all over the country, and the media anti-alien propaganda is overwhelming. It seems it will be impossible. I won't make a public statement right now. You can tell other leaders unofficially where I stand, but make sure that they know I am not optimistic that I can convince Congress."

"Now, I have a request of you," President Cortez said. "I mentioned we need to build a relationship with the aliens. I want to meet Ellie Keys. They won't deal with any nation individually, but if they know how to help humans save ourselves, I would like to hear it."

"I think," Cortez looked at the man, "it must involve the United Nations. That's why reform is important. The aliens understand the Assembly is required for success. They would not meet with the Security Council. We five former super-powers are the problem from their point of view. I'm hoping at least to learn something to save my presidency and maybe restore the old order."

In the anteroom, Mary grimaced at the President's words. She no longer saw any good in the old order. Her pregnancy with a hybrid baby had softened her and given her a galactic perspective.

I'm not in Iowa anymore... Mary had reminded herself.

"I want to meet Ellie one on one and with no publicity." Cortez looked at the Secretary in expectation.

"I'll go to Ottawa next, then Mexico City. The Canadian Prime Minister might be more open. Even though he is your boy, he represents the rich middle powers. I will ask him to ask Ellie."

The Canadian Prime Minister stretched protocol and accompanied the Secretary General to the airport. The volatile political situation reduced the visit to a low profile event with no press conference.

"Are you representing the United Nations or the United States today?" The Prime Minister knew, but would the Secretary General admit it? He leaned back in the limousine and waited.

"Both," the Secretary said, "it is in our interest to pacify the aliens."

"I'm about to call an election," the PM said. "The political situation will only get worse and the extremists are already splitting the country. Most think we should negotiate with the aliens and that is my ground. I might not get a better opportunity for a mandate to do that. The public seeing me as the important diplomat between Earth and them would help. I'll fly to Goderich to negotiate with this Ellie entity."

"The US President says you need to use your two intermediaries or the aliens won't talk."

The Prime Minister did not answer. They emerged from the car, dodged the horde of reporters, and shook hands at the gate where the Secretary's charter waited. The Prime Minister did not wait for the boarding.

"Get the Air force to have my plane ready tomorrow morning. Call the mayor of Goderich and tell him to pony up that Ellie creature to meet me." The Chief-of-Staff rushed away.

The Prime Minister saw a chance to by-pass the annoying junior MPs and take the initiative. An election would rid him of Liz Dafoe and Dawn Waasnodae. If everyone saw him showing strength, it would offset the blame for the collapse of the industrial weapons economy. He would fly back from Goderich, triumphant and with Ellie.

The Goderich mayor panicked at the phone call from the Prime Minister's Office. He did not know where Ellie Keys had gone. He knew her father worked for Mike Hammersmith, and he set a record speeding to the factory. Mike and Charlie laughing at him did not help his mood.

"It's okay, Jack," Mike Hammersmith said, "Ellie is in London. Charlie will ask her to call you, but Ellie won't meet the Prime Minister. At least I don't think so."

"Jack," Charlie called the mayor an hour later, "Ellie won't be here, but they have arranged for someone to meet the PM. Tell his office they will be at the airport at 9 AM."

"Thanks, Charlie."

"Oh, Jack, I wouldn't go anywhere near the airport tomorrow."

At ten in the evening, Ellie Keys buzzed Liz Dafoe's apartment from the front entrance.

"Why are you here?" Liz had heard nothing of tomorrow's event with the Prime Minister. She and Dawn had just decided it was bedtime.

"I have to escort you two on a quick trip. You are our representatives in Canada and the PM has by-passed you. He tried to meet me, but I will not go. You two will be there, though, but it's in Goderich."

"We don't have time to get there for tomorrow," Dawn said.

"Dawn, remember the story you told me of the old man back home who always talked about being called to the mother ship? You are going to get your ride on something like it tomorrow morning. The three of us must be out front about 7 AM."

A parade of RCMP vehicles arrived at Goderich Sky Harbour airport overnight. They formed an impressive array in the main parking lot and well down Airport Road.

Captain Fontaine received an order for her troop to go to the airport to support the police. Ghislaine hurried downstairs and found RoH sitting in the living room.

"I see they involved you," RoH said. "That's good. I was going to go by special means," she glanced at the ceiling, "but I'll ride with you instead. It will be a bit of a show, so bring snacks. All you'll have to do is watch."

"They ordered me to appear to be an honour guard for the Prime Minister but to have loaded weapons."

"I think they have some half-baked idea of capturing Mother." RoH giggled. "I don't think the Prime Minister watches news on television."

RoH and Ghislaine spent the night playing chess. The captain had taught her the game and RoH learned quickly. On principle, she avoided probing to discover Ghislaine's moves ahead of time. It would not be fair, and RoH wanted to experience her un-enhanced human side. After these few weeks, RoH would win about half the matches.

"Chess is war," Ghislaine said when she won, "and I'm a professional."

They always shared a laugh at this running joke. Once, when Ghislaine had lain RoH's king down in victory, the piece rose on its own and sidled into the square with Ghislaine's king.

"Brothers of the heart," RoH said. "It is sad that war is your job. You know we will put you out of work if we are successful."

Ghislaine closed her eyes.

"I once thought I had an important job," the captain said, "but you star people have taught me power is relative, and it also demands responsibility. They train us to use what we call command and control, so that we use our power in a planned way. The important thing there is the command; we think it must be top down. I know you control the immeasurable power you all have from the bottom up. Each of you, individually or by joint decision, controls your actions. Your power scares the hell out of me. You taught me the more important lesson that we don't need fighting. I just don't see how we get there."

RoH suddenly brightened and her thoughts, what she would later claim to have been an inspiration from a dandelion, flashed through the fleet.

Mother, would step-daddy like to head the Institute for Galactic Study?
Sigh...

"Ghislaine, how would you like to become a galactic historian when your day job becomes obsolete? You could work with Dr. Jorgensen and teach humans how we did it. Maybe you could teach humans how to succeed."

The Prime Minister stared glumly from the airplane window. He had expected his usual large air force transport, but settled for this small business jet because of the short Goderich runway. The aircraft ferried the Joint chiefs, so had luxurious appointments. It gently touched down in Goderich, with screaming reverse thrust and the braking chute dragging them to a stop. Ghislaine's force rolled their APC into the parking lot. The Mounties who had been lounging about suddenly came to life. Ghislaine dealt with the over-officious RCMP commander. RoH stood quietly and watched as the jet whined to a stop on the apron. She decided that the terminal building would be the best place to meet. RoH made it halfway to the door.

"Stop," ordered a Mountie, "show me your hands."

RoH turned to the man, and he suddenly found something better to do.

"Where's the mayor and that Ellie woman?" The Prime Minister's Chief-of-Staff demanded. The wind gusting off the lake watered her eyes.

"There's no one here yet," the cop said.

"We ordered the mayor to be here for nine. It's ten past. Get them here."

The Mountie sent a car to town to find the mayor. The Prime Minister wandered between the plane and the fence separating him from the terminal, his tie flapping annoyingly in the breeze.

A cop struggled to light a cigarette, but the wind suddenly died. At the same instant, a bright glow flowed in over the trees at the lake. The alien craft made no noise as it hovered directly above the stunned crowd. The familiar purple column touched the ground. Ellie, Liz, Dawn, and Johnny Bray descended between the Prime Minister and the building. RoH hugged them.

"We'll get together soon, Sweetie," Ellie called to RoH and slowly rose back into the ship; however, the craft did not move. The purple glow suddenly expanded into a circle that included the Prime Minister. The Chief-of-Staff rushed to aid her boss. An unpleasant tingle repelled her as she touched the glowing wall. The police ran around, guns drawn, but the confused commander issued no orders. Ghislaine stood her troop down, broke out the tasty snacks that Elsie had provided, and sat beside their armoured carrier to watch the spectacle.

"Welcome to you all," RoH said. "Hello, Johnny."

She had not met Liz and Dawn before, but needed no introductions. RoH felt the women's minds in case she needed to comfort. Her connection to Dawn startled. She found something there she had not expected, not in the woman's mind, but in Dawn's body.

Could it be...?

"Prime Minister, please follow us inside. I think there are enough chairs." RoH headed to the door without waiting for a reply.

"I demand to see Ellie," the Prime Minister paced about the threadbare room. Everyone had taken a chair, chrome-framed auditorium things that once had been in the town hall. The politician looked down at the others, thinking he had the authoritative position. He glared at the two backbench MPs, did not know who Johnny might be or why he had arrived from space, and he puzzled at RoH. The other three looked at the little girl as if she were in charge.

A girl! He thought.

RoH stared back at the PM. He suddenly felt uncomfortable. Her eyes penetrated, and he could not look away.

"I speak for my mother," RoH said. The PM froze.

"Your mother is Ellie?" He put his hands on his hip. "I don't talk to children... get her here."

His tone impressed no one.

"Crikey, mate," Johnny said. "You ain't tumbled to the situation, have you? You couldn't find reality if it were a snake in your boot."

Liz and Dawn laughed. The Prime Minister frowned at the coarse comment from this rough-hewn man with an accent.

RoH stood, and suddenly Ellie looked the man in the eye.

"Is this better?" she asked.

"Yes," his voice shook.

"But this will have to do," and RoH now stood in front of him.

"Sit," she pointed to a chair. He sat; RoH looked him directly in the eye.

"The American president wasn't as arrogant as you are when I met him. He did not have to prove his importance. He's dead and you're here for President Cortez."

"I'm here on the behalf of the Secretary General of the United Nations."

"Prime Minister, we won't get far if you aren't honest. The Secretary came on a mission from the American President."

A snippet from the meeting between Emalia Cortez and the Secretary General suddenly played in holographic clarity to one side of the room. The conversation clearly came through.

"How..." the PM slumped in his chair.

"You think meeting my mother will help your election chances? You had planned to kidnap her and claim victory."

"No..."

"Yes," RoH smiled. "Why is it that human leaders think kidnapping people will help them keep power? Frankly, that is becoming tedious. We gave up kidnapping decades ago." RoH looked at Johnny.

"Damned good thing." Johnny rubbed his beard and smiled.

"I never planned that," the PM said. His mouth had gone dry.

"I'll get you some water." RoH extracted a flask from her pack.

"How did you know I was thirsty?"

"You had eggs for breakfast, tripped on the cat, and couldn't decide what tie to wear. Your wife had to tell you. So, I know you planned to kidnap Mother."

The Prime Minister felt helpless.

"Will someone meet the American President?" he muttered.

"Let's talk about the election first," Liz Dafoe said. "Will you oppose or advocate for the visitor's cause? Will you advocate human survival? At least make Canadian policies that will help and work to reform the United Nations into a real democratic institution?"

"My advisors tell me to oppose the aliens."

"There are enough bigoted parties already," Dawn Waasnodae spoke, "and you are being blamed for the economic disaster. If you fight on their ground, they will defeat you for sure. Your advisers live in the old world and think what worked in the past still applies, even with the presence of stellar visitors."

The PM believed her. "The opposition is screaming that if we change, we will have surrendered to the aliens."

"Maybe it's just surrendering to life on Earth," RoH said.

"That's your counter line," Liz exclaimed. "Choose life, not war. You can add, especially not a losing war."

"Look," RoH said. "If we decide humans are going to take the wrong path, we will leave, disappear... poof. You will have all your toys back as fast as you can rebuild them, but you will be dying. The climate disaster will kill off most humans before you can make one new atomic bomb."

The Prime Minister had three problems. His cowardice exceeded his belief that he was the smartest man in Canada. The third was that his Chief-of-Staff was not here to tell him what to do.

"I would fire that Chief of yours," RoH smiled. "She's more delusional than you are. She thinks she's the boss and is fuming outside, thinking she should be the one in here talking to us. Your Chief would stab you in the back in an instant if it suited her. By excluding her, we made her hate star travellers even more."

The Prime Minister did not like to hear it said, but he had known it for a long time.

"So," he did not know what else to say. "Will someone meet with President Cortez? She has demanded that Ellie meet with her."

"I know Emalia Cortez is smart enough not to demand." RoH said. "She has good advisers whom she trusts. They are honest women, by the way." RoH made a show of glancing at Liz and Dawn.

"The President knows negotiation and alliance of purpose with star travellers is the right way to go. Alliance, in this case, does not involve the usual human ideas of war, conquest, and greed. You should have a frank chat with her. She should have you visit Washington."

"Tell the Secretary General to inform President Cortez that my mother will meet with her, but here in Goderich. We will not go to any capital city. Tell them to bring all the President's women. Oh, and give Liz and Dawn a ride back to Ottawa."

The Prime Minister left by the front door. He eyed his chief-of-Staff. She scowled at the two MPs walking beside him as she rushed forward. The PM ran a short list of potential replacements through his mind. Liz Dafoe's name stuck.

"Get a line to the American President," he snarled at the woman. "When we get to the office, draw up my request to the governor general to dissolve Parliament and call an election. Call a caucus meeting. "

I'm going to lose anyway, he thought. *I might as well get it over.*

Liz and Dawn entered the plane ahead of the PM. Dawn chuckled as the plane lifted into the late morning sunshine. She felt like it was a movie, and even if the sun was not setting, she and the other politicians on board were flying into the sunset of their political careers.

Dawn Waasnodae looked at Liz with love and thought about home with her Anishinabek. The last hours with the Prime Minister and RoH had startled and encouraged her. RoH had never appeared in her alien form, but Dawn had seen her mother, Ellie, in shimmering grey. Dawn believed that RoH was a miigis, a descendent of the original miigis, the shells or the alien guides and teachers from long ago, or perhaps a new mentor and guide. As the plane arched above the puffy clouds, Dawn knew that her real quest had just begun. She had yet to learn who the actual child of the miigis was.

CHAPTER 23

Hi Ho, Hi Ho, it's off to...

President Cortez purposely, and Sam Rice accidentally, planned to meet an alien. Their logistics problems for travelling only differed in scale. Both had to arrange transportation, and both had to overcome anti-alien demonstrations. Travelling through cities had become more complicated. Riots of conspiracy believers and jobless defence workers had become daylong events. The extra police hiring absorbed some of the newly released military personnel.

"If Harry were still here, he would never agree to go, cap in hand, to some backwater to meet an ordinary person." President Cortez sat with Mary and Daisy.

"I guess it's humanity's good luck that Harry is gone." Mary did not smile. She took no satisfaction in the death of her former boss. Mary had loathed the man, but she grieved, never the less.

"You won't be meeting anyone ordinary," Daisy encouraged. "This may be the most important event of your career."

"If you campaign on hating star travellers like all of your opponents," Mary said, "then you will lose the next vote. Despite the mess on the streets, there is support for the aliens. That's your only chance. These folks have not taken to the streets. They fear the conspiracy nut-bars will kill them. There's still a lot of ammo around."

"We are working on a plan to get that ammunition and as many assault weapons as we can. The army and the police need them." Cortez had issued a secret executive order as her first act after becoming President.

"The polls show that over half of the population supports some sort of friendly relationship with the aliens." Mary continued. "Tap into that and build it into a movement, a popular wave towards equity and away from greed. Your opponents all think they can fight to regain their wealth."

"Considering we don't have any actual weapons," Cortez frowned, "we don't even have the option. How do I get to this Goderich place?"

President Cortez confronted the same problem as the Canadian Prime Minister. Goderich Airport could not accommodate Air force One. Her solution meant postponing meeting Ellie for a week or two.

"Teddy." Emalia Cortez held the handset to her ear. "I need your yacht in the Great Lakes."

"No, I don't want to go sunbathing in Michigan in April, and you don't need to be there. Actually, you can't come."

Cortez frowned. Her billionaire benefactor, Theodore Rockford III, had been more than free with his hands in the past. His money bought many women, and he had assumed that when he donated to Emalia's senatorial campaigns that he had free access to her body. She had held him off only by supplying a porn star as an option. Since she had become vice-president, he had behaved. Emalia believed that her developing wrinkles had something to do with it.

"The tub reeks like an onion, this time of year," Rockford said from his lounger on the Bahamas beach. "It'll take two weeks to get her ready."

"Two weeks...?" Cortez nodded at Mary. Daisy opened the itinerary.

"You meet the Saudi king on the 15th; there are three days after that."

"Can the boat be in Port Huron on April 16th?"

"Okay, I'm just sailing across the lake to Canada. My people will brief your captain. Send the bill to the White House. You name the amount."

"Yah, I love you too, Teddy."

Cortez frowned. The big boat sat in winter-idle in Chicago, and it would need the time to be ready and reach Port Huron. Mary issued an executive order commandeering the boat and paying with administrative funds. A Secret Service detail would fly to Chicago.

"Get hold of that Ellie person. Do I need a gun?" The President asked.

"Why do you think a gun would help?" Mary asked the obvious.

Sam Rice did not know he wanted to meet an alien, or at least a hybrid human-alien. He would confront a hateful preacher who instigated Mandy's murder. Sam did not know the reality of Robert Orville.

Money also limited Sam. It had been expensive to bury Mandy, and although the church fund helped, Sam and the family suffered badgering by the funeral home. Sam's pastor threatened never to use them again for a parishioner burial and that held the greedy undertaker at bay. The funeral home owners had no sympathy for Mexican aliens, but money trumped bigotry. The owner made a huge profit by directing destitute grieving families to pay for funerals with high-interest loans from a company he also owned.

Sam worked all the over-time available, but could only keep a small part of the wages for his trip to Dallas. It would take another month.

"I need a handgun," Sam Rice pressed his cell phone to his ear and whispered. He sat in his car in the middle of a sports stadium parking lot with no other human within sight.

"What makes you think I can help?" The disembodied voice did not sound Texan. "Why would you need a gun?"

"The stores have sold out of guns. I need an automatic."

"Semi-auto," the voice said. "You don't know much, do you, kid?"

"I'm taking lessons," Sam said.

"How did you get my number?"

"Guy I work with, Bill..."

"No names..." the voice rose. "It'll cost a thousand."

Sam gulped. "They are only four twenty-five in the store."

"There ain't none in the store, as you say."

Sam did a quick calculation.

"I can only afford 800."

"You sound like a nice kid," the sarcasm dripped. "Do you know where the Horny Hoof is? It's a gay bar, cowboy theme...meet me there ...bring 800...cash...no bigger than twenties...4 PM...Try to fit in. Wear a Stetson and tight pants, and carry a shoulder bag with the money. I'll be wearing a red polka dot bandana."

"Yes... I'll be there."

He had the cash, but the transaction would set Sam back a week or two in his plan.

Maybe Lila will lend me some money.

"The insurance company got lucky. The foundation is still good." Lila smirked. Sam had caught up with her at the site of her demolished house. Inadvertently, Sam had already done more physical damage than the star travellers had done in many decades. Sam wanted to hold Lila's hand, but Lila's husband stood on the far side of the construction and harassed a labourer who struggled to square a floor joist.

"You men, y'all think you know how to build. Maybe, with any luck, the guy will throw Bo-Bob into the hole." Lila laughed.

"Why's the church not being worked on?" Sam turned to look at the rubble of the once proud building.

"Apparently, good old pastor bought the cheapest insurance he could find. The company says that terrorists destroyed the church, like the cops think, and they have a clause that says that voids the contract. It's making lawyers rich. Plus, the feds still call it a crime scene."

"It's weird. Lee's lawyer father is representing the church, getting richer on it. He never cared about the kid. That's why he became a crazy."

"The whole thing's a crime," Lila gazed wistfully at her new house. The original had made some wonderful memories. She turned to Sam.

"Strange thing," she said. "Someone called to warn me about the blast." She locked eyes with Sam.

"That's strange, wouldn't y'all say, Sam Rice?"

Sam fought to stay calm.

"Maybe he called all the neighbours. Maybe he had a conscience and didn't want to hurt anyone."

"Yes, it was a man," Lila smiled warmly, "not a woman, but I guess y'all just assumed that. He only called me."

"Y'all never told the cops about the call. It would have proved the terrorism angle."

"First, he called to protect me, so I figure I owe him the same courtesy. Second, I take care of friends."

Lila's eyes told Sam that she knew.

"How did y'all know my last name? I don't think y'all ever asked."

"Y'all aren't my first lover, lover, and y'all likely won't be the last." Her eyes asked another question.

"One guy is a cop. I showed him the call on my cell and he tracked it to a tower on the south side. Funny, he chased it a bit more and found that's the neighbourhood where the young woman who Noah killed lived, with her parents and her brother."

Her look convicted Sam, and then she glanced towards the pile of sacred rubble across the green space.

"I never liked that church or the idiot pastor. We only went because we liked the cheap mortgage. Thankfully, that's done now. The terrorist did us all a favour. Bo-Bob there is happy. He's a philandering jerk, but pays the bills. I hate the church's bigotry. Bo-Bob," she looked at her husband, who was now being berated by the site foreman, "has no convictions. He's as bad in the head as he is in the bed."

Lila laughed loudly.

"He doesn't know what he's missing." Sam looked at Lila and thought about how attractive she looked even in conservative slacks and a blouse.

"I bet the guy who called is happy y'all didn't rat him out."

"I hope so," Lila glanced at Sam, "and we both owe each other, I'd say."

"Speaking of owing," Sam hurried into his reason for being there, "I was hoping I could owe y'all a bit of money for a month or two. I guess, though, y'all would be short, with all this." He nodded to the construction.

"How much... and when...?" Lila asked.

"Only about 500. I need to make a trip to Dallas in about a week and need gas and a motel."

"Okay, meet me Thursday evening. I'll give y'all the cash and a bonus, and a motel practice run. Come to the Hilton at the airport, about eight."

Lila brushed Sam's hand and then quickly withdrew. She made a mental note to find out what Sam wanted in Dallas.

Sam walked into the Horny Hoof looking like he belonged. For tight-fitting pants, he only had his old high school football uniform. They were imitation silver lamé and outlined his muscular calves and thighs. On top, he had a checked shirt overlain by a leather vest. A large grey Stetson topped off the costume. A rather attractive middle-aged man sipping a fruit drink at the bar ogled and whistled as Sam sauntered past. He had not felt this exposed since dropping that touchdown pass in the city championship game. Sam spotted the table at the back where a slim man in a red polka dot kerchief gulped beer from a bottle. He tried to remain casual as he made his way deeper into the gloom.

"You got the cash?" Polka Dot asked.

Sam un-shouldered the bag and laid it on the table.

"Y'all got the gun?"

"Never say that word," Polka Dot hissed, and then nodded. He reached for the bag.

Sam grabbed his wrist.

"Show me..."

Polka Dot opened his denim jacket to reveal a pistol handle sticking out of an inner vest pocket. Sam released his grip.

"Wait here," Polka Dot took the bag and disappeared into the washroom.

Am I being ripped off...?

"What'll y'all have, sweetie?" the waiter wore spandex that left nothing to the imagination.

"Lone Star..."

"Oh, that's creative." The sarcasm dripped. "I like creative stuff."

The waiter winked and undulated towards the bar.

The beer and Polka Dot arrived at the same time. The waiter rubbed Polka Dot's shoulder as he set Sam's beer between them.

"Hang around after," he said to Polka Dot.

"Sure, until the Ace of Spades gets here."

"So y'all have money," the waiter looked from Polka Dot to Sam and back again. "Y'all know I don't like it when you're on that stuff."

The waiter huffed away.

Polka Dot set the bag onto the table. It made a muffled thud. The gun had replaced the money.

"Who's your cute friend, Tex?" The ogler from the bar swished past towards the washroom.

"You should stay," Polka Dot said. "You would have fun."

Sam decided that although they called Polka Dot Tex, he seemed to have a California accent.

Sam gulped the Lone Star and stood.

"Thanks..."

"I already fed the baby," Tex said. "I threw in a bonus. You sure you don't want to stay?"

Sam tried not to run out the front door. He had seen nothing to compete with Lila. He glanced up and down the street, half-expecting a swarm of cops to arrest him. Sam knew that having a gun would be the last thing they would arrest you for in Texas, at least if you were white skinned.

CHAPTER 24

Chicken Dance

Kerri welcomed her brother, Gary, at the front door. She glanced past his shoulder to make sure Jody did not wait in the car.

"Don't worry, Sis, Jody's knee deep in the re-building plans for the church and hating aliens… ridiculous. They have long prayer sessions to help Pastor George out of the coma, but plan something else."

Kerri escorted Gary into Charlie's living room. A woman he only knew from television sat in a comfortable rocker.

"Hello, Gary," Ellie stood to shake his hand. "Kerri tells me there's something going on that involves star travellers."

"You hardly fit Pastor George's picture of the devil's angel." Gary sat and eyed the woman who everyone in the church hated.

"My daughter was there, but didn't hurt Pastor George. Another hybrid human-alien has turned bad and caused that problem. Kerri says the fresh problem has to do with the UFO worshipers."

"Yah, it's the cult off Highway 8; our zealots are going to attack them. They think those folks torched the church. That isn't true, though."

"So we have one cult attacking another." Kerri's contempt came through. "Are you sure they didn't burn the church?"

"I'm sure," Gary did not hesitate. "A member of our congregation is in the cult, covering all their bases, as they say. They are sure no one there did the arson."

"Since members can come and go, they aren't really cults, just mislead people looking for comfort and confirmation." Ellie said.

"My daughter's in charge of dealing with the rogue hybrid; my specialty seems to be chicken dancers." Ellie laughed. "I need to know when they plan to attack."

"Jody likes to brag. They'll visit the UFO nuts tomorrow night, just before they begin their hoe-down."

"I guess actual aliens need to appear," Ellie pondered. "A small scout ship should do. I'll be the centre of attraction."

RoH

Yes, Mother...

I have a minor job for Captain Fontaine and her squad and for you.

Oh, goody, can I play farmer again?

No, this time you will play doctor.

Two members of Ghislaine Fontaine's force lay in the woods near the edge of the Holy Spirit Immersion of Huron's construction site. They watched the parking lot fill with vehicles. Pickup trucks sported huge Canadian flags and would lead the mob down the few kilometres to the chicken barn. One watcher described the scene through a sat-com head set.

"Captain, there are more coming all the time. We count a hundred."

Ghislaine Fontaine and her troops lounged at the APC in a field entrance opposite from the direction to the church and out of sight of the chicken farm lane. Ellie had created a simple plan that she hoped would not involve shooting and would knock the fight out of everyone. RoH had assured Ghislaine that her mother did not plan any violence.

Ellie arrived with Bobby Briscoe and Jimmy Smith. They waited with the soldiers. Most of the chicken barn members had already arrived.

"Okay, the pack is on the move," Ghislaine's receiver muttered. "We have seen long guns. We'll be a minute behind them."

Four pickup trucks jammed with parishioners led a column of of fully loaded vehicles from the church parking lot, horns honking. A minute later, a dark SUV slid from the trees and followed the mob towards the chicken farm.

A young girl walked through the front entrance to the Royal London Medical Centre. The guard, in place since the pandemic protocols, watched a young female in doctor scrubs approach. He had never seen her before, but many unfamiliar people had privileges.

"Can you tell me how to get to the sixth floor west?"

"Take the elevator around the corner and go out the back door when it gets to six. You're new here."

"They appointed me to consult on a special case." She flashed her I.D. hanging on a lanyard from her neck. He noted Doctor Clara Solis in his log.

"Pastor George," the soft voice soothed, but the catatonic preacher did not stir. RoH leaned close to his head and probed. It only took an instant. George's eyes snapped open.

"You're..." he gasped in recognition. "Where am I?"

He struggled to get out of bed, to get away from this devil's angel.

"In a hospital in London," RoH softly replied, "but I'm taking you to your flock."

"You'll kill me or brainwash me and make me your slave."

"No, Pastor George, you can do and say whatever you want, even the ugly lies. Take this as a show of friendship."

RoH smiled. Pastor George proved to be a rougher dandelion, but she always had hope. None of the star travellers would ever turn a human into a robot. Humans were useless as slaves. They had either to live or die of their own free will. For RoH, it risked sadness, but she thought that better than any artificial victory. They had chosen her grandfather, Charlie, because his family had hated and fought alien meddling.

George wore the standard hospital gown open at the back. The three nurses at the station and several others along the way did not notice the passing of the wild-looking man in a blue gown and the young girl who held his hand. They avoided the guard station by using a back entrance and stepped into the gloom of a late April evening. When the alarm went out in the hospital a half-hour later, it did not matter. Pastor George had already experienced a ride in the purple light.

Ellie, Bobby, and Jimmy walked up the farm lane and into the celebration building just before the church mob arrived. Since she had been a little girl, Ellie had wanted to stop violence and suffering. She had to stand between the chicken dancers and the mob. It reminded her of a night in Texas, long ago. It had been a horrible night. The trio waited in the vestibule between the exterior doors and the hall entrance.

Horn-blaring pickup trucks roared into the farmyard. The parade veered into whatever spaces were available and the line spilled out into the lane. The music inside could not hide the incessant honking. Dancers surged towards the entrance. Ellie led them outside. Bobby and Jimmy went to opposite corners, facing the mob with cameras rolling.

"Come on, you bastards, you alien lovers...fire bombers, come and get yours, come meet the Lord." He waved a sinister looking 12-gauge pump-action shotgun towards the crowd of horrified cultists. The horde from the convoy roared in support. Shouts echoed from the barn and washed over the mob.

The worshipers of aliens and flying saucers cowered. For many years, it had been fun, but now guns pointed at them.

Ellie stepped forward.

"Who the hell are you?" The armed insurrectionist growled.

"I am your pastor's jezebel, whore, and sinner. I am Ellie."

"The alien..." both the cultists and the zealots murmured. Suddenly the chicken dancers felt braver. Their saviour had finally arrived. The anger of the pack shifted from the humans to the actual object of their hate.

"Get her," someone shouted while safely standing at the back. "In the name of God, get the devil's angel."

"You are protecting these arsonists. These sinners burnt our church. They have to pay and you, too." The man worked the slide-pump on his shotgun. The sounds of shells slamming into chambers came from behind.

"She and those sinners are the devil's angels, alien slaves." More pushing forward followed the shout from the rear, but the front echelon sensed alien danger.

"We have, in this farmyard, a reflection of the sad situation of humanity. We have two groups," Ellie swept her eyes from the cargo cultists to the mob of believers, "both willing to fight, maybe to death for beliefs. Neither of you are acting from knowledge or thoughtfulness. It is this that may doom humans to extinction."

"Liar, alien whore, Jezebel," roared the horde. The cultists once again cowered back to the barn wall. Several mothers hurried children inside. The rear of the mob pushed forward, lusting for carnage. They pressed against the leading cohort. Although these were the ones with guns, they all eyed Ellie with a touch of fear and resisted the insistent supporters. They had seen RoH fling tractors and trucks aside on Suncoast Boulevard, and they believed she had turned Pastor George into a frothing, gigantic dog. This Ellie, the little girl's mother, had to have more powerful than her daughter did.

From the corner of her eye, Ellie saw the owner of the chicken barn sneak from his house and held a hunting rifle at the ready. It would not take much to start a shooting war.

Ellie had scripted the scenario as carefully as a Hollywood melodrama, and the cavalry rode in. Actually, a two-pronged intervention arrived almost together. Ghislaine Fontaine and her troop rushed down the lane. Armed with real automatic assault weapons, they had enough training for the ten of them to neutralize this mob if they were ready to shoot down civilians. Warnings screamed from the rear of the horde as the Alien Guard spread out along the fence, weapons raised and clicked safeties off. Ghislaine prayed that the mere threat would be enough to stop bloodshed.

More impressive than the Canadian army, a star ship shrieked over the highway. It arrived in a blinding burst of light, with a debilitating sonic boom that persisted as a wall of sound. The craft passed above the yard and dropped behind the barn. The barrage of energy threw many people in the barnyard to the ground, temporarily deafened and somewhat blinded. Exposed skin tingled from the heat. The star travellers normally stayed below the speed of sound and avoided super-heated air inside the atmosphere. Ellie had decided that a little shock and awe might be useful.

"They used my landing pad," only the farmer at the house gate could see past the barn. "That's wonderful."

He rushed towards the ship. All of his planning and work became worthwhile.

The ship arrived so quickly that neither Bobby nor Jimmy captured it. Jimmy had recovered from his shock and hurried around the corner, recording video. The small vessel, although larger than the barn, hovered just above the yard. A man and an alien stepped from a purple light. RoH pointed, and the man began an uncertain walk towards Jimmy. RoH disappeared into the ship.

Jimmy had seen Pastor George on New Year's Eve and knew that he had been comatose in a London hospital. Considering Jimmy's experiences with aliens, the pastor's appearance in a Huron farmyard seemed unsurprising. The aliens' purpose in delivering him into the middle of the stunned insurrection remained a mystery.

George walked in a daze towards Jimmy. He loomed up to the camera, spectral in his flapping hospital gown and unkempt black beard, and created a sinister impression. George ignored Jimmy and headed to the mob-filled yard with his bare backside to the camera. Jimmy laughed, but he kept recording.

Pastor George stumbled around the corner into his parishioners' view.

"Praise the Lord," echoed from the barn.

The throng roared in recognition, but their cheers faded as the pastor made his way to Ellie and squeezed her hand. Confusion replaced joy.

"What...?" someone shouted. A growl of anger swept the mob.

"What's the pastor doing? Pastor, what are you doing?"

Pastor George turned to his congregation, and in the bombastic tones usually mustered for a sermon, he said, "I was wrong about these visitors."

Angry shouts of disbelief drowned a cheer from the chicken dancers.

"They have brainwashed, Pastor. He's now one of them." The man with the 12-gauge turned to the mob. "They will get us all."

As if to confirm the man's fear, the alien craft slowly rose above the barn and hovered in sinister domination.

"God protect us," a woman cried, raised her hands to the sky in supplication, and then bolted for her car.

The scene that followed would have done justice to old silent film slapstick comedy. It happened in a roar of fearful screams and desperate curses of pushing and shoving as the panicked crowd fought to escape. Vehicles jammed the lane, with minor collisions and more cursing. Ghislaine ordered her troops well away as panicked drivers jostled towards the highway. One terrified pickup driver charged through the fence, but the truck became bogged in the soft field. The riders piled out and fled, screaming across the pasture, towards Highway 8, expecting an alien death ray to strike at any moment.

Eventually, the yard became quiet. The ship slid away to the south and out of sight. The farmer stood at the landing pad and watched the craft leave. His heart filled with pride. Captain Fontaine's force took out snacks and leaned against the fence, watching.

The chicken dancers formed a circle around Ellie and a dismayed Pastor George. He had remained silent as the desperate panic swept over everyone. The fiddler played, and the caller sang in a burst of creativity...

Bow to the alien
That got light hair.

Ellie cried. *It seems hopeless.*

In the panic, a trio of Pastor George's parishioners stood firm. These were two elders and the ever-faithful secretary, Mary, and they knew they had a problem. Although the three had easily signed contracts with Mike Hammersmith and others to rebuild the church, the Pastor had appeared. He had all the legal signing authority for the Holy Spirit Immersion of Huron. They held desperate hope that, somehow, George was competent and would not subvert their plans. These were not cynics and held genuine belief in the pastor and his message. Mary still hoped for more. They were also practical, even as they confronted a total dislocation of their faith. They pushed through the dancers.

"Pastor, what are you saying?"

"These visitors are not the devil's angels. They mean us no harm. No one does. I will deliver that message on Sunday's service at the church."

"How can you say that? These burned the church to the ground." He made a disdainful wave at the circle of dancers. "Freaks."

Ellie searched the minds of the four men, and she understood. Pastor George, now certain of the harmlessness of the star visitors, struggled with a major crisis in faith. His internal Satan had stood him on the lofty tower of certainty, and the fall seemed more fearful because of it. The three parishioners had not recovered from the shock and focused on the practical for temporary relief. Mary came forward and took his hand.

"These folks didn't do it," Ellie intervened, "at least only one."

Ellie looked at the dancer hidden beneath the green alien suit. She would deal with Gar, Gary Grenier, later.

CHAPTER 25

Wayfaring Strangers

Robert Orville sat on a bench in the front yard of the Church of Heavenly Enlightenment. He enjoyed a double chocolate dipped ice cream cone from the vendor at the park. Relaxing did not fit into Robert's normal day, but lately, ever since the narrow escape in Canada, he had been introspective. The strange little girl seemed to be an enemy, but Robert knew he could defeat a youngster. Everything in his plan for revenge appeared to be in place, and now he had little to do but keep his congregation loyal and wait for the right time. The developing Texas separatist movement encouraged him. Robert needed to bait the aliens into exposing themselves to his power. He thought that petty human politics would not do it. He, Robert Orville, would be the triumphant destroyer of the aliens, the fist of vengeance for the horrible life they had inflicted on him. His first attempt had collapsed. He needed the aliens to come to him.

Families with playful children lined up at the vendors by the park and took Robert into the unhappiness of his memories. The engaged fathers and mothers, happily scolding and hugging their children, only reminded him of the deprivation of his childhood.

His mother's bitterness made it impossible for her to give Robert joy. In his recollection, she had been working or angry. Robert could not understand why his mother's anger would swell whenever she looked at her son. He had visited her at work once, when he was in high school, and

173

resented that it was there that she seemed to be happy and carefree with her workmates and customers. Robert did not understand that he had seen the real Ruth Orville, and could not relate her unhappiness at home with him. He mistook it as Ruth not loving him as much as she loved others.

Robert savoured the icy treat, but he did not return to the present.

After Robert's 18th birthday, he wanted a driver's licence like his friends, but they were too poor to afford a car. His mother did not want to tell him where he had been born. He had lashed out, accusing his mother of being a failure. She collapsed in tears and then sobbed out the entire story... that his father was an alien. He had not believed it and added mental illness to the list of grievances that he held against her, but the story had stimulated curiosity. Robert had not known that she had conceived and given birth to him in Rachel, Nevada.

Other than pilfering the odd pack of gum, Robert had committed his first actual crime by stealing a car. In Vegas, many drunken people left keys in ignitions, and that made it easy.

Robert stopped the car beside the Texaco service station in Rachel, Nevada. He found a dusty spot to the rear of the little diner attached to the north side of the service station. A passing cop would not notice. The older woman behind the lunch counter smiled as Robert sat.

"A pie and a coffee." Robert eyed the tempting treats beneath the glass covers on the counter. He ended up with cherry "fresh from California" and over-sweetened the drink.

"I am wondering if you knew Ruth Orville," he began. Everything he knew about investigating came from television. In 1985, that questionable police college did not emphasize finesse.

The woman hesitated.

"Do you know Ruthie?" she asked.

Robert decided that admitting he was Ruth's son might cause problems. He had no desire to have a relationship with anyone in Rachel.

"I go to school with her son. He heard I'd pass here and asked me to ask."

"Well, she lived here. In fact, she's my cousin. Half the town is an Orville or married to one. Ruthie got pregnant and took off with a kid, baby boy, as I remember. No one's heard from them since. No wonder as the church pretty well ran her off, and the doctor right after."

Robert's questioning look encouraged the woman.

"Story goes the Orville clan first settled here and named the town after our great something or other grandmother. Not sure that's true, but there is a Rachel way back in the family bible."

"Ever hear tell of any aliens around here?"

The woman dropped the tea towel she had been folding.

"No," she said, too quickly.

"Okay, but Robert told me that there were aliens around when his mom lived here."

"Hey, Bert," the woman shouted to a man in a back booth. "The kid here wants to know about aliens."

The few other patrons laughed.

"Bert claims he saw some. We all think he's nuts," she whispered. "He lives on his own out there towards the base." She nodded towards a spot hidden by a wall. "Go talk to him."

She turned to busy herself with straightening soda glasses, glad Bert had been available for her to dump the kid onto. She did not want to go down the gopher hole. Robert took his coffee and headed to the back booth.

"I don't want to talk about it," Bert said. "You'll laugh, like all the rest."

"I won't laugh," Robert smiled. Robert had not yet discovered his special abilities, but when he looked Bert in the eyes, the man felt safe.

Bert leaned closer and examined Robert.

"Yur Ruthie's kid, ain't yah? Yah, you look lots like Ruthie."

"Shhh," Robert glanced around, hoping no one had heard Bert.

"I guess I can talk to you. Ruthie claimed some alien knocked her up with you, I suppose. We think it was that young doc, but maybe Ruthie was right."

Bert suddenly stiffened. He had just realized that the young man in front of him might be part alien. Robert felt Bert's fear.

"I hope it was the doc." Bert hoped he was not talking to some alien bastard. "We all thought Ruthie was crazy. Now they all think I'm crazy."

"I'm not alien, don't worry. You saw aliens?" Robert pressed on.

"More than saw them; their damned ship blew me over. One night, out on the range, I see this saucer come over and hover, not a hundred yards from me, no sound or nothing, nothing like what the movies show. Next thing I knew, a little green alien walked out of the dark and they beamed it up, scared me to death, and then when it shot away, it blew me onto my ass. I never saw no more."

"Are you sure he was green?" Robert's mother had described his father as being grey.

"I ain't sure of nothing, but I told everyone it was green. That's what the movies show them. That's what folks expected."

"So he could have been grey."

"Yah was too dark to see, really. I couldn't tell if it were he or she."

"Was that when Ruth left town?"

"Nope, she birthed her boy nine months later; that's when she left."

Robert had trouble sipping the last of his coffee. His hands shook. The old geezer had verified his mother's story. Some alien jerk had made her pregnant and then abandoned them both to a life of poverty and resentment. Robert's anger deepened. He hated aliens, his father, more than he loathed his mother. They both had destroyed his life. It never occurred to Robert that Bert might actually be crazy, or that the ship had received an alien other than his father.

How did I know Bert was afraid? Even though Robert could not yet admit it, talking with Bert had opened the door to understanding exactly who, or what, he was.

Robert made sure he arrived home when his mother would be working. He scribbled a quick note of goodbye and drove the stolen car east.

To hell with them all...

He sold the car to a no-questions-asked scrap dealer in Phoenix and bought a bus ticket. Dallas became his destination, and there he had stayed.

Robert munched the soggy bottom of the ice cream cone. Reliving childhood trauma weighed on him. The first time he had knowingly used any sort of mental manipulation had been in tricking another 100 dollars from the scrap man in Phoenix. It took Robert a few more years to realize how to use his special abilities. Making the judge let him go on a vagrancy charge had been the start of his new life.

Long ago, thought Robert.

He briefly considered buying a taco, but headed inside the church instead. Robert had a hotel reservation in Aspen.

Sam pushed through the glass doors into the lobby of the El Paso Airport Hilton. This place, although not luxurious, was above his pay scale. The text on his phone said room 414. Sam tried to be casual as he crossed the polished ceramic floor and fake Persian rugs past the reception, hoping the clerks thought he had headed to the bar. He had never met a woman in a hotel and did not understand the knowledgeable indifference of the staff.

He turned to the elevators.

Sam had two reasons to be here. He tried to believe the important one was the 500 dollars that Lila had promised to lend him. That would finance his trip to Dallas. Sam tried not to think that his lust for the middle-aged woman exceeded everything, except his grief for his sister and his hatred of Robert Orville.

Sam had showered and sat on the edge of the bed, buttoning his shirt. The clock said a few minutes past midnight.

"Here's the money." Lila handed Sam a thick wad of bills.

"It's a thousand," Sam exclaimed. "I don't need that much. I'll just be in Dallas for a day or two."

"Two people being there make it more expensive."

"Two...?"

"Look, Sam Rice, I know who you are, what you did, and what you want to do, and I love you like an old perverted aunt. I want to keep you safe. I'm so sorry about your sister. Of course, I should be mad at you for blowing up my house, but you were sweet and called, so..."

"But..."

"Shhh," Lila sat beside him and ran her fingers through his damp hair, "I enjoy being with you a lot, so I want to keep you alive, at least until a better offer comes along. I don't know how we will deal with that preacher who instigated Noah Lee's murders, but I don't want you to kill him. I don't want you hung."

"I'm not planning to kill him unless I have to do it, but I want to make him suffer like he caused me...others...to suffer. How did you know?"

Sam had a fleeting thought that Lila had turned police informant. He glanced at the door, expecting a loud knock.

"I just put two and two together, Sam. Once I knew who you were, and why blow up the church, it all made sense. Now there is a preacher you might have accidentally offed with a clear conscience."

Lila laughed. "The cops linked Orville in Dallas to Lee, so why you wanted to go to Dallas seemed obvious. I just guessed, really."

"You are a beautiful and smart woman, Lila. How did you end up with a husband like Bo-Bob?"

"My father abandoned us when I was a little baby. I never met him, and I stopped hating him long ago. Mother worked hard and loved me. We had little, but I had this..." she tapped her head. "I did well in school and went to college to be an accountant. That's where I met Bo-Bob. He graduated in finance and, unbelievably, he was sexy and fun back then. I knew he would give me the luxurious life I had always wanted."

"So what happened?" Sam did not see Lila's husband as a rival. Sam was not even sure he contested for Lila. Their relationship seemed improbable, and he had decided being in lust did not equate to love. Sam's pastor had discussed that in their youth group's sex and marriage sessions. He had even used the example of Samson and Delilah to show the bad side of lust. Sam thought Lila felt the same.

"Bo-Bob discovered he loved money more than me, or sex, although I think he has a few women spread around. He's out of town a lot."

"You aren't the first," she kissed Sam's ear, "and probably not the last, but you are now. I need to be with you in Dallas... stay the night."

"I need to be up early for work."

Lila picked up the phone and asked for a wake-up call.

CHAPTER 26

The plot thickens

Theodore Rockford III, "Teddy" to those who thought that he was their friend, only had two objectives: profit and prestige. Of the two, status exceeded every desire. Teddy did not have friends, only prospects. He was about to meet another who would consider him as an opportunity.

As the appointed representative of the billionaires' club, he had called this gathering to ensure both desires. Of course, there was no such thing as a club, but simply a conglomeration of oligarchs. They could unite if needed, but normally would try to steal each other's money.

The club needed to counter the common threat of the star travellers. Trillions of dollars of assets had evaporated with the collapse of the defence industry, and everyone wanted the wealth back. For this, the narcissistic elite stooped to mingle with those they considered inferior and purchasable. Teddy saw the Aspen effort as simply buying servants. Only a small amount of money would be required. Those billionaires, who Theodore thought of as opportunities, referred to him as "small potatoes" in their world of higher privilege. They had sent their useful inferior to deal with the riffraff.

"I'm Robert Orville. Theodore Rockford III has reserved a room for me."

The clerk at the polished rosewood counter examined the offered driver's licence and tapped his touch-screen. He thought Orville did not measure up to his usual posh customers. The clerk did not like the way Orville stared at him.

Robert examined the clerk's mind with disdain and resisted the thought of giving him a little tweak. In his annoyance, Robert missed the essence of the man.

"Suite 606 has a view of the mountain and is just down the passage from Mr. Rockford. Welcome to Aspen."

Robert signed and accepted the key cards. A dozen other church leaders had arrived, along with all three of the deputy directors of the Texas Department of Public Safety. In addition, there was a liaison person from the governor's office. An attendee Robert knew was an assistant chief in the Dallas police department. The man was a loyal member of Robert's congregation.

"Is Mr. Garcia here yet?"

"Let me see…. yes… Suite 602."

"Thank you." Robert left a ten on the counter. A deft hand snatched it.

The clerk watched Orville disappear towards the elevators and added Robert's name to a list in his cell.

"Cover for me please, Sheila," he tapped in a number as he walked towards the rear service doors.

"Something's up here," he spoke without greeting when someone in Washington answered his call. "Rockford III is here, along with about a dozen other creepy types. Everyone has arrived and in suites paid for by the Travers Foundation. I'm texting the list."

The clerk played a key role in the FBI surveillance in Aspen. The resort town hosted clandestine business activities, including arms sales with Russians as one of many customers. Aspen also harboured a high-end sex service for the rich and famous. The Travers Foundation sat at the centre of both investigations. The FBI had connected Theodor Rockford III to the foundation, and he visited frequently.

"It's all set up at this end. The suites are hot." He returned to reception. Ten minutes later, a huge RV parked beside the hotel. No one got out.

"Welcome, gentlemen. I'm glad you were eager to see me." Theodore's grifter smile shone from the head of the table in the intimate dining room. "We have reached the time to act, but first, a toast… to success."

Everyone raised glasses, sipping excellent whiskey. Drinks had been flowing freely as the visitors gathered. Several of the pastors had lectured against the evils of alcohol. Apparently, they did not consider Jack Daniel's as the Devil's spirit. All had been jovial when Rockford III walked in.

He waved at the steward, who refilled glasses as waiters brought lavish plates of veal. Teddy preferred cheeseburgers, but his belly, torturing the buttons of his jacket, suggested that he enjoyed any food.

"This reminds me of the time the King of Saudi Arabia honoured me… me… the King… me… yes, I'm somebody…"

The man who would be king, Robert Orville thought. *Such people are simple.*

The head steward stood by the door, directed service traffic, and eyed the conspirators. The FBI did not know why Rockford had called the meeting.

"Gentlemen," Teddy talked as he ate, "you all know bits of the plan, but this week I'll flesh it out, and you will all have your part."

"What's in it for y'all?" The Texas drawl annoyed Rockford.

"It will make the President weak and likely resign. I hate her, a woman president, a woman," Teddy flushed, "but she is cozy with the aliens and that has cost me… us all a lot. We think the aliens will the leave and we can return to normal, with Texas as a country and a wall defending us against those hoards swarming the border. You might say we'll be dealing with all the aliens at once."

He laughed at his wit and waved his hand around the room, as if expecting applause.

A weak voice managed "Praise the Lord".

Teddy swept his eyes over the table. His staff had built a file on everyone. The public officials were no problem. They were long used to doing the bidding of their owners. The pastors were another issue, but Teddy felt comfortable in dealing with others who shared his greed, narcissism, and sexist values.

He frowned at Robert Orville. This one differed from the rest of the opportunistic, self-interested preachers. He had invited him at the insistence of Richard Garcia, Regional Director for the Texas Public Safety Commission covering Dallas. Orville owned neither a mansion nor a personal jet. If Robert's humility was real, then he could be less controllable. Teddy had little experience dealing with principled people.

That is a dangerous man.

His gaze lingered on Robert a bit too long, and Teddy found himself absorbed by the preacher's dark eyes. At that instant, Robert had Theodore Rockford III.

Orville is the key to success. The sudden thought came to Teddy. He hesitated. The plan suffered a sudden revision.

Rockford III, a polished public speaker, stumbled. He never suffered a loss for words, even if his usual rambling seldom made sense. Teddy struggled to recover.

"Gentlemen, let's eat. My staff will present the details of the plan tomorrow." He sat and focused on his plate but not tasting the food. A feeling of dislocation overwhelmed him.

After dinner and more drinks, the gathering staggered to their suites. Rockford III approached Robert.

"Come to my suite about nine. We can discuss things then." He paused as Robert stared at him. "I'll have Mr. Garcia there as well."

The room emptied.

Robert tapped on Rockford III's door at 9:10. He intended to be late. Showing Teddy disrespect formed part of his preparation. Garcia, being a well-trained civil servant, had arrived on time.

"You're late," Rockford III flared.

"I have important things to do," Robert sat without invitation, as if Teddy's anger had no importance. Robert waved a hand, and the others sat.

"If I am to lead this effort, you can't keep questioning my actions."

"Of course," Teddy said. Garcia remained quietly subservient.

"Now here's the plan," Robert leaned forward. Even he could not subdue his excitement. In the RV in the parking lot, an agent inserted a timestamp into the digital recording and made a note.

"… we are going to move next Thursday. There is a big state-wide rally planned then and that will turn into the noble fight for Texas' rightful place as a country. Roadblocks have appeared on major highways. They must confiscate all guns they find. If the gun owners want to join, that's even better. With thousands in the streets, we will take over every federal office and military base in the state."

"You," he turned to Garcia, "must send the Rangers to the border and take over the immigration offices. Close the border at the Rio Grande."

"Rockford," Robert spat the name, "we need more money. Send a million to the church. We will use it for bribes and mercenaries."

"The Feds will not like it. They'll fight." Garcia finally spoke.

"The Feds don't have a clue," Orville laughed. "It's the aliens we need to deal with."

The agent in the RV inserted another time stamp.

CHAPTER 27

In all the infinite galaxies

The white phone on Mary's desk, the direct line to the F.B.I. demanded attention. Mary answered with the speaker and recorder on. She nodded at Daisy, who took a notebook and pen in hand.

"Is this line secure?" The deep male voice asked. Mary raised an eyebrow; Daisy nodded.

"Of course, Director, what's up?"

"Do you remember a mass shooting in El Paso about six weeks ago?"

In the avalanche of disasters in the previous few months, the El Paso incident had been horrific enough to remember.

"Yes, some kid thought he was shooting aliens."

"Noah Lee killed a few human aliens, but no space invaders. We have been on that case and are building a case against a preacher in El Paso. It seems someone blew up his church."

"Good..." Mary fell short on sympathy.

"That's for the local cops to handle. We have an accessory case against the pastor, but a new lead came up. There is another church in Dallas that is more of a danger."

"Dallas... what's that got to do with El Paso?"

"The Dallas bunch is on television, and the Lee kid contacted the pastor, Robert Orville. The guy preaches anti-alien hate, but at least he knows the difference between illegal immigrants and spacemen."

Daisy narrowed her eyes. RoH's rogue enemy had attracted the FBI.

Things are getting complicated.

"Orville has an army in his church. They all act like zombies. Our man on the spot has seen Orville stocking weapons. They are ready to fight for Texas succession, and we need to take them down."

"We have solid evidence that big money backs this Orville character. We were investigating Theodore Rockford III on criminal matters when we discovered the link to the Dallas church. The plot is huge, involving many states, but Texas is the first. Funny, though, Orville thinks that Texas fighting will somehow involve the aliens, and he'll be able to fight them. The guy's a nut."

Not a nut, Daisy thought, *but dangerous to humans.*

"How can the President help?" Mary had not heard of this Orville problem before. Rockford III being involved might complicate the President meeting with the alien on his boat.

"We need a lot of manpower. We need the President to send troops."

"That's illegal. We can't use troops against citizens. What about the Texas national guard?"

"Haven't you been following the news?" The man scoffed. "With Texas close to separating, the guard won't cooperate. They plan to join Orville. This is deeper and more sinister than you can imagine. Every Texas agency is in on the insurrection. Look, send military police and we can swear them in as agents."

"How many...?"

"At least 200..."

Mary gulped. It would take a secret executive order. That would eventually expose President Cortez to a political attack. Mary wavered.

"These are special times," Daisy leapt into the vacuum. "She may not have any option. We could consider this Orville character a terrorist and make it a secret under the Homeland Security Act."

Mary nodded. It was a logical way out. She had become used to Daisy knowing her thoughts.

"When...?" Daisy asked.

Daisy contacted a ship. RoH needed to know about the expanding FBI operation, and the agents would be powerless against Robert's abilities. RoH and her interstellar cousins had hoped to deal with Robert without involving humans, but that seemed to be a fading expectation.

"In a week," the agent thought the voice was Mary.

"The President will want to follow the action, but she will be in a sensitive meeting then. Can you delay it?" Mary had just completed the agenda for meeting the alien woman in Goderich.

"No way, Orville is ready, and it surprised us he hasn't moved yet. There's a big separatist rally scheduled in Dallas. We want to take him down the day before, on Wednesday. Otherwise, it might be too late. He has dreams of leading a free Texas."

"Oh, another thing, their plan is to take over all federal offices, military bases and so on. You need to reinforce them. The ones at the border are important. You should send reinforcements to Fort Bliss at El Paso, and to Brownsville and all other major crossings. All federal employees are in danger."

"I'll get the troops. Send us the full report. Keep me filled in on Rockford." Mary hung up.

"What has Texas separation got to do with our alien problem?" Mary looked at Daisy.

"Orville thinks if he is head of a Texas government, it will draw out star visitors. He wants to kill us."

Mary frowned and lifted the handset on the secure line to the Pentagon.

"Yes, Mary, what do you need?" Colonel Thomas was the White House's man in the Pentagon to advocate for the President's plans.

"Colonel, President Cortez is issuing Eyes Only order to send military police to support the FBI in Dallas next week. It will be under the Homeland Security Act. Also, a detailed order will come later for sending troops to reinforce every base in Texas, especially near the border with Mexico."

"We don't have enough," Colonel Thomas said. "They have furloughed all the troops returning from overseas."

"Find them… bring them back… now."

Daisy had already typed out the order and only needed President Cortez's signature.

"The order is under number 96-245. We need 200 of them on the ground on Wednesday. They should be in civilian clothes, but armed. The details will be in the order."

"I'll send a courier to pick it up." Colonel William Thomas reached for another phone. "I'll have the orders issued right away."

"Use Love Field down there. We don't want any attention. Contact the FBI director for details on that end. We are sending a NAAP member down as well."

"What the hell does this have to do with aliens?"

"I'm not sure," Mary guarded the secret of Robert Orville, "but we think it might attract their attention, so we want an expert on the ground."

"Who…?"

"General Ringwald, we are flying him in from Canada."

"That will create command confusion, and besides, I think he's a traitor."

"He isn't a traitor, Colonel. He's on our side, but the aliens trust him, and he's one of our contacts with them. If aliens get involved in Dallas, we need someone to interact with them. Ringwald is familiar with that. He'll only be there to observe and keep the FBI from shooting aliens."

"I still don't like it."

"Relax, Bill, I should arrange for you to visit NAAP. We are beyond Harry's thinking of fighting the aliens. There must be a way to work with them for everyone's interest. If not…"

Mary had no desire to explain her epiphany regarding the star visitors. She had been the instigator of Harry's old hostile policy and now had invented the new strategy. Others might call her actions capitulation, and if anyone knew she was carrying an alien hybrid baby, she would be a target for death.

"Isn't NAAP where Ringwald got brain washed?"

"No, Bill, he saw the light after the CIA tried to use him. You can blame them, not the aliens."

Mary played the inter-service rivalry card. With the FBI versus the CIA, it was one unpleasant scene, short of shooting. The military disliked them both.

"Saying 'Saw the light' makes you sound like a convert. We have lost everything because of the aliens."

"What did we lose, Bill? What is the purpose of the armed forces and the nukes? It was supposed to protect us from attack. The aliens have fixed it so no one can attack anyone. There are no threats now. I'd say that requires a military re-think."

"I think they are still a threat."

"Colonel, our assessment is that the biggest threat they have made is to withdraw and let us behave as before. They say we will end up destroying ourselves, and they don't want that. The human-alien hybrid mother and daughter are their main reasons. So far, they seem sincere."

"By the way, for your ears only, President Cortez is meeting with Ellie, the alien hybrid mother. We might have a better idea after that. No one is to know about it until we announce it."

"I hope you aren't playing with fire. I have to issue the orders."

"Bill, stop thinking like a soldier and start thinking like a human."

Mary sat beside Daisy.

"Daisy, I trust you, but I know nothing about you. Why do I like you so much? Have you twisted my mind?"

"Mary, I have done nothing to your mind. Your real thoughts are too valuable for us, and humanity. We would learn nothing if we interfered, and you would never build a true and lasting understanding of us. Mental manipulations, quantum tinkering, I call it, decays and at worst, would leave you confused and incapable of doing anything. Our friend, Robert Orville, seems to have done it to his followers. RoH says he spends a lot of time reworking their brains to keep control."

"So, what's your story on Earth?"

"I was involved in the clean-up after the fiasco in 1947. The crash of the ship was a disaster for us. It has caused the loss of three of us and severely hurt a fourth. It took several decades to recover all the artefacts and two bodies. Earth had a low priority in our galactic work. Just recently, our child, RoH, rescued the injured one and recovered the third body."

Daisy suddenly looked agitated.

"What's wrong?" Mary held Daisy's hand.

"They treated the survivor cruelly and dismembered the body. The air force had hidden them both at Groom Lake. Not even NAAP knew. Until RoH discovered them, we did not know. We thought we had recovered everything we could decades ago. Ellie will reveal that to Emalia Cortez. Humans are lucky that we aren't vengeful."

"You were part of that earlier recovery?"

"Yes, but our plans changed in 1947. We understood humans better. We contrived to have Ellie born and later give birth to RoH. Since then, they are teaching us and have advanced things more than we predicted. Ellie and RoH give us skin in the game, as you Americans love to say. That makes Earth and humans more important than any other we discovered."

"We established surface operations, with some of us assuming Earth identities. I infiltrated the CIA while others focused on various things like NAAP. That began when we took Ellie at the insistence of her great grandfather. He had insight the collective lacked."

"His genetic line that has resulted in Ellie and now RoH is not based on some careless lust when he crashed. He had some understanding of what it might mean, and he loved the woman who saved him. Believe me... I know a bit about human lust."

Daisy patted her belly, but it still refused to betray the pregnancy.

"I can't believe that you people are anatomically similar to humans."

"My actual form would repel most humans right now. With time, that revulsion would go away, but humans focus on superficial differences. That's the basis for much of your bigotry and racism. We are warm-blooded, bi-pedal and bilaterally symmetrical, like technology developing species everywhere. Our anatomy is like humans, including sex organs. It seems to be a consequence of our common DNA that we have found everywhere in the galaxy. Even those sentient species that killed themselves off had that genetic and parallel physical structure. We postulate a common origin, probably in some long-lost planetary system that destructed billions of years ago. There is a possibility that it originated in another, older galaxy, but we have no data either way. It could easily be just a result of the laws of physics, which are universal."

"All life is valuable no matter where it exists. It might be the same in the entire galaxy, perhaps in all the galaxies."

"How many of you in disguise live on Earth?" Mary had a twinge of fear.

"Don't be afraid, Mary. None of us wants to hurt anyone. Including recent deployments, about two dozen are here full time. Some come and go as needed."

"How do you feel about Earth and humans?"

"Earth has been a popular assignment amongst us for about a century and for another inter-stellar species for thousands of years before we came. It is one of only a few thousand similar planets in this part of the galaxy. A few million planets support life, but the Earth-like ones are special. We don't admit to feeling joy, but just being here on the surface brings pleasure. It was that way before Ellie and her great-grandfather taught us about what there is to love here."

"Our RoH thinks this is a playground and brings mischievousness to that joy. Our star fleet in the solar system has coined a slang expression for the merriment that RoH brings. Her mother, Ellie, calls it 'the RoH show'. Amongst the stars, she is so young that she seems unimportant, but here on Earth she is formidable. When she is serious, doing some serious task, her understanding of both humans and star travellers makes her the most effective of us as individuals. We would struggle to surpass her. I probably can't, and on Earth, no human can hope to oppose her. Again, pride is another emotion we do not have, but we feel a deep privilege to be working with her."

"You will be happy to know she loves humans. RoH does not see any human that does not have worth. She is the best thing that could happen, both on Earth and in the stars."

"How do the rest of you star travellers feel about humans?"

"We are learning," Daisy hesitated. "We made lots of mistakes that hurt and even killed some humans. Ellie and RoH feel remorse. In the cold calculations of our community, we classify it as a null experimental result. Changing that thinking is why we need more RoHs in the galaxy. Earth can supply them and now with less suffering than Ellie and her parents experienced… if you humans survive."

Daisy squeezed Mary's hand. "We hope that little Nathan in your tummy will be one, or at least an Ellie."

"Why have you been dealing with the USA and not the other powerful countries?"

"Why do you think we aren't? You have separated yourselves from other species on Earth and divided humans into many tribes. From the perspective of the stars, you are one tribe. In the universe's perspective, we are all; humans, every other species confined to planets and all species of star travellers in this galaxy, one tribe. Sometime soon, at least soon in star travelling time, we may find out if all life is but one tribe on all planets in all the infinite galaxies."

CHAPTER 28

The painted darkness

Johnny Bray startled awake from a deep sleep. What he assumed to be a dream seemed deeper. He threw off the covers that kept him as warm as when sleeping on his summer cot in Alice. He fought to control his trembling.

Crikey, drongo, get a grip.

The bedside clock glowed 4 AM. The London Ontario summer sky had just lightened to the east. Steven and Ellie's house remained quiet.

Something brushed Johnny's mind.

What...?

The fleeting feeling did not return, but it had seemed to be the darkness Johnny painted, evil, threatening, the feared Yowie.

This awakening marked another, deeper awakening in the old man from the Jannali. Johnny had felt his difference. After his interaction with Ellie at the coffee shop, he knew he had some ability deep inside, but at this instant, he felt power, an alien essence, and his mind sought.

Suddenly, Johnny felt many minds talking, but not to him. He reached out, probing the darkness.

Johnny, Ellie's thoughts came louder than the rest. She had been asleep in the next room. *We will talk about this in the morning. Robert Orville was dreaming, and he projected. Try not to focus outside your head. He might feel you. I'll teach you the trick to shield your mind tomorrow.*

Johnny closed his eyes. Ellie, like her daughter RoH, could soothe. Johnny returned to sleep, but his mind remained filed with turmoil, a light show of brilliance and shadow. The thoughts were disquieting, and Johnny lived Robert Orville's story.

Thousands of kilometres away, in Dallas, Texas, Robert Orville dreamed. It was a deep dream and nothing registered on his consciousness. The dreams echoed Robert's anger, frustration and hate, but they also projected a profound loneliness. In his awakened state, Robert felt he had always been alone, as if he floated high above, detached, and watched his life unfold. He had no friends, only useful tools or associates. To make a friend would mean giving up control and nothing scared Robert more than not being in control.

It had come at an early age. Robert sometimes thought he had always feared vulnerability. He had surrounded his emotions with high walls of anger and hate, and he had allowed no one to pass. In his unconscious sleep, Robert radiated his anguish. At these times, the fortifications crumbled, and his underlying need for companionship escaped his guard. The images were always of conflict between his longing and his fear. The dreams were violent and horrible, a story that no movie producer could make without going mad. Such were the things that flew from Robert's mind to Johnny.

Johnny writhed on his bed. He woke with the sun in his face and the bedclothes twisted into knots, soaked. Johnny had never sweated as much in the scorching outback summer. His hand shook as he tried to dress. He could not remember the dreams, but he felt the horror.

"Johnny, you look like crap," Steve Jorgensen helped Johnny into a kitchen chair and hurried to place a coffee in front of him.

"What the hell happened?" Steve ignored his toast.

"You dreamed more, didn't you, Johnny?" Ellie touched the old man on the shoulder. The trembling stopped. Ellie frowned, and a tear formed.

"I can see the horror." Ellie said.

"What the hell happened?" Johnny sipped coffee and grasped the mug in steady hands.

"Just now, I calmed you, but last night, somehow your mind and Robert Orville joined, or at least talked. So far, no one on the ships can discover if that ever happened before. RoH and I are in touch like that almost constantly, but we shield to keep from driving each other crazy. My mother and I have a link. It seems your mind opened to Robert's thoughts, or probably dreams. I don't know why."

"I do," Johnny said. "Robert and I are brothers."

"That's a puzzle, since you both had different mothers and fathers. RoH pulled Robert's father from a vat at Groom Lake."

"I don't mean actual brothers," Johnny frowned, "but we are of the same generation, the first hybrid bunch. I think that somehow links us."

"Yes, there was a pair like that on the record," Ellie said, "in Alaska. They were twins and had a deep connection where they just knew what the other was thinking. One experienced a horrible death. The other went mad when the scared locals murdered his brother, and then they murdered him. Last night might be a danger signal. RoH has to deal with Robert in a few days. He might die."

"no… he can't…" Johnny trembled.

Ellie sat and stared at Johnny. She became detached in a condition that Steve had seen several times. Ellie was in deep discussion with the linked alien minds that populated the solar system.

Mother…?

Yes, RoH…?

We must keep Robert alive, for Johnny's sake.

We all agree, dear, but how? He seems so lost. When you confront him, he may kill himself.

Johnny… RoH's thought came immediately. *Johnny can keep him alive.*

I think I can. Johnny's thought came through clearly.

"Your mind turned on," Ellie said aloud.

"I think that's what happened last night. I felt it before, with you at the café, remember? Robert did nothing special, but my mind woke up. I suddenly knew what you and RoH were thinking just now. I always felt pre-sentient, as if I knew what people would say. Now I know why."

It can be scary and dangerous. RoH's thought came.

"Crikey," Johnny exclaimed, "last night could make a bloke suicidal."

Why are you tuned to Robert? RoH wondered.

Johnny paused, his mind racing into deep places.

I think it's because Robert and I have a deep connection, brothers. Don't ask me why. I think we are supposed to come together sometime, somehow.

The image of Johnny's extended family, the photograph on his studio wall, flashed before him and thus into Ellie and RoH's consciousness.

"I had all that… have all that," Johnny said aloud, "but Robert has had none. He has wallowed in profound loneliness and longing all his life. I need to heal that, to show him the possibility. Someone needs to give him that companionship."

"Is it you?" Ellie asked.

"I need to show him what could be," Johnny said, "but I'm not sure we can be mates. It might be too late for that."

He looked into Ellie's eyes.

"He needs a soul mate, a dinkum cobber, someone to love. I have a strange feeling, at least a hope that there is another who will do that. Robert has a deep pit of darkness in his heart. Someone who survived the loneliness and resentment that owns Robert needs to massage that heart, someone who understands. I was too happy despite it all. I might get him to go through the door, but another needs to be there for him on the other side."

For a moment, RoH and Ellie saw an old Australian aboriginal elder contemplating beneath the shade of a gum tree. His hand extended as if greeting an invisible soul as Johnny conceived a new painting.

Who is that special someone? RoH, Ellie, and Johnny united in the question.

Mother…?

Yes, RoH…?

I think we can save Robert. I think Johnny can save him.

Perhaps, Ellie pondered. Mother and daughter had separated themselves so that no one could overhear.

Mother, I know Robert took his best shot at me in Pastor George's church. The congregation saw a monstrous dog, but Robert could not touch my mind. I only saw George making a suicidal leap at me from his pulpit. Robert would have killed him, but I suspended George and let him fall gently. Robert retreated. He knows now that I am more powerful.

He was not ready for you, my sweet. What would he do if he expected you?

I hope to have a distraction.

Johnny…?

Johnny…

That day, Johnny began a new painting. He covered the canvas in dark, swirling confusion, full of danger. It was the first angry image he had created since arriving in Canada.

CHAPTER 29

Head to them thar hills

"Get out of the truck, sonny," the burly Texas Ranger fingered the gun handle in his open holster.

"What's the problem, Ranger?"

The driver of the rusted out F-150 did not move, but his hand slipped down to touch the butt of the 45 Chiappa revolver beside him on the seat. His leg hid the weapon from the cop, but the trained man noticed the slight movement. He reached for his sidearm.

The cowboy had practiced a front seat quick draw, and his weapon pointed at the Ranger whose gun had only cleared the holster.

"Y'all want to put that gun away, cop?"

As famous last words, those of the cowboy were not remarkable. Six slugs from a LaRue assault rifle, held by the Ranger's backup, shattered the windshield of the F-150. Only one missed.

The Texas Ranger ran to his car and called for reinforcements. The six Rangers on this roadblock on Interstate 10 west of Van Horn, Texas, waited to check a long line of vehicles. So far, they had confiscated three dozen weapons for the separatist arsenal; the dead cowboy contributed another and a hundred cartridges. Ten new recruits had gone into town to register, and the rest passed without their guns. This had been the first shooting. Most Texans supported the independence effort, even if they resented surrendering their weapons. Many had more at home, anyway.

Lila sat behind the wheel of her pert SUV and fumed. She and Sam headed along Interstate 10 to Dallas, but traffic had jerked to a halt about three kilometres west of Van Horn. This Tuesday would give them a night in a motel and Wednesday, Sam planned to confront Pastor Orville. Sam's pistol hid beneath the front seat. Their left lane moved faster than the right. Big rigs jammed the right lane as they waited to go through the weigh station. The westbound side of the Interstate had little traffic.

"What the hell is going on?" Lila did not expect Sam to answer. "There must be a terrible accident," she answered herself.

"Can't tell," Sam muttered.

Lila tapped the LED display and switched the radio from Texas twang music to the satellite news. The car flashed its location to the space-based network, and the source focused on west Texas news. With her paid service, Lila did not have to endure the usual five minutes of advertisements for guns, beer and pickup trucks. Fortunately, the news via New York did not filter out anything, but repeated feed from local sources, with the usual bias for the exciting and tragic.

"We have increasing reports of road blocks in Texas," the smooth announcer said. "Civilian insurrectionists have blocked roads and take weapons from travellers. Apparently, although we cannot confirm, the Texas Rangers are doing the same thing on highways, including the interstates. We received a report, also unofficial, that the Rangers have shot and killed one person at a checkpoint on Interstate 10 west of Van Horn, Texas."

"Damn it," Lila exclaimed, "that's probably what's up ahead."

"They'll take my gun," Sam frowned.

A Texas Ranger patrol car sped east on the westbound side with its siren blaring. A shiver went down Lila's back. As a kid living in a tougher neighbourhood, she had developed a danger detector. It sounded at full volume. She glanced into the median ditch, guarded by an insurmountable steel barrier that would defeat her SUV.

She looked at Sam.

"We need to get off this road. I think we should get back to El Paso and go to Plan B."

"There's a Plan B," Sam asked.

"There soon will be," Lila laughed, despite the feeling of doom.

"How...?"

The line moved forward. Just beyond the next vehicle, Lila saw a service crossover from the east to westbound lanes. It created a gap in the barrier. She gently eased towards the paved left highway shoulder.

Take it easy, she thought. *We don't want to get the guy behind us mad.*

The line lurched forward.

Just a bit more ...

The line moved. Lila turned the wheel.

A Texas Ranger car appeared westbound, crawling.

Damn...

"That guy is counting the cars along here," Lila tried to breathe. "I hope he gets a move on."

The line moved again, but Lila held her ground. The Ranger needed to be out of sight.

Just a little time...

A horn blared from behind as if a few meters of ground meant something. The cop car topped a slight ridge and disappeared to the west. Lila jerked the wheel and sped across the median onto the westbound. There was no traffic to stop her as she zipped into the entrance of a scenic lookout park.

"We need to let that guy get well ahead of us. I'm guessing he'll pull a U-turn at the end of the line and come back the wrong way."

"So, Plan B..." Sam wondered.

"Y'all hold your horses, lover. Let me think."

Lila leaned over and kissed Sam on the mouth. They lingered, but the scream of a siren from a Ranger patrol car disturbed their moment of diversion. The cop flew the wrong way past on 10 but then made a hard braking turn and shot onto the ramp to the parking area.

"Damn..." Lila seemed to have adopted the word, "just what we need."

The patrol car eased to a stop behind Lila's SUV. A lone Texas Ranger got out and approached.

"I'd like y'all to get out of the car," the Ranger did not sound hostile, but he left no doubt he had given an order.

"Where y'all headed?"

The man pushed middle-aged but seemed to be in good shape. He looked more like Cowboy Slim than Sherriff Bull.

"El Paso," Lila smiled. "Is there something wrong, officer?"

"Where y'all coming from?" He ignored Lila's question.

"Dallas," Lila neatly reversed their morning's intentions.

"So you came through the check down there," he nodded towards Van Horn.

"Seems so," Lola said.

"I don't think so," the Ranger stared at Lila.

"Y'all got nothing better to do than bother innocent folks?" Sam interrupted.

"Watch your mouth, kid." The Ranger suddenly tensed. "What's your story?"

He stepped towards Sam. Lila frowned and moved aside.

"Just enjoying the desert morning," Sam smirked, "at least was."

The Ranger took a quick step, grabbed Sam by the neck and slammed him against the SUV. Being a good macho Texan, he discounted the woman as a threat.

"I think y'all up to no good," he hissed and reached for his zip tie restraint.

Lila's blow hit the Ranger in just the right spot. He crumpled into a pile on the asphalt.

"Why the hell did y'all have to rile him?" Lila spit. "Now, we have a problem."

"He didn't buy your story. Where the hell did y'all learn to hit like that?"

"Martial arts, state finalist, and a tough neighbourhood," Lila said. "We learned the difference between the killing spot and the just 'knock y'all out' place. Of course, we weren't supposed to hit at all. But we learned how… just like the Navy Seals."

Lila completed the sleeping Ranger's reach for the zip tie and bound the man's wrists securely behind him.

"Another surprise… y'all knowing how to tie him like that? Where would y'all learn that? Are y'all a cop?"

"Remember, my bedroom… Bo-Bob like to play games. I'd tie him up a lot, at least before he lost interest. Y'all blew my house up before I could do it to you." Lila laughed.

"Help me get Wyatt Earp into the back of the cruiser."

"That was Arizona," Sam quipped as they struggled to deposit the man into the back of the car.

They drove the patrol car into a pit area just off the exit road to the overlook and wound down all the windows so the unconscious man would not cook. People could see the car from the highway if they looked.

"I hope they don't find him for a few hours," Lila slid behind the wheel of her SUV. "It's over an hour back to El Paso. I think I have a new plan."

She sped onto the main road and back towards the city. The eastbound line-up had extended another kilometre.

"If he called in your plate, they'll be looking for us."

"I'm more worried about another checkpoint this side of El Paso."

Fifteen kilometres up the road, Lila exited to Sierra Blanca.

"There's a good road that takes us up to State 62," Lila maneuvered through the light downtown traffic. "It's good because 62 will take us where I want to go."

"Through those hills…?" Sam was sceptical.

"Yahoo, we're heading for them thar hills, away from the law," Lila laughed, "but then, to the El Paso airport."

Lila found her friend in the maintenance hangar of Royal Air Services. Ross owned the company but took pride in being hands-on. Any of his hundreds of employees could expect him to show up unannounced. He did not micro-manage and made no one feel as if he did not trust them. In his 60 years, he had learned how to build loyalty.

"Hi Ross," Lila hugged him, "How are y'all?"

"As if you care," Ross frowned. "When's the last time we got together?"

"I've been busy," Lila laughed. "Someone blew up my house."

"So I heard," Ross frowned, and noticed Sam. "Is this your new guy?"

Ross seemed resentful. Sam guessed at the story of Lila and Ross.

"This is my sister's oldest," Lila squeezed Sam's hand. Her ability to spin a convincing lie on the spot amazed him.

"We need a favour," Lila hugged Ross again and kissed his ear. "Sam here has to be in Dallas tomorrow morning to register at school, but crazies have blocked the roads."

"Likely story," Ross frowned again, "commercial can get you there."

"I'm trying to avoid them," Lila winked.

"It's expensive," Ross laughed. "Unless…"

"For sure," Lila giggled, "… soon."

"I tell you what," Ross brightened. "I need to test fly this baby," he pointed to a trim Lear jet with an engine cowling off, "I can run you over to Love Field as a test… early, about seven tomorrow morning."

"Deal," Lila hugged Ross. "Bo-Bob is out of town next week. I'll call y'all."

"Have y'all zip-tied good old Ross?" Sam sounded annoyed even though he knew his relationship with Lila had no future.

I'll likely be dead tomorrow anyway…

"I never kiss and tell." Lila leaned over and kissed Sam. "Let's give Bo-Bob's credit a workout at the Hilton."

CHAPTER 30

Those magnificent women in their flying machines

President Cortez, Mary, and Daisy slipped out of the White House service entrance. A parade of delivery vehicles screened their comfortable Secret Service SUV on Pennsylvania Avenue. The pool reporter did not watch the back entrance and missed the departure. They noticed Vice-President Hilfreich arriving at the front entrance at the unusual time of six in the morning. Everyone in the president's political staff believed Cortez might go into harm's way, and the VP needed to be available. As Siglinde2 entered her office in the White House, Air Force One departed Joint Base Andrews.

"How are we going to handle this?" Emalia asked. An awakening Virginia passed below as the plane turned to the north-west.

"I think the question is, 'How will Ellie handle this?'" Mary opened a file. "The aliens may see this as a simple courtesy, although I doubt they would bother considering our behaviour since New Year's Eve. I think they want you to do something."

Daisy said nothing. The situation was more of a hope and less of a plan for the star people. Convincing Cortez that she was powerless would be easy. Encouraging her to take the political risk and advocate the correct path would depend totally on the courage of Emalia Cortez.

The Russians, Chinese and the Europeans presented a more difficult problem. They believed that they still had power. It would take more than

Ellie to change them. All had a history of direct, violent repression to keep that power, and that would likely be their first response. Daisy felt sorry for the star people on those assignments.

Collapse of the powerful countries would create the turmoil for change. It saddened the star visitors that the change would not be peaceful, but at least there were no nuclear weapons. Intervention would be pointless and probably make things worse. The galaxy did not need or want colonial subservience.

The USA would certainly fragment quickly. Star travellers hoped President Cortez could influence foreign governments before the internal collapse. The American federal response to a violent insurrection at home would be the same as the others if she did not lead to another path. In the end, if nothing changed, Russia and China would follow the USA into disintegration. Given the speed of climate collapse, the Earth might not have two years. Most humans would die within a decade. Daisy and the others had seen the tears from Ellie and RoH over that probability. Their empathy influenced the fleet.

Immediately, Texas was a problem. It would be the inspiration for more uprisings and the aliens had no interest in choosing winners. The only priority was to keep Robert Orville from becoming a leader with alien abilities that might cause bigger problems. The visitors had to deal with Robert. Long ago, alien bumbling had created him and his hatred. They must isolate Orville or kill him.

"Let's go," Lila tapped her credit card for the waiter and stood. Sam followed her from the Hilton coffee shop and into the El Paso morning. He loved the cool quiet of the morning in south-west Texas, but today his agitation ruined it. He feared how the day might turn out. Sam wondered if Noah Lee had had self-doubt before he murdered Mandy and the others. The thought of Mandy's death stiffened Sam's resolve for revenge.

The Lear jet lifted off at El Paso about the same time Air Force One touched down at Selfridge in Michigan.

"Why are y'all really going to Dallas?" Ross looked at Lila in the co-pilot's seat. "The news claims there's going to be a coup, starting in Dallas, to take Texas to freedom. Are y'all part of that?"

Ross glanced back at Sam, who had sunk into a luxurious seat. He clutched the bag that hid his gun.

"Would y'all be upset if we were?" Lila touched Ross' hand.

"A bit," Ross scowled. "I have a good business here, been down a bit since the aliens kiboshed the weapons, but still good. Texas separating would likely put me out of business. No, I would not like it, if y'all were into that."

"Don't worry, Ross. We are doing the opposite, at least a little thing. Sam has a personal vendetta to settle. It involves a potential separatist troublemaker. Y'all wouldn't be able to fly us out of Dallas in a day or two, would you?"

Ross looked at Lila. "For y'all, sweetie, I could arrange it, if no one blows up the airport. Y'all wouldn't even have to hop into bed with me for it if y'all can stop the succession. Otherwise, I'll be hiding in Mexico. Most of my money is already there."

"I'll call if we need y'all," Lila looked down at the rough Texas landscape. Ironically, they passed just south of Lubbock where the alien project had accidentally begun in 1947.

Sam and I might not be around to need a ride. Lila shivered.

General Daniel Ringwald stared from the passenger terminal at Love Field. He had arrived in Dallas at sunrise, flown in from Goderich at the request of President Cortez on a Canadian air force executive jet. He watched over his breakfast as he waited for the FBI to meet him. A group of people crowded into the lounge just outside the café door. They all wore casual black windbreakers and matching ball caps set squarely and precisely on each head.

Military, he thought, *but not in uniform.*

The FBI finally arrived. The lead-agent escorted Danny to a waiting car, but the military mob ended up at a line of five coaches idling outside the terminal entrance. A sergeant in civilian clothes who Danny slightly knew from a posting in Africa oversaw the loading of the buses. Large, heavy duffle bags ended up in the bus baggage holds.

Weapons... Danny knew the look.

"General Ringwald, the President specifically ordered you to be here." The agent shared the rear seat with Danny. "Why?"

"Washington thinks there's an inter-stellar alien connection to Robert Orville. I'm only here to advise if that turns out to be true. You might say I'm an expert. Actually, I am sure there will be alien involvement today."

"Why…?"

"The aliens told me," Danny smiled. The agent nodded. In the past six months, everyone knew that aliens existed, and that some lived on Earth. He also knew about General Ringwald and the NAAP. He thoughtfully eyed Danny.

"So, did they tell you what would happen?"

"Nope, we are both winging it," Danny smiled at the agent. "I would suggest that if, I think it's really when the aliens show up, we just wait and see what happens. I can tell you they do not want shooting."

"We're ready to shoot if necessary," the agent scowled.

"So I noticed with that gang of grunts that got on the busses. How many people will you have?"

"About 400…"

"And ready to kill…," Danny muttered.

"Ready to kill…"

"Can you wait for my order on that?"

"My orders are to neutralize this Orville guy by any means needed. They also ordered me that, if aliens show up, you are in charge. Are you going to talk to the aliens?"

"My job is more to explain them to you. Tactical decisions will be yours. I think we are going to be surprised."

The small convoy edged through a gathering mob in the downtown. So far, the separatists had not blocked the streets. The handguns in open holsters worried Danny and the FBI.

"It might get bigger than anyone thinks," Danny said.

"400 might not be enough." The agent patted his shoulder holster. "We might have to fight our way out. These folks don't like the feds."

"You will need more than pistols," Danny frowned at a few open-carry AR-15s wandering along the sidewalk.

General Ringwald and the FBI had just left Love Field when Ross gently set the Lear onto the runway. He taxied to a commercial hangar near the outside road. Lila and Sam joined him in the office.

"This is where I leave y'all," Ross hugged Lila. "I'll be waiting for your call."

"You'll get it, sweetie." Lila kissed him on the cheek. Sam looked away and busied himself with a map on his cell. Five miles separated them from The Church of Heavenly Enlightenment.

"We need a ride," Sam watched Ross hurry out the door.

Ross had a feeling there would be big happenings and wanted to be on home ground to get his family to safety. That old army Buffalo transport sat ready and loaded in the hangar. It could easily handle the dirt strip at Cerro Blanco, where his rich Mexican friend would keep them safe. He hoped Lila, and maybe the kid, would be alive at the end.

"I'll call for a pickup," Lila glanced outside as the Lear rolled towards the taxiway. "Let's get to the street."

The ride service sent a self-driving vehicle. Lila gave the car the address of the Church of Heavenly Enlightenment.

"There is a problem downtown." The car had an alluring female Texas drawl tailored for tourists. "I'll have to take y'all around the long way. It is a higher fee. I have to drop y'all a block from that address."

A number flashed on the view pad in the back.

"Do it," Lila said, tapped her credit card, and the AI engaged.

"The customer has agreed to the offered fare and route," the car said.

President Cortez's helicopter left Selfridge base heading to Port Huron as Ellie and Johnny piled into Steve's little car. The Mounties followed them out of town and north to Goderich. At the farm near Goderich, the Canadian force stood ready.

"Let's go…" Captain Fontaine had assembled her squad in front of the farmhouse. They piled into the three waiting SUVs that were on forced loan from the CIA. Their owners languished in detention as the Canadian and American governments exchanged diplomatic insults.

RoH watched the force disappear up the dusty road. The usual small bunch of gawkers at the gate, "UFO nuts" as Ghislaine called them, made way. Fontaine had left one of her force on guard cradling a mean-looking assault rifle so that the people would not decide to do something silly. RoH had gone to chat with the curious crowd many times; they were simply more dandelions to be nurtured. The farm's alien babysitters, Elsie and Jake thought the people at the gate a non-threat and served treats to them. RoH had nothing to do until Johnny arrived.

Steve maneuvered the car into the drive-through of a Goderich doughnut shop. They had some time before President Cortez's boat arrived.

"Do you see that car behind us?" Steve asked the window clerk. "Here's another twenty to cover whatever they want. They're with us."

Steve eased forward and the two Mounties on their tail received free coffee and donuts.

"Crikey, I'm liking this Canadian tucker." Johnny sipped a sweet tea and eagerly munched a blueberry fritter. He had become so used to dealing with tourists back home in Alice Springs that he thought in an Australian dialect. Steve, the linguist, found it fascinating, and he encouraged Johnny to use slang. He thought it lent enthusiasm to everyday speech.

"No use rushing." Ellie looked back at the cop car. "The president won't arrive for a bit."

President Cortez shared a billionaire's snack, what ordinary folks might call luxurious, with Mary and Daisy. A steward in a crisp white uniform hovered nearby. The Secret Service agents lounged on the after-deck and enjoyed similar treats on paper plates. The boat had long cleared the entrance to the St. Clair River and would soon be at Goderich. At high speed, the craft had a slight lift and an annoying vibration.

When the Presidential boat throttled back along the Goderich harbour mole, the effect resembled floating on a cloud. The presidential party gathered on the aft-deck as the luxury yacht swung around opposite the grain terminal and eased into the wharf. The escorting Coast Guard boats formed a protective ring. One moored past the bow and another stern of the yacht while two more hove-to on the harbour side. Workers at the grain elevators gathered on the far wharf to watch the parade of Yankee flags.

Captain Fontaine's honour guard, in battle dress with loaded weapons, formed a smart line on the road. A small electric car slide down from North Harbour Road. The trailing Mounties joined people at the boat launch who stared down the wharf.

Despite its size, the boat's deck barely rose above the edge of the wharf. A small gangway extended and several Secret Service agents deployed alongside, eyeing the Canadian troops. A steward hurried down the gangway and planted an American flag to one side and the Presidential Banner on the other. Ellie emerged from the car and frowned at the bunting.

"Darling," Ellie stooped to the open driver's window, "drive Johnny to the farm. He has to go with RoH. Jake and Elsie make a tasty breakfast. You can practice your alien, and RoH wants to hug her step-daddy."

"What are you doing with the President?"

"We are going for a boat ride, or more realistically, a flying boat ride." Ellie giggled.

RoH, you're a bad influence on me.

Sorry, Mommy... you have fun.

This is serious work, girl.

Then be sure you make her laugh.

Ellie kissed Steve and turned towards the boat as Mary, Daisy, and President Cortez descended.

As the President stepped onto Canadian soil, Fontaine barked an order and her squad snapped to attention and saluted with rifles. Cortez, from habit, saluted back.

"That's for you," Ellie said. "We don't demand that kind of honour."

President Cortez offered a perfunctory handshake. Ellie responded with more sincerity.

"Okay, young lady, what's your alien aim?"

Ellie walked past the president towards the gangway. Both of the banners flanking the ramp flew sideways to languish on the asphalt. Cortez suddenly felt awkward and saw no option but to follow her guest. Ellie stepped onto the boat with the President behind.

"Mary," Daisy said, "you have to be with the President, but I must stay on the wharf. Don't worry," Daisy reacted to Mary's concerned look. "I'll be going back to Washington with you. No matter what happens, you will be safe. No one is getting hurt today. You and I have a special connection." Daisy patted Mary's slightly bulging stomach. Mary hurried up the gangway.

Daisy went to Captain Fontaine.

"We haven't met, but I'm here to protect you."

"We thought we were protecting everyone else."

"I'm only making sure no one accidentally gets hurt. We want to keep those guns as decorations. Please have everyone stand away from the boat, over there by the railway cars."

Ellie crossed the narrow deck and into the luxury lounge. She found a spot on a comfortable couch. Cortez sat at the farthest end and leaned away from Ellie. Mary stood, uncertain of what protocol might dictate. It said she should be near the President, but something made her want to be nearer Ellie. Cortez hated the unknown, and the woman staring at her exuded mysterious confidence.

"What makes aliens think you can just do what you want on Earth? Do you think you can overpower the USA so easily?"

Emalia abruptly felt as if she sat in a slowly rising elevator. She looked out the panoramic window and watched the grain elevators on the far side of the harbour fall away. A warning bell rang loudly from the bridge and feet pounded the deck. Someone tried the door from the outside, but it had locked. Terrified screams came from all directions. The captain revved the engines, trying to save his ship.

As the yacht rose from the surface of the harbour, lines stretched and snapped. A cleat tore away from the boat. The sound mimicked shooting and the US coast Guard crews streamed ashore with rifles and handguns ready. The Secret Service agents on the shore drew weapons. An enemy did not appear, so they turned their anger towards Ghislaine's force. As they levelled their weapons, Captain Fontaine gave a battle signal.

"Hold fire," she barked. The rules of engagement held her troop ready for either her command or a shot from the supposed enemy. Half of the Canadian force took cover beneath rail cars, rifles ready and on automatic. The rest spread out in a wide arc, weapons at the shoulder and sights on the target, safeties off. The Americans raised weapons.

Daisy ran between the forces.

"Stop," she cried out, "there is no fight here."

The presidential yacht hovered a kilometre above. Its engines finally gave up turning the screws and made a loud backfire. This caught the attention of everyone but the Canadian troops, who kept their eyes and their guns firmly on the threat.

Cortez contemplated Ellie.

"Point taken..."

"We won't harm anyone," Ellie said, "my daughter and I ensure that, but there never had been a plan by star travellers to do more than observe Earth. My existence and RoH's has added a new desire to have humans succeed. You won't do it by killing each other or trying to kill us."

CHAPTER 3l

Healing hearts

"Daddy," RoH squealed and ran to hug Steve Jorgensen as he climbed from his car.

"Don't make fun of me, kid," Steve laughed, "although I would be proud to be your father."

RoH let go and watched Johnny round the back of the car.

"I brought your sidekick," Steve claimed another hug.

"I'm more like Johnny's sidekick," RoH said. "Johnny, I think you are the key if we're to have a good outcome today."

"We either save Robert, or I have to kill him." RoH's eyes watered.

Steve contemplated the little girl who seemed so far beyond everyone. He could not reconcile the RoH he knew with a killer.

"Can you…?" Steve asked.

"Robert is a menace," RoH looked thoughtful, "but none of this is his fault. We star people are responsible. Death could be a sad necessity, but I will do all I can to save him. Johnny might have the key to the darkness in Robert's soul."

Steve hugged her once more. She looked as self-possessed and yet also as uncertain as her mother had been in the Dakota captivity so long ago.

"Johnny and I must go," RoH pulled away and took Johnny's hand. "Johnny, let me show you my flying machine."

Almost instantly, a purple light descended and engulfed RoH and Johnny.

"Steve, do you want some breakfast?" Elsie called from the front porch.

"What do y'all intend to do?" Lila asked.

The robotic car had dropped them a block up a side street from the tree-lined boulevard that ran past the Church of Heavenly Enlightenment. They had now turned towards the church. Lila did not like the bulge beneath Sam's windbreaker. Texas allowed open carry of any gun, but Sam hid his. Open carry gave the opposition too much information.

"My plan is to wing it," Sam said. "I'm not sure I want to kill the guy, wound him in the knee or just yell at him and leave. This is just for options." Sam patted the bulge.

They did not hold hands as lovers might in their last desperate hours. Lila had smitten Sam, but he knew they only had a temporary arrangement. Lila's maturity and self-certainty attracted and held him as much as their physical adventures.

If only I knew someone my age, like Lila.

"I don't want y'all to come in with me. I don't want y'all hurt."

"No way y'all are dumping me at the altar," Lila laughed. "Y'all would have to tie me down. I want to keep y'all safe."

Sam had imagined no one there but him and Orville. The complication almost made him leave. Then, he thought of Mandy. They reached the taco and ice cream trucks.

"I'll buy second breakfast," Lila approached the taco van. Only in Texas would anyone consider a taco to be breakfast.

The meal allowed Sam to look over the church. The lack of activity reassured him. He hoped the door was open.

They found the front doors locked, but the side door nearest the offices swung free. The secretary always left it unlocked for Pastor Orville.

Danny Ringwald and the FBI commander watched the strangers enter the church.

"Who the hell are they?" Danny wondered aloud.

The FBI man sent a ready command, just in case.

"Orville usually shows up about lunchtime." The FBI incident commander said. "So far, general, there is only the secretary and those two strangers inside."

"Who are y'all?" The secretary felt a twinge of fear, but a well-dressed, middle-aged woman calmed her. Maybe they wanted to join.

"We are not accepting any new members," she said.

"We are here to see Orville," Sam spat. "Where is he?"

"Pastor will be here soon," she managed a reply. "I'll make an appointment, and if he will see y'all, I'll call."

Sam pulled the gun.

"We are here and not leaving. Where is he?"

The secretary glanced at the door to the pastor's study, wondering if she could hide there. Sam took it the wrong way.

"In there," he waved the gun at the woman. "We'll wait in there."

"Get the ice cream guy out of there. We are moving soon." The FBI commander's call went to the taco truck.

"Hey, y'all," the taco server sauntered to the ice cream window, "there might be some bad doings here. Y'all should leave."

"Why is that?"

"That pair that just went in is up to no good."

"They seemed nice enough. Business is slow, and I hoped they'd buy on the way out."

The ice cream alien knew only what the cops did. He thought the pair's arrival might be a coincidence. They gave off some negative thoughts, fear he thought, but nothing concrete and he did not think it worthwhile to report. The FBI's concern changed that.

RoH, get here soon. The FBI is about to move.

"Y'all know I'll be safe," he stared at the taco vendor.

"I guess y'all will be okay," the man walked away.

Robert Orville had passed a police roadblock two streets down, but thought nothing of it. He felt a growing disquiet as he approached his church, a general fear that came from the building. He slowed and surveyed.

The taco and ice cream trucks were still in place. He did not sense the FBI operation hidden behind the trees. Robert turned and hurried into the church. The ice cream vendor followed him in his mind. He had discovered how to use Robert's senses without Orville knowing. The past weeks had been uneventful. Now, something was up.

The fear came from his office. Robert sensed three humans there, his secretary and two strangers. All were afraid. Robert pushed the door open.

Sam had been watching the door from the pastor's chair behind the desk. Lila sat against the far wall and the secretary trembled near the door where Sam could see her and the entrance. The opening door hid the woman from Orville.

"Who are you?" Orville growled.

"Come in and shut up, killer," Sam shouted, louder than he intended.

A communications cable connected a tent to the taco truck. An FBI agent listened to the conversation in the church. They had not put bugs inside the building, but the sensor technology listened through the sound vibrations against the church windows. The man switched the feed to the speakers. Ringwald and the commander could hear it all.

Robert probed and smiled.

"Kid, you do not know who you're up against."

Before Sam knew what happened, the gun flew from his hand and landed on the floor halfway between the desk and the trembling secretary. Sam felt a sudden crushing against his chest. Lila squealed as her lover turned white. She then realized that she could not move, but something threw her to the floor.

More quickly that anyone thought, Orville was on to Sam, grabbed his collar and threw him down beside Lila on the opposite side of the desk from the gun.

"Y'all are…"

"Only part alien," Orville snapped, completing Sam's thought.

The horrified secretary cried out in terror, fell from her chair and curled up into a foetal ball.

Pastor… an alien…

"Only part," Orville frowned at his secretary.

"No wonder Lee turned to killing…" Sam cried.

"Who's Lee?" Orville asked.

"He killed my sister in El Paso, because of y'all." Sam wanted to attack Orville, but he could not move.

"Oh yes, that preacher in El Paso... incompetent fool. Well whoever she was, I guess I get to kill her brother," Robert steeped towards his victim. "Do I kill her mother too?" He nodded at Lila.

Lila gasped in helpless fear. She grasped Sam's hand and squeezed hard. No one in the pastor's study expected the cavalry disguised as a little girl and an old aboriginal artist.

The ship deposited RoH and Johnny in the park well behind the FBI force. The cops focused on the church and missed the spectacular alien arrival. RoH and Johnny passed unseen through the police line. They materialized in front of the ice cream truck.

RoH nodded to the ice cream seller and stared at the church. Anger, fear and hatred met her probing. She turned to the ice cream vendor.

It's bad in there. What happened?

A young man and a woman went in and forced the secretary into an office. Robert arrived a few minutes ago. He used his ability to neutralize the visitors and now seems ready to kill. The FBI will attack soon.

Who were the couple?

I don't know, but they aren't friends of Robert.

"Where the hell did they come from?" The FBI commander drew his handgun and stared through the trees at RoH and Johnny.

"I told you," Danny chuckled, "that aliens were certain to show. That's RoH; she's half alien and Ellie's daughter. I do not know who the old black man is. Put that gun away. Let RoH do whatever they plan to do. Don't let her little-girl-look fool you. She has abilities we can't imagine. We might get out of this yet with little fuss. Whoever our enemy might be, it's not her."

Robert probed Sam and Lila. Sam's purpose was plain, but the woman presented complexity.

On the surface, Lila felt horror at the reality of an alien controlling them. She did not understand Robert's status as a hybrid and monstrous space invaders flashed through her mind. His power seemed enormous. Probing deeper, Robert discovered Lila's life history. Lila did not know Robert could read her memories. She had buried them deep. They only surfaced in her dreams. Robert translated her memories into a story.

My father disappeared before I was born. Mother never said why, but he had gone to prison for life and died there. Mother loved him and did not blame him. She only longed for him and never married. It was hard. We always were poor, but Mother lifted me up, sacrificed and made me a success. She behaved like a good soccer mom, but with little money.

My weakness was in wanting the good life, and so I married Bo-Bob. He's a good man but loves money more than me. I guess that's karma for me marrying him because I knew he would be rich. I thought he had father-qualities, the ones I missed as a kid, but that disappeared. He never really loved me, and I realized I never really loved Bo-Bob. We drifted apart, and I found fulfilment where I could. Sam is probably the son I never would have.

In Robert learning Lila's story, he had accidentally shared his upbringing in return, the source of his anger and hate stretching all the way from Vegas. Even in her fear and loathing, even though her father had been human, Lila saw a common longing. Empathy, her mother's greatest gift, defeated her fears and her mind tried to soothe. Robert felt it. For the first time in his memory, he felt a flash of unconditional care. This feeling distracted and calmed him. Robert hesitated.

RoH sensed danger. The crisis had matured.

"Come on, Johnny. We have little time."

Despite the urgency, RoH eased through the outer office. She sensed the conflict in Orville's mind. It no longer appeared to be the pure evil that she had encountered in Goderich the first time his mind had touched hers. It seemed different from the Robert she had encountered in Pastor George's church. A long buried yearning for love struggled against Robert's hate. She kept her mind guarded. Johnny surprised her by taking the initiative as they entered Robert's office.

Brother… Johnny thought.

Who…? Robert jerked his head towards the doorway as Johnny's mind penetrated like a bullet.

"You don't know me," Johnny said aloud, "but you should. Our stories are the same. I lost my father, an alien, and then my mother."

"My mother hated me. I hated her."

"At least you had a mother, mate. Mine disappeared into her nightmares… no father, no mother."

Robert tried to command Johnny's mind, but the strength of Johnny's ability, tutored by Ellie over the last few weeks, resisted. Then Johnny merged his mind with Robert's. In an instant, each knew the other's story.

"Your mother loved you." Johnny whispered.

"I… I… I know…" Robert sobbed. "I could not love her."

Johnny covered his face with his hands as grief and longing for his long-suffering mother overwhelmed him. Unlike Robert, he had loved his mother as she faded into alcoholic oblivion.

We are brothers; we grieve and long together. Let go of the darkness.

RoH overheard it all and thought back to her first day on Earth, when she had sung to a dandelion in her grandpa's backyard. She had to sing to Robert. She searched for the words and entered Lila's mind. RoH trembled. Lila was not alien, but her story paralleled Robert's. RoH touched Lila's thoughts.

Lila is the song for this dandelion.

Lila released Sam's hand and crawled toward Robert. She touched his arm.

You're not alien, Robert's thought shouted at the blurred image of Lila.

"No, that's where we differ," she said aloud, "but our fathers disappeared. Robert, your mother and mine suffered the same in a lost love. They both tried to pour their love into us, you and me, but my mother hid her anger. She shared with me her genuine love for my long gone father. Yours could not. Her suffering and anger fell onto you and destroyed what you could have been. I want to share my love with her with you. Then you will feel your mother's love."

Lila told about her childhood, her mother's love. Strangely, the telling filled her void that money and easy sex had not accomplished.

Odd, RoH thought, *sometimes the song reflects from the dandelion to the singer and heals both.*

RoH... the alien at the ice cream truck sent the thought. *The people out here are about to attack. Some of the church members have arrived too.*

We need a few minutes... delay them.

As was usual, Robert's congregation showed up for afternoon work duty. They found the doors sealed and keys would not work in the locks. The ice cream vendor stepped into the street. Muffled sounds came from the trees behind the truck as the FBI force rushed forward and formed a line between the park and the church. The commander walked into the street. He drew his weapon. The ice cream man raised an arm.

In an instant, the dozen churchgoers in the yard turned to the street and sang.

"How many roads must a man walk down...?"

The police froze in bewilderment.

The parishioners picked flowers from the front of the building and went to the street, smiling and all the while singing the pacifist folksong. They handed flowers to the rifle squad.

The chime on the ice cream truck performed the song's melody like well-tuned guitars.

Danny Ringwald rushed into the street.

"Commander," he yelled, "the aliens are in charge here."

RoH needed to hurry things along. Lila and Robert went rigid as their minds merged. In an instant, they collapsed into each other's arms, finding comfort in shared sadness and longing.

RoH entered Robert's head.

Robert, here is your father.

The story of RoH and Jas at Groom Lake unfolded in Robert's head. He saw the alien floating in the tank, the open roof and ascent into the waiting ship.

A weak, distant entity appeared in Robert's mind, smiling in the pale, alien way... *Robert, son, I am your father. Come home to me.*

Robert clung to Lila. Letting go would destroy him... destroy all hope.

Lila gasped in Robert's grip. She heard the call for Robert to go home.

Sam Rice eyed the gun lying on the far side of the room. He crawled. RoH touched his hand and felt his mind.

Sam, let hate leave here today. You are grieving. Feel for Mandy. What would she do?

Sam's tears joined Johnny's, Lila's and Robert's.

RoH hugged Sam.

Sam, more than ever, there is a need for good people in the world. Your sister was one. Follow Mandy's heart.

"How many times must the cannon balls fly?" The singing crept into the church.

CHAPTER 32

What Floats Your Boat?

Siglinde2 sat quietly with her eyes closed, following the morning's events in both Goderich and Dallas. Of the two, the situation with Robert Orville seemed the most urgent. They planned Goderich as a humbling and perhaps an encouragement for the President.

A panicked voice joined the insistent banging on the door.

"Vice-President Hilfreich, we need you in the ops room. It's urgent."

The chief security adviser banged again without waiting.

The V-P rose from her comfortable chair and opened the door.

"What's the panic, Charlie?"

"The aliens have kidnapped the President." Charlie seized Siglind2's hand and almost dragged her towards the operations center. "Vice-President, you may be president by noon."

The live feed from the Secret Service stranded on the Goderich wharf showed the presidential yacht hovering high above. A stream of commentary from the Goderich dockside added up to the simple phrase, "we don't know what's happening".

There was nothing from inside the boat. It hovered, cut off from the universe. Considering the physics of how the star travellers had levitated the craft, that idea came close to reality. In one sense, the vessel and its passengers floated in a different universe.

"I don't think we should panic," Siglinde2 examined the large LED screen. "As long as we can see the boat, Emalia will be fine."

Siglinde2 took her usual seat next to the unoccupied presidential chair. She smoothed an arm of her smart, black suit-top.

"We should instruct the Secret Service and the Coast Guard to be patient and do nothing. I doubt there is anything effective they could try. My knowledge of the aliens says they will not harm the President."

President Cortez' wisdom in appointing an alien expert as V-P suddenly became apparent to the gathering.

"So, what do you want?" Emalia Cortez tried to smile.

"Nothing," Ellie said, "except for humans to learn to take care of everyone and stop trying to exploit and kill each other, and save life on Earth."

"Tall order…," Emalia said.

"Yes, a tall order…" Ellie seemed frustratingly agreeable. President Cortez wanted to be angry, but felt helpless. She looked out the window. Goderich seemed beautiful.

"You think intimidating me will help you win?"

"We aren't trying to win. For star travellers, there is no fight. Before my genetic line began, before me and now RoH, they had little interest in Earth as more than an anthropic curiosity, with some future promise. Star travellers saw it as a low priority research operation. RoH and I loving Earth have made this planet, its life and especially humans, important. My daughter and I long for survival of all life on Earth. The star community, our other family, now supports this."

"We are not conducting war. We are trying to show the way to your survival and success. You have been living without major weapons for four months. Aside from plotting to get them back, governments have done little. You cannot threaten each other because of that disarmament. Of course, illegitimate governments struggle to keep control at home. That is happening in your country."

"How can you call my government illegitimate?" Cortez flared.

"Texas will be gone by the end of the month." Ellie ignored the president. "The rest will unravel. European countries and all the artificial ones like Canada, patched together by colonialism, will also fall apart. Your rivals, in the old order of things, will follow quickly."

"This is going to cause horrific violence. It will mean many deaths and much suffering." Cortez came close to tears.

"Emalia," Ellie whispered. "For the whole of human recorded history, when did most people not suffer? When did anything other than brutal repression maintained short-term stability and prosperity? Don't hold your country up as an example. Honest evaluation shows it."

"You and all governments will waste your time trying to suppress your populations. It would be better if you worked on what to build from the fragments of your former countries, and fewer will die."

"There are a lot of evil players; people who will try to become kings." Cortez said.

"Yes again, and focus on dealing with them while you still have power. The FBI gave you one name, Theodore Rockford III. I suggest you start with him. The good news is that, with no outside interference, local populations will exhaust their desire and ability for violence. They will make other arrangements. It would be better if you did that before killing starts."

"Many will be dead before that." Emalia said and wondered at the strangeness of the aliens and the FBI agreeing.

"Many will be dead." Ellie now had her turn to suppress tears. "Reducing death and destruction should be your primary concern. Leading the way to those new arrangements is your best option."

Emalia looked over at Goderich, spread out in the sunshine below.

"It's beautiful," Ellie said, "with all the trees, but it also represents a scar on the natural world. Every species alters its habitat. Human power is such, unlike any other species, that you can destroy your home and every other creature in it, the whole of life on the Earth and die with it. Humans must learn to use your power with wisdom. So far, there has been little of that, at least in the last ten-thousand years. You must find wisdom."

"Humans always search for hope. I would hope," Ellie smiled at her joke, "that you hope for success as a species on Earth, together, other than to want some higher power to fix it."

"The United Nations is about to hold a big climate summit, COP-42. That will be the answer to saving the climate." Cortez genuinely believed.

"Forty two," Ellie said, "the number is discouraging."

"You all will make gracious speeches and make big promises. Like the other 41 times, they will be meaningless hot air. Your media will shout about progress. You'll all have a fine dinner that over half of the world doesn't even dare dream about eating, and you will go home, where, as you see, it won't be business as usual."

"Perhaps they will cancel 42 due to weather." Cortez and Ellie shared a laugh.

"Nothing real will happen without you being forced to do it, without outside pressure. That force should come from the masses of humans, but I suspect it will be the climate. Earth itself will force you, and probably too late for humans."

"Why can't you stop it, if you can do things like this?" She waved at the window. "You are that outside force. You could just take over the world."

"We could, but we are not shepherds and you are not sheep," Ellie frowned. "It would achieve nothing if we replaced all world governments using the same threat of repression, domination, and violence. It is not the next step for the Earth. You either save yourselves or kill yourselves. It would tear my heart out, but that must be the way. I have no desire to be a good witch in a fairy-tale future for humanity."

"You star people are not Walt Disney."

"We don't pander platitudes and mythical nonsense to make money. Wealth means nothing to us, and we replace meaningless sayings with reality. For instance, your government cut up one of my star cousins and put her parts into jars at Groom Lake. I feel bad for her and probably her suffering, but death comes to all, no matter what the lifetime of the species might be. Platitudes usually have a dark brother, revenge. We avoid both. There is no reprisal to be sought, even for that horror."

Cortez had not heard of the Groom Lake situation. Ellie seemed to have repeated something from science fiction or from a nut-bar conspiracy.

"Is that Groom Lake story true?"

"RoH retrieved the body parts and rescued another cousin you kept alive, floating in a tank."

Ellie stared at Emalia and the story of RoH's adventure in Nevada ran through the president's mind. She burst into tears.

"I didn't know. Why didn't NAAP tell me?"

"NAAP didn't know either, and neither did we. RoH discovered it all by following a hunch and sorting out local stories. It's the dark part of your government that will betray the president. They will try to exploit the coming fragmentation. Put dealing with them, Rockford III and the others like him, on your list to do before you lose too much power."

"Who can I trust?"

Siglind2 sat amongst a gathering of security and political staff. A dozen monitors covered one wall of the White House situation room. Except for the live feed from Goderich, most depicted large cities in Texas. Most came from helicopters, although one security camera showed the State House in Austin. That coverage followed a huge gathering filling the park in front of the legislative building. The mob waved Texas flags, and the scene shifted to a television camera view of a platform constructed on the front steps. Huge Texas banners waved, but not one union flag. The governor had scheduled a speech in the afternoon.

The staff gathered in the White House focused on the boat hovering over Goderich. Vice-President Hilfreich ignored that. She watched the aerial observation of Dallas and the ground live feed from the FBI opposite the Church of Heavenly Enlightenment. Siglind2 knew what would happen in Goderich, but the situation in Dallas was fluid. It all depended on RoH.

On the screen, General Ringwald and the FBI commander stood in the middle of the street, and the small group in front of the church behaved strangely. Siglind2 waited. She did not know what was happening inside the church. RoH had more important things to do than tell the fleet.

Outside the situation room, the Chief Justice waited to swear in Hilfreich as president. The judge shared the gloomy mood with the top ranking politicians and the increasing number of arriving cabinet secretaries. The death of President Harry Ascue had shaken the city. To have a second event in a few months seemed horrific. A steward emerged on his way to refill the coffee carafe.

"What's going on in there?" the Senate majority leader demanded.

"They are just watching television," the steward hurried to the kitchen. None of the important people in the outer room had security clearance to match his, and the President herself had sworn him to secrecy. As with everyone who worked in the building full time, he had survived the rigorous questioning by those two women, advisers to President Cortez.

"Loyal people, especially Mary, Daisy and Siglinde Hilfreich, surround you." Ellie nodded at Mary, who quietly sat near a window. "They have made sure others near you are on your side. Discuss it with them."

"Another reason we won't interfere is because we don't fully understand the nature of human interaction. The Roswell tragedy in 1947 interrupted our attempt to learn more about that. Perhaps, if we had, we might create an intelligent intervention. RoH and I think that you solving it all would lead to a better future, even if we could constructively mould you."

"Your human history and culture have put you into a feedlot. We have just opened the gate and shown you the pasture."

"Sounds like you still think of us as sheep."

"Not sheep, but maybe wild horses penned up."

"I am about to set the boat back in the water. I will not leave you with any demands or advice. You are on your own. Follow your heart and listen to good people."

"I had not planned to meet you, but you asked. We won't normally talk to any single government, so we made sure that the Russians and the Chinese knew about this meeting. It's up to you if you want every other government and the public to know. Tell the Russians and Chinese what we talked about."

"I know," Emalia laughed. "I received irate calls yesterday. They would like their Mars people back, the ones you have at your farm."

"They sent representatives some time ago, and they saw the people are fine. Those individuals declined to go home, and we supported their decision. The Chinese and Russians have since appointed them as ambassadors to save face. They still believe that we hold them hostage to trade for who knows what. After all, that's what humans would do. They are free to go anytime they choose. Tell the premiers that."

"What if they try to take them by force?"

"They did."

Ellie laughed. It was her turn to wave at the window. Cortez joined in the laughter.

"Great," Ellie said. "RoH told me I had to make you laugh at least once. I did it twice."

"That's quite the little girl you have there."

"She's bigger than me; more important; more powerful, but we love about the same."

RoH, I made her laugh… twice. How are you doing?

You imp… RoH laughed in return.

It was hard, Mother, but we are nearly done. Johnny and two humans I had not known about helped Robert. Humans won't have an alien trouble maker and we have a new human cousin. We are leaving soon.

CHAPTER 33

Mine eyes have seen the glory...

Lila tried to stand, but Robert clutched her to his chest.

"I need you." He embraced her as if he was a small boy.

All her life, Lila had used others to fill her heart's void. This status, someone needing her for anything but the physical, had never been with her before. It felt new. It felt...

Wonderful

RoH travelled with both their thoughts and feelings. She had hoped that dandelions could help each other; the world depended on that, and here were two, one withered and suffering, and the other in their prime supplying each other's needs in a strange fulfilment.

RoH smiled. For a sweet instant, her mind travelled the eleven years of her life. She remembered the many planets and stars she had seen, and her travels on a ship. She learned and grew, and the wonderful day they had arrived on Earth with its tumble of uncontained, living exuberance. The stars were her home. RoH had always felt love, but now Earth had claimed her heart. In that instant, she saw her purpose, and once more the vital flaw in the star travellers, the cold void that they must heal.

Humans had the reverse problem, the wildness and strength of individual energy that humanity must temper with mutually caring. RoH felt like a path to fill both their needs. She knew she had to carpet the path with dandelions, like Lila and Robert. The stars needed them, and her, and they needed the stars. RoH suddenly saw her star-travelling cousins as dandelions.

Am I above it all? The thought seemed ridiculous. *It would hurt to leave Earth. Who did she belong to?*

RoH did not yet understand the breadth of her role in the galaxy.

"Stop," the secretary shrieked. In a recovery of clarity, she had taken the opportunity of RoH's distraction to roll over and snatch Sam's gun. She leapt to her feet and levelled the ugly weapon at Robert.

"I'm going to end this." She eyed Robert, a man she had loved and trusted as a pastor. She had invested her soul in this man and it now seemed he was a minster from the devil. Pastor Orville had betrayed her. She stepped forward and raised the weapon, ignoring the others. Her finger found the trigger.

RoH looked into her eyes.

The woman's face contorted. She snarled at RoH, but then threw the weapon against the wall, propelled by an unseen power. The pistol tore through the polished mahogany panel, destroyed the plaster beneath and lodged, barrel first, in the brickwork beyond.

The secretary collapsed in fear and frustration. The monsters here horrified her.

RoH approached and touched her shoulder.

"Sue-Ellen," RoH said, "you have nothing to fear here. You are safe and with friends, not monsters."

The woman looked up at RoH, who then knelt. Their eyes were level and Sue-Ellen stared into a child's face. Lila and Robert sobbed quietly. Sam watched in disbelief. RoH stroked another dandelion.

"Sue-Ellen, you joined with Pastor Orville from a loving heart. Your faith and your desire to do good things drew you in, and Pastor Orville's hatred exploited and captured you. That hateful control is no more. Robert is a new person. You are free, and so is he. Follow that love in your heart. Much bad is going to happen, but you can work to reduce the pain. You do not need to fear star travellers, but only human evil. Work to have human good overcome that darkness. We think there is much more good than evil in humans. Prove us to be right."

RoH turned. "You too, Sam, do as Mandy would want."

Father...?

Yes, RoH, Z263-A is an option for Lila and Robert.

They must understand what it means to go there.
Lila can return any time, but not Robert
I will ask them, Father, I need to show them.
We need them on the ship for that.

"Robert, you cannot remain on Earth," RoH looked at the couple. "Learn and heal. We will help; there is much to redeem to you by star travellers, but we will not leave you here. There is a place, a planet, far away, where you can find peace. Lila, I think you need to travel with Robert. Your heart and his will heal together."

Lila looked at Robert. The years between them exceeded the age difference between her and Sam, but age did not matter. It was a trifling thing. She and Robert did not have an Earth romance, but a melding of need, love and hearts. Lila considered her earthly life with Bo-Bob, El Paso, her dead mother's grave and even dear Ross. The thousand little things of a life lived.

She decided.

"Sam," Lila said, "it has been fun, wonderful, but I must leave. What y'all gave me covered my hurt, but another can fill that hole," she turned to Robert, "another who knows the pain."

Johnny went to the pair and laid his hands on both of their shoulders.

"Brother, sister, mates, my travels will soon take me home, but so will yours. Home is where comfort and belonging soothe. One day, I will visit."

"We'll send a postcard," Lila smiled through teary eyes.

"Johnny," RoH said, "you can go with them. You will have a life of comfort and perhaps much longer than on earth."

"Dear cousin," Johnny smiled at RoH, "I could not live without my family. It would be hell, not heaven, to be there and leave their love here. A few more years with them would be my reward beyond even immortality. I will return to Alice, and in the end I will sleep beneath a place where my grandchildren dance and laugh in love over my grave. They will plant a ghost-gum tree over me. In my sleep, I will dance as a ghost in the moonlight to remind them of my love."

Robert and Lila walked out the front doors, holding hands. The FBI readied their weapons. Several of Robert's followers gathered around and threw dandelion flowers over the couple.

The couple paused. Robert had never heard the tune before. Old hymns had not been part of his liturgy. They more reflected RoH's taste. His worship music had been closer to country rock, simple and repetitive. On the far side of the street, the ice cream vendor stood in front of his truck, waving his hands like a choirmaster. The small group of adherents sang the old hymn in such a sweet melody that even Danny Ringwald teared.

"I always loved a church wedding," Danny said to no one in particular.

"What the hell…?" the FBI commander said.

"I would stand down, commander." Ringwald replied. "It won't end well for you and your people otherwise."

"Will they kill us?"

"No," Ringwald laughed, "but you all might be singing kumbaya."

The sound of a mob up the street, far away, infiltrated the cheerful scene.

"I think," Danny said, "that we will soon fight someone else."

"Tomorrow is the day they plan to revolt." The FBI man holstered his gun. "That's a bunch of rioters. Orville had planned to lead the attacks here in Dallas. We'll deal with them."

RoH intervened in the mystifying celebration. She separated Lila and Robert from the choir and led them into the middle of the street. Instantly a purple light engulfed the pair, and they rose into the sky. As she disappeared, Lila blew a kiss towards Sam, but gripped Robert's hand and tried not to be afraid.

"Commander," RoH walked up to Danny and the FBI chief. "You should not fight those people down the street. Retreat and wait for orders. There has been too much killing already. Texas separation has to happen. Fighting in the streets will not change that. Many will die if you fight. President Cortez will issue orders soon."

General Ringwald had never liked the word retreat. He did not oppose tactical withdrawal, but somewhere, in a drawer back home, he had a medal for valour, earned during a retreat. It left horrible memories that a bit of ribbon could not erase.

"Why should I listen to a little girl?" The FBI man asked.

"Don't start," Danny laughed. "RoH could put us all on our asses in the park if she wanted to."

The power connection between the ice cream truck and the taco mobile snapped apart. The sound of the hinged awning above the ice cream counter slamming shut reverberated from the stone of the church façade.

"Get back," RoH commanded.

Danny and the FBI retreated to the park gate.

RoH, Johnny and Sam gathered beside the ice cream truck. The ice cream vendor reverted to a grey alien. In an instant, all, including the ice cream truck, shot skywards. The generator on the taco truck sputtered to life. On the far side of the street, the impromptu choir burst into song:

Mine eyes have seen the glory...

CHAPTER 34

Hell in a handcart

The large boat gently settled into the dark water of Goderich harbour. The onlookers gasped, but none suffered physical harm, no shock waves, no sound and no sunburns. Quantum gravity manipulations created no side effects, unless the star travellers wanted them.

In theory, they could make a quantum weapon. In their deep-rooted lack of aggression, and throughout galactic history, they could not conceive of the need. They could dismantle anything physical, like peeling an onion. In a common quantum mining technique on the uncounted dead bodies of the galaxy, aliens would fragment metal ore from the inside. To use such a thing for killing held an abhorrence that humans would have to embrace if they wanted to survive.

The gathering in the White House cheered at the sight of the President waving goodbye to Ellie, but they overflowed with questions. No one but the vice-president knew the answers, and she said nothing.

The president's boat hurried from the harbour. President Cortez and Mary sat together in the lounge, where they had met Ellie. Both gazed at the receding Goderich shore and contemplated the challenge presented by the aliens.

"It's our only choice," Cortez said, "but how do we convince the country... the world?"

Daisy declined an invitation to join them. The American humans had to come to the right conclusion independently of her. Instead, Daisy walked to the stern sundeck. Lake Huron rippled gently and gurgled against the hull as a soft north-west wind washed her face. The air carried the pungent odour of flotsam and fish. She had experienced similar conditions on many planets, but because of Ellie, Earth held a special feeling. The morning sun bathed her, and Goderich receded in its quiet beauty. The reproduct... *no, my baby in me...* neared term; she would soon spend time on a ship.

Daisy's pleasure came to an abrupt end. Footsteps, the soft sounds of deck shoes only audible to alien ears, followed the breeze around the corner of the cabin. Daisy peeked. A sailor in white, holding a vicious handgun, eased along the deck and reached for the door that separated the president and Mary from death. His hand closed on the chromed handle. Daisy probed... a hired assassin who had killed many times. His mind held the image of the recently dead president slumped over his desk.

"Mary," President Cortez said, "draft orders for the confinement of all federal forces in Texas to bases. Send a message to the White House calling a full cabinet meeting as soon as we return."

"Tell Colonel Thomas at the Pentagon to issue specific orders as they see fit. I want most units gradually withdrawn from Texas. We don't want more killing."

Both women were oblivious to the horror unfolding just meters away.

The intruder reacted as Daisy stepped into view. He turned the weapon and rushed towards her.

"Put the gun down. You don't want to do that."

"I'll do you first, bitch. You're just a bump in the road."

The pistol with its ugly silencer rose towards the new target. A seagull squawked overhead and the large American flag on the stern snapped in the wind. Life left the man's eyes. He turned towards the water and flew headfirst, gun in hand, already dead, over the edge of the boat. The body sank as if propelled, finally wedging into the mud, never to rise again. The assassin earned the dubious status as being the only human a star traveller had directly killed since 1947.

Appalled and sickened, Daisy retreated to the stern deck and sat sideways on a recliner, slumped and staring at the deck. Her physical appearance flickered between Daisy and her alien reality. Daisy's anguish swept over the thousands of star travellers who swarmed the solar system.

RoH's image filled Daisy's mind. The girl said nothing, but washed Daisy's pain away with love.

Not all dandelions are salvageable. Daisy felt RoH sooth. *Humans must determine events.*

On a ship high above, RoH had interrupted her goodbye to Johnny to embrace Daisy's grief. She thought of the horrific night at Groom Lake. She briefly sat once more in grandpa's kitchen with Rick, a withered flower she had saved. It did not ease her pain that the dandelion Daisy had killed had been irretrievably dead in his spirit.

"This is as far as we go." The Captain in command of the LAV and ten trucks sent from Fort Hood stood at formal ease in front of Danny Ringwald and the FBI commander. "We're ordered confined to base to wait orders."

Danny withdrew his military identification and flipped the case open.

"General," the officer snapped to attention and saluted.

"I'm not in uniform," Danny returned a half-hearted salute and read the name on the battle dress, "Captain... Sanchez, but I'm now in charge." "I'm going to clarify the order, field authorization. You and your trucks will load here, and we will proceed to Little Rock Air Force Base in Arkansas. You will then be at a base, and I think they will evacuate Fort Hood. There are about ten tons of weapons in that church. I want it seized, and it goes with us. Use some of it to arm your men. We may have to fight."

The captain hurried to direct his trucks to the back of the church. Danny frowned at the text on his cell.

I ordered a retreat from Texas. Re-join NAAP by best possible... It was beneath the presidential seal.

"This is as far as I go," RoH gripped Johnny Bray's hand.

An alien carried Johnny's luggage, and some carefully protected sketches he had made in London and placed them at his feet.

"I'll miss you, cousin. You sure added some excitement to the old man's life." He went to one knee and hugged RoH. She seemed taller than just a few months ago.

"I'll always be with you, Johnny Bray.... always... you in my heart. Your ride is ready. I'll visit soon."

Johnny felt a gentle descent, but it seemed in an instant he stood in the middle of the hot, dusty street in front of his studio in Alice Springs.

"Grandpa…" a small girl, about RoH's age, shot into his arms, unkempt hair flying, and hugged. Her eyes flashed and her black face glowed from perspiration. Her grandfather's sudden materialization did not seem to bother her. *She's a one-eighth alien,* Johnny thought. *Like Ellie.*

"I have a new dance to show you."

She helped Johnny carry his baggage into the store. A painting of ghost gums beneath bright stars and children dancing formed in his head. The whistle of an arriving tourist train sounded from over the way.

"Damn, I seem to specialize in fighting retreats," Danny said. He clutched an assault rifle and divided his attention between the approaching on-ramp to I-30, and the quiet, threatening houses along this street. He shared the third vehicle in the line, a substantial SUV that trailed a similar one. The LAV led the column of five coaches, ten army trucks, and several SUVs. Fortunately, Fort Hood had treated Danny's request for transport as an exercise in a war zone. They sent one fighting light armoured vehicle along for practice. The officer had armed the weapons, and the mission had become real. None of the soldiers relished having to defend against civilian insurrection.

"My men won't shoot unless threatened," General Ringwald said to the FBI commander. "The military aren't supposed to shoot civilians inside the USA. That's what you cops are for."

"That may be so, General, but I have a feeling before today ends. We all will have done our share of shooting. It looks like the entire world is going to hell in a handcart."

The little convoy raced up the ramp onto I-30 eastbound.

On I-30, the convoy from Dallas approached the intersection with Texas 69 in Greenville. The vanguard in the LAV called a halt about a half-kilometre short of the overpass. A line of Greenville police vehicles diverted all traffic onto the ramp to I-30 Frontage Road. Danny and the FBI commander walked to the LAV and surveyed the barrier with glasses.

"What do we do?" the FBI commander deferred to the General.

"General, the Captain in the LAV jumped down. We have been getting updates from Hood. These roadblocks are going up everywhere. They are seizing guns and ammo and trying to recruit fighters. Some idiots tried to do it at a base gate."

"What happened?"

"The road is open. It didn't go well for the idiots."

Danny frowned. "The star travellers did not want to kill anyone, but it seemed they're causing a lot of dying, anyway."

He examined the police barricade.

"Captain, I believe you have a hardened hull on this thing."

"Yes, sir…"

"They have a thin line of light vehicles. Can you ram through?"

"That's part of our training. I never thought I'd do it for real at home."

"Okay," Danny said. "Set up a wedge line with the LAV at point and two heavy trucks on each flank and slightly behind. Knock the middle cars aside. When the first trucks pass the block, stop and cover the rear."

"Then what…?" The FBI man asked.

"You and I, my friend, if they aren't shooting, are going to walk up and try to talk that bunch into behaving. We deal with them and move on. The buses have to wait for us to clear it."

The Greenville police cars could not resist the LAV. It slammed through, aimed at the gap between two of the vehicles. Patrol cars flew sideways. The following trucks completed the job of spinning them to the shoulders. Four cops ran for the roadsides.

Danny did not approach the demolished barrier as if this were a western shoot out. Soldiers with raised assault rifles moved with them on each flank. The LAV on the other side had swung about so its 50 calibre dominated the scene. A rifle line from the two trucks stood ready.

"Come here, son." Danny found a cop who seemed in less shock than the others did. "What's your name?"

"…Lenny, sir."

"Lenny, we're going through here. You boys aren't to bother us, okay?"

"Y'all can do what you want." Lenny had no fight.

"Give your weapons to that nice Corporal over there."

"Captain, check all the cars and take any weapons. Break the radios and bring the keys."

The SUVs, trucks and busses passed through the barrier under the watch of the LAV and the rifles. The police gave no trouble. One of Lenny's team ran down the ramp to the checking station where the police harassed travellers. It would take a few minutes before any radio call could go out.

"That was easy," the FBI man said.

"Too easy… if we get out of this without shooting, it'll be a miracle."

CHAPTER 35

From the heart of Texas

"You'll never get re-elected." The judgement from Cortez's Secretary of the Interior thundered down the cabinet table. Heads nodded and most of the cabinet mumbled agreement. In an anteroom, watching and listening via video, Mary frowned. Daisy took notes.

"Ladies and gentlemen," Cortez sat calmly, "I have made that calculation. Anyone who wants to jump ship, go. I won't condemn you."

No one moved.

"Washington is about power and influence, but that is no longer the game. The survival of the United States of America is the only thing in play. Every government around the world is in the same boat."

"Those damned aliens have screwed everything up." The Secretary of Agriculture, a holdover from Harry's administration, stood. "Everything's going to hell in a handcart."

"Or heaven, sort of," the Secretary of State replied. "We assess that there are now no direct external threats against us, thanks to the aliens."

"We can't say the same for our interests overseas. We don't have the resources to deal with growing local unrest. Our bases are all under threat."

"Just like Texas," Cortez said, "internal collapse and exposed forces all over the globe."

"What's the solution?"

The Secretary of Defence had become the unlikely ally of common sense. He reluctantly agreed with President Cortez. He rose slowly.

"In war, we have three options: attack, hold our ground or pull back. A good commander does what is tactically necessary to achieve the strategic aim. Here, we pick the third option and redeploy."

"Retreat…" sneered the agricultural secretary.

"Yes, retreat, save what forces we have and leave nothing behind that the other side can use."

Emalia smiled. The defence secretary had not used the word enemy. She could not conceive of Americans, the people of Texas specifically, to be enemies.

"I have already issued the order to withdraw from our Texas bases. The Pentagon prepared a plan to bring our forces home from abroad. We have brought many back over the past six months. It's time to get the rear guard home for their safety."

"The voters will crucify you." The judgement thundered once more, this time with less support. Serious people considered the options.

"I say we nuke 'em," another hold over from Harry's cabinet said.

President Cortez frowned at the woman. Most of the Harry's secretaries for non-key departments… *mostly lightweights*… had remained. She had not wanted to bother fighting Congress for new appointments. She now regretted that decision. These shallow opportunists were a drag on honestly acting on the alien advice.

"Here's reality," the Secretary of Defence handed out a document with the words "Eyes Only" stencilled across the top page.

"I don't have clearance," came from several of the group.

"I'm declassifying this for you to read," Cortez said. "I'll do the paperwork later. Considering the lack of military might, I don't see any security issues."

"Page one simply says that nothing larger than a 50 calibre machine gun works. There is no ability to produce ammunition of any type, so we have limited supplies. The last paragraph suggests we seize any ammunition from civilians that we can."

"That violates my rights," the secretary from the heartland exclaimed.

"Let's move on," Cortez wanted to keep that argument to later, and seizures had already begun.

"Page two is the important one, and yet meaningless," the defence secretary continued. "We discovered they disabled anything military depending on electronics. The aliens did something to every military circuit board, everywhere. We don't know what they did, but there seems to be no damage, no radiation… nothing. They just don't work."

"Can they mess with the laws of physics?"

"I have been told by reliable sources, the aliens themselves," Cortez said, "that they can't change physics. Whatever they did, they haven't told us."

"Here's the interesting part." The defence secretary said, "A circuit works fine if we don't install it in a weapon, aircraft, navy ship and so forth. We tried replacing everything in an F-16, at a backwater base in North Dakota. It worked, and we thought we had beat the bastards."

"So, why aren't all the planes flying?"

"Aside from the fact that we have nowhere near enough replacements for more than a handful of systems, our celebration ended spectacularly. They flew the F-16 for a test. It got to about three thousand feet and suddenly everything died. The pilot didn't know what happened, but he ended up standing on the tarmac back at base. That plane is a hole in the landscape now. See paragraph three."

"What happened?"

"We believe, and a guess might be all we have, the aliens took a few minutes to realize the F-16 was operational, and then they just disable it, mid-flight and rescued the pilot."

"So we are back to square one."

"Worse, a few hours after the crash, that base went dark, and they fried every electric circuit. We need to get our troops home. They could close every one of our foreign bases if we don't behave."

"That leaves us vulnerable to the Russians and Chinese."

"No," Emalia Cortez said. "Those dictators have repressed their populations for decades. Some of those folks are revolting. Their versions of Texas are uglier than ours are, with a lot more chaos and killing. I have ordered our diplomats home. The aliens don't play favourites. I'm sure the Russians, Chinese and others have more disabled bases than we do."

"That's why we need to get out of Texas, and perhaps a few more states that follow their lead. We don't want a shooting civil war like 200 years ago. Spilling blood will make it harder if we have any chance to heal."

"Shooting might not be our choice," the Defence Secretary handed the latest field reports from Texas to Cortez.

"General Ringwald is leading a convoy of military and FBI to Little Rock. The last report says separatists have pinned them down at a roadblock and it looks like it will mean fighting. We expect casualties."

Daisy carefully placed her notebook on the table and rushed to the Rose Garden.

"Do we surrender, negotiate, or fight?" For the second time that day, Danny examined a roadblock on I-30. The little convoy had stopped a half-kilometre short of where the highway passed beneath North Jefferson Avenue. Mount Pleasant, Texas, was an hour from the Arkansas border. This one looked serious. Guns, a mixture of hunting and military weapons, bristled around a blockade of heavy trucks. A huge Texas flag flew from the bridge and more fighters flanked it.

"I used to be a hostage negotiator," the FBI commander said, but those aren't small time punks or crazy husbands.

"I'm sure there are a few of those up there," Danny said, "but who's in charge?"

"General," the Captain ran up, "they blocked the road behind us too, the underpass at Highway 271."

"They're trying to force our hand," Danny snarled. "I don't see any option but to talk. Let's run a white flag up there."

"I'll go," the Captain said. "I've been in Texas long enough to understand the locals, and I speak Spanish. What do I say?"

"We are on official army business," Danny replied, "and we want to get to Arkansas by noon."

"Should I add that if they don't, we'll kick ass?"

General Ringwald re-examined the blockade.

"There might be some ass-kicking today, but it might be our asses. Don't make any threats."

The Captain advanced, clutching a white towel in a raised fist. A sniper in hunting camouflage lying on top of a garbage truck kept him in the crosshairs.

Danny ordered the LAV to focus its 50-calibre gun on the truck. The Church of Heavenly Enlightenment had supplied a 30-calibre machine gun Ringwald deployed to face to the rear.

"Is anyone a machine gunner?" Danny asked the truck crews.

No one admitted to the skill. Danny picked three.

"Okay, only fire on my order. Pick one target, send a few rounds at it, then another target, and do the same. Don't spray the damned thing around like in the movies."

"Do you see any of them on our flanks?" Danny asked a sergeant.

"Looks open and we could get the trucks and the LAV off-roading, but the busses won't make it."

The Captain had reached the barricade. A person in a Texas Ranger's uniform met him. It was too far for Danny to hear, but they argued. The Captain finally threw his arms up and turned back towards the convoy. He made it halfway before a bullet hit him in the back, knocking him to the pavement. The 50 calibre sent a quick burst at the garbage truck and threw the sniper backwards. A tracer shell ignited the truckload of garbage as it penetrated the flimsy steel bin and the fuel tank. Black smoke billowed and supplied a screen between the forces. Aimless shooting came from the smoke, but Danny's force had no visible targets and held fire. A hail of undirected bullets flew from the front and the rear.

"They have no discipline and not much training." The FBI commander observed. Everyone had flattened on the ground.

In the excitement, no one looked skyward.

"General Ringwald," the soft female voice startled Danny, "I'll take care of this."

Feet appeared to Danny's left. He turned his head and looked up from a pair of black, high-heeled shoes to the short woman who wore them. Daisy had dressed in a business suit for the cabinet meeting in the White House. A prim Yankee secretary seemed out of place in the heat of a dusty Texas highway.

"Who the hell… oh, I know you, from Fort Belvoir."

"Yes, I was Gary's secretary."

A bullet ricocheted off the LAV and buzzed just overhead.

"Get down," Danny yelled.

Daisy waved her hand. A purple glow descended around Danny's force and absorbed the bullets.

"Get ready to move forward. You won't need to shoot."

The sporadic shooting from the blockades ceased as shock gripped the rebels.

"I'm going to rearrange the furniture."

Daisy walked in a protective glow towards the barrier at Jefferson. When she reached the body on the asphalt, Daisy paused and the captain flew skyward. At the barrier, she noted that the 50 calibre had not hit the sniper. The impact on his perch had flung him off, but left him alive.

"Who the hell are you?" A Texas Ranger stepped from behind a truck. He levelled his rifle at Daisy. The weapon flew from his hands and embedded barrel-first into the roadside.

"We didn't want to intervene, but we don't enjoy killing. The general in that convoy must reach Washington. Let them through."

"No," the ranger ignored the fate of his rifle and reached for his handgun. "Long live free Texas."

"Freedom's just another word for nothing left to lose." Daisy pointed.

The cop joined his weapon on the shoulder with his revolver somewhere in the weeds. All the trucks and a few dozen gunners ended up on the westbound roadway. Several made a screaming retreat behind the overpass embankment.

Daisy strolled back to the convoy. The insurrectionists cowered in fear; the 400 cops and soldiers surrounding the vehicles scrutinized this strange woman with awe. What had happened resembled what they had seen on television on New Year's Eve. No one had expected to meet an actual alien, especially this "hot-looking city chick".

"General, bring everything through and don't shoot. I'll escort you to Little Rock. From there, get a flight to Washington and report to the White House."

"And the captain...?" Danny asked.

"I'm not sure."

CHAPTER 36

Dawn
The stirring of ancient drums

Saving Robert Orville had accidentally become RoH's major distraction. Now that he and Lila had left for Z263-A, RoH planned to return to what she had imagined being her primary task. She had embraced her project to show humans the way to survive, to cultivate her dandelion garden, but she had found a new distraction, Dawn Waasnodae. Before the meeting with the Canadian Prime Minister at Goderich, she had only thought of Liz and Dawn as her mother's friends. When she had connected with Dawn at Goderich Airport, RoH discovered something strange, a thing both exciting and terrifying. Dawn was more than she seemed, and more than Dawn knew.

At least she isn't evil like Robert.

RoH had been careful to keep her discovery from the vast organic intelligence of the star travelling fleet. That would come when she had enough information. To be sure, RoH had to meet Dawn again. First, RoH needed her mother.

"We haven't been physically together much since last September." Ellie held RoH's hand. Mother and daughter sat on the bench in Courthouse Square where RoH and Emily usually chatted.

A passing stranger would instantly recognize the pair as mother and daughter. Ellie once joked that RoH looked exactly like her and exactly like her father whenever RoH assumed her human or alien body. On the ships, the mind differentiated, not looks, but most humans had wrongly observed, "All aliens look alike".

"RoH, you are growing fast," Ellie examined her daughter. RoH now showed secondary sexual characteristics and had increased at least 20 centimetres in height since their arrival. "I think your human and star genes are playing games with each other."

"Jaden has given me advice about human puberty. I have adopted her as a sister. Hybridization seems to speed up human development."

"Something bothers you." Ellie said.

"Mother, when you met Dawn, what did you discover about her? Did you examine her?"

"Our minds touched, that's all."

"The day we met the Prime Minister, I looked deeper. Her native entity intrigued me. I wondered about subtle differences in physiology and found something strange. Mother, shield your mind from the group. I want to understand more and talk with Dawn before we share this."

"What is it, Sweetie?"

"Dawn is different."

"Of course," Ellie laughed, "so are we."

"That's too close to what I mean. Dawn has other genes... different from the other humans I know... different from us. Since that day at the airport, I have examined a few. Robert and Johnny have some of our genes. Of course, there are the other reproducts, but all other humans are, well, human, except Dawn. She's different. I can't identify where those other genetics came from."

"Is she a mutant?"

"Spontaneous mutation might explain it, but other humans should have strange differences too. I found none to match Dawn. Mutations are usually fatal."

"We should share this with the fleet."

"Not yet, Mother, not until I talk with her. Did she say anything about her ancestors?"

"Not her family history, but the tribal ones and the old stories."

"What old stories?"

Since the first evening with Ellie ten months before, Liz had become used to strangeness in her life. The insistent tapping on her sixth-floor balcony door in Ottawa only slightly startled her. She let RoH enter.

"Don't tell me you are a monkey too, or a witch. Should I check for a broom out there?" Liz glanced at the balcony and laughed.

"I'm just an imp, but there are too many people at the lake today. It would have been the purple pillar of panic. Where's Dawn?"

"Dawn, have you ever felt that you were different? Did you ever feel something strange about yourself that others did not have?"

"Nothing…"

"Think back. Does anything about your life still seem like a mystery?"

"When I was little, when I was walking down a path, I used to get the idea that I knew what was around the corner. It always appeared as I imagined it."

"Anything else…?"

"I could tell if someone was bad or good. There were many bad people around the community. I always knew, just as soon as I met them. I was never wrong."

"Can you still do that?"

"I usually guess right, just like I did for Liz's love and your mother once I got over being jealous."

"I don't think it's a guess, Dawn. I would like to know your life."

"Where do I begin?" Dawn leaned forward. RoH stirred things that had lurked deep inside for many years.

"Dawn, you can say no, but can I please share your mind? I won't hurt you, but it will save time."

"That sounds scary… Liz?"

The conversation mesmerized Dafoe. She had felt Ellie's power and experienced her mental explorations. RoH's stunning ability and her empathy seemed deeper than Ellie's.

"It's safe," Liz said. "I trust her."

Dawn nodded to RoH. It ended in an instant.

"Dawn, I must meet your family."

"What is going on?"

A touch of fear crept into Dawn's voice.

"Part of you is old, older than anyone could imagine."

"Old...?" Dawn asked.

The old man on the dock did not turn around. He flicked his fishing rod gently and half-cocked his head.

"You have come." He did not sound surprised.

Dawn and RoH stood on weathered planks a few metres towards shore.

"We are here," RoH said unnecessarily.

"You want to know about my daughter, and the ancients."

"We want to know about the ancients. I know your daughter is special."

The old man set down his rod and rose from a folding lawn chair that seemed ready to collapse. In contrast to his frailty, he strode forward and embraced Dawn tightly.

"Welcome home, daughter. You have travelled far and seen sights. You bring the stars to me."

He looked at RoH.

RoH gazed around the bay. The deep blue of the water in the inlet of Lake Huron ran to shining white rocks at the shore where spring ice had scoured up to the trees. Steep green carpets rose on all sides, and ended in the shining blue sky. The wharf extended from the park-like openness of the community commons. A fire pit surrounded by split log benches took centre stage beneath the trees, along with various structures used for meetings and powwow. The lapping water, the occasional cry of a bird, and the hum of shore insects amongst the rushes drew her in.

Her alien family could not reproduce such peace amid the stars.

Earth is special.

RoH focused on the spot where the ancient quartz quarry hid behind the trees, and she felt the jewel-like crystals and wondered.

The old man followed RoH's gaze.

"You have come for peace and knowledge. You bring me peace and understanding. I longed to know and tell. Come to my house."

"I grew up in this house." Dawn looked about the comfortable kitchen. She ran her hand over the simple pine tabletop. Worn spots marked where siblings' hands had rested beside plates, and rings marked where many cups and mugs had stained the polished wood.

"That has always been your spot." Dawn's father turned from the work of boiling a kettle. "Her mother sat there."

He pointed to the table's head, where a place setting remained undisturbed. Fresh, braided sweet grass on the plate effused its delicate aroma.

"My siblings had a different mother," Dawn said. "I'm the youngest, born after their mother had died and oosan remarried."

"Her mother came to me in my grief," father said, "and healed my heart. She had that gift. Dawn shares her ability."

"Some say that when a loved one dies, they take a piece of our heart. That is not so. Love in any form only enlarges our hearts. When the object of that love departs, dies or walks away, they do not take that back, but leave an ache in it. Happily, as time passes, the warmth of remembered love overwhelms the hurt. I loved them both, and they loved me."

His tender gaze on the table's head accompanied cups for tea and a mug.

"You like hot chocolate," he rustled in a cupboard.

"Dawn and you share that talent," RoH said, "you know."

"Sometimes," he replied, "it comes and goes. If it were constant, I would always know where to fish."

"Did her mother know things?"

"We shared that, yes. My first wife, my first love, did not."

"Dawn is special." RoH took her hand across the table.

"You are the girl from the stars." He placed a full mug in front of RoH, poured tea for Dawn and himself, and sat beside his daughter.

"I think part of you both came from the galaxy." RoH blew on the steaming chocolate, "and Dawn's mother did too."

The old man nodded.

"I used to think the stars held the same wonder for everyone that they do for me. I sat on that dock with others, beneath the stars. As a youngster, I noticed, the way they described them fell short of my feelings, except later when Dawn and I shared the sky."

"I always thought oosan," Dawn leaned over and kissed her father's cheek, "had taught me that. Now, I believe father shared, not taught."

"Tell RoH the stories, the old ones from long ago, the special ones."

"No doubt the original events were different," he began. "Winters are boring, the fires bright, and the stories grow larger."

"The canoe story starts it," Dawn encouraged her oosan to stick to the theme.

"It may have been the first contact for this place," he continued. "Maybe it was the first ever, but I think not. The shells on our path say differently. A great shining clamshell, some stories say, in the shape of a canoe descended above the bay. Even in the daytime, its light cast shadows against the sun, just as when you two arrived today. The light of your arrival cast my purple shadow onto the water."

"The people feared and hid in the forest. Creatures from the spirit world, as the stories say, shining grey and similar to people drawn on rocks, left the canoe. They walked over the water directly to the hiding spots. 'We come in peace.' They said, speaking the language of the people as if they were Anishinabek. 'We wish to know.' Then the visitors sat and extended hands in friendship."

"A warrior panicked and flung a spear, but it flew high and then plunged its point deep into the soil between the visitors and the people. 'Let us bury our fears with the point of the spear, and be friends,' they said and showed no anger for the warrior."

"All this happened in just a few minutes. The people emerged and sat in a circle with the spirit people. So began many years of gathering, sharing, and friendship. Our word for them is miigis, the shell guides. They also made children with the people, so the stories tell. The special people, they called the children, the children of the miigis."

He suddenly frowned.

"There are so many stories," he said, "but we have no time."

"But then the visitors left." Dawn added.

"The visitors left," her father continued, "untold generations after their arrival. They had come and gone often, but then, they never returned. I have tried to date when that happened. It seems too long, but I guess over a thousand years ago. Gradually, expectation faded and the rituals that implored their return paled to nothing. No one has performed them for centuries."

"I am not supposed to tell you these stories," he said. "We keep them guarded. I would normally fear I had done a great wrong, but you," he reached for RoH's hand, "are from there. You are one of them."

"I think only their cousin," RoH said. "But it seems you are more of them. Can I look inside you, oosan?"

RoH focused on the father and daughter opposite, only for an instant.

"You both share genes from them."

"What good is it?" Dawn asked.

"I do not know," RoH said. "We know little of those. They secluded themselves about the time they left your people. If they are like my star family, you exist for a purpose, as I do, perhaps a great purpose. Possibly my star family is to them, as humans are to us." An image of Z263-A came to RoH, a place she had only visited once.

"I think they wait."

CHAPTER 37

Jigsaw

"They are waiting for us to attack," General Ringwald watched the bank of screens displaying action, or the lack of it, from Texas. The video feed showed a large force of armed Texans camped at the Oklahoma border.

Danny had finally made it to Washington and found himself escorted to the White House instead of NAAP headquarters.

"Well, general," President Cortez said, "they will wait a long time while I am in command."

Cortez had given General Ringwald the new title of "Senior Security Advisor for Alien Affairs". Danny described his fancy title as "Chief Retreat Coordinator".

The president and general shared the situation room with Mary and Daisy. Daisy had not offered Danny a ride on a ship when she had "beamed out" of Little Rock. Her leaving in a pillar of light at the air base gate caused some consternation. He eyed her with curiosity and some concern. He had become used to aliens and hybrids in Canada, but this situation caused discomfort.

Does President Cortez know one of her trusted staff is an alien?

"I have a lot on my plate," Cortez continued. "We have bigger problems than a threatened fight. So far, they have not cut off the oil, but that may be because they haven't organized enough. Other states are getting restless."

One image came from the situation assessment group at Joint Air Defence Operations Centre. Since defence was impossible, they converted to global threat assessment. It had analyzed the separatist threat inside the USA. The display of the continental USA showed all the states, colour coded. The colours showed levels of insurrection and separatist activity, and went from a blazing red Texas, a hot pink Florida to cool greens of the northeast. Vermont had an unsettling shade of yellow.

"I'm meeting with the Secretary of Commerce soon. The key problem with Texas is the oil refining and NASA. Other than that, they can keep their gophers, longhorns and snakes."

With no other politicians in the room, Cortez felt safe saying something that she could never do in public. Mary and Daisy were her allies, and the Texans had shot at Danny.

"What are you going to do?" Danny hoped it would not be an attack.

"Negotiate," Cortez said. "It will depend on how soon they sober up and see reality. So far, it has disrupted nothing but travel in and out. They will play the oil card, so we need to be flexible. A free trade agreement would be good, if I can convince them and congress. My first problem is to find someone to negotiate with."

"They have some problems too," Mary said. "Their high-tech cars, refinery industries and the spaceport on the Rio Grande require national markets and federal money. We have some leverage in negotiations."

Daisy knew there would be another factor that would soon upset the Texas corner of the puzzle. A low-pressure wave had left the shore of West Africa. It made a slow trip south of the Cape Verde Islands on its way west. In seven days, it would enter the Caribbean Sea as a category one hurricane and gather strength as it curved north between Mexico and Cuba. In the Gulf of Mexico, it would explode into a category five, and then drive over Galveston, deep into the heart of Texas. She did not smile. It would be a disaster, but Daisy knew that this would reset everyone's thinking. Nature held the aces.

Danny looked back at the display.

"The country resembles a jigsaw puzzle with a piece fallen under the table and more on the edge."

New Mexico blinked to red.

"Is the puzzle marked 18 to 80 years?" Cortez asked. "Perhaps it should be for thousands of years old." She imagined aliens completing the puzzle.

"The aliens say all this has to happen," Mary said.

"They told me they won't get involved," Danny spoke to Mary, but looked at Daisy.

"Ellie said the same thing." President Cortez said.

Mary flicked a switch and the display from Anacostia-Bolling showed a global view with many red splotches, mostly inside Russia and China.

"They are having it worse than us. A bully fails as soon as they don't have power," Cortez said. "The Russians and Chinese have fought their people. I sincerely want to avoid that horror here."

"There is a lot of bluster and anger in Congress," Mary said. "They have expelled the Texas reps from Congress. You might have to veto a declaration of war."

"Can I do that?"

"Do it anyway. You're the Commander-in-Chief. You need to address the nation today." Mary replied.

"Arrange it for tonight. Can we at least get talking to Texas before then?"

Mary and Daisy disappeared.

The global display showed red expanding rapidly as countries revolted that had had stability imposed by violence. All the Middle East was pink or red, India and Africa appeared to be larger jigsaw puzzles than the USA. Over half of Canada turned several shades of pink.

"Danny," Emalia sat beside the general, "can we trust the aliens?"

"All I am sure of is that they will abandon Earth before they do anything big to help us or hurt us." He thought of the incident on I-30. "They might offer to save our personal asses, if that becomes necessary, and if we want to go. Otherwise, we must save ourselves."

"That's what Ellie told me. She said she would be sad if that happened."

"Ellie and RoH are the only reason they even bother with us," Danny said. "Those two are of special importance to them. We too should respect them. I love them."

Danny thought of his grandchildren and how big a refugee group he might have to muster.

CHAPTER 38

The new world disorder

President Cortez tried not to think about the next twenty minutes. She would give the most important and likely futile speech of her life. They had prepared well with notes written in bullet form by Mary and printed by Daisy in large font. The television crew counted down to 6 PM, airtime. She would not hide in the Oval Office. Accredited reporters jammed the pressroom. Many more gathered outside the White House, watching on large screens. Emalia closed her eyes and deeply breathed as her mindfulness guru had taught. The plush chair gave such comfort she would have fallen asleep in easier circumstances. She thought most would reject her message, perhaps violently, but she believed if she spoke clearly and with confidence, there might be hope.

"Madam President, three minutes…"

Emalia Cortez rose and grasped her notes. Out front, her press secretary did the warm-up, trying to control expectations.

"Thank you all for coming on short notice," Cortez swept her gaze over the rows of expectant journalists.

"My fellow Americans," Emalia looked into the camera with the red light, "and people of the planet Earth. Thank you for joining us."

Mary had written the words "people of the world," but Emalia gave it some galactic perspective. She needed to draw her fellow citizens from the normal inward looking view to a global view, and, she hoped, for a star view. She wanted more than a global perspective but wanted to take her audience further, to see Earth as a small fragile planet in the darkness of space. If any hope remained, it required her to inspirer the baseball fans of Baltimore; the wheat farmers of Kansas; the pot-smoking sophisticates of California; and those rebellious libertarian Texans to imagine a greater good.

"I know times are hard for many of you. Economic disruption, beginning with the aliens destroying military industry, has hit hard. We should think about why our economies depended so much on war."

"I must remind my fellow citizens that the entire world is in the same situation. To help at home, I have issued an executive order to use federal funds to distribute food where needed and to begin employment programmes for the greater good. These will be simple at first, the clean-up of streams, streets and highways. The longer term will be a plan that various departments are developing for initiatives to help the environment, mitigate climate change and to adapt to its growing impacts while creating jobs. The goal is to work together for the common good, for us and for the Earth. We will send legislation to Congress as soon as possible."

Cortez hoped that the last item would reduce political attacks. Already, in some homes and public places, viewers hurled the words commie… idiot… crazy Cortez and more at television sets. She had not yet said the words that many would reject.

"The immediate crisis, and probably why all of you are here," she frowned at the reporters, "is the insurrection in Texas. You have heard sabres rattling, especially from Congress. As you know, the House and the Senate both expelled Texas representatives. The constitutionality of that will end up at the Supreme Court. I think they made a mistake."

"Worse than this action, many have called for a war against Texas. Some people think our forces, equipped with rifles and pistols, should fight their force armed the same. In my calculation, that would be a greater tragedy. I hope you agree with me, we want to avoid another civil war. I have no desire to lead Americans against Americans. Once we spill blood, we will find it harder to heal. Frankly, we never healed from the last one."

Emalia dropped the big bomb.

"I have ordered a federal withdrawal from Texas and am actively looking for someone in authority with whom to negotiate. They have yet to sort out who might be in charge. I am hopeful, but so far, we must wait. I hope those of you with relatives in the forces, or are serving your country, appreciate how many lives and how much grief this will save."

"Other states have followed Texas' lead or are thinking of it. We must deal with that and perhaps consider another continental conference as in 1776. The aliens have given us a respite from external threat. We should make use of it."

"I have referred to the aliens. It divided you into hating them or being friendly with them. First, they are here, and no amount of dreaming is going to change that. Whether they are angels or devils is for God to decide. We cannot decide that in the streets." Cortez glared at the camera. "We must deal with reality. We must engage with them."

"The first lesson is to learn humility in the face of a superior entity. This is especially hard for the United States of America, Russia, China and the European Union. We, the powerful, have, for centuries, ruled the Earth for our benefit. The aliens have reduced us to secondary powers. We are used to bullying other countries and our first instinct is to expect the aliens to bully us, to use their superior abilities to enslave us."

Cortez paused for effect.

"I have met with their representative, the person we know as Ellie Keys. She is actually mostly human. She agreed to meet at my request. We must be clear on that. The star travellers will not deal with any of the formerly major powers, but only through something like the United Nations, a reformed United Nations."

"Our meeting seemed like an audience with an emperor, but she did not act like a master or Queen. She only agreed to meet to make sure I, as president of the most powerful country in the world, understood exactly what the aliens want."

Again, Cortez paused.

"They want nothing. I want you all to understand that. They can get all the resources they need from dead worlds around the galaxy. That includes water. They make food from these basic materials. They do not want to eat us."

A giggle rose from the gathered reporters.

"I'm serious," Cortez frowned, "that stuff made for exciting horror movies, but that is all. Ellie Keys made it clear; they do not want slaves or human sheep. They won't herd us or manipulate us into their bidding, but will leave us free to do what we want."

"I need to answer a question before you ask it. The aliens have not taken over my mind. That's another exciting theme from science fiction. Fiction must be simplistic, but a complex reality faces us."

"There are two things they want from Earth. One is to absorb human empathy and togetherness. They have decided they lost that, and it is something essential to survive among the stars. They began that with an accidental breeding with a human near Lubbock, Texas in 1947, yes Roswell and all that. That accident has resulted in Ellie Keys, and they extended it with her daughter RoH. Apparently, more of that is going on, but unlike another titillating movie theme, it does not involve sex slaves. Ellie told me they only achieve useful results if the human and the alien actually feel mutual love. I'm sure there will be an entire branch of study at universities over that one."

"The second thing they want, and that is because of Ellie Keys and her daughter RoH, is for humans to survive and perhaps reach the stars. I think this is their chief aim. I embrace the idea that we must change how we behave on the planet, from how we damage the environment to how we exploit each other. Not only is this the most important, it is the hardest to do and probably politically impossible. Whether we do the right thing depends upon intelligent action from Congress and other governments. It also hinges mostly on you; what ordinary people around the planet want to do. The aliens don't give us much chance of surviving, but Ellie and RoH are part human and they care. Because of them, the rest of the aliens care."

"Whatever time I have left as president, I will strive to save Earth. That involves making life better for everyone, including peaceful cooperation in this land we call America. I hope that might gain your support and extend my time in office, but it is more important than my political future. From today, my work will focus on that and not our usual selfish greedy ways. That has probably ended all of my political funding, which normally comes from those with greedy self-interest. They are used to buying politicians. I am no longer for sale. If Congress impeaches me, so be it."

Emalia took a long sip of water and waited. The murmur in the room subsided. She had gone to the mountaintop and now had stepped off. She hoped the last statement might prevent Congress from removing her.

"I hope that all of you, at home and around the world in your own circumstance support this approach. Do what you need to do. If you don't want to do anything or just fight each other, you will get what you want and the aliens will leave in disgust. Ellie and RoH will leave in tears. I think we will have chosen suicide, personally and for humankind."

"My fellow Americans, we have stars on our flag. We can also have the stars in our future. Through struggle, hard work and compromise, taking care of our precious Earth and each other by working together, we can reach those stars. Thank you and God bless the whole green Earth."

"Questions…"

"What if we save life on the planet but still don't get to the stars? It would all be a waste."

"Mr. Alvarez, do you know how stupid you sounded with that question?"

President Cortez, in a symbolic sign of her message of compromise, had allowed a reporter from Texas the honour of asking the first question. Emalia Cortez; however, was in no mood to be nice. She had probably killed her career without preventing the likely violent end of the country she loved.

In the situation room, the video feed from the front of the statehouse in Austin attracted General Ringwald's attention. In response to Cortez's pleading for understanding and cooperation, the Texas mob had fired defiant volleys into the air.

"Good," Danny said to Mary. "The more ammo they waste shooting ducks and sunbeams, the less they have to kill us."

"There's hope," Mary said. "Texas wants to talk, although I don't think the old governor is in charge. Someone from the separatists has taken over. He's an ex-police official. Their pre-condition to talks is that we free Rockford III and send him to Texas."

"I'm suggesting we agree, as long as they promise not to let him out of Texas." Mary laughed. "It's a beautiful state, but for a puffed up man like Rockford, living in Texas would be worse than death."

On screen, a man and a woman at the front of the Austin mob seemed to argue. Both had guns. Soon, both appeared to be dead.

Somewhere, Danny knew, RoH would be crying. He flipped the view to the standoff at the Oklahoma border. He did not know that RoH would soon shed her tears in an anguished night of goodbyes.

CHAPTER 39

The gift to the miigis

The farm that had become RoH's home sat just five kilometres from the spot where RoH and Ellie had first appeared to Charlie Keys. The gap would never close. Necessity of duty would soon separate RoH by light-years from her places of heartfelt comfort.

As RoH had sipped chocolate with Dawn Waasnodae and her father, an enormous spacecraft had left a star system in the Sagittarian arm of the galactic spiral. It lay in a small group of middle-aged stars with stable planetary systems and life-saving distance from any killing super-nova.

The massive craft curved above the spiral arm . Then it made a graceful descent between the Sagittarius and Perseus arms where other mature stars shared a relatively sparse bit of space. The ship would rendezvous with the third planet of Sol.

Although a familiar route, no ship had made the journey for many Earth centuries. They had waited for a beacon. A signal finally came as hoped, but from an unexpected source. The Long Contemplation had ended. The galaxy had become interesting once more, and there was, of course, the Andromeda galaxy, which the beings on the ship knew as The Great Companion.

By the time the Sagittarian ship reached the inner solar system, several vessels from Ellie's star family escorted it. The chaperons felt no threat, but an honour to accompany the ancients. Word flashed around the system and drew RoH into the vision of an exciting but frightening opportunity. The Sagittarians wanted RoH.

RoH drew her family and friends close. Only in their comfort could she overcome her distress. RoH had once taken Siglinde Hilfreich to a place of a similar grand decision, to fly on hope from a high cliff. Siglinde, in her bravery and curiosity, had made that leap. Now, at an even more fearful edge of the unknown, RoH found strength and comfort in Siglinde's bravery.

It had to be at the farm. RoH knew that any place connected to her leaving would hold lingering sadness and loss. It might not be as horrible for Lisa and Charlie this time. It might not be as wrenching as in that Texas pasture near Lubbock. She did not want any of the happier places blemished, although for her, the farm would never lose its happiness. RoH wanted her goodbye to be from that sweet place.

Her mother would be fine no matter where. Ellie had made a more fearful decision those years ago at Lubbock. Her mother's enduring longing would be for RoH to return to her. Only Ellie and RoH knew why RoH had called for such a huge gathering. Mother and daughter had already shared their tears.

RoH had made a trip to Alice Springs to explain it to Johnny. His family overwhelmed her with hospitality and deepened her love of Earth. When she explained what lay in her future, Johnny drove her to the site of a transmission tower, high on the MacDonnell Range above the Todd River gap. Alice spread out to the north. Elsewhere, the red land and blue-shadowed hills ran to the horizon.

"This land is forever," Johnny said, "like the universe. You are standing where it calls you. Fly, my cousin, fly to where your heart brings joy, where RoH will fill the need. But, like me, return to your place, your roots, where you will always dance in the moonlight in peace."

"I'll be back, cousin."

"There," Johnny pointed to a patch of green in the dusty valley west of the town, "you'll find me there when you return. Dance with my grandchildren beneath the trees."

The old man and the young woman hugged and cried. RoH left Johnny on the hilltop. He stood on the lofty peak, gazed over the baked red earth, and contemplated eternity.

"I won't be gone forever, Mother." In the subdued gathering, RoH had talked with everyone, one on one. She and Ellie sat on the top step of the porch. The balmy night had drawn them all outside. No one partied. RoH had announced her departure at the start and the gathering seemed like a wake. Laughter sometimes broke from hushed conversations.

"We know nothing, really." Ellie sighed. "I may not be here too much longer. Everyone may have to flee. Cortez made a powerful speech, but some want to impeach her. Events in Russia and China are more disheartening. Our people there can find no influence over those humans."

"I'll know where you are, always." RoH hugged her mother and touched the crystal hanging from her neck. She wondered if it could span light-years.

"Mother, where did our crystals come from?"

Ellie paused as she asked the fleet for information.

"Jewel, my love, the people of Z263-A sent them. It's their technology."

RoH thoughtfully fingered the stone and contemplated the sky. She thought of Dawn Waasnodae's childhood home with its quartz quarry, and RoH felt a piece of the great cosmic puzzle click into place. She knew how, but not why the Sagittarians had called her.

"I just wish I knew what they need me to do. Am I that important? How did they even know about me? We call them the Sagittarians, but only by default. I know little about them, but I know Dawn, and that is comforting."

"We have sketchy records." Ellie said. "They distanced from our people long ago. Perhaps we were primitive in their eyes, and they let us to grow, just as we are letting humans mature. Maybe we have qualified to be their equal. Maybe your existence did that. I think you are more than that, more than they are. Your great-great-grandfather is with them now to be a bridge, but you will eventually travel alone."

"Mother, I love Earth. I don't want to leave."

RoH had shed more tears tonight than she had ever before. She and her mother shared more.

The time drew near. RoH sought Jaden and Dawn and took them away from the bustle. They sat together on a bench that Ghislaine's troop had installed beneath the big oak. Fireflies danced above.

"Jaden," RoH began, "I drew close to you the instant your grandmother showed me your picture. You had a broken heart; I saw the need in your eyes. Now, I'm thinking there is more, but I cannot know why. You have a greater purpose. I'm not sure what your future holds. I wish you could come with me. You are my most important dandelion."

"Me too," Jaden whispered.

"Remember, Jaden, when I talked to you about perhaps having a child? Then it seemed to be a logical idea for someone as smart and brave as you are. I still think that it is your future, but now, perhaps, not with my people, but with these unknown visitors. We will see, but in the meantime, spend time with Dawn. She has some of their blood, and she will comfort you."

The news shocked Jaden. She had been grieving the impending loss of her best friend. To discover that Dawn had star blood stunned her. Jaden could not speak.

"Yes, Jaden, not only am I of two spirits, I am of two species. RoH is the core of it all. She revealed it to my father and me. We were ignorant. I will travel among my people and want you to be with Liz and me. We will meet others I now think are, like me, children of the miigis. There are stories you must hear if you are to decide."

"We don't even know if the Sagittarians want that," RoH said. "I will find out soon enough."

"RoH," Dawn took her hand. "That is not their name. My people called them the miigis because it sounds like what they call themselves. The stories that father could not tell reveal that."

"The miigis are from our past. The stories call the shells that my ancestors found everywhere along our path, the miigis. They guided us from the east to the centre of Turtle Island. Considering what I know now, perhaps the other star people took that name from my ancestor's minds and used it to be familiar. Perhaps they left the shells as a guiding gift; perhaps they call themselves something else; perhaps they were the shells."

"Then you and your line are a gift of the miigis," RoH said.

"You are our gift to the miigis," Dawn smiled.

"Christian religion refers to the alpha and the omega, the beginning and the end." RoH said. "I am neither, but perhaps in the language of science I am the delta, the change."

RoH suddenly stiffened and looked beyond the hill.

"The delta is larger than one, larger than me." RoH said. She then reached beneath her shirt and took out the crystal. Carefully, she raised its thong over her head, the string grasping at her long hair as if reluctant to be free. RoH looked at Dawn.

"Here," RoH said, and slipped the cord over Dawn's head, "here is a gift from the miigis to you. Dawn, you are part of the delta, the part that lives on Earth. I don't know what this means, this jewel, but it binds you to the future. Even though we are apart, we will be near."

"It's your jewel," Dawn said. She moved to give it back, but RoH laid a hand on hers.

"I won't need it after I leave. I will always be near to you and mother." RoH glanced across the yard to her family, gathered in their sadness. "This will tie you to mother and bond humans and life on Earth to the miigis."

Again, RoH became calm, looked at the hill, then to Dawn, Jaden, then to her family, and finally swept over the yard full of all she loved.

"We will all meet again."

The three women sat silently, holding hands, feeling the approaching goodbye. RoH, who a year before had appeared as a little girl, suddenly, in Dawn's eyes, was a woman, not only in her blossoming body but also in her being. The miigis had a reason to seek RoH. She did not know why they had picked Dawn Waasnodae. Dawn knew it had to be something that spanned the galaxy. It seemed RoH manifested the galactic soul.

Yes...

The thought came so clearly, Dawn thought it to be her own.

"Did you say something?" Dawn asked RoH.

"No," RoH said, "but I also heard it from there." She pointed beyond the hilltop to the east. *You heard it because of the jewel. It is home with you.*

The first sounds were so faint that only RoH, Dawn, and Ellie heard them. Then they grew from an unknown source beyond the hill. The night had no clouds and here in the valley, the stars brightly shone. The darkness beyond the sky absorbed all light until the first ship shot over the pasture.

"It is my father." RoH left the bench and went to watch the craft. Her father travelled in the same small ship that had brought RoH and Ellie a year ago. To humans, it seemed massive. It moved off to the northwest, making room. RoH knew for something else.

Be brave, daughter. All will be well.

RoH gathered her mother, grandmother, and grandfather together in the middle of the farmyard.

"Your father says to be brave. I know you are that," Ellie hugged RoH.

"I got that from you, Mother."

Lisa and Charlie shed tears. It all seemed so familiar.

"Grandma, Grandpa," RoH took their hands. "It is not like when mother left. Great grandfather will be on the ship and will travel with me for a bit. He eased mother's journey and will do so for me. Remember, the stars are my home as well. The miigis are a promise, not a threat. They need me, but I have not learned why. My importance drew them from their isolation when they knew of me."

"New Dust That Spreads New Life," Ellie translated RoH's star name.

"I'm still a little girl and wish I could stay here and not sure there are dandelions beyond the sky. I wish I could take a dandelion with me."

She looked at Jaden, who cried beneath the tree. RoH's tears flowed and mingled with the rest.

With a subdued rumble, the edge of a spacecraft eased into view above the hill. In contrast to her father's ship, this was indeed massive. Her star-family fleet had none so huge. The rim of the ship appeared as a straight line until it raised enough to show a curve. Perhaps the edge passed five kilometres away over Goderich. It moved silently, majestically until it hid the sky. Aside from a few perimeter lights and the reflection from the yard lights, it was dark. It stopped and a circle of light appeared in the hull, above the brow of the hill.

Come now, RoH. I am here. Great-great-grandfather's thoughts reached RoH and Ellie.

"Goodbye," RoH hugged her family. "I will return."

RoH turned and walked towards the fence. Her face lifted towards the light on the hill and her steps were sure. In an instant, she was over and slowly climbed the hill towards the circular light.

"Dress warmly," Elsie's shout softened the sadness.

Mother... RoH's mind touched Ellie. *Elsie has a sense of humour. That's great, and hope for the stick-in-the-muds. Get her to like hot chocolate.*

*Never...*came from the shimmering grey shape on the porch.

RoH's youthful form diminished up the slope. In her heart, RoH felt sadness. She had dreamt of saving life on Earth. She did not know her greater purpose. Every human she loved stood in the farmyard. Almost everything she loved clung to this blue ball of Earth. Her steps were firm. Her heart raced, and her mind questioned.

“She looks so small,” Lisa sobbed. Ellie took her mother’s hand, but neither found comfort.

Two figures appeared from within the ship. An alien accompanied great-great-grandfather. The miigis looked similar to RoH’s star family, perhaps a bit more blue, taller, had defined ears but somewhat larger eyes.

RoH paused and looked back down the hill. She waved at her mother and raised a hand over her head. Above the farmyard, fireflies swirled and undulated in a brilliant pulsating cascade. The light reflected from RoH’s eyes. Ghislaine’s troops shouted a farewell.

RoH had decided that no matter what the future held, she would always keep her human form. She reached the two figures. The miigis lowered their eyes, perhaps in greeting, perhaps in honour. Then they looked into RoH’s eyes expectantly.

“I am here. My name is RoH.”

“RoH, we need you. Come with us, to Z263-A, to our Jewel.”

Those in the farmyard watched the three silently stand; it seemed forever. Then RoH turned, looked down the hill, beckoned and called out.

“Jaden, come, we have a hill to climb.”

From the next story set on the moon planet, Z263-A, or Jewel

Z263-A

A Galactic Honeymoon

For small creatures such as we, the vastness is bearable only through love. - Carl Sagan

CHAPTER ONE

Space

"The void is the enemy," Siglinde said, "the infinite vacuum with no life, no love."

When did I become a poet?

The dark void had a few bright dots and the distant smudge of a local galaxy. She turned away from the vast near-empty darkness filling the view port and to her alien lover, now in the form of a human, astrophysicist Adonis. At least, Siglinde saw Ted, her love in his human form as the "hot hunk" that her friend Liz described. Of course, Ted was much more; a mind that held the quantum understanding that he could not share with Siglinde who merely had a human brain. The desire for that knowledge only added to her lust and love.

That new world of emotion and giddiness proved to be a comfortable place to Siglinde, the normally matter-of-fact physicist. Still, it seemed as alien as the craft that carried her to an even more mysterious world. The events of the past few months, the actual arrival of aliens on Earth, en-mass, and the revelation that her love Ted was a star traveller, had collapsed the un-certainty of her life of theory and experiment. Siglinde felt that it had transformed her from experimenter to the experiment, a quantum speck in fuzzy orbit about a mysterious reality.